S0-BBC-935

THE GODMOTHER'S WEB

WEB

Elizabeth Ann Scarborough

ACE BOOKS, NEW YORK

THE GODMOTHER'S WEB

An Ace Book / published by arrangement with
the author

PRINTING HISTORY
Ace hardcover edition / February 1998
Ace mass-market edition / February 1999

All rights reserved.
Copyright © 1998 by Elizabeth Ann Scarborough.
Cover art by Tara McGovern Benson.
This book may not be reproduced in whole or in part,
by mimeograph or any other means, without permission.
For information address: The Berkley Publishing Group,
a member of Penguin Putnam Inc.,
375 Hudson Street, New York, New York 10014.

The Penguin Putnam Inc. World Wide Web site address is
http://www.penguinputnam.com

Check out the ACE Science Fiction & Fantasy newsletter
and much more at Club PPI!

ISBN: 0-441-00600-0

ACE®
Ace Books are published
by The Berkley Publishing Group,
a member of Penguin Putnam Inc.,
375 Hudson Street, New York, New York 10014.
ACE and the "A" design are trademarks
belonging to Charter Communications, Inc.

PRINTED IN THE UNITED STATES OF AMERICA

10 9 8 7 6 5 4 3 2 1

Dedicated with respect to the Hopi and Navajo Nations, and to the other First Peoples of the Southwest.

Acknowledgments

This is in chronological order rather than necessarily being in order of importance. The gifts people give of themselves when they share aspects of their lives and culture are too important to rank.

First of all, I would like to thank my friends and colleagues from twenty-five years ago when I worked as a nurse at Gallup Indian Medical Center as it was then called:

Lupita Bennally (Navajo/Cochiti). You were right, Lupita. I have regretted ever since that I had to leave New Mexico without accepting your invitation to the initiation of your niece into the medicine clan. But I have always been so honored that you asked me and took the trouble to arrange it. I hope to see you again some day. Lonciana Ondelacey (Zuni), who gave me a little insight into life in Zuni. She was a fine nurse I was proud to know as were Mrs. Romancita and Mrs. Marianito and our head nurse, Lucy Jopling, who kept me out of the Gallup jail.

Thanks also to Julia Lopex for her friendship and kindness; Carmelita Sanchez, Chief Nurse, whose parting words have warmed my heart ever since.

I would also like to thank the first nurse's aide I worked with over at the white hospital, the night Mr. Cutnose took the IHS emergency room hostage. That night you told me about your horrifying experiences in boarding school and I have never forgotten what you told me.

My gratitude as well to all my other colleagues who probably can't quite remember my name either but who made my professional experience in Gallup one of the happiest in my nursing career.

During the same period, I am indebted to my Navajo weaving teacher, Noel Bennett, for teaching the culture with the weaving. From her I first learned of Spiderwoman and I thank you, Noel, for the many lessons I have kept close to my heart throughout the years and for introducing me to the writings of Gladys Reichard. Also I thank Tiana Bighorse, Noel Bennett's teacher, collaborator, and mentor, for sharing with me through Noel the stories of your parents. Besides your weaving books with Noel, I read *Bighorse the Warrior,* your father's story.

In recent times I wish to thank: John Swan, veterans' counselor in Fairbanks, Alaska, for helping me connect with Cliff Balenquah (Hopi) Veterans' Readjustment Counselor at Keams Canyon. Cliff's insights were invaluable in presenting a contemporary Hopi perspective for this book, including the care of the elderly and the viewpoint of a person who is progressive in wanting some of the advantages of the outside world for his people, while remaining a traditional Hopi in the religious and social sense. Thank you also, Cliff, for sharing your dream.

Valerie McCaffrey, for sharing her friendship with her Navajo sister, Teresa and Teresa's family, the Chees. These folks put me and my research assistant up for ten days in the home of Teresa's parents (whom I also wish to thank for their hospitality), told us much about Navajo kinship, something about ceremony and family structure, took us out to visit the relatives and to Canyon de Chelly and Wide Ruins, shared their concerns and food with us, let us play with their kids and pet their dogs and cat. I am indebted to you, particularly, Teresa, for sharing your insights into contemporary problems in the Navajo Nation and for the wonderful visit to see your grandmother's weave. Special thanks to you, Al, for your memories of how things used to be done by traditional Navajo people, the ceremonies, and for the pleasure of seeing you care for your livestock.

Laverne Lizer for her insight into Hopi/Navajo relations and how folks with spinal cord injuries fare within the Navajo Nation, as well as for her recounting of the miracle at Rocky Ridge and her kindness and friendship.

Anna at the museum in the Hopi Cultural Center for recommending books and sharing a bit about the women's side of her culture; Neva Reece for sharing her viewpoint as a volunteer at Big Mountain.

The many authors and contributors too numerous to mention that I used in filling out the background for this book. Special thanks to my local Port Townsend used bookseller,

William James Booksellers, for acquiring for me the works of Father Berard Haile and most particularly to owner Jim Catley for saving for me the truly inspiring book, *They Sang for Horses, The Impact of the Horse on Navajo and Apache Folklore* by Laverne Harrell Clarke.

My deepest appreciation goes to my friends who accompanied me as research assistants on my trips to the Southwest, Tania Opland and Tara Raynor. Thanks for driving, sharing, and listening as well as baggage schlepping, baby-sitting, observing and keeping the car running. Thanks for the hospitality to Anita Del Valle in Albuquerque for putting Tara and me up the first night off the reservation and sharing her insights as well.

Thanks also to Dr. Anne Biedel and Cindy Brown for reading my medical scenes for any possible errors, to Maris for reading the manuscript and helping make Cindy Ellis behave like a real horsewoman and for being, along with Al Chee, my head wrangler for the horses in this book.

Last but not least, thank you, Cliff, Teresa, Al, Laverne, Maris, Tania, Mom and of course, my editor, Ginjer Buchanan, for reading and commenting on the early drafts of the manuscript, and Carol Lowe, the very thorough copyeditor who kept me from making a fool of myself. And thank you as always to my agent, Merrilee Heifetz at Writer's House, for keeping me going long enough to finish.

AUTHOR'S NOTE

Grandma Webster is based on a complex and ancient being, who appears as a Hopi Holy Person long before the Navajos came to the Southwest and learned to weave from her. Because she helps both peoples (as well as the other Pueblo peoples of the Southwest) in this story she simply borrows the dress of the tribe with whom she is spending time, sometimes the Navajos and sometimes a mixture of Navajo and Hopi dress. If she had made a visit to the Hopis in this book, she would have dressed in their traditional clothing.

ONE

Beauty and the Menagerie

*F*ROM THE NORTH *comes the sun-haired maiden. She is changed from a mouse. She is changed into a far-flying she-eagle. She lands in Flagstaff and is changed once more into a maiden.*

Her skin is made of white shell. Her eyes are made of deep waters. Her mouth is made of carnelian. Where the sun kisses her cheek, the white shell changes to carnelian. Her hair is the color of rabbit brush blooms. Her hair is the texture of rabbit fur.

Her body sits straight as a lance. Her touch on the rein is gentle as a warm breeze, but firm as the red rock rising around her. A valuable blanket made of soft wool and rainbows cushions her saddle. She is riding the sun's own blue horse.

In beauty she rides along the flowing highway. The cars flash like wish-granting fish among the eighteen-wheeled leviathans. The darting minnow motorcycles weave it into a single undulating fabric of noise and motion, this highway along which she rides.

The highway's banks are studded with turquoise and silver placed on bright blankets in flimsy wooden stalls by sleepy Native Americans. They have just left hogans and trailer houses down rutted paths from the stalls. Signs of painted wood that say "Half price!" "Buy here!" "Navajo made!" "You've Gone Too Far" and "Nice Indians" fish the highway for silver and green tourist money.

To the south are the cities of Flagstaff and Sedona, and the land where the blue horse was born. To the west are the sacred mountains. To the Anglos and the Mexicans, they are called the San Francisco Peaks. To the Navajos they are the Sacred Mountains of the West, Light Always Glitters on Top, and are made of abalone. To the Hopi they are the place from which the kachinas dance, bringing rain and corn and other good things to the Hopi, who by and large say nothing of such matters to those who are not Hopi. To the north lies Seattle, whence the maiden came.

To the north also lies the Grand Canyon. Within it are the Colorado River, the images on many postcards, the footprints and less fleeting reminders of many tourists, and the place where the Hopis originally came into this, the Fourth World.

To the east are what is left of the lands of the Navajo, the Din'eh, the People and what remains of the land entrusted by the gods to the Hopi.

To the east the maiden is looking with her deep-water eyes. To the east she is guiding her blue horse with her warm-breeze touch.

Then from the west, where the abalone peaks stand sentinel, an old woman strides across the desert.

She is dressed in velvet, despite the heat. Her skirt is like yellow corn pollen and does not show the dust of the desert at its bright hem. Her moccasins and her silver-trimmed blouse are the red of the canyon walls. Her hair is black obsidian and streaked with strands of white shell. With white yarn bindings it is tied into the shape of a bumblebee. At her ears, wrists, waist, fingers, and neck are strands and nuggets and beads of the purest sky-colored turquoise. A rainbow-colored blanket is folded over one of her arms and in her hand she carries a spindle.

Across the shimmering sands she walks, and her small moving draws the attention of the sun-haired maiden on the blue horse. The sun-haired maiden thinks the woman from the west must be nuttier than a piñon stand in Santa Fe, for, although it is late autumn, the air is hotter than a red chili ristra.

However, the maiden has learned that some old women are not what they seem. Some of them can change Harley

Davidsons into horse trailers. Some of them can create from thin air crystal horseshoes that cure a favorite pony's lameness. And besides, the sun-haired maiden is a kind girl. She does not like to see someone's grandmother walking in the heat like that, and she worries.

Later, she knows she was right to worry. The old woman is a great deal of trouble, even for a sun-haired maiden on the sun's own blue horse.

TWO

THE SUN-HAIRED MAIDEN'S name was Cindy Ellis. She was neither Navajo, nor Hopi. She was not a citizen of the state of Arizona, the state of Utah, the state of New Mexico or the state of Colorado. Nor, strictly speaking, was she a maiden.

In the lore of the dominant culture, her story might begin: *Once upon a time there was a young woman who was as good as she was beautiful.* It probably would not say that many people found such a person damned annoying, and sometimes so did Cindy. She was blessed with both a modest disposition and an embarrassment of riches of the nonmaterial sort that, in the olden days, it would have taken an entire fleet of good fairies to bestow upon her at her christening.

It was not just that she was a good rider, a fine artist, had perfect pitch and sang like an angel. It was not merely that she was graceful as a doe, gentle as a dove, kind and thoughtful. She was good at other things too. She had a gift for languages and no math block. She could wire a house, fix the plumbing, put up sheetrock, make a cake from scratch and a wedding dress by hand.

She also had a handsome prince. Princes don't get where they are by being dummies and Cindy's beauty, courage, versatility, good humor and intelligence had drawn the attention and affection of Raydir Quantrill. He was not only a prince but the King of the Alloy Rock.

Her beauty and goodness did not annoy Raydir, of course. He was far too self-involved to be annoyed by anyone who didn't, for instance, screw up his sound system during a recording session. But some of the less lovely females in his entourage found his new stable manager-sweetheart a bit hard to take.

"Cindy," said the young woman's social worker friend, Rose Samson, when they met for lunch to discuss Rose's bridesmaids' dresses for her forthcoming nuptials, "it's a classic case of you reliving your family drama except now that your wicked stepmother and stepsisters are out of the picture you're doing the same thing with the women in Raydir's entourage—trying to please them instead of making them look at their own stuff." Rose could sometimes be very firm about what other people needed to do.

But Cindy had to admit her friend probably had a point. Trying to get her stepmother and stepsisters off her back was how she had *acquired* so many of her skills. There was no need for them to hire anything done when they had a live-in slave to torment.

Cindy's love of horses and counseling from Rose had eventually helped her escape their clutches, but she was beginning to feel she'd jumped out of the barbecue and into the four-alarm chili, as her old stable boss, Pill, used to say.

She had no friends at Raydir's estate except Raydir, and though he had many good points and made her heart pound like Silver's hooves when the Lone Ranger was riding to the rescue, he could also be a major pain. Plus he was gone a lot.

One morning after her second riding lesson, she tripped lightly between the rows of rhododendrons, madroñas and weeping willows that lined the palatial estate. In her hand was a posy of wildflowers for her love, who surely would be awake by now, as it was well past his usual crack of noon rising time.

Raydir was indeed awake. Bejeaned and bare-chested in their bower, he was hastily stuffing leather pants and T-shirts into a piece of luggage with lots of pockets. "Hi, babe," he said, tossing in a hand-beaded vest and a pair of custom cowboy boots.

"You're leaving?" she asked. "I thought your gig wasn't until the sixteenth."

"Yeah. Neddy set up a couple of promo things on the local back-East stations before rock fest gigs, the concert at Carnegie and the guest spot on David King."

"Oh," Cindy said. She had been hoping they could enjoy a meal together away from the mansion—breakfast for him, lunch for her—at one of their favorite romantic hideaways—the Denny's north on I-5 between the mansion and Edmonds.

"Wanna come?" Raydir asked, putting his arms around her waist and rocking her back and forth. Usually that made her very happy, but she was busy feeling abandoned—again. He'd just returned from a weekend gig in L.A. and San Francisco and she'd barely had time to welcome him home.

"No," she said. "Who'd look after the horses?"

"Those stablehands you said I needed to hire. Whatsername—Ginjer—and the little girl. You've trained them pretty well."

"Not that well. And Courtney's just twelve, Ray. She has school. She's only working in exchange for lessons."

"Well—that old guy you used to work for, what's his name? Call him. I *need* you there for me, babe."

Oh, sure, she thought. Like a horse needed a second tail. She'd heard him say that before, and happily gone with him to his gigs, where she'd spent all her time ducking and backing into corners and dodging, trying to keep out of the way and not interrupt. Before and after the concerts there was the endless waiting while he talked to sound engineers, lighting designers, stage managers, other tech crew and, of course, fans. The stampede of groupies nearly trampled her as they grabbed for Ray, pushing their phone numbers and room keys on him and asking him to sign their underwear and cuddle with them for a photo.

The concerts themselves were worse. She *hated* Alloy Rock. The lyrics were whiny with worse language than Pill had used the time he was thrown by the mare he bought to rent out for kiddie rides. Besides, the music was so loud it hurt.

"Well, I'll think about it," Cindy said. "But Pill's pretty busy."

"I'll pay him for his time. A lot."

Ray thought that money would take care of any problem. What worried Cindy was that from what she could see, he might be right.

"Just call him. Okay? Think about it, huh? Then say yes, call me and hop on a plane. I'll send a limo to pick you up."

He gave her a confident but hardly passionate goodbye kiss, and left.

She wandered out into the kitchen to see if there was anything to eat. The housekeeper was there, having lunch with the cook.

"Hi," she said. They both looked up.

The cook, or rather chef, was a burly, bearded man with an eye patch and about forty tattoos on his arms, the most outstanding of which was a tree growing from the roots at his wrist, the branches wrapping around his meaty forearm. An animal or bird sat on each branch, and across the back of his hand a treasure chest spilled booty onto his fingers. Today there was a full color something in the crook of his elbow above the highest branch. He saw her looking.

"Like it?" he asked, opening his arm so she could get a better view. "Just got it yesterday. It's the Tawa sign the Pueblo Indians use for the sun and the colors of the four directions—see, yellow, blue, black and white. Only I had them put in red where the white was because it didn't show up very good."

Cindy inspected it appreciatively. "It's really nice," she said. "I didn't know they could do all those colors."

"The process has been around," he told her.

"Don't just stand there bragging about your skin, Hogeye, get the child some of that great stew you whomped up for lunch. She's been working all morning, poor kid, and Raydir just ran off and left her again," the housekeeper said, pointing to the stove with a dainty hand. She kept house while wearing three-inch stiletto heels and skintight pastel shorts and a halter, or leather miniskirts and a shirt three sizes too small, depending on the season. For formal occasions, she wore a black spandex catsuit with crystal-enhanced zippers from neck to crotch and ankle to waist on each leg. She was about ten years older than Cindy, putting her at thirty-five or so, and wore her white-blond hair in a messy pile on top of her head. Racoon rings of smudgy blue shadow, and black liner around cold blue eyes belied the endearments she used when speaking to Cindy. Her name, supposedly, was Pagan Platero, though Ray's daughter, Sno, told Cindy that when Pagan's mother, Mrs. Grossnickel, was alive she used to phone and ask to speak to her daughter Phyllis and Pagan always took the call.

Cindy missed Sno, who was in Ireland studying to be a fairy godmother with the strange lady in gray named Felicity Fortune, who was herself a fairy godmother. At least, Cindy didn't know what else you'd call someone who changed a Harley Davidson hog into a 4 X 4 and horse trailer before her very eyes *and* made a magic shoe that had cured Punkin's lameness. Felicity was responsible for saving Sno's life and for Cindy meeting Raydir and finally escaping the influence of her stepsisters and stepmother for good. She had also helped Rosie Samson become head of Seattle Social Services and find true love with Fred Moran, now her fiancé. Everybody was supposed to live happily ever after now, weren't they?

"Poor little Cindy Éllis," Pagan cooed through her burgundy-colored lipstick. "Slaves all morning in a hot stable only to have Raydir go romanticus interruptus on her again."

"He asked me to fly out and meet him later," Cindy corrected her. "He has a living to make, after all."

"That's not all he's making, honey," Pagan told her with a worldly wiggle of her eyebrows. "If I were you I'd hop that plane right now. You gotta be nuts not to have gone with him. He gets *lots* of attention." She sighed and stood. "Guess I better go fluff a pillow or something," she said, and tottered off, hips swaying as she balanced on her pointy heels.

"Don't mind her, honey," Hogeye said. "How about some of that stew anyway? You look a little skinny to me."

"No thanks," Cindy told him. "I lost my appetite all of a sudden. Bye. Time to go muck out the stalls."

"Well, okay. But hey, if the boss wants to play, there's more fish in the sea, y'know?" He blinked his good eye in what she assumed would have been a wink except for the patch. "You get lonely, you just come see old Hogeye."

That was the kind of offer to make shoveling horse shit look downright attractive. Cindy was weary of how every time Raydir left, the people who worked for him or who were semipermanent houseguests insisted on providing her with details of what they assumed he was doing, based on their superior knowledge of his past, which was almost twice as long as Cindy's and apparently a great deal more colorful. She knew he had made some mistakes—Sno was quick to remind him, in case he forgot. But their relationship was their relationship and it was special and different.

She was beginning to feel a little more relaxed when Belinda Benedict, Ray's West Coast publicist, arrived to ride her Thoroughbred, Quantrill's Fiery Lawrence, or Larry, as he was usually known. Cindy had never spent much time around the woman, who was always intent on conversations with Raydir or too busy trying to snatch an hour or two to ride Larry to chitchat with Cindy. Cindy didn't much like the way Belinda parked Larry as if he were a car and expected someone else to take off his tack and groom him. And Courtney said she'd seen the publicist strike the horse. He was skittish.

So Cindy kept heaving manure when she saw Belinda arrive, expecting her to go straight to Larry's stall. Instead, Belinda, in white jodphurs and shirt and black riding boots polished into obsidian mirrors, tripped down to Punkin's stall. She was smiling and flicking her riding crop, playfully making flies crash and burn. She needed only a long red scarf and she could be the Red Baroness, Cindy thought.

"Hel-*lo,* sweetie. How are things today?" Belinda asked in a musical voice that probably made people want to phone her.

"Just fine," Cindy said, planting her foot on her shovel and scooping up an odoriferous mass.

"I'm surprised to see you here, Connie. I thought surely you'd have gone with Ray-dear."

"It's Cindy. And I'm the stable manager, not the stage manager," she said. She was beginning to feel trapped in the closeness of the stall.

"Of course you are. Anyone can see that," Belinda said, making her agreement sound somehow insulting. "No one would mistake you for another boring supermodel afraid to ruin her manicure."

"I don't think they'd ask me to be spokesmodel for designer perfume either, right now," Cindy said, dumping the load off the shovel and jabbing the blade under another pile.

Belinda laughed as if Cindy's remark was a lot funnier than it was. "How refreshingly earthy you are, dear. I can see why Ray-dear thinks you're so different even though, purely superficially of course, you're the same type as all of his other women except his wives. Smallish and blondish, that is. Well, there's Pagan, of course, but she's just a convenience."

"I guess housekeepers are supposed to be convenient or people wouldn't have them," Cindy said. She had been her stepfamily's housekeeper (as well as carpenter, plumber, electrician, seamstress, laundress, chief cook and bottle washer) and had tried to make herself extremely convenient to them, knowing that otherwise she wouldn't get much to eat. She also knew that wasn't what Belinda was getting at, but she was trying to ignore the nasty tone and get on with her work. She'd had a lot of practice trying to deflect nasty remarks when she lived with the steps.

Belinda had long, curly red hair, presently encased in a snood that added to her air of elegant superiority. Cindy had heard someone say that Belinda's family was very wealthy and she only did publicist work because she was bored and liked associating with famous and talented people.

"Oh, you're not at *all* like Pagan. That slut may be convenient but she's utterly useless as a housekeeper. I swear the sheets on Ray-dear's bed hadn't been changed for a week the last time I stayed over. You're *much* better for him. So wholesome and practical. It's so nice to see someone here who doesn't care about her looks or spend all her time trying to be glam. Someone who fits in better with horses than Hollywood. Someone who obviously is a thrifty clothes shopper and doesn't mind getting a little mussed. You're just so— charmingly ordinary, Connie. In a nice way, of course."

Cindy wasn't sure how her shovel slipped, seemingly of its own volition, tilting sideways to dump its load of horse manure onto Belinda's pristine white pants and shiny boots, fouling them with dung. "Oops, sorry," Cindy said, grinning for the first time that afternoon.

Her satisfaction was short-lived, however. She finished the stalls with difficulty since she had to quit from time to time to brush away angry tears with the sausage-sized finger of her work glove. Trying to regain her composure, she'd taken Punkin out for a long ride and when they were done, she loosened the cinch, cooled him down, unsaddled him, removed the bridle, replaced it with the halter and let him have a good roll. After putting him in crossties, she checked his feet, then brushed him first with the rough brush to get the worst of the dirt out of his coat, then with the Dandy brush for initial shine. Next, she used a rag to buff him up, then rubbed him with her hands until his coat shone like rose gold. Finally, she oiled his feet.

Her heart still ached so badly, she felt as if a horse were standing on her chest, so she cleaned and oiled all the tack, and still she felt horrible. First the step-relatives, then Raydir's entourage—she always seemed to be at the mercy of people who thought they had more right to be where she was than she did. She wasn't very good at fighting back either. A shovel full of shit didn't begin to cover the depth of her aggravation.

Finally she went into Sno's room to pet and talk to Puss, the street cat Felicity Fortune had once empowered to talk to people. Puss had been with Dico Miller until the boy went to Ireland to study music. Sno had persuaded her father to let her take care of the cat, now silent except for the standard cat noises. She'd made Cindy, her fellow animal lover, promise to talk to Puss sometimes, figuring the cat must miss human conversation even if she could no longer be a comprehensible participant. Cindy wasn't sure if Puss minded that or not, but right now Cindy needed the comfort of the cat's purring warmth. Puss usually preferred to nest in Sno's room, though of course, like any self-respecting cat, she had the run of the house. The minute Cindy opened the door to Sno's room, the cat came barreling down the hall and jumped up on the bed, onto the cat fur-covered quilt that had belonged to Sno's Grandma Hilda.

The girl's room was the most normal one in the house. The bed was surrounded on two walls by bookcases stuffed with portions of the library Sno had also inherited from her grandmother. A stereo outfit, with a record player on top of the cassette, radio, and CD components occupied the frilly dresser.

Beside it was part of Sno's inherited vinyl album collection. The rest of the collection sat in stacks all over the floor.

Puss nudged Cindy's hand, sniffing the smell of horse that clung to her fingers. Cindy stroked the cat's head, scratching her behind the ears and under the chin. "Oh, Puss, I wish we were in Ireland too, don't you? Someplace else anyway, where people have better things to do than be nasty to us." Puss rubbed down the length of Cindy's arm, then settled awhile in the small of her back.

"This place really is not big enough for me and them, you know? I rode Punkin all over this ranch of Raydir's and there still wasn't enough room to work off any steam for Punkin or me either."

Puss made a *prrt* sound and the weight on Cindy's back disappeared, followed by the sound of books clumping together on the shelf as the cat jumped up to the top shelf, to do a little lurking.

The phone rang. Cindy ignored it, knowing one of the others would get it. But a few moments later, Pagan's affected voice called, "It's for you, Ellis. A man. But don't get excited, it's not Raydir. Just some old goat."

Cindy picked up Sno's phone and switched from the girl's private line to the one for the main house, indicated by the blinking red light. "Hello?" she said cautiously.

"I don't know who that gal was," said a familiar raspy voice, "but she wasn't brung up too good, was she? I'd rather be a nanny than a ninny myself, is all I can say."

"I'm so glad to hear from you, Pill!" Cindy said. "How's the stable?"

"I ain't hardly had time to find out," he told her. "Just got back. Been down visitin' an old saddle-pal of mine who's got a place out by Flagstaff. He was talkin' about somethin' made me think of you, wishin' you wasn't tied up tendin' your boyfriend's polo ponies or whatever the hell he's got up there."

"It's mixed," Cindy said and proceeded to tell Pill, gratefully, about every horse and rider in the stable.

"Sounds like you got your hands full. Too bad. You're the only one I could think of when my old pard asked if I knew anyone could train a cayuse of his for long-distance trail riding. You've done you quite a bit of that, haven't you? "

"Some, when I first moved out of Dad's house and before I got the job with you and the house-sitting job in Wallingford."

They talked a while longer about his trip and she tried to sound cheerful about living at Raydir's and Pill sounded distressed, as if he didn't believe a word of it. He could read her pretty well. She had just hung up when something tumbled down from the bookcase and fell on her foot, followed shortly by the thump of Puss's paws landing on the bed.

Cindy looked down to see what had fallen. It was an old book called *To the Foot of the Rainbow* by a man named Clyde Kluckhohn. The subtitle read "A Tale of Twenty-Five Hundred Miles of Wandering on Horseback Through the Southwest Enchanted Land."

Puss *prrrted* at her again and she reached over and scratched the cat's whiskers, then gave her a kiss on top of her head. "Who says you can't still speak human?" she asked.

Cindy got one of those Mr. Spock cat looks from Puss in return as the cat swabbed a paw across her whiskers as if to say, So what else is new? Once magic, always magic, and settled down for a nap alongside her human companion.

Cindy spent the rest of the day reading and petting Puss until her belly told her it was time to eat something.

Before she risked wandering into the kitchen, however, she thought she'd try to call Raydir. It would do her good to hear him ask her to come out to meet him again, even if she didn't want to.

She tapped the button that dialed his cell phone automatically. A woman at the other end giggled and then said breathlessly, trying to imitate an answering machine, "I'm sorry, but Raydir can't come to the phone right now. Please leave your name and number after the click." And she hung up.

Cindy looked at the phone, and looked at the Kluckhohn book, then called Pill back.

A week later she and a wrangler oddly enough named Bill Gates headed up north of Flagstaff where he parked the truck and horse trailer by the side of the road. Gates released the rope binding the horse to the trailer and Cindy opened the trailer door. When the horse backed out, she grabbed the lead rope and led her new pupil out onto the grass. His name was Chaco and he was a good Arab-quarter cross stallion with a gray body, white stockings and a white star on his forehead. This gray was the color the Navajos sometimes called blue, even turquoise, Gates had told her.

Well, he looked gray to Cindy. After consulting with Pill's friend Hank, Chaco's owner, she had reluctantly decided to forego the route Kluckhohn had taken. For one thing, she was going in the wrong direction and for another thing, Hank said, riding across the Navajo Nation wasn't an easy thing anymore, what with all the fences the BIA had put up for range management purposes. Much as she hated abandoning her more adventurous plans, Cindy agreed to stay along the roads and well-marked trails on the reservation. It was still going to be a pretty interesting trip, since she would be seeing the Indian country of the Southwest for the first time. Besides, as Hank had pointed out, she was a woman alone on a good horse that didn't belong to her. He made it very clear he much preferred that she stay close to phones, food, water and other conveniences, and have the luxury of pacing Chaco as she thought best, rather than as necessity dictated. At least doing it this way she could manage without the burden of a pack horse.

Hank had asked her specifically to use a Western saddle, as he was six feet two inches tall and weighed 230 pounds. The heavy Western saddle, coupled with the well-packed saddlebags, would help make up the difference between his weight and Cindy's. Normally Cindy would have preferred a McClintock saddle for long-distance or endurance rides, as they were lighter and easier on both horse and rider, but those were measured specifically for a custom horse/rider fit and since Chaco was Hank's, it didn't make much sense to have a saddle fitted for Cindy.

She smoothed the freshly cleaned saddle blanket across Chaco's back, slung the saddle on top of it, fastened the cinch and settled the saddle into place before tightening the cinch.

Gates had brought a five-gallon container of water and a bucket in the truck bed and Cindy poured the water into the bucket and offered Chaco some water, which he wisely drank.

"Okay, fella, put your head down," she said, and he graciously acquiesced. Nice guy for a stallion, she thought. Hank usually rode him with a D-ring snaffle. That wouldn't have been Cindy's choice either, not on a stallion, since the snaffle didn't have much whoa to it—no way to enforce your command to stop. The bit was very gentle and most people, including Cindy, preferred a more authoritative bit, especially in unpredictable circumstances. However, you didn't fix what wasn't broke when it came to tacking up a critter who was already used to a certain kind of gear.

Finally, she took the heavy saddlebags from the side of the truck bed and hoisted them up behind the saddle, evened them out, and tied them on. The horse was fifteen hands high and Gates had moved in to help her but she waved him away. She'd have to manage by herself out on the trail. Might as well start now. When Gates saw that she had matters well in hand, he saluted her with two fingers to his hat brim and drove away. She mounted, gave Chaco a companionable pat and headed his nose north.

In her saddlebags, Kluckhohn had been joined by Douglas Preston's *Talking to the Ground*. She had found a special map of the Navajo and Hopi Nations as well, and that was folded in her hip pocket. She'd wanted a Navajo dictionary but her boss pointed out that most of the Navajos she met probably spoke better English than Pill did and that the language was not an easy one to pronounce, so she wouldn't have much luck figuring out what to say or what was said to her by consulting a book.

She was just taking in the countryside, the jewelry stands, the distant red cliffs, the cracked desert, the hogans, and to the southwest, the San Francisco Peaks, when she saw the small figure of the old Navajo woman in the red velvet blouse, yellow velvet skirt and the fortune in turquoise jewelry strolling across the desert toward her, brandishing a long, pointed object with a round disk near the end of it as if she were Mary Poppins, swinging her brolly and out for her morning constitutional. Even though it was well into fall by then, the mountain cool of the morning had already worn off and it was, to Cindy's Pacific Northwest internal thermometer, ungodly hot.

The Navajo lady, almost looking as if she expected to see Cindy there, raised the hand with the pointed object in it and called, "Hi there!"

"Hi," Cindy said back. It only seemed polite to wait for her. For someone so ancient, the woman had crossed the stretch of desert between them with amazing speed.

"Where you goin' on that pretty horse?" the old lady asked as she drew abreast of Cindy and stopped. To Cindy's surprise, the woman wasn't even breathing hard, but looked perfectly calm and serene, except for regarding the horse with a slightly quizzical air.

"I'm taking him up to Tuba City for a training ride across the reservations."

The old lady's hand went to her lips and she grinned a white grin around her fingertips. "A training ride. Tee hee. Who's gonna train who?"

Cindy laughed. "It usually ends up being mutual, that's for sure. Do you live around here?"

"Me? No, I live clear out by Canyon de Chelly. I been visitin' my sisters over across that London Bridge they got down to Havasu City. My grandsons was s'posed to meet me at the bridge, but they didn't. Guess they got into mischief someplace."

She didn't seem in the least put out about it. Instead she gave Cindy a calculating glance. "I need a ride, I think."

"You didn't walk all the way from Havasu City, did you?" Cindy asked. She'd looked at enough maps lately to know that was on the far western border of Arizona where it met with California, a good 200 miles or so away.

The old lady shrugged.

"Wouldn't you rather ride in a car or a truck?" Cindy asked.

"Why? You got one?"

"No, but, I mean, all I have is this horse and . . . "

"Looks like a good one to me," the old lady said. Suddenly she sank down so that her skirts spread in the sand. "Gee, I sure am tired."

Cindy wasn't tired. She wanted to get started. Not to get anywhere exactly, because if you wanted to get someplace fast in this day and age, horseback wasn't usually your first choice of transport. She was anxious to begin her journey though, away from the cities. This trip was what Rosie would call process oriented. And part of the process was taking what came along, getting to know people. And here was a person who evidently was all too ready to get to know her and who, moreover, seemed to need her help.

"You could ride my horse for a while," Cindy offered. "At least till we get you to a bus or something. You won't want to go with me. I'm going to be on the trail for quite some time."

She was dismounting as she said this and was bending down to make a stirrup of her hands to help the little old lady to mount, only to find that with little more than a hop, the woman in Navajo dress was already in the saddle. Cindy looked up at her, and for a moment, her impression of great age was challenged by the woman's actual appearance, which could have been that of a mature forty-year-old or a well-preserved woman in her eighties, though probably one with ready access to spas, expensive cosmetics and plastic surgeons.

The impression of elderliness—or maybe just elder-ness—was more in the way she carried herself, as if her body were an old couch whose upholstery was worn but whose springs, though rusty, were still good. Although the rustiness seemed not to apply to mounting horses.

Her eyes said "old" too—but there was an expression in them that seemed familiar to Cindy, if eyes full of timeless secrets and stories from unmappable places could be said to be familiar.

The woman winked at Cindy and Cindy felt an almost imperceptible dip and shift in her reality, making her just the slightest bit dizzy for a moment. It was the heat, she decided. Flagstaff and its environs were in the mountains—this was desert. The heat was dry and crept up on you. In spite of the coat of tan she'd laid down over her Seattle pallor in the last few days, she still needed #30 sunscreen on her face and the backs of her hands.

She blinked up at the little old lady sitting astride her horse. "That's okay," the woman told her. "I'm not in a hurry."

"Oh—uh—that's good," Cindy said, regaining her equilibrium. After all, she didn't want to seem ungracious. She would be traveling through land belonging to the Navajo Nation and it probably wouldn't look too bad to be seen helping this elderly lady. Old people seemed to like company and maybe this woman could tell her a little about the places she was going.

"I'm pretty hungry and thirsty," the old lady said. Cindy handed her one of the plastic sippy-cap bottles of water she'd brought along. Canteens looked good, but they didn't keep the water cold the way the insulated carrier around the plastic bottles did, and a canteen tended to give the water a metallic flavor. She also dug out the salami sandwich she had meant to keep for her own lunch, and an apple.

"This is good stuff," the elderly woman said, chewing busily on the salami while clucking to the horse so that it climbed onto the road, crossed between cars and trotted down to a trail along the other side, with Cindy keeping up on foot. "We can go cross country this way. It's quicker."

Cindy didn't like the idea of departing from her scheduled route, especially since the old woman was liberally chugging her water and had left nothing of the apple but a core, and nothing of the sandwich but the crust. "Here, put these back for yourself," the woman said without a trace of irony. Cindy did so, her eyes narrowing as she reflected that she seemed to have already acquired another evil-mother type who was going to take advantage of her. But the old lady, as if hearing her thoughts, said gently, "You're a very kind girl. My sister said you would be."

"Do I know your sister?" Cindy asked and then, before the woman could answer, she began thinking that maybe the poor old thing was confused, an Alzheimer's patient who had wandered away from her caretakers. Wearing a fortune in turquoise no less! She could have gotten mugged. They both could get mugged as it was now. "Look, where does your sister live? I know you said across London Bridge but, well, do you have any relatives close by here we could call? Just to let them know you're safe? Maybe we could stop at someone's house and they could call your grandsons to come and get you?"

For a long time the old lady looked straight ahead, and Cindy thought she had offended her. Then, with a little sigh, the woman said softly, "I'm related to most everybody in these parts. We can see if my grandsons are in Moenkopi at the dance, maybe."

"Moenkopi? That's near Tuba City, isn't it?"

The old lady nodded.

"What do I call you?" Cindy asked.

The old lady was silent again for a long time and then said, slowly, "When I was taking care of relatives who had to go to Bosque Redondo or to Santa Fe, some of the white people called me Grandma Webster." She regarded Cindy impassively for a moment, but warmth and humor kindled in her ancient-seeming eyes and suddenly she smiled, a flash of the strong white teeth in the finely tooled leather of her face. "But you should just call me Grandmother. Everyone around here does."

"Nice to meet you—Grandmother," Cindy said, reaching up with her free hand to take the one the old woman extended. Her handshake was a bit limp but Cindy put that down to age. "I'm Cindy Ellis."

"Yeah, I know," Grandma said mildly.

Out in the desert, a whirlwind gathered sand and weeds into its ever-lengthening cone and gyrated off across their path toward the cliffs in the northeast.

"Wow, look at that!" Cindy said, as the cone reached up toward the clouds. "That's the biggest dust devil I ever saw."

"Dust devil? Hm," Grandma Webster mused and Cindy sensed, rather than saw, that her face, too, was turned toward the sand-filled maelstrom. She studied it. "You see how it is rotating against the sun instead of with it?"

Cindy tried but couldn't really tell. "I'll take your word for it."

"This shows that it is a dark wind. The good kind is just called a Darkness. This sort is called the Rolling Darkness."

"That's pretty omnious for a whirlwind, even a big one."

"Well, actually, it's a ghost," Grandma said. She was silent a long time and Cindy thought she had said all she was going to say. Finally, after the whirlwind disappeared over the horizon, Grandma continued. "There's different kinds. That one—she twitched her lips in the direction the wind had gone—"is Rolling Darkness. There's Coiled Winds and Revolving Winds and Striped Winds too. When a spirit departs a body and turns into one of these winds, it can go into someone else and make them act wild, behave crazy, say bad things."

"I've heard of some people going crazy because of winds before," Cindy said. "Like the noise and the agitation get to them. Is it like that?"

Grandma didn't answer directly.

She held up one of Cindy's hands, palm up, and touched the tip of her ring finger. "These," she said, tracing Cindy's fingerprint, "are the tracks of the wind that blew life into you. You got the same tracks on your toes. That's good wind. Bad ones can blow into you, though, and mix up the good winds inside you. We've had lots of them lately."

And she was silent again for a long time, turned inward, though her lips were moving, as if she were singing to herself, or chanting.

THREE

The Rolling Darkness

For three years a Rolling Darkness sweeps over the world. It dries up the water in its path. It blots out the stars in its path. The doors of houses are blown open by it. Sand scatters before it.

It enters, stinking, through the noses of the sleeping people. People strong with resolution and good thoughts cast it out. People weak with drink or despair are made weaker.

It comes rolling into the Navajo Nation. It comes rolling to Gallup, to the bars and the cheap motels. It comes rolling as far north as Shiprock and Farmington, to the streets and the jails. It comes rolling to these places in Page and Grants, in Aztec and in Winslow. Carrying evil in its whirlwind, it comes rolling.

Into men carrying evil it comes rolling.

Into women carrying evil it comes rolling.

Over all of the Navajo Nation, it is rolling.

Rolling over old men, beaten and battered it comes rolling. Over young women, raped and left for dead, it comes rolling. Over animals, mutilated and dismembered, it comes rolling. Over land cracked with heat it comes rolling. Over stillborn crops it comes rolling. Down creek beds dry as the castoff skins of snakes it comes rolling, carrying its evil.

And evil that once had been unthinkable becomes commonplace.

A Navajo father, in a drunken rage, kills the children he had loved dancing with. He did this only to spite his wife, who had wearied of his drinking and left him. And lies were spread, and spite became a good reason to do almost anything. Skinwalkers sang to the moon and witchcraft flourished.

This was not the gentle Wiccan people dancing in the moonlight, nor was it Satan worshippers with their dreams of power and pain. This was one person with a jealous grudge sickening and poisoning another person, his children, his animals, causing his house to burn and his heart to fill with killing fear.

Good people were blamed and vilified while bad ones abused their power and everyone else.

On the Hopi Partitioned Lands, it was as bad as everywhere else, and worse.

When the Hopi elders made their way to their most sacred spring in the summer of the second dark year, they found a wall closing it off from them.

And in the third dark year, at the time when Cindy Ellis sees the whirlwind, another group of Hopi elders visits another sacred shrine. The shrine is hidden in the deepest woods where the juniper grows thick enough to furnish boughs for the masks and headdresses of the kachinas. From hiding, someone watches, sneering as the elders honor their shrine.

When the elders leave, this person enters the shrine that should have been secret, and the wrongness is made worse. Laughing, the person leaves the ruined shrine behind. Laughing, thinking how the Hopis won't like what they will find when they return.

The very soles of the person's feet are dishonored by the sacred pollen stamped into them. And afterwards there is another whirlwind of the bad kind. In its grip are the eagle feathers, the painted sticks and the white cornmeal that had been offered to kinder beings.

Sometimes this sort of thing, the desecration of shrines, is done by people who are angry, into whom the darkness has crept because they feel wronged. Sometimes someone with a bad heart has spoken to them and angered them more than they might be ordinarily. On the particular day when this particular shrine is desecrated, the person with pollen on his feet is one who feeds on hard feelings, who picks at them to make them fester, who incites sabotage, who loves to make bad go to worse.

This person is a witch, a kinwalker, The One Who Is Also a Wolf. Once he was a man, like others, with a job and a life and a family. But the dark wind inside of him blew that away. He makes sure that no one knows who he is—or not all of who he is. If they knew, they would find a way to destroy him. And he does not wish to be destroyed. His place is to destroy, not to be destroyed.

In his old life, he had a cousin, now dead. His dead cousin's wife is out herding the few sheep she has left. Her face is hard and angry as she thinks about how many sheep she used to have, before the BIAs said that was too many for the land and took them away. Didn't even give her the money. Said she owed *them* money.

Today she has one less sheep because the witch was hungry and he needed some meat. At night, if he wishes, he turns into a wolf and takes what pleases him, kills who displeases him.

Today he is a man. "Yah-ta-hey, Alice," he says. He has walked close enough to her to make her jump when he speaks from behind her.

She whirls but his face is in shadow, though the sun is hiding. He is casting the shadow himself, but most people do not see this right away. She squints up at him and glares as if he were a BIA, instead of what he is, which is even worse. Much worse. But she doesn't know that yet.

He smiles, a wolf's smile, showing lots of teeth. His eyes do not crinkle. "Hey, it's okay. I'm one of your husband's relatives. I heard you talking at that meeting held by those AIM people, the American Indian Movement folks from the Plains and back East, who came to help out. I danced with your sister's son's wife at the girl dance."

Alice Begay squints harder. She still doesn't know him but doesn't want to say so, the witch can tell. "Oh," she says, in a voice smaller and more puzzled than her angry one. Her eyes do not meet his, though she is known to be a bold woman. "What do you want?"

"I want to help you. You're a brave woman but you're up against powers you don't understand."

"You got that right. Even the *biligaana* don't understand their government."

"I mean the Hopis. They're the ones behind this. They have strong powers that are helping them take your home, even though they don't want to live on this land. You need strong powers, too. I can help you."

"How?"

"I can tell you what to do to become strong enough to fight them off."

"You live out here too? Why don't you use this knowledge to fight them yourself?"

He chuckles and it sounds like the friendly chuckle of an ordinary Navajo man, the same way the roar of a panther sounds like the mew of a housecat. "Nobody's gonna bother me. You could see to it that they don't bother you either."

She doesn't ask how she can do that. She knows him for what he is now. Maybe she knew from the start but didn't want to admit it. Denial. That's what the counselors call it.

"Maybe that would be just as bad," she says finally. She is staring straight up into his face, but the shadow conceals him, he knows. "Maybe I don't want to be like that. Maybe I don't want to do those things you do that would let me do what you say."

He shrugged. "I hear the New Lands aren't bad if you like little cluttered villages with a lot of people with nothing to do but collect utility bills and wait around to die. You're probably tired of the sheep anyway. And who knows? It might be good to live in a radioactive area. Maybe you could grow great big corn, like that Killer Tomato movie." He dug in his hip pocket and pulled out a small plastic bag, the kind people kept beads or little stones in for setting. It held a single off-white bead the size of a BB. "I got a present for you," he said. "You can use it to pay your union dues, supposing you want to join. You know what to do with it."

She wouldn't touch the plastic bag, so he dropped it on the

ground and walked off. He knew, without seeing her, when she picked it up.

Beauty's Rose and Blue Corn

After a long period of poverty for the whole family, Beauty's father heard that one of his ships had been saved from the storm and had landed in port, laden with rich cargo. He asked each of Beauty's sisters what gift they would have him bring them. "Beautiful dresses of the finest silk," said the eldest. "Jewels and gemstones, the biggest and rarest," said the middle sister. "And you, Beauty?" the father asked, for his youngest was secretly his favorite. "What would you have me bring you?" Beauty said she wanted only his safe return, but when he pressed her she said finally, "A rose then. Bring me a single rose."

Hub Honahni was a legend to Carl Loloma. Hub had been a handsome young man when Carl was an adolescent boy, a brooding hero returned from Vietnam before Carl got drafted, and had already established himself as an innovative jeweler and artist who brought the attention of big-time dealers to Hopi while Carl was still drinking to forget what he learned in the war. Honahni was born into one of the traditional priestly families, but favored progressive ideas to better the lives of his people and had contributed much of the money he made toward educational programs, libraries, food programs in time of shortage. By the time Carl moved away from Phoenix, back to Polacca, Honahni had himself moved away, to be closer to his gallery in Santa Fe, a showcase not only for his own work, but for the finest in Hopi jewelry, pottery, baskets and kachina carving.

He had to be a good ten years older than Carl, but he didn't look it, sitting across from him in a booth at the Rainbird Hotel restaurant, where he had invited Carl for a breakfast meeting. Hub wore a Western-style jacket over a cowboy-tailored shirt, jeans, a silver inlaid bolo and bracelet of his own distinctive design. His hair was still worn Hopi-style, straight across the front and long, but cut by a good hairdresser so the effect was the kind that, on a movie star, people would imitate. Unlike Carl, Hub's features were regular and fine. They'd been almost feminine when he was younger but had weathered to a distinctive handsomeness now. If Hopis had planned to have a poster-boy celebrity, something they weren't likely to do, they couldn't have picked one better than Hub Honahni. Carl had been surprised by the phone call inviting him to breakfast, and pleased.

"I hear good things about you, Carl," Hub said. "People say you've really taken a leadership role in getting this land issue settled, in getting the Navajos to let go of our land."

Carl cleared his throat and said noncommittally, "Well, it looks like it's about settled okay."

"Thanks to the perseverance of people like you. You heard my cousin isn't going to run again for tribal chairman?"

"Yeah. That's a shame. He's been doing a good job." Even if he hadn't, it wouldn't have been a very good idea to say so. But as a matter of fact, he and Carl agreed on quite a bit.

"Well, has he talked to you about trying for the job?"

"He sort of joked about it," Carl said.

"He wasn't joking. Trust me."

"How about you, Hub? You'd be a good chairman. Everybody respects you. Ever think of coming back to Hopi?"

"Not everybody," Hub said uncomfortably. "And since Amy died, what with my folks gone, I feel like an outsider."

Carl could see how that might be. Amy Honahni, Hub's first wife, had been killed in a car accident just before Carl moved back to Polacca. He'd heard she'd been drinking. Her parents both had problems like that, and so did her brothers, and they'd all hated Hub and still didn't have a good word to say about him. Carl didn't know them very well and the ones he did know he didn't like very much.

One of Amy's cousins was a client of his in his capacity as a substance abuse counselor and Carl found him particularly difficult to deal with. Manipulative didn't even start to describe it. Hub's parents had died in a fire when he was fairly young. Though his clan and lineage were good, and he could have had an important role in a religious society if he wanted to, several of his relatives had been suspected of witchcraft at one time or another. But many people who did much of anything with themselves were.

Hub was smart to stay away, Carl guessed, if it didn't bother him to do so. Carl had tried life outside for a long time and found that only back here at home did he feel centered, strong and confident enough to stop screwing up his own life and maybe do something to help other people with theirs. If you had to start somewhere, your own family, your own community, and your own people were a good place.

Hub said, "I think you should seriously consider the idea. You have a feeling for this kind of thing—you care about the welfare of our people, and you understand the balance between tradition and what is simply a decent life for them now, with plumbing and electricity and a good hospital for things that need AMA-type cures. You explain us well to outsiders, make a good impression for us—like Abbott used to do."

Carl was so flattered now, he would have felt suspicious if the speaker had been anyone but Honahni. Abbott Sekaquaptewa had been an enormous force for positive change in Hopi—the Hopi Cultural Center was largely his project, among others.

"I'd really like to hear more of your views, Carl. Just because I don't live here anymore doesn't mean I don't care about what's going on with our people. I was wondering if you might have the time to come up to my place in Santa Fe for the weekend, spend some time, eat some good food, meet a few friends."

"Sounds great," Carl said.

Two weeks later he was floating in Hub's turquoise pool, drinking Scandanavian mineral water. Hub had been a great host, showing him around the jewelry studio, the grounds he had landscaped himself in the shape of a great Hopi rainbird with feathers made of flowers and vegetables. Carl had been glad to see that Hub raised a little corn, blue, red, yellow, white and spotted, the traditional sacred corn colors appropriate to each direction in each segment of the garden. The house was Santa Fe-style but also Hopi-style, if Hopis had been wealthy with more beautiful things than they could make. One soft blanket in three desertlike colors, no more. A small collection of exquisite pots in various sizes. Kachina dolls on their shelves as they would be in a proper Hopi home, overseeing the household activities. A painted feather here—like a prayer feather, an artistic reflection of a sacred object Hub was too respectful to display, a drum beautiful in its wooden and white simplicity, a stack of pumpkins, a plain bowl of golden clay with red berries arranged like flowers, pink adobe, whitewash, red brick, and soft dark wood. A sudden burst of color from a striking painting suggestive of ceremonial life.

This was the work of Hub's second wife, a beautiful and gracious Zuni woman, also a jeweler. Her hair was pulled straight back, worked into a long braid down her back and clasped at the nape with a silver and turquoise barrette of Zuni needlepoint design. She wore white clothes—loose white pants, or a long, flowing white skirt, and a loose tunic top, cinched when there were special guests, with a breathtaking concho belt, and on less formal occasions a green and black, red and white Hopi sash. For around the house, the tunic was worn unbelted, with bare feet or maybe sandals. She wore big silver hoops all the time except for special occasions, when the earrings hanging to her shoulders matched the belt and barrette, the rings and bracelets she put on to make her white things party clothes. Elegant woman. She suited Hub.

Though Hopi men were always advised to marry Hopi women, a Zuni was the next best as the two were closely related by blood as well as custom and had a deep historical bond. Several other people were staying at the house, including a couple Carl recognized as being part of the law team that represented Hopi interests against the Navajo Nation regarding the Hopi Partitioned Lands, or HPL.

But mostly he and Hub talked about their childhoods, of Hopi history, of the future, the things they'd like to see preserved, the things they earnestly hoped would change, and how the prophecies of the elders supported the changes—or not. Not that the prophecies, strictly speaking, ever really supported anything. Who knew what they meant, whether their coming true brought everyone closer to the end of the Fourth

World or perhaps were the proper thing to do to prevent the end? Some elders said one thing and some said another.

It was good to be able to discuss these things with Hub, as if he were an admired and respected older brother, as if, almost, they were in the kiva together. This house, Hub's whole way of life, showed that a Hopi could be successful and also religious—could live in the outside world and remain Hopi, could be apart from the gossip and innuendo and backbiting and yet still be one of the people, still care about them. And yet have sophisticated, helpful insights as to how to help them. Both Carl and Hub knew that the choice the Hopi had made when they accepted their stewardship of this world from Masaw was being interpreted a bit too literally in this day and age.

Even though Carl had spent many years away from Hopiland, the creation story was repeated often enough that he knew it by heart. The classic portion, which told why Hopis lived where and as they did, was the story of how they chose their corn. He could almost hear his father's voice telling it.

Of all the people who emerged from the Third World into this, the Fourth World, Hopis were allowed to choose first which food we would have. Our people were shown all the kinds of corn and all the colors, red, yellow, white, blue and spotted. The red, yellow, white, and spotted ears were fat and juicy with kernels, long and perfect in shape. Only the blue corn was small, its stalks far shorter than the other types, its ears stunted and tough. "We will have the blue corn," our ancestors said. And by picking the poorest corn that could grow in the most arid soil under the most difficult conditions, they ensured that, although we Hopis would never be wealthy and often would go hungry, we would always be able to survive.

In the same way, the Hopi ancestors had chosen Hopiland, the most arid portion of all the lands they had roamed long before the white man, long before the Spaniards, long before the Navajos, long before even the other Pueblo people. All of these people had more arable land, more water, than the Hopi did. Carl's people had deliberately chosen to be poor, to have to work hard to live so they would not fall into the same error they had in the previous three worlds. This way they would not become bored with an easy life or have the leisure to think of bad things to do.

It agreed very much, in some ways, with the Christian feeling that "idle hands make the devil's work."

And yet, hands as old as his father's needed to be idle at last at the end of life. And why should it be hard to clean him, if water pipes were available? Why should Carl's niece Sela not get a good bilingual education, with tools she needed to help her own people and to make her living in the white world, if need be? Why must there be so few opportunities, so little stimulation in his land that the young people moved away and fell into trouble? These days they didn't even have to move away. Only a few days before, a classmate of Sela's had OD'd on drugs the other kids swore had been offered to them by people in a sleek BMW, as payment for jewelry, carvings, and fine pottery. Not having enough to survive the outside world was surely as dangerous to their souls and to the fate of the world as having too much.

Hub's voice broke into Carl's thoughts as he floated in the pool. "Carl, some guys just came who want to meet you."

"Yeah?" he answered, surprised. He didn't think Hub would be acquainted with anyone outside of Hopi who would even know of him. It was probably some hotshot Santa Fe writers or anthropologists—the kind of people who might make friends with Hub. The kind of people who would come out to Hopi. Carl trusted Hub's judgment enough to be pretty sure it wouldn't be some New Age guru. Those were the three types of people who were usually the most eager to talk to Hopis. With only a few thousand Hopis, and more writers and anthropologists coming out of the schools and cities all the time, a Hopi person, even the rare one with no relatives, need never get lonely. Just stand around long enough and some *pahana* would come and study you or interview you or sit at your feet to learn your wisdom.

They were usually flattered when they heard that they were

called *pahanas*, or white brothers, after the one way back in the days of the Hopi migrations who migrated to the East with a piece of the stone tablet Masaw gave the Hopis as proof of their right to the land. He was "the" *Pahana*, and so far had not returned—the Spaniards had not met the qualifications, nor had the other North Americans, nor anyone the Hopis had yet encountered. Just the same, all non-Hopis who were not some other kind of Indian were called *pahanas*, sometimes with considerable irony.

These *pahanas* who came to study Hopis always, of course, most wanted to study the elders. The ones who really knew something special were usually obliged to keep what they knew to themselves or within their kiva. He knew a couple of old guys who were, well, just OLD, not necessarily high up in the men's societies or priests or anything, but they were old so the *pahanas* figured they had to be elders and would believe anything the old guys said. Whether money or goods changed hands, nobody was ever entirely sure, but it kept everyone concerned entertained anyhow. Carl was getting into middle age now. Maybe these friends of Hub's figured he was an elder-in-training.

He climbed out of the pool, momentarily wishing his niece could have come to enjoy it too. She had stayed home to take care of her grandfather and besides, at sixteen she had her own agenda. Unfortunately part of it was a weasly Navajo kid Carl had little use for but that's the way it was with kids.

He pulled on his pants and shirt, leaving the latter open, finger-combed his hair to dry across his shoulders and padded barefoot across the cool red tiles into Hub's auditorium-sized living room, where Hub and a couple of guys in alligator shirts sat around on hand-crafted furniture Hub had traded a painting for with a woodworker he knew. The rustic wood contrasted with the honey colored handwoven upholstery and the Navajo-rug style cushions in soft natural dyed colors of sage and gold, brown and gray.

Hub, also barefoot and wearing a T-shirt, stood when Carl entered the room. "Gentlemen, this is Carl Loloma. Carl, this is Ed Abercrombie and Micah Firestone. They plan on doing some work up around your area soon and had heard you might be a good man to know."

Carl lifted his eyebrows in Hub's direction. Where would these guys have heard something like that? Hub shrugged. From him, of course. Well, maybe they really were friends. Though they didn't impress Carl as being artistic types, or even collectors. There wasn't a shred of imagination or style in the way either of the men dressed or tamed their bald spots.

Carl nodded, smiled, and leaned forward to shake their hands, then curled up on one of the blond cushions. Hub's wife came in with more margaritas for Abercrombie, Firestone and Hub, mineral water for Carl, and nachos for everybody to snack on. Good nachos with three kinds of imported cheese, two kinds of beans, olives, tomatoes and salsa.

"Congratulations," said Abercrombie—or was it Firestone? Were they doing that on purpose? Looking so alike it was hard for him to tell them apart? "We hear you were pretty instrumental in moving those Navajo squatters off your property. Tough job."

"Well," Carl said slowly, not liking the way that was put, "it was bound to be. Anybody who's been squatting for a hundred fifty years or so is bound to be a little stiff. And the people who are signing the leases are staying, of course."

"But the others are being evicted?"

"Slowly. And very carefully. And with every attempt on the part of the Bureau of Indian Affairs to get them to sign instead. They've had a lot of publicity, attracted members of the American Indian Movement, lots of environmental activists. We've tried to minimize the hazard, but nobody wants violence and nobody wants news photos of Navajo grandmothers being forcibly carried from the hogans they were born in."

"Very wise," one or the other of the men said. "We wouldn't want that either, of course. That is, the company wouldn't want that."

Uh-oh. He'd *known* they weren't art lovers or New Age gurus. Or even anthropologists. Not nearly scruffy enough. "What company is that?" he asked softly, using the same voice he sometimes used to ask clients how they thought their wives might have felt after being hospitalized with "accidental" stab wounds or bruises from falling down the stairs in a hogan or a one-story dwelling.

"Mutual Energy Enterprises," said the one in the blue alligator shirt—Firestone, he thought.

"Or MEE, as we like to call it," added the one in the red alligator shirt, who by process of elimination was probably Abercrombie, with a condescending smile.

"Yeah, I know," Carl said. "They explained what the initials meant in the newspaper."

"What newspaper was that?" Maybe-Firestone asked.

"*The Wall Street Journal*," Carl said, enjoying their reaction.

"Uh-huh," Abercrombie said. Yeah, Abercrombie. He was the first one introduced and he was on the left, in the red shirt. "Well, then, if you read the *Journal,* you probably are also aware of what our company does and what it stands for."

Carl nodded sagely, one broker to another.

"Well, then, Carl—you don't mind if I call you Carl?"

Carl waved his hand, palm up, graciously. He would have called the man by his first name and said, Not at all, so and so, but though he was very good at remembering names where clients were concerned, there was something very Teflon about these guys and nothing about them was sticking with him.

"Well, then, Carl, if I may be perfectly frank. Hub tells us that you're a man who cares deeply about his people and their future. Which is why I think you'll be pleased to learn that despite the disappointing results of the experimental drilling that was carried on with your tribal chairman's permission a few years ago, we have good reason to believe there are resources on the land being vacated that will be far more valuable to your people than cattle fodder."

"*Really*?" Carl said. They weren't wasting any time. Well, he was surprised they picked such an indirect method of going about this and, more surprisingly, chose to talk to him, and here. "That's interesting, gentlemen. Gosh, does Hub's cousin, our tribal chairman, know about this?"

"In a general way. But the particulars won't be of interest to him if he steps down from his position this year. We were told you were extremely interested in helping engineer future prosperity for your people and we'd like to help you do this. We realize that campaigning for office, and then, once you're instated, inspecting the sites, taking extra meetings, arranging the particulars, might take more financial resources than you have available, and we'd like to assure you that the company is more than willing to advance you whatever you require . . ."

It was all Carl could do to keep from laughing out loud. Not that he didn't like money, or prosperity for that matter. But these guys obviously hadn't even talked to the anthropologists or even read a book about his people, or they'd know that showing up for a new office with a new pickup when you'd just quit your job was like showing up for a Christian church service with the number 666 branded on your forehead.

"Hub," he said to his host and former idol, shaking his hand sincerely, "it's really been a pleasure to see you and your wife. My niece is home taking care of my dad and he can be a handful, so I think I'd better get back. Maybe since I have to rush off you'd be willing, if you remember it, to tell these gentlemen how the Fourth World came to be created. Mr. Abercrombie, Mr. Firestone. See you around."

He was gratified to hear, as he gathered his socks and boots and thanked his hostess, that Hub Honahni was still Hopi enough to enjoy the joke. In a serious voice, he was leaning forward and explaining to the men from Mutual Energy Enterprises the Hopi emergence myth, the value of choosing the rockiest, most arid part of the desert as home in order to keep out of trouble. Hub was just getting to the part about the blue corn when Carl closed the door behind him, climbed into his truck and started the engine.

While the two *biligaana* from the energy company talk to their flunkey, The One Who Is Also a Wolf watches and listens.

The white men have landed at the mesa in their helicopter. Since they land at a place leased by their company, no one else pays any attention. The flunkey knows where to meet them because they called him up on his cell phone. He likes gadgets and luxuries. He used to work for the Navajo Nation until he bought a few too many luxuries with money from his budget. Everybody did that kind of thing but the People picked on him and took away his job and house and everything. He had to leave, but one of the *biligaana* guys he used to take bribes from gave him a job with his company. The flunkey kept it for a while, but even though it paid good it didn't have the status his old job had. He was going to quit, when the guy who'd hired him, Ed Abercrombie, offered him a chance to get back at the Navajo Nation for making trouble for him and firing him. Now he got paid to make trouble for the People. Also for the Hopis. Just to stir things up, make sure the people who might want to make peace with each other stayed mad instead.

The One Who Is Also a Wolf thought this was a pretty good joke. Those *biligaana* believed they were using the flunkey to serve them, because if all the Indian people were mad at each other, they wouldn't pay any attention to what the *biligaana* company was doing. The company could make sure one side or the other won. If the Navajos won, well, Navajos already had a lot of mines on their land and probably the Navajo Nation would let the company mine the land they wanted on the HPL. If the Hopis won and kicked the Navajos out, there was a good chance some people among the Hopis might lease the land to the company too, not only because of the money but also because the Navajo resisters didn't want them to. Indians fighting each other seemed to be a good thing for the *biligaana*. A good thing for the flunkey too. He made real good money doing what he wanted to do anyway. Besides, he'd invested some of that money he'd stolen from the Navajo Nation in the *biligaana* energy company. He would win all the way around. The only thing the flunkey didn't like about all this was that Abercrombie seemed to have forgotten that at one time their positions had been reversed. Now that the guy was now one of the flunkey's bosses, he had this memory lapse about all the times when he used to come to the flunkey with money in hand, asking for favors. Abercrombie seemed to think that along with his tribal government job, the flunkey had lost some of his marbles, or at least IQ points. Every time the two got together, it seemed more likely the boss would begin the conversation by saying, "How. Me come in peace."

Instead what he said was, "That Loloma guy you tipped us off about is a real smart-ass."

"Yeah?" said the flunkey. He was a tall, good-looking Navajo whose longish hair was pulled back for this meeting and tucked under a red tractor cap with MEE FIRST embroidered in white on it. He also wore jeans and a red plaid shirt and running shoes, as well as a turquoise watchband on one wrist, a ketoh, or bow guard, on the other one, and a turquoise ring on each hand. Good stuff—the old deep blue-green with rust-colored matrix. His belt buckle was sand-cast, with a big stone that matched the others. All the jewelry had the patina of dead pawn, the jewelry pawned and never redeemed because the people who pawned it had died, freeing the trader to sell it. But the One Who Is Also a Wolf knew that though this jewelry was from the dead, it had never been pawned, never been redeemed for money, but taken directly from dead necks and wrists and fingers.

"Yeah. He didn't even hear us out. Just told Honahni to tell us some Hopi fairy tale and said he had more important things to do. Who the hell does he think he is, anyway?"

The flunkey shrugged. "Maybe the next tribal chairman, like I told you."

"He mentioned a niece and a father. Sounded like an invalid. You know anything about them?"

The flunkey scratched his ear. "The girl's in high school. Name of Sela. Gets gossiped about some because she sees a Navajo kid. The old man apparently is a pretty important Hopi elder but not one of the ones in favor of letting us Navajos stay on our land out here."

Actually, the land the flunkey stayed on belonged to his dead mother. He had never lived on it or wanted to until he became persona non grata with the Navajo Nation high muckymucks in Window Rock.

"Girls that age get into trouble sometimes," Abercrombie's sidekick, a guy named Micah Firestone, said thoughtfully.

The flunkey enjoyed shaking his head. "Not that one. She does good in school, well liked, seems to get along with everybody. The only thing anyone ever says against her is her choice in boyfriends."

"He bad news?" Firestone asked.

The flunkey lifted one shoulder, let it drop. "Not especially. Doesn't know who his people are, hangs around too much. Drinks a little sometimes. Loloma doesn't have much use for him, I hear. Afraid he'll corrupt precious little Sela."

"Hmmmm. . ." said Abercrombie.

The flunkey added slyly, "Guess Loloma doesn't like the kid drinking either. Used to be a lush himself, before he got to be a born-again Hopi. That's when he became a substance-abuse counselor. He tells you all about it when you first go to him. Like you're supposed to bow down or kiss his ass or something."

"That what you hear?" Abercrombie asked.

"Soon as I heard he was someone you might be interested in, I got to feelin' real bad about my taste for fine wines. Went to see if he could straighten me out like he's done so many other folks." The flunkey shook his head. "Guess I'm a hope-less case, though."

Abercrombie smiled politely and Firestone made a face, like he was too good to talk to an Indian who might be a drunk sometimes. People got moral about funny things, The One Who Is Also a Wolf thought.

The flunkey said casually, "Guess it's no wonder he worries about the girl. Probably would just about kill him if she took to drink, too—or maybe even drugs. People would think he only cared about helping folks he was paid to help. Couldn't take care of his own family. Who knows, they might even think he was a dealer himself. It's happened before, counselors being pushers. Good setup when you think about it. And some of the kids out here are getting bad habits now, from what I hear."

"I hear that too," Abercrombie said with a self-satisfied grin. "The Arabs have told me the same thing—seems like everyone they go to buy jewelry from would rather have dope than money these days. Wonder if that niece of Loloma's makes jewelry."

"Probably," the flunkey said. "She does everything else. You should check it out."

"We will. Thanks for the tip."

They continued chatting about how sad it was the Hopi shrines were getting desecrated, Hopi cattle mutilated or killed, a trailer burned up. The One Who Is Also a Wolf watched with the flunkey as Abercrombie and Firestone boarded their helicopter, sure that peace between Hopi and Navajo was in no danger of breaking out any time soon.

FOUR

Cindy knew as soon as they were out of sight of the road that she had made a mistake in letting Grandma Webster lead her off the path she'd mapped out. "Look," she suggested as tactfully as possible, "if we go back there, I can flag down a car, maybe get someone to go find one of your relatives to come and get you."

The old woman gave her head a slight shake. "No need. We will find them. You'll see. Say, don't you think it would be a good idea to take this horse up to the Grand Canyon first? It's nice up there. You'd like it."

"I went with my family when my dad was alive," Cindy said. "It's pretty much off the route I'd been wanting to go. I'm trying to follow this book, see?" She reached over and pulled the Kluckhohn book from her saddlebag.

"Oh, that one. You'd have to do it backwards or only from the other end. I been around here longer than anybody except maybe the sun. You should go where I tell you if you want to see what's really something."

"Well, thanks," Cindy said, trying to be diplomatic. "It's not that I don't appreciate it, but I have planned for only just so long and I actually meant to go alone. And my first goal was Tuba City."

"In one day?"

"No, of course not. I was going to stop and camp along the way."

"We should go to Wupatki, then. I used to have relatives there."

That brightened Cindy's day considerably. Maybe some of the relatives still lived there. She could tell someone at the visitors' center to notify the authorities, who were probably searching for the old lady now. Much better that she find them before they found her. All Cindy needed was to be accused of kidnapping a geriatric Native American! And lots of people in the cars that passed them on the road before they turned off would have seen them together. She forced the worries to the back of her mind and smiled up at Grandma. "Okay. Let's look at my map a minute."

"It's not far," Grandma said. "Come. You are tired. Ride with me."

"I don't want to burden the horse too much this early on the trip," Cindy said, looking longingly at the horse's back, as if it were a featherbed.

The old lady leaned forward and said something in a language Cindy supposed must be Navajo. The horse gave a nicker that sounded like muttering.

"He's very strong," Grandma told her, sitting back up in the saddle. "He thinks he could carry us both, easy."

Cindy held out for another hour and Grandma didn't press the issue, but Cindy's feet began burning and her boots were lumpy with the grains of sand she and the horse kicked up high enough to go into the boot tops as they walked. She sat down and pulled off first one boot, then the other and emptied them; then with some difficulty pulled the boots onto heat-swollen feet. When she rose, it was to find Grandma's hand stretched down to help her up on the horse. She took the hand and mounted without comment.

The Coyote Who Tried to Be a Bird

One time Coyote was really hungry, when he saw some birds. They were picking up seeds and putting them in a basket, then blowing away the chaff, winnowing the seeds clean to store for the winter, because they were industrious, like that. The birds noticed Coyote and said, "What are you doing around here?" Coyote said he was just admiring what they did. Well, the birds weren't stupid and they started to fly away, but Coyote said, "Oh, I wish I could fly away, with you, but I don't have any wings. If I had wings I could be like you . . ."

Puss in Boots

Once upon a time a miller died and left behind his only son. He had nothing to leave him but a cat, but the cat was very clever. "Dress me up like you, with a hat and fine boots, and I will make our fortune," the cat said to the miller's son . . .

One time there was an infant who was abandoned at the door of a trading post, with no clue to his true parentage. The only thing his real parents left with him when they went away was a really smart—or at least it thought it was smart—animal. It wasn't an animal you could see. It was an animal spirit that lived inside of him.

The trader was half Navajo, a man by the name of Charlie Smiley, so when he took the boy to the orphanage, they gave him Smiley's last name. The director of the orphanage, who had watched way too many Saturday morning cartoons and had rather a cruel sense of humor, gave the baby the first name of the Roadrunner's unfortunate antagonist. Therefore, the poor orphaned baby boy was called Wiley Smiley. Before long, however, baby Wiley's animal spirit guided his actions so that he looked cute and bright when a childless couple looking for a baby came by, and he got himself adopted. These new parents, who were white, didn't know anything about the animal. It was a Navajo thing. Wiley was sure of that much, because he was pretty sure he was Navajo. He didn't know exactly which animal it was. It might have had something to do with his clan, except Navajo clans didn't always have animals, and anyway, Wiley wasn't sure what his clan was.

His white parents were a Mormon Amway-sales couple from Cedar City, Utah. They were honest folk who thought they were being culturally sensitive by letting Wiley keep the name he'd been given at the orphanage, and when he was old enough, they told him all they knew about his past. Later, when Wiley left their home, he went to see what he could learn about himself, but he didn't find out much. Smiley's trading post wasn't there anymore and Smiley himself was long gone. There was a Safeway there now. That was progress for you. And yet, Wiley had always had this animal spirit living inside him, whispering in his ear. Where other people might have a mother's or father's voice urging them to do one thing or another, Wiley's animal spirit was always encouraging him to try something, be daring, take risks, leave the hard, tedious work to others and be bold. Far from feeling deprived because of being an orphan, or having less sense of self-worth, Wiley felt, as his Mormon mother would have said, empowered and entitled to the best he could manage to get for himself and the animal spirit, whatever it was, that lived in him. It always sounded good when the spirit told him to do something, and it always got him in some kind of trouble, which was why he wasn't welcome at the home of his white parents anymore.

Wiley decided one day to go see his girlfriend, Sela, a Hopi girl who lived with her mother's brother and her grandfather at Polacca. Sela's uncle, Carl Loloma, who was an important man among the Hopis, maybe the next tribal chairman, didn't like Wiley much. He came out of the house when Wiley walked up and said, "She's in the piki shed. Don't stay long. We're leaving soon."

Wiley went out to the little lean-to where Sela was making piki. Sela was always doing something. She was a hard-working girl. Wiley figured that was because she was Badger Clan. It made her hard-working. Her uncle was a badger too, but it just made him mean.

He had to stoop down to walk into the little shed. It smelled good in there. Hot grease, funny smelling, cooking cornmeal and other smells, old smells, Hopi-type smells. And there was Sela, dipping her hand in the blue-corn batter, smearing it quickly across the flat black stone that sat over an open flame. After a moment, as quickly as she had smeared the batter on, she rolled it up and off the stone in a scroll thinner than the onionskin writing paper his Mormon brother had written home on from overseas.

"Hi, Wiley," Sela said, without looking up.

"Hi. Making the piki bread again, huh?" he asked.

"Yes. Where were you the other night?"

"What night?"

"We were going to go to the dance. Remember?"

"Oh. Oh, gee, Sela, I'm sorry. Something came up. I had this business opportunity."

"Another one?" She didn't have to sound like that. It wasn't as if he had been with another girl. Well, not on a date anyway. The girl made jewelry for TVM, the home-shopping network and she started telling him about how they operated. Then she'd invited him back to her place to see a Western jewelry show on cable and explain to him how the whole thing was produced and what kind of products they used and so forth. And so forth.

Well, he couldn't help it if women liked him, could he? He was a good-looking guy, or thought he was. Since he'd moved back to the rez, he wore his thick black hair long, in a ponytail with a red tie, like it was a statement or something, which, actually, it wasn't. When his reflection looked back at him, where some might have seen a skinny, hatchet-jawed boy, to Wiley he looked lean and mean in his jeans, into which he ironed creases, and his black or navy cowboy shirts. He kept his black boots and his rodeo belt buckle shined to a high gloss. Anyone who looked at the buckle closely would see that it was actually for winning the cowgirl barrel-race competition. Wiley had won it off a guy in a card game. He didn't know where the guy got it, but it looked good and most people didn't read that close. One of these days he was going to get himself a handmade silver-and-turquoise buckle and maybe a bracelet and ring, but right now he had other priorities.

Like coming up with a product they could sell millions of in a few minutes' presentation. Jewelry was his new lady friend's specialty, but unfortunately for him, Wiley had to be about the only Indian on the whole rez who had no talent for silverwork, pottery, carving, painting or weaving. He was an entrepeneur, something he'd learned—well, mostly learned—from his adoptive family. He just had to find the right thing to market.

Watching Sela make the piki he had a sudden inspiration. "This is just blue cornmeal, right?" he asked.

"Yes. You know what it is. I've made it lots of times."

"Yeah, but I never had it right off the stone. Can I have a roll?"

"Sure. But just one. It's for my cousin's wedding." The reproach she put into the word "wedding" was lost on him as he touched his lips to the film of cooked cornmeal. It flaked off into his mouth and melted with a subtle corn flavor, dry and wispy but still very corny. It was nice. Healthy. Organic. And as thin as it was, it had to be low calorie. There was no place to put any fat in it. It was exotic. It was from his culture—well, Hopi culture, not Navajo, but how many white people sitting in front of their TVs made the distinction? Besides, he thought, looking at Sela in a new way, *Sela* was Hopi, and pretty in her rounded sweet-faced way. She could demonstrate while he did the selling. They would get rich. They would get married. They would name their first child after either his white mother or his white father and then he would be welcome in their home again. Or his adoptive parents could come to *his* home, which would be one of those beautiful adobe palaces like you saw in Santa Fe, with beautiful blankets, baskets and pots around just for decoration, a state-of-the-art TV, and a computer to keep track of his money. "How hot does that get exactly?" he asked Sela.

She shrugged. "Hot enough to make piki."

"That's not very scientific. Don't you know?"

"What do you care?" she asked, laughing.

"I'm curious about everything you do, is all," he said, placing a kiss in the hot, moist crease of her neck. "I think I'll go get a thermometer someplace and see, okay?"

She shrugged again and went back to making the piki. Once he found out how hot the stone was, he'd know how hot he had to make his product—with adjustment for different sea levels, he supposed, like on the cake mix boxes. He wondered, too, what kind of stone it was made of, and what the best simulated material would be . . . He hurried off to get the thermometer.

He left just in time to see Carl Loloma heading for the piki shed, and hear him say, "Sela, if you're going to be finished soon, I'm going up to Moenkopi to pick up those railroad ties from Ralph Sakiestewa."

Sela smiled over her shoulder. "I'm at the end of my batter now, Uncle. I'll ride with you as far as Hoteville."

Wiley walked off whistling. It was his lucky day. With both of them gone and only Sela's invalid grandfather at home, he could give that stone a good going over.

Sela Loloma was not much like your typical beautiful Hollywood Indian princess, as she was neither Italian, nor Jewish, nor Lebanese, nor Mexican, but a real Hopi girl, round and dimpled, her hair as black and shiny as a raven's wing, her eyes the spicy brown of a chili bean, her skin the scrumptious cinnamon color that harmonized beautifully with the golden sand and red rocks and deep auburn shadows of her surroundings. Furthermore, her hands were quick and talented, she was very smart, and also very kind and good-natured. Everyone said she would make some man a fine wife. But though all the boys courted her, she chose no one. She had always told her uncle that this was because she wanted to go to college and learn something that she could bring home to help her people.

That was until a certain skinny Navajo came sniffing around. Though the girl who was not a princess turned down Hopi boys of good families, who were fine jewelers and weavers, who were learned in the ways of their people and good at picking up the better ways of the outside world as well, who showed promise and enterprise, she wouldn't talk seriously to any boy except the Navajo. She said he made her laugh. The uncle, advanced though he was in years and wisdom, still couldn't figure women.

When his niece got in the car, the uncle, who was the same Carl Loloma that Wiley Smiley regarded as more of a wicked giant than a good and just leader, asked with a very studied carelessness, "So how's ol' Wiley Coyote doing?"

His niece knew he didn't much like the scrawny Navajo kid hanging around her, but he was smart enough not to come down so heavy that his disapproval drove her closer to the boy.

Sela smiled affectionately. "He came to bum some piki. He really likes it."

"Any left for your poor old uncle?" Carl asked. He gave her the playfully pleading puppy-dog look that had always been as successful on nieces as on other ladies in his all-too-distant past.

"Oh, sure. He's the funniest guy. He wanted to know how you make it. He once told me he doesn't know who his parents are. Wouldn't it be cool if he found out he was part Hopi?"

Carl grunted, disgusted. He hoped that if Wiley did turn out to be Hopi, he'd find out he had clans in common with Sela so he'd have to go away or commit technical incest.

"Well, he *could* be," Sela protested. "Why don't you like Wiley?"

"You know the story about the coyote who tried to trick the birds into thinking he wanted to be a bird so they would give him their feathers and help him fly so he could catch them?"

"Uncle Carl! That's just an old story, not about real people. And anyway, those birds never were fooled and just as Coyote got airborne, they plucked all their feathers off him and he fell to the earth again and was killed. I always cried at that part."

"You would," Carl said.

"Well, you're wrong about Wiley. And he wasn't trying to kill anything. It was *only* piki."

This was followed by indignant silence on her part, and Carl realized that he had pushed a little more than was prudent.

Sela changed the subject. "When do you get the new bull?"

"As soon as I get this fence built for him."

"You think those people are going to leave it alone?" she asked, referring to the Navajos who lived nearby and had, until recently, used Carl's grazing land as *their* grazing land, which was one reason he was going to have to haul food for the cattle to supplement what the sheep had left of the grass, which wasn't much. Not that the drought had left much for the sheep either. A warm, dry winter and an early hot summer with no rain had left Hopi land as cracked and dry as a sidewinder's long-discarded skin.

He shrugged. "Well, I saw a couple of them out there and they kinda gave me a dirty look. So I told them, 'Hey, I got no problem with you being here. Just don't mess with my livestock or tear up any of my stuff and we'll get along fine.' But we'll just have to see. You know how they are."

Sela didn't say anything. She wasn't afraid of her uncle, but she was a little in awe of him. It wasn't as if she had grown up knowing him. Her mother's brother had been away from the Hopi mesas for many years, first in Vietnam, then off in the cities, where he said he had made a lot of mistakes. He didn't get down on people very quick, but when he did, there didn't seem to be any turning back. She knew he tried to be and thought of himself as a forgiving man. He said it was because he had done most of the unforgivable things a man could do already. And he was pretty forgiving, okay, about the little transgressions committed by nieces and nephews, or the crankiness of old people, or the falling off the wagon of a twelve-step friend. But if he took against someone, Sela had yet to see him revise his opinion.

He was a smart man, and a pretty good judge of character, she knew. But he wasn't infallible. And he wasn't right about Wiley, for instance. Or Shirley.

"Is your friend Shirley still putting all that stuff on the Internet about how Hoteville's rights are being violated by the sewer line?"

Sela nodded. "It's what her elders tell her. The workers are being disrespectful. They moved the *nakwakwusi* and the *pahos* the elders put down to mark the path of the Creator to the sun."

Her uncle cocked an eyebrow at her. "Well, at least they didn't cut off the water, like the utilities companies did to Shipaulovi," he said, with a nod to the second mesa village, which had been dry due to nonpayment of old debts the present utilities board suspected had been embezzled by the previous board. Carl hated it that the infighting of village politics was depriving the sick and the elderly, as well as babies and their mothers, of a commodity most people outside took for granted. But of course that was why the Hopi had chosen to live in the particular place they occupied in this, the Fourth World. Previous worlds had been too easy and the people had become corrupt. If hardship was all it took to make them pure, by rights they should be so pure by now that there would be no liars among them, much less embezzlers.

"Water should be cheap here, Shirley says. If only the mine at Black Mesa didn't use millions of gallons in that slurry line it runs."

Carl smiled. "Isn't Shirley being a little inconsistent, not wanting the sewer but blaming the mine because some people have no water?"

"They should have a right to it, even if they don't choose to, she says," Sela informed him. "And anyway, they didn't have to move the prayer sticks and feathers to put in the sewer. And they didn't have to dig the line during the winter purification period, when no one is supposed to dig."

Carl smiled again at her somewhat confused vehemence. The kids understood Masaw's austerity plan for the Hopis in theory, but they saw how other people lived, on TV, and how easy life was for people in adjoining towns, even for some of the Navajos, and they couldn't help but wonder why it had to be quite so hard for themselves. The ancestors had chosen a hard path. Eventually, after years away in the deceptive ease of the cities, Carl too had opted for the relative spiritual peace and certainty of his birthplace over the outside world. But the kids had to choose for themselves.

"So I take it from your tone that our traditions do matter to you after all," he teased, "and you're not actually going to convert to Catholicism or Mormonism or whatever, any time soon?"

"Of course not!" she said, then leaned forward in her seat to peer at a car that had pulled off the highway and was headed up a dusty road leading to a collection of ramshackle wooden buildings. "Wait! Uncle! There's that car I was telling you about!"

Carl braked. "That silver rental job? Is that the one that was at Joey's house the day he died?" He approached the turnoff very slowly. Joey had been a friend and classmate of Sela's, a talented artist. He'd started to change in the last few days before he died and Sela had confided to her uncle that some of the kids couldn't figure out what was with him. Carl had noticed the relapse of some of his clients, particularly those who were artists, into drug or alcohol abuse, but when he suggested that possibility to his niece, she had defended her friend, arguing that Joey's odd behavior was probably due to his concentration on the awesome entries he was preparing for the Hopi Market in Sedona. But when Joey's mom came home from her job at the Hopi Cultural Center restaurant one day, Joey was dead and the projects he had been working on were nowhere to be found. Drug paraphernalia had been found near the body, though Joey's mom said he had never to her knowledge used drugs. The autopsy revealed that although there was little evidence of repeated drug use, and the boy had not used enough coke to kill most people, evidently he was allergic to the drug, which had produced anaphylactic shock and killed him. The poor kid had been unlucky enough to be allergic to almost his first dip into recreational chemicals.

Unfortunately, the people who had dropped out of Carl's counseling sessions didn't want to talk about it. Carl tried going to the homes of those with whom he had spent considerable time, including Wyatt Emory, a young jeweler whose work was already appearing in some of the finest galleries in Taos and Scottsdale. Wyatt had grabbed Carl by the arm and led him away from his home. "Don't come here around my brothers and sisters talkin' to me about this stuff, man," he said.

"I'm glad you care about them enough to want to shield them, Wyatt," Carl told him. "But what if the guys you're buying from start selling to them too?"

"What are you talking about, man? I'm okay."

"Tell it to somebody who hasn't been there, kid. A boy's dead because somebody who didn't give a shit about anything but what he could produce for them that day started him on drugs—"

"Bull. He could have got them himself. And he was allergic. It was a freak accident."

"He's dead and the people who killed him have the work that represented money to support him and his mom, plus a lot of the beauty in his soul that they didn't give enough of a damn about to give him clean stuff. Help me out here, Wyatt."

He refused. But later his sister told Sela about seeing a silver car pull up on the highway and Wyatt talking to the people inside. Later, she noticed the stunning concho belt he'd been polishing was missing. Along with a silver necklace that was a series of double-sided pendants, each side representing one of the kachinas and matching earrings, bracelet, and ring. That was a lot of silver and represented most of the money Wyatt had earned from his other work so far. Yet, though the work was gone, he still didn't pay any of the bills and begged cigarette money from his sister a day afterward.

"Okay, that gives us something to go on," Carl told his niece. "A '97 silver Beemer, New Mexico. License plate number—" He shaded his eyes and squinted in the direction of the vehicle.

Sela read the number for him. He was still too vain to wear bifocals.

"Write it down," he told her. "Write it down and hang on!" and he made a U-turn and headed back toward the BIA police station at Keams Canyon.

FIVE

The Red Rooster
(Male Counterpart to the Little Red Hen)

THERE WAS THIS young Navajo man named Michael Blackgoat
who came from a big family, with lots of brothers and sisters,
aunts and uncles and cousins. Unfortunately, it wasn't a very
happy family when he was growing up and both of his parents
drank too much and let their land and their livestock go to
hell. The young man loved his family anyway, but left home
as soon as he could to seek his fortune, or at least escape, by
joining the military. He did pretty good at that, but one day he
heard his mother and father had died, so he went home to see
what he could do to help out.

His sisters and brothers and aunts and uncles already had
most of the land divided up between them, but nobody wanted
the two old skinny cows which were all that was left of his
parents' cattle.

It was dry that year, like always, and the cattle were so hungry and thirsty that the young man, at first out of pity, began
feeding and watering them. He asked his younger sister, the
one he liked the best, if he could build a house on her land and
she said that he could. She was married and lived far away,
anyhow.

So he stayed there. He didn't have enough money to buy
food even for the two cows for very long, but he remembered
a steep, rocky canyon nearby, not far from where his grandmother used to have a sheep camp. The sides of the canyon
were almost straight down, covered with rocks and cactus and
probably snakes, but he herded the cows down there to eat the
good vegetation that benefited from the little bit of drainage
that ran away from the rocks and dust and seeped into the

canyon floor. The cows got fatter, and sleeker, and healthier, and pretty soon he was able to breed them and they had calves, and the next year they had more calves and then their calves had calves. He sold off one or two for food and did the best he could.

One winter it froze real bad and he asked his brother if he could give him some money to buy food for their parents' cattle, but the brother said, "Why should I? I can't afford to feed a herd of cattle. There were only two to begin with. You got them. You earn the money to feed them."

So the young man did. He hired out as a carpenter to a retired rodeo clown who wanted to build himself a house, and earned the money to feed his cattle.

The next summer was really dry and his pickup broke down so he asked his auntie if he could borrow hers to go get water for his cattle, but she said, "That will take a long time. I need my pickup to get to town. You were the one who decided to take care of the cows, so it's up to you to do it, not me."

So he did. He got a friend to lend him his pickup, and in exchange for promising a calf for the friend's daughter's *kinaalda* ceremony, the friend helped him haul water all that summer until his own pickup was fixed.

One time there was a bad storm and all the cows got scattered. He asked his uncle to help him round them up, but his uncle said, "I'm too busy to fool with cattle. You wanted to be a bigshot cowboy, you herd them."

So he did. It took him four nights and four days in the pouring rain, pulling cows out of mud and flooded ravines, but after losing only one, he rounded them all up again. He caught pneumonia in the process, but the herd was safe.

That was when he realized he had to have a horse. He'd had one once, but it tore its belly open on a rock the first time he rode it into the canyon. He figured it was because it was one of those horses they teach to herd cows on the plains, but that don't know nothing about the desert. He needed a good reservation pony.

This time he asked his mother's sister's eldest son, who was what was called in the Navajo way his cousin-brother,

Morris Blackgoat. Morris was from the western part of the reservation originally, and he used to have a lot of horses but sold them off when he and his family moved back to the ancestral lands of his mother.

Morris scratched his head. His hair was just growing out in a black thatch from his summer brush-cut. "I need to talk to some people, Michael," he said, "but I ought to be able to come up with something."

It was only right that this time Michael Blackgoat would get help from his family. In the European way of telling things, three is the magic number, but among the Navajo and Pueblo peoples, it's four that's the charm.

Morris got back to him two weeks later and said he had a horse lined up for Michael to see, but it was up by Jeddito. "The guy's name is Etcitty, Charlie Etcitty. He's a good horse trainer. Hopi Rangers been giving him lots of trouble about how many he runs though. His rangeland is up by Black Mesa."

Michael nodded.

"You can go see him any time. He says he's got a good one and since you're my cousin-brother, he'll make you a deal. Better take a horse trailer with you."

That turned out to be a problem. Nobody had one, or had one to spare. He went to see his friend the retired rodeo clown, who told him, "I got a trailer sitting at my sister's place in Flag, but you'd have to go down there and get it."

"That's okay. The guy I got to see is out at Jeddito so I'll go by and see the horse and if it's what I want, I'll go get your trailer and pick the horse up on the way back."

So Michael got in his pickup, took the four hundred dollars he'd saved from his last carpentry job, and went to see the guy, see what he had.

That was when he fell in love for the first time.

Etcitty's place was a little off the highway, the usual hogan and trailer arrangement, with a corral in the dusty side yard. No horses were in it. Etcitty came out to meet him. "My string is up at my mom's place at Two Tracks." He hopped in Michael's pickup and said, with a lift of his chin toward the north, "It's that way."

So they drove out there. It was a little bit of a hassle because the Hopi Rangers, claiming there was a major fire hazard because of the drought, were stopping people going off the main highway like they were at some kind of international border crossing or something. Since Etcitty had family out at Two Tracks, they let him and Michael go through once they'd checked IDs and looked suspiciously into the truck. Michael wondered what they thought the men could be hiding. Horses? Little bitty ones, maybe? A coal mine? Some of those white environmentalists who came up from Phoenix to protest or those Sioux people who came to do Sun Dances for them?

"Assholes," Etcitty said, referring, Michael figured, to the Hopi Rangers or maybe just to Hopis in general, as they drove away. "They've got their stone villages and their mesas, what the hell do they need rangeland for anyway?"

Michael shrugged. The Hopis had their villages, but other than their jewelry and kachina dolls, he didn't really see how they made a living out here. It was even drier than Window Rock, and you had to haul everything uphill.

"They're confiscating animals without the proper notification, on all kinds of phony excuses . . ." Etcitty went on.

"Probably why they need rangeland," Michael joked, trying to lighten him up a little, "to graze those confiscated animals on . . ."

Etcitty laughed, and after a long dust-choked and bumpy ride, they came to a stopping place, where they got out of the pickup, took a feed bucket, a saddle and a halter from the back end, and went looking for the horses.

They weren't hard to find. In fact, the little pinto Etcitty had in mind for Michael came right over to them.

Etcitty slipped the halter on, saddled the horse and jumped up on its back, riding ahead while Michael negotiated the rocky road in his pickup. They went as far as a herd of Hopi cows.

"My family's been out here for a hundred years," Etcitty said, "and this guy just asked his politician relatives for a lease on our land and they let him have it. He says it's okay if we stay here if we don't bother his cattle. Hah! Well, we won't bother 'em any. Just herd 'em a little."

Etcitty put the horse through its paces. Or maybe it was the other way around. That was the smartest damned horse Michael had ever seen. It seemed like it read minds, both cow minds and men's minds, and did what was necessary to cut an animal from the herd, stand pat while Etcitty hog-tied the beast, and drive a herd in such a pretty line you'd think it was that pig from the kids' movie Michael had taken Morris's kids to see in Gallup.

When the dust settled, Michael said, "He's kinda small, but I like him. How much?"

"I'll let you have him for a couple thousand, since you're Morris's relative."

"I got four hundred."

"Nah, I gotta have more than that. A thousand five hundred at least."

"I only got four hundred. Maybe I could get a little more, in a couple of weeks."

"I never know when the Hopis are going to claim I'm over-grazing and take some of my stock. I'm not sure I have a couple of weeks. So I'll make it easy. A thousand."

"Five hundred."

"This is a smart horse."

"I know."

"Seven fifty? Can you raise that?"

"I'll try. I got to rent a horse trailer too, though."

"Okay, six hundred. Can you get that?"

"I'll get it," Michael said. "Give me a week, okay?"

Etcitty agreed. Michael decided to go to Flag for the trailer and look for work while he was there. He wouldn't even go home. He could call Basha's grocery in Window Rock where Morris's wife worked and ask her to get Morris to look after Michael's own stock for a while longer.

He was just about to wind down into Keams Canyon when he saw a green Camry by the side of the road. A little girl clutching a stuffed animal stood to one side, looking on curiously as a long pair of golden tanned legs and a shapely butt encased in shorts moved back and forth in the steam the car was emitting.

Michael pulled up in front of them, got out of his truck and walked slowly toward the car, so as not to scare the kid.

The little girl, who looked to be maybe seven years old, said something and the butt straightened up to reveal a pretty woman in a tank top. She put one hand on her hip and, blowing a stray strand of black hair out of her face, stared at him. Both she and the kid looked hot and frustrated.

"Looks like you got a problem," he said. "Need some help?"

"I could use a lift to the IHS hospital," the woman said. She didn't have a Navajo accent that he could hear, but she looked Navajo to him. The child didn't as much—her hair was light brown and her little face was heart-shaped, whereas her mother's was broadened more at the cheekbones before it tapered into a determined chin. He'd seen that kind of chin before. That's why he was pretty sure she was a Navajo woman.

"Your little girl sick?" he asked.

"No, nobody's sick. I just need to go there."

"I'm pretty good with cars," he said, pointing with his lips in the traditional way, at the open hood.

"So am I," she said, not real friendly this time. "But the radiator has boiled over and that's not going to improve without water. So I still need that ride to the hospital, if you want to help."

She sounded pretty cross for somebody asking for a favor, but the little girl looked as if she was about to cry, so he said, "Get in."

The woman said, "Just a minute. Help me load this stuff in your truck, will you?" and began hauling out luggage and clothes bags and laundry baskets full of stuff, and boxes from the trunk and the back seat. It only took the two of them about five additional minutes, though.

"You moving here?"

She nodded. Grimly. But she didn't offer any other information and he didn't ask, but dropped her at the hospital, before heading on to Flag.

By evening he had the trailer hitched to his truck, but no leads on work at all. Everybody he knew said construction was at a dead end right then because the price of materials had risen so much. Seems the logging companies had sent all the trees they clear-cut to Japan, so there weren't enough to keep the mills open in all the places where they used to get materials. Well, he only needed a couple hundred dollars. Michael figured he might have better luck making that closer to home. So he headed back up the highway.

SIX

The Origin of the Snake Clan

At park headquarters at the entrance to Wupatki National Monument, Cindy dismounted and Grandma followed her. She led the horse through the parking lot and to her surprise found a hitching rail. A sign on the curb beside it said RE-SERVED.

"It's okay," Grandma said. "The politicians here are always going someplace on horseback to show they're like other people. But they're not."

Cindy tied up the horse and went in, followed by Grandma, who looked this way and that, curiously peeking around corners and under things until she wandered off into the exhibit room where displays showed how the stone structures had been built.

Cindy approached the desk just as a tour bus full of people came crowding into the area. It then occurred to her that there was probably a pay phone somewhere nearby. The desk at the gift shop was busy too, so she ducked back outside the building to look around. A pickup truck with a horse trailer was pulling up opposite where she'd left Chaco.

An Indian man got out of the truck cab, stretched long legs and looked around. His gaze stopped a blink's worth at the spot where Cindy stood—or was it where Chaco stood? And then he seemed to be surveying his surroundings in general, just unwinding from the drive. About that time Cindy felt a tug on her sleeve. "You want to see where my relatives used to live?"

"You can find it?" Cindy asked. She'd meant to go back in and ask the rangers if anyone had lost an elderly lady.

"Oh sure. The spot where they used to be. It is well known. But they don't live there anymore."

"Okay. But maybe we better rub Chaco down and find him a drink. We should refill our own water bottles too. Is it far to this place?"

Grandma made the little lopsided lip gesture to indicate it was off to the right, whatever that meant. "Not far." Then the old lady took the hem of her skirt and started rubbing Chaco's hide with it. Cindy fished her curry brush and rags out of a saddlebag and handed them to the woman, who gave a grunt of approval, and let her hem drop so she could use the rags instead. "My daughter who loaned me this dress will be glad not to have horse sweat all over it."

Cindy nodded and took the plastic bottles and collapsible bucket into the ladies' room to fill them with water.

When she came out again, the Indian cowboy from the pickup truck was visiting with Grandma, helping her curry Chaco. They were talking in one of the Indian languages, Cindy guessed, though she really couldn't tell.

Grandma performed introductions in English. "Michael, this is my niece Cindy. She's one of my white sister's girls. Cindy, this is Michael, one of my Dine'h great-grandsons. He likes your friend's horse."

Cindy patted Chaco's neck and gave him a short drink. "He's pretty nice, isn't he? I'm training him for an endurance ride by taking him across the reservation."

Michael nodded and patted the other side of Chaco's neck.

"Say, if Mrs. Webster is your great-grandmother, you wouldn't mind giving her a lift home in your truck, would you? It's a long horseback ride and I'll be camping rough and it's not really fair to Chaco to ask him to carry two on a long ride like this."

The man gave her a look that clearly asked, *Isn't it?*

And Grandma patted her on the arm. "Maybe later I will ride in Michael's truck. Right now, I will go with you and show you the way."

"Oh, and you've been so much help already," Cindy lied politely and then said, "Could I speak with you privately, Michael?"

He gave her a half-amused look and stepped to one side. She joined him and pulled him away from Grandma, who was now carrying on an animated conversation with Chaco.

"Frankly, Michael, I'm not prepared to take care of your grandmother. She's a dear, but I'm afraid she's wandered off from the people she was staying with and they'll be worried about her. She might be on medication. I didn't come prepared to care for another person when I'm supposed to take care of this horse."

Now he was openly grinning at her, and looked about to laugh. She had a thought and said, "Look, I could pay for your gas, if that would help."

But he waved his hand and said, "She won't come. Maybe later. Don't worry, lady. She'll take care of you."

And he turned on his heel and walked back to his truck, pausing only to turn and give Grandma a wink. Grandma waved at him as if she were sending him off to kindergarten.

Cindy was furious that a family member had been so callous about the old lady's welfare and entrusted her to a stranger. But then, Grandma had introduced Cindy herself as a niece so maybe the man thought she was in good hands. Or maybe, and she now suspected this was the case, he was no more a great-grandson than she was a niece. She was about ready to go in and question the rangers again when another tour bus showed up and she was buffeted by Japanese tourists on their way into the visitors' center and bathrooms.

When the sea of tourists parted, Grandma was already sitting astride Chaco, the reins in her hand. "We should go now," she said.

They rode for several more hours, first through the monument, a well-defined rubble of a stone pueblo-style dwelling, with funny-looking round walls in the middle of the open space. "I wonder if those were gardens?" Cindy mused. But when she read the plaque placed in front of one, it said they were ball courts similar to those found in Mayan ruins.

Grandma pointed out a petroglyph of a snake. "You see? This was made by my relatives when they lived here. They were Snake Clan people, the ones who came through. They brought their dance to make rain here."

"Is that the one where they dance with live rattlesnakes in their mouths?" Cindy asked, shuddering. "I saw a National Geographic video about that once."

Grandma frowned. "It's a holy dance. It should not have been shown. People don't understand. You don't understand. Snakes are not evil. They're not good either. They're snakes. They have a purpose. For one thing, they have the secret of bringing rain."

"Snakes do?" Cindy asked, skeptically. "I never heard of that. One of my stepsisters was into goddess religions and claimed all sorts of healing powers and stuff for snakes, but she never said anything about rain." Having Perdita extolling snakely virtues was as good a reason for disliking the critters as any, for Cindy.

"Well, I don't know about that. Maybe they don't do it for white people, only us, because of the marriage and all."

"Marriage? To snakes?" Cindy asked.

"You're young," Grandma said placidly. "And all of this happened a long time ago, when even I was much younger. Get down. I want to tell you something." Cindy dismounted and so did Grandma, who sat down on the edge of a broken wall, and the spindle reappeared from a fold of her skirt where she'd evidently kept it during the journey. Furthermore, it had a tuft of wool on the end of it and she began spinning this against her thigh into a length of yarn. The sun beat down on them and a few clouds scudded by as fast as highway traffic. "There was this young man who was restless. He wanted to travel, to go see something new. He specially wanted to see the Great Water—what you know as the Pacific Ocean. It wasn't a bad journey then because at that time the Hopi people, having left the *sipapuni,* the place of emergence, which is in the Grand Canyon, where I *told* you we should go, were migrating from one place to the other. Back then his people lived in what's now called California."

"Emergence from what?" Cindy asked.

Grandma sighed. "And tourists always wonder why we don't try to tell them much about ourselves! There is much to explain. Do you think the world was always as it is now? Even my white sister knows better than that! Before this world, we lived in another. But it was destroyed because people were wicked."

Cindy sighed. Just her luck. She had fallen in with some kind of a religious nut.

"The Creator was kind, however, and did not destroy all the people. Some were allowed to come into this world. They were the ancestors of the Hopi, Pueblo and Navajo peoples. They came up from the lower world, and as they emerged, Mockingbird told them whether they would be Hopi, Supai, or whatever."

"A little bird told them, huh?" Cindy asked.

"How can I tell you these important things if you talk?"

"I'm sorry," Cindy said immediately. She was very polite usually, especially to older people, but this trip was not starting out very well. She was hot and tired of walking and wondering how she'd feed them both. Funny about that man refusing to help with the old lady. She'd always heard how respectful Indians were of their old people. Maybe he just meant that elderly Indian ladies were a lot tougher even than young women who weren't Indian. "Please go on, I'll be quiet."

Grandma gave her spindle an impatient twist or two, then shook her head and sighed again. "I should be used to it. My grandsons aren't very good listeners either. They're real naughty sometimes. Anyway, like I was saying, this young man wanted to go see the Great Water. His mother and father thought this was a real good idea. His father even told him that he'd known since the boy was born that he was supposed to take this trip. And his mother told him that shells, coral and turquoise were really important to the people and that the Woman of Hard Substances, the one who loaned me this jewelry, lived by the water and he should ask her to give him any shells and stones she could spare. He said he would. His father helped him get ready to travel. They found a hollow tree, cut it down and made a lid for it, and the young man crawled into this with all of his supplies and the *pahos* his father gave him to give to Huruing Wuhti, the Sea Woman, in exchange for the stones and shells his people wanted."

"I thought you said he got that from the Woman of Hard Substances?" Cindy asked, confused.

The old woman had a long strand of fine spun yarn. From somewhere in her voluminous skirt, she pulled out a puff of fluffy white wool and, spreading the end of her yarn so that it fanned out again, she quickly smoothed the fibers of the puff together with those of the yarn end, and with a couple of twists, joined the two so adroitly that Cindy couldn't see where the yarn left off and the puff began.

"The two are one. An—alias, like they say on the cop shows. You can think of her as Huruing Wuhti also known as Sea Woman also known as Woman of Hard Substances. Okay?"

Without missing a beat or a word, Grandma Webster had begun spinning again.

"Okay."

"Taking these *pahos,* the young man crawled into the hollow log-boat and floated in it. Finally he came to the Great Water. He crawled out of his log and took what was left of his food and the *pahos* and looked around. I had a little place with a sea view then, back among the rocks just beyond the tide line. If I'd been able to hang onto it, it would be worth a lot of money now. The boy saw it and came over to my place."

Cindy wanted to ask how long ago this *was* anyway, that people traveled in hollow logs, but she didn't want to interrupt again. Had to keep the old lady happy until she found someone responsible to take custody of her.

"He knew who I was. People did back then, more than now even. Everybody did, even if they never had met me. So he came into my place and told me he wanted to see my daughter, Huruing Wuhti, who's sometimes called Sea Woman and sometimes Woman of Hard Substances. He told me his mother had asked this of him and he offered me four of the *pahos* his father had made and some very good piki and tushi his mother and sister had made for him. Such a nice boy! Such good manners! And so obedient and mindful of what his parents had told him. I tell you I was pleased to meet such a one—so different from those grandsons of mine, who are always sassing me back."

Grandma added another puff of wool as she had done before.

"I pointed out to him the island where Sea Woman lived. He was pretty worried how to get to that place, because the log had already drifted away and it would take a long time to make a boat. But I made a bridge for him from a rainbow and he crossed over. He did fine."

Cindy thought she understood now. Either the old woman really believed in putting herself into these stories she told—after all, how many Napoleons and Madonnas were there walking around in and out of therapy?—or maybe this was a past life experience she was relating. Or maybe it was traditional when people told legends of this kind to do some of it in first person. Cindy had no idea, but she wasn't about to speculate aloud.

"I see by your face that you don't believe me. I'll bet if I made you a rainbow bridge, you'd be afraid to set foot on it. But this young man, as I say, was a polite and obedient boy and he thanked me. It's no trouble to do something for somebody like that. I told him that when he was ready to come back to shore I'd help him again. He went over there and I guess he was pretty impressed by her house. She always builds with only the best quality turquoise, so her house is bluer than the sky and the sea put together. I saw him stand there looking for quite a while before he went inside."

Another puff. The fine-spun yarn filled up the bottom of the spindle whorl now. Cindy wished she had remembered to get something to eat at the ranger station, and reached into her saddlebag, expecting to find only the sandwich crust and the apple. Evidently they'd fallen out, but she did find two additional sandwiches and two more apples which she'd apparently forgotten packing. Her fingers encountered a can as well, and an opener. After the sandwiches and the apples, she extracted the can. Peaches. She set an apple and sandwich beside Grandma and began munching on the other sandwhich herself as the old lady talked.

"He was over there all night long. That Huruing Wuhti, now, she is a lusty woman, but she's also particular. Well, you get to be that way when people are always asking you for favors, and everybody likes nice jewelry, don't they? She moved out to that island to keep from getting pestered, so she had to test people who came wanting something from her. So when she answered the door for the boy, she had made herself up to be real disgusting—like, what do you call it, you know, the things in those Living Dead movies my grandsons like to watch?"

"Zombies?"

"Right! Just like a zombie. She had flesh falling off her and sagging and big sores and she made herself smell real bad. She was a mess. But this boy gave her the *pahos* anyway and told her what he wanted. Then she told him what *she* wanted and she said the look on his face was priceless. She told him she might be able to let him have the stones and shells his village needed but he'd have to sleep with her. So here's this boy, probably never been with a girl before, ready to sleep with a woman he thinks is not only ugly but could probably turn him into something nasty if she wanted to . . ."

Cindy stopped chewing. Grandma looked up, her head cocked to one side. "Nothing," Cindy said. "Go on." Turn him *into* something? What was she? A witch? Or could she be, maybe, a fairy godmother like Felicity Fortune, whom Cindy had seen interacting with a frog Felicity claimed had once been a hit man, before *she* got ahold of him.

"Of course, by that time, Sea Woman had had time to freshen up and slip into something more comfortable and she was her usual beautiful self. That was one relieved boy, she said, and she said he was good too . . ." The old lady chuckled. "He said later that when he woke up that morning, the pretty maiden he'd made love to was gone but there was a blanket loaded with beautiful shells and turquoise nuggets and branches of coral. He came out of her turquoise house carrying the blanket like a bag. I'd been watching for him and sent the rainbow over to the island and he walked across it to my place."

She held the apple in the palm of the hand whose fingers held the end of her yarn. Cindy noticed suddenly that those fingers were about twice as long as her own, though the old lady was a much smaller woman. Grandma's fingers seemed to have at least one extra knuckle, and were extremely slender. With the palm cupped over the apple and the fingers dancing on the yarn, the hand reminded Cindy a little of the spiders her father had called daddy longlegs. The old lady paused in her story and spinning only for the time it took to bite, chew, and swallow a nibble of apple, then continued smoothly.

"He was feeling pretty pleased with himself, I could tell. Cocky, you know? That can be dangerous but it's not always a bad thing in a young man, not if he's truly brave and just looking for his next adventure."

Cindy wanted to say that young women could look for their next adventures too, but Grandma was clearly about to tell her what the next adventure was, and besides, it was up to *Cindy* to be politically correct. Elderly female persons of minorities didn't have to be.

"When I gave him something to eat, he said that he was trying to find out what he was supposed to do next. Surely his destiny, the one his father had referred to, hadn't brought him all the way out there just to get jewelry? We'd been talking before he went to meet Sea Woman, and I said something about the Snake People. Now he asked where they were, as he hadn't seen any people except me and Huruing Wuhti.

"Now, in those days, it wasn't like it is now, Cindy. There was no TV or radio, no highways, no books even. People had a long time to think and much to think about and they really knew how to concentrate. I tell you this because maybe you will think it strange when I tell you that some people could change themselves into other things."

"Like toads?"

"Yes. Or snakes, or spiders, lizards, bears, coyotes. All kinds of things. We changed sizes that way sometimes too. It was easier to show this boy than to tell him, so I made myself small and went with him."

"Uh-huh."

"I guided him to the village of the Snake People, which was a bit east of my house. I warned him that he'd see a lot of snakes, but not to be afraid of them, because they were just curious, and not to step on them."

She finished the apple, handed Cindy back the core and nodded toward the saddlebag. Cindy didn't see why she couldn't just toss it—surely critters would eat it. But she did as Grandma indicated. Grandma took a bite of the sandwich and added another puff of wool.

"That boy was sure jumpy when he saw all those snakes. Bull snakes, rattlesnakes, copperheads, water moccasins, all kinds of snakes writhing around there on the ground. They didn't crawl away when they saw him either, just watched and waited. Then when we got to the village, the old man appeared."

"What old man?"

"The kikmongwi—the leader of the Snake People. The young man told him about his long journey and how he had been directed to the village. The old man told him he was welcome and invited him inside the kiva. I whispered in the boy's ear to follow the kikmongwi down the ladder and to give him four of the prayer sticks. When he was inside the kiva, the old man introduced himself and said that they had to talk.

"The boy told him the name of his village and that his father was kikmongwi there, and gave the Snake People kikmongwi the *pahos.*

"The old man thanked him for the *pahos* and said they should smoke. The tobacco those Snake People use is really strong and the boy wasn't used to it. I helped him a little, so he'd make a good impression on the Snake People."

"How'd you do that?" Cindy asked.

"I crawled down to his anus and drew the smoke out so it wouldn't overpower him."

"Uh-huh," Cindy said, trying, and failing, to picture the old lady crawling on hands and knees down the boy's back and buttocks. "Then what?"

"There were a lot of other people in the kiva besides the old man and my young friend. They were very impressed with how strong he was. I think they suspected maybe that I was helping him, or that someone was, and this impressed them even more. So then he was asked to tell of his journey, which he did, telling how he wanted to find what lay where the river meets the Great Water.

"The old man said, 'Now that you know about that, we will show you something else. We are the Snake People and we are very different from your people or anyone you have met before.' Then his people stood up and took down snakeskins which had been hanging along the wall and they went into another room.

"I said to the boy, 'They're just testing you. They don't mean to hurt you.' But when those people came back, wearing the skins they'd put on, they were real snakes and they looked as if they meant business and were going to bite him. But he was one brave boy. He just sat there and let them crawl all over him, sliding along his legs and brushing his arms and even his face, putting their heads in his lap. When he didn't react, the kikmongwi signaled his people to return to their human form. The people went next door again and did that, and came back walking on two feet."

Their sandwiches were finished—almost. Grandma left a bit of crust on hers and handed it back to Cindy, who had been about to take her last bite but stopped, and put it with Grandma's crust, back in the bag as the old lady indicated. If saving apple cores and bread crumbs was some sort of Indian custom, she felt she should start observing it too. Grandma balled up her yarn with deft spins of her long-fingered hands and nodded to the peaches. Cindy picked up the can and opener and went to work. Granny popped another puff of yarn on the pointed end of her spindle, gave it a couple more twists, and began spinning and talking again.

" 'Now you see what we're really like,' " the kikmongwi said.

"The boy nodded and said he did.

"The old man told him that because of the way he had acted when the people were around him as snakes, they knew he was a good person, had a good heart, and that they would adopt him as one of their own. The old man made him a nephew. And the boy, with his good manners said, 'My uncle, I thank you.' He stayed with the Snake People four more days while they taught him their ceremonies, their prayers, how to bring rain. They also taught him how to talk to snakes and handle them, how he should dress to perform the snake rituals. They told him the healing secrets of their people and the ways they knew to lead a good life.

"He was a quick learner and at the end, the old man was pleased with him and said, 'That's all we have to tell you. You're one of us now.' Then he proposed something a little like your story about that girl named Cinderella and Prince Charming. Only this time it was my young friend who was the prince and the snake girls who were the ball guests."

Cindy looked at her strangely and also kept a watch on the sun-baked rocks. It made her nervous, all this talk of lots of snakes squirming around on the ground.

But Grandma Webster was continuing, "Then the old man said, 'So you must have a wife of our people to take home with you. She'll help you remember the ceremonies and assist you in the preparations.'

"The snake girls in human form were as graceful and sinuous in their movements as they were when they were snakes. They were slender and fair featured too, and the young man wasn't displeased at all to have one of them for a bride. He said he'd be glad to take one of them for a wife.

"I knew, of course, that only one girl would be the right one. So when the kikmongwi sent for all the unmarried girls to come to the kiva and they put on their snake skins so that once more the floor was squirming with snakes, I told the boy, 'Choose that gray rattlesnake. Pick her up the way they showed you and—that's right, stroke her with the feather to calm her down so she doesn't bite you in her excitement. Then tell the kikmongwi you choose her.'

"He did this and when the kikmongwi asked him why, the clever boy said that not only was this snake girl beautiful but he could tell she was very learned in the ways of her people and intelligent as well. That pleased both the old man, who complimented him on his choice, and the girl. It's nice to know your husband thinks you're smart."

Cindy had set the open can of peaches beside the old lady. Grandma swallowed half the can in one long drink, held it back out to Cindy with a satisfied smile, wiped her mouth on the back of her sleeve and kept spinning while Cindy fished out the remaining peach slices and popped the cool sweet fruit, slick with syrupy liquid, into her mouth.

"As soon as he chose, all the other girls went out, took off their snake skins, and came back inside the room again. I left them at that point, but I heard that boy and his Snake Wife did good and took their knowledge back to the boy's people."

"That's nice," Cindy said, saving a peach slice, in case that was part of the custom too, and crunching the can down over it before putting it and the opener back in the saddlebag. "Did they live happily ever after?"

"Almost. The only problem was, when they had kids they took after their mother's side of the family. Sometimes they bit their playmates and made them die so they had to move on after a while. But that leads to another story and we have paused here long enough."

"Well," Cindy said, rising to her feet, which had begun to go to sleep. "That was quite a story."

"Normally, my people don't tell stories this time of year. The Navajos only tell them in the winter, and for the Hopis, storytelling is done only in December, when the evil things have frozen in the ground. But that's because they're talking of things that they consider magic. This was just a little anecdote, I think you'd call it, of something that happened to me one time. So you'll understand the country better."

"I appreciate it," Cindy said.

By now Grandma had another whorl full of yarn and she wound this off too and popped it back somewhere in the folds of her skirt, along with her spindle. "We better get going," she said chidingly, as if it was Cindy's fault that their journey had been delayed.

SEVEN

The Looking Glass

ONE THING ABOUT Sela's friend Shirley was that she was always easy to find. She spent most of every day tapping away at the keys of her state-of-the-art computer. Sela walked the long road up to Hoteville and crossed the plaza to Shirley's house. It looked the same on the outside as the other little adobe houses, but inside it was comfortable and pretty. Shirley's mom was a very well-known artist who had her pottery in all the big galleries in Phoenix and Scottsdale, Santa Fe and Taos. She gave back to the people too, plenty, but she still liked nice things and had a lot of them.

You'd never know from the way Shirley dressed. She was rounder than Sela, her brown eyes large and startled-looking, as if seeing life outside a computer screen was an astounding thing. She wore her black hair cropped into severe bangs and bowl-cut sides with a long braid running down her back. Sela thought privately that if it wouldn't have taken so much time away from her computer, Shirl would have worn her hair up in the old-time maiden style—like Princess Leia in *Star Wars*. She wore dusty black jeans and a black T-shirt with a Natchat logo on it, the new one with the two beaded computers hooked together by a coral red ray of light to symbolize the conversation between First Persons surging back and forth across the net. Her feet were bare and even dustier than her jeans.

"Shirl, we saw them . . ." Sela began from outside the screen door, since she could see her friend sitting at the recycled kitchen table that held her computer.

"Sela! Just a sec. I've been online with Milt, from Portland? A bunch of the AIM guys have asked Raydir Quantrill to do a concert in support of the Navajo resisters. Won't that be way cool?"

"Maybe *it* will be cool but Uncle Carl won't. He'll shit a brick when he hears about it. Everything those people do makes him mad."

Shirley sniffed. "Your uncle is one of those progressives who want to tear up our land for water lines and electricity—"

"The kind that runs that thing?" Sela asked innocently, gesturing to the computer.

"You know what I mean," Shirley said. She wasn't dumb. She knew when she couldn't reconcile her political stance with her lifestyle. The trouble was, for Shirley, brought up in the computer age, computers *were* part of her traditional lifestyle and what kept her in touch with Lakota braves, whose talk was a lot more interesting than anything she heard in Hopi. Well, usually. "So?" she asked quickly. "Who did you see?"

"That car that you saw when Joey was killed—we got the license number."

"Cool!" Shirley turned back to her screen and said, "Give it to me and I'll run it."

"The police did already. It's rented to some people who've been dead for three years."

"Oh, the old graveyard trick. Yeah. Well, I'm putting it up on the net anyway and telling my buds to watch for it. You never know."

"They'll probably change cars," Sela said, sitting on the arm of the overstuffed rocker that was Shirley's mom's favorite chair. A serape in muted shades of tan and gray covered it.

Shirley shrugged. "You never know. The more data you put out, the more chance there is of catching them."

"I suppose so. So, did I tell you what Wiley did today? He's so cute . . ."

Shirley said, "In a homeless puppy kind of way, I guess. Did I tell you that if they can do the concert here, Milt will probably come down with the support crew?"

"No. What's this guy look like?"

"What does that matter? He's a great warrior who helps our

people, very committed, very intense, really up on all the latest issues of First Peoples."

"And you didn't notice anything else?"

Shirley grinned. "Okay, so he's also a major babe but our relationship isn't based on that."

The Emperor's New Hospital Gown

Though Michael Blackgoat could not have known it, the woman with the long legs and the broken car was a warrior, one who had dwelled in another country for a long time learning of life and death and what's important and what's not, so that she came away changed, never completely one of the alien society and now feeling that she was also not completely Navajo. Warriors get to be like that, when they spend too long in battle. But she wasn't into killing. Quite the contrary. Unlike her more traditional ancestors, she was not afraid of death. She spit in death's eye and snatched victims from it every day.

She was a doctor and tried to be a good one. She found it very strange that when a person with her skills was so badly needed, people who were supposedly making policy that would better the lives of all Navajos felt obliged to get in her way.

Before the cute guy with the truck drove away, she and Dezi, her daughter, had unloaded their stuff. The guy jumped out and helped them without a word, and got back in his truck again. She knew she'd put him off but she didn't seem to be able to help it. The whole world was making her lose her temper these days, and only Dezi was good at working around it so that she didn't have to be a bad mother as well as a bad partner, and, if the Navajo hospital administrators in Window Rock had their way, a bad doctor.

She knew better of course. It was all politics. But she was going to be in the middle of it again if she didn't let the administrator here know that she was signing in as planned. Furthermore, they needed to show her where her housing was so she could get Dezi settled and enrolled in school.

Meanwhile, the two of them carried their boxes and bags

into the tiny lobby—just a hallway really, at the hospital, and she left Dezi sitting on them while she slipped into the ladies' room to change.

Then she returned to the desk and said, "I'm Dr. Maria Chee. Would you please tell the hospital administrator that I'm here? I believe I'm expected."

The woman looked at her blankly for a moment, then rose. "Couldn't you just call him?" she asked, a little impatiently. It was hot in the hospital too and Dezi had begun to droop over their household goods.

"This is faster" was all the woman replied as she left the desk. When she came back she said, "Yes, Mr. Nakai is expecting you—he said your appointment was for two hours ago, actually."

She started to sweep past the woman, who she felt was being unnecessarily intrusive and nasty, but then realized she was going to have to work with her. So she explained, "We had car trouble."

Edison Nakai was a little older than she was—mid-thirties rather than early, maybe. He had that Mexican look to him that some Navajos did—curly hair, for one thing, and something about the shape of his features and eyebrows. But he was very much like some of the men she'd encountered in Window Rock.

He didn't look up, but kept frowning into his paperwork. Finally, taking a deep breath, she stuck out her hand and said, "Hi, sorry to interrupt. I'm Dr. Maria Chee, your transfer from the Window Rock clinic. I'm supposed to start work here tomorrow. Just thought I'd come in and introduce myself and see if you could point me to my quarters. It's been a long day and my daughter's exhausted."

Nakai looked up, ignored her hand, and his frown deepened. Finally, reluctantly, he stood, extended his own hand, and then indicated a chair facing his desk—much like the chair meant for an erring child called into the principal's office.

"Dr. Chee, Maria? I'm a frank man and I'm going to speak to you in a frank way."

"Fine, Edison," she said, since he wanted to be on first name terms. He frowned again and she thought to herself, maybe it was just *he* who would want to be on first name terms but she'd learned all about that kind of power play in Feminism 101 at Berkeley where she'd done her undergrad studies.

"You have a reputation as a troublemaker, Maria. Now, I'm not saying we can't use another doctor here—I've requested one regularly every quarter since I took this position five years ago. But we're a small, close-knit team here at Keams and we don't need uncooperative staff members who consider themselves prima donnas. Do I make myself clear?"

"A troublemaker? Me?" she asked innocently, then decided that maybe she would try another tack, that it was a small place and she really did want to get along with people, regardless of reports to the contrary. "No, seriously, Edison, I very much appreciate you sharing with me what's been said from my previous post. But I think perhaps you should understand where I'm coming from. I graduated in the top third of my class and could have had postings at several large California clinics. But the Navajo Nation paid for my education and I wanted to practice here, where I could do my people some good. Unfortunately, some people see a Navajo woman doctor as a curiosity to be exploited. Also unfortunately, some of these people are in high positions in the Navajo Nation. I believe most of this trouble started when I refused to falsify the medical records of a certain high-ranking official so that he could use his department's budget to take sick leave supposedly to seek a consultation elsewhere . . ."

It pained her to talk about this even while it filled her with indignation. A liberally inclined Californian to the bone, Maria Chee was idealistic with a strength of conviction that was almost religious in its zeal. Before returning to the reservation, she had earnestly believed that her people, the Navajos, would have most of their problems dealt with best with other Navajos running the government. She had a sort of romantic notion, as she saw it now with a certain amount of embarrassment, of an American Indian Utopia brought about by the process of the tribe educating its young people who brought their gifts home and bettered the lot of the people

with all of the benefits of outside society and none of the at-
tendant ills.

Unfortunately, it seemed, the only people who had been
willing to assure the power to represent a people who had formerly, with fierce individualism, represented themselves
solely on the basis of personal, family or clan affiliation, were
the people who were not fit to wield it. This was familiar to
Chee from state, local and national elections she'd heard her
family, friends, and teachers discuss within the dominant culture. The first thing some Navajos had learned from the outside world was how to abuse their power. The unfairness of
this so rankled Chee that any diplomatic skills she might have
possessed were overwhelmed by her contempt for the men
who stooped to this sort of thing.

"How could you be so sure he didn't actually have that
medical need?" Nakai asked.

"Because there's no facility in Las Vegas that specializes in
any of the things he claimed were wrong with him," Chee
said, trying to keep her voice level. It also angered her that
these crooks had decided to lengthen the shadow they were
trying to cast over her career so it covered her new post. Even
in exile they wanted her punished, and for what? Refusing to
go along with their crooked schemes!

"But there was a petition signed by Navajo staff members
testifying that your handling of your communications with
them was demeaning and abrupt."

"I was forbidden to ask what that was all about," she told
him. "But one of the people involved came to me and voluntarily told me that she had been under the impression it was a
petition for improved lunchroom facilities at the clinic."

"I see. Well, that's not what Commissioner Becenti says
here in this report but. . ."

"Commissioner Becenti was caught by two nurses with his
hand in the controlled substances cabinet. There's an incident
report on record," she said, thinking privately that there was
unless someone had tampered with the records, not unheard
of. Even though it was federally controlled, the Indian Health
Service had always had as many indigenous people as it could
hire in key positions, and these days that meant a lot of the ad-

ministrative staff as well as nursing staff—Navajo doctors were still fairly rare, given the traditional Navajo bias against dealing with death and dying.

She didn't think she'd rouse Mr. Nakai's sympathy by telling him that when she tried to interview Commissioner Becenti about the incident, at the urging of the nurses, he had chased her around the desk and backed her into a corner. A knee effectively placed in an anatomically vulnerable area had taken care of that, but she didn't want to tell this to Mr. Nakai. She couldn't be sure it wouldn't give him ideas of his own and anyway, she didn't like to start a professional relationship off with that sort of personal revelation.

Nakai cleared his throat and changed the subject. "In light of all this, we were not sure how long you might be staying. The Keams Canyon Hospital, as you may or may not be aware of, Dr. Chee, services all patients who live in the area regardless of tribal affiliation. In light of historical and recent conflicts between the two dominant cultures here, ours and that of the Hopi, this is a difficult assignment and extraordinary tact and fairness are needed to deal with many situations that would, in other places, be strictly medical. So far, your record does not show that you possess this sort of tact."

"Nevertheless, here I am," she said.

"I see. However, our allocated housing is full. There is a bulletin board in the staff lounge that sometimes posts vacancies in what housing is available. So you're on your own there, Dr. Chee." And he returned his attention to his papers, unable to completely suppress a smug little smile.

"Mr. Nakai, I have a daughter . . ." she began and then stopped. He didn't care, obviously. The more difficult he made things, the easier it would be to get rid of her, which was what he wanted. Well, it wouldn't work. Her father had relatives around here somewhere. One phone call to California and she'd get directions and maybe have someone to call on for help. Or she hoped so. But when she returned to the lobby, a woman in a wheelchair was talking to Dezi, asking her questions and smiling.

"Mama, this is Nicki," Dezi told her in the adult fashion Maria had taught her from an early age. "Nicki, this is my mama. She's a doctor."

"Hi," Nicki said, smiling. Maria felt her heart melt to see a truly friendly smile after all the guardedness and hostility she'd been subjected to so far. "I have a pickup, if you need help moving your stuff. Dezbah says your car's in the shop."

"That's kind of you but we couldn't put you to the trouble," Maria began, with California manners.

"No trouble to me." Nicki grinned. "I have a teenage son and daughter to do the grunt work."

"I apparently have no place for you to move them to right now," Maria said, "but I sure do appreciate the offer." She was going to go then and make her call and start arranging her life, but nothing would do but that she explain.

She took Dezi and Nicki outside to tell them what Nakai had said to her about the housing. Nicki was as angry as Maria wanted to be. "What way is that to treat you when you come here to help us? Wait a minute till my kids get back and we'll load your stuff in the truck. It may be a little rough and a little crowded, but my mother would be angry with me if I didn't get you to come home with us for supper and stay at our place until you can find your own."

EIGHT

Rumplestiltskin and the Creation of the World

At Lomaki Ruin, Grandma Webster turned Chaco's head due north. "We'll take the shortcut," she said. "We can stop at the river to wash up and give Chaco a drink and you will see more of our land instead of just the highway."

According to Cindy's map, the land around the Little Colorado River was not on the reservation, for the most part, but ran along the western edge of the Painted Desert. They had gone about five more miles when they saw first a fence, then a scattering of sheep grazing on occasional patches of short brown grass, and finally a group of buildings. A rectangular cinderblock house, an arbor made of poles and covered with a tarp held down by evergreen branches, an old Airstream trailer, and one of the eight-sided Navajo houses Hank had told Cindy were called hogans, the traditional Navajo dwelling. This one was made of logs chinked with mud.

Just outside the tarp's protection was a tall frame half filled with a rug in colors that matched the surrounding desert, the red cliffs beyond, and the yellow rabbit brush that grew along the sides of the washes where nothing else would.

A Siamese cat lay on the tarp, its paws hanging off the edge as it watched them approach. Two dogs, barking and wagging furiously, ran out to meet them.

"Yah-ta-hey," Grandma called to the woman at the loom.

"Yah-T'ey," the woman replied, and waved.

Grandma spoke to her in what Cindy presumed was Navajo and the other woman shaded her eyes against the sun and kept waving vigorously, a big grin developing on her face as they drew nearer and nearer. The woman leaned to look around Grandma at Cindy, who was still riding behind her companion.

"What did you tell her?" Cindy asked.

"I told her the horse was tired," Grandma answered. "I said could we rest at her house."

A voice called out sharply from within the house and the weaver called back something.

A weary-looking young woman, in her teens, emerged from the house, wiping her hands on a dishtowel. She wore jeans, a T-shirt, and an open red plaid flannel shirt with the elbows out. "Speak *English*," she said to the weaver in a complaining voice. From behind her, a middle-aged woman and man, an older man, and three teenaged boys came from the house and stood outside with arms folded, not looking happy.

But three little kids, grandchildren of the weaver judging by their ages, ran out of the arbor and up to the horse. One of them stroked the animal's nose.

Cindy slipped back, swung one leg around and jumped lightly to the ground, again prepared to help Grandma, but Grandma was already heading for the woman at the loom, her arms outstretched to envelop the other woman in an embrace, as if she were a long-lost daughter.

Cindy decided to let them talk while she loosened the cinch and lifted the saddle's cantle and blanket momentarily to let the air circulate beneath them and cool Chaco's back. The little girl who had been stroking the horse's nose held out her hand for the currycomb and rag.

The teenaged girl came over to Cindy and asked, "What do you want?" in a tone that was less than friendly.

"Just to water my horse, maybe buy a little feed for him."

"You got money to pay?"

Cindy did, but she wasn't expecting the question. The river was about fifty yards from the house, and though it was little more than a ditch with a stream connecting little pools and mud puddles, the grass surrounding it was less brown and more plentiful.

The girl saw her look and said, "Or maybe you'd like to buy a rug or some jewelry, huh? My husband's auntie makes good rugs. She's slow, though." She shot a look at the weaver.

The weaver suddenly looked up from her animated chat with Grandma and said something sharply to the girl in Navajo.

"Guests don't get to have guests. You should stop talking and get back to work," the girl snapped. Everyone at the door but the older man glared at the weaver.

"We don't mean to cause trouble," Cindy said. "But I hadn't planned on having my horse carry two when I met this lady." She indicated Grandma with a nod. "She was wandering across the desert."

The girl, to her surprise, gave her a pitying glance. "She's probably just like these freeloaders, then," she said. "Let the Hopis and the government take their land and then expect us to support them when there's not enough here to support us. You should make her sell some of that fancy turquoise and buy her own horse."

Cindy said nothing, but the older man frowned and nodded at one of the boys, who came and pulled the girl away.

Cindy wanted to tell Grandma it was time to go but she was still talking to the weaver. The kids meanwhile were having a great time fussing over Chaco.

Grandma and the woman were now carefully inspecting the weaving and Grandma suddenly sat down and began doing something extremely businesslike with the yarn. It looked as if she intended to stay a while, despite the teenaged girls lack of hospitality.

Well, Chaco could use a good long break after carrying double the load he was supposed to. Cindy finished removing his tack, unsnapping the bit from the bridle. On this special endurance model, once you removed the bit, the bridle became a halter. And it was even whippier than that. The reins could be converted to a lead rope, so you didn't have to carry a ten-foot rope around the horse's neck while on the trail.

A little boy of about nine said, "He's thirsty, I bet. Shall I take him to the river for a drink?"

"I think I'd better do it for now," Cindy said. "We've just had a long hot ride and he's real thirsty, but if he drinks too much cold river water all at once, he could colic."

"We know *that*," a girl maybe a year or two older than the boy said. "We had lots of horses before the BIAs took them away and we had to move here."

Grandma nodded sharply to Cindy, who protested, "He's my responsibility."

Grandma said a little pityingly, "You're a good horse girl but these children are probably better than you even. You watch. They know what they're doing."

"Could I ride him there?" asked another little boy, this one about six. Cindy set him up on Chaco's back and was going to lead Chaco to the river herself, but the little girl took him. Cindy watched while the children very carefully did exactly what she would have. Grandma was right. The kids knew how to handle horses.

Over by the loom the two old ladies, Grandma Webster and the weaver, sat talking. Cindy walked over toward them and under the shade of the arbor, where in one shadowy corner a girl in jeans and a sweatshirt sat spinning with a spindle like Grandma Webster's.

Since she didn't speak Navajo, and the kids were handling Chaco like seasoned wranglers, Cindy watched the girl for a while and then rose and went over to watch her more closely. Piled around her was skein after skein of yarn.

The older man, the girl, and the middle-aged couple from the house stood under the edge of the tarp, watching them all with what seemed to be a mixture of wariness and disapproval.

The weaver gestured toward Cindy and spoke to Grandma in Navajo.

Cindy smiled at her and said, "Grandma Webster, please tell the lady I hope I'm not being rude, but today was the first time I ever saw anyone spin like this. It looks like it would be fun to learn."

The girl who had first spoken to Cindy snorted and the middle-aged woman's frown deepened. They were joined by a boy who took a swig from a can of Coors.

The girl in the sweatshirt smiled ruefully and said, "It *was,* while we had our own place and wove for ourselves."

"What do you mean?" Cindy asked.

The weaver said something that sounded like a warning and the girl gave Cindy a helpless look and returned her eyes to her spindle and wool.

The weaver gestured to Grandma Webster to join her beside the girl who was spinning, and spoke rapidly in Navajo. Grandma clicked her tongue and sat down cross-legged beside the girl. The older woman took up a spindle herself and sat down next to them.

The girl didn't look up but steadfastly concentrated on her work. Grandma said something to her in Navajo in a gentle tone, and the girl blinked up at her, as if in sudden recognition. She started to point to something nearby, then used her mouth instead to indicate a pair of rectangular boards with a handle on one side and spines on the other. Grandma nodded, picked up the boards, and grabbed a handful of raw wool from the sack beside them.

"What are those?" Cindy asked, feeling safe asking Grandma, at least, a question.

"Wool cards. They have a lot of spinning to do. I'm going to help them out. This is how you card the raw wool to make it ready to spin."

Grandma's pace seemed slow and steady as she brushed the wool between the cards and laid it in fluffy rolls between the two spinners, but before Cindy could blink again the wool sack was empty and the little fluffy rolls were stacked in a bale as high as the women's shoulders. "Wow, you're good," Cindy said admiringly.

Grandma smiled and waved her hand modestly. "Oh, child, I should be. I invented spinning and weaving."

At the time, Cindy assumed she was speaking figuratively.

Then Grandma touched the girl's shoulder and took the spindle from her. With deft movements she unwound the partial skein the girl had spun and took it from the spindle. Just as quickly, she wound on a hank of her own wool and spun it out long and fine. When it was time to add a second hank, she handed the spindle back to the girl. Then she took the weaver's spindle and did the same. The old woman looked as if she was about to kiss Grandma's feet, but Grandma said, "Just use what I have given you. It will be enough."

The older man spoke to the middle-aged woman, who walked over to the spinners and asked a question in Navajo. Beaming, the weaver seemed to be introducing Grandma. The woman's tight expression broke first into scorn, then, watching Grandma spin, incredulity, and then something like awe, and she hurried back to the others, said a few words and dragged the plaid-shirted girl by the arm back into the house.

Grandma, meanwhile, sat down at the loom and began working on building the pattern begun by the weaver—stripes and crosses and diamond shapes in rows of soft golds, tans, rusts, grays and white.

Cindy sat down beside her. The men closed in a little but stayed a respectful distance beyond.

"Do you mind my asking what's going on here?" Cindy asked.

"The weaver of this rug is one of my children. Her name is Nell Tso and she lived all of her life on her land near Big Mountain. The girl is her daughter, the children her grandchildren. They were told by the government men that they had to move, that their land was not theirs but belonged to the Hopi.

"Nell didn't want to move but they told her they would give her a house in Flagstaff. She didn't want to disobey the law, so she went, but they wouldn't let her take her sheep or horses. The BIAs took them away. Her son-in-law said it would be all right, that he would find a job and that the children could go to city school.

"At first she thought it would be okay. There was an indoor toilet, and lights you put on with a switch, and her son-in-law bought a television for the children. He even got them a phone.

"But then the bills started coming, and he still didn't have a job. Nell and her daughter Denise sold a rug and that kept them going for a little while. But with no sheep of their own, they had to buy wool and there was nowhere to get the good stuff in town like they used to be able to get at the trader's if they needed something special. There was no place to pick the dye plants in the city either.

"Pretty soon the son-in-law left, and the bills kept coming

in. Then the government took back their house. The only place they could come to was here, where Nell's brother lives in the house that used to belong to his wife before she died. Now it belongs to her daughter.

"They have good land, and water, but they say Nell's family makes too many people and they really don't want them here. Nell thinks if only they can weave four rugs and sell them within the next month, that maybe the family will let them build a hogan of their own a little way from here and support themselves and contribute to the family income with the weaving. Her brother made them say they would give her a chance."

"That's awful," Cindy said, with a sympathetic glance at the two women earnestly spinning away in the corner. The yarn pile was quite a bit larger. "How come the government took their land? I thought all that was over with and they had their own country now, sort of."

Grandma nodded, her fingers continuing to weave. From the house now came the smell of cooking. One of the boys came out with two cans of Coke and set one down beside each woman. Grandma inclined her head toward Nell and Denise and the boy said, "Oh, right," and went back in the house, returning with two more Cokes for them.

"It's a very long story, Cindy Ellis. You see, when the People came into this world from the old one, they did not come all at once."

"No?"

"No. I can see that you need to be told more about this." She looked around. All of the family except the weaver and her daughter were now standing around the loom, looking at her over the top, through the warp, and at the sides. The expressions on their faces were uncertain and uncomfortable, but fascinated, Cindy thought. The middle-aged woman and her daughter hovered at the edge.

The children had quietly returned with Chaco. They'd been carefully hand-grazing him, grass interspersed with caresses and whispered conversations, and now one of the boys yelled to Cindy and pointed to the little run-down circular corral made of railroad ties stacked end-over-end log cabin style. It was about a quarter filled with new grass, maybe a hundred yards from the house. He nodded to Chaco and to the corral with a questioning look on his face and Cindy smiled, and called, "Better tie him up. We don't want him to leave without us."

"Yeah," the boy called back. "You'd sure have a long walk."

When Chaco was safely ensconced, the children, one by one, came to sit cross-legged between their elders and the loom.

"I don't suppose very many of you speak good Navajo, do you?" Grandma asked.

Everyone but Nell Tso, even Denise, looked a little embarrassed.

"No, I didn't think so," Grandma said with a put-upon sigh as she made another joint in her design and pushed her shuttle through the space her batten had just opened between warp threads. "Okay, for the sake of my niece here and all of you Navajos who don't speak Navajo, I will give you the one-oh-one version of the Cliff notes of creation."

"Cliff notes!" One of the teenage boys laughed. "Good one—get it?—Cliff notes, and the mesas and—"

His elders were giving him a dirty look but Grandma smiled at him with approval. "We might make a Navajo of this one yet. He has a sense of humor. Do you know, my grandson, that you can make triple puns in Navajo if you ever bother to learn it?"

The boy lowered his head, not knowing whether to expand the smile that lingered on his face or be ashamed because of his ignorance.

Grandma continued. "Okay, everybody but Cindy here probably knows that all of the people here today got kicked out of the last world, the Fourth World for Navajos, the Third World for Hopis, because some of them had been very wicked. Not all of the people were wicked, and so they got help from the gods getting out of that other world, which was being flooded.

"They came up through a hole in the sky, first climbing up through a reed and then on a ladder woven of spider silk.

"Well, all those people having to be evacuated, it took a really long time. And a lot of discrimination to figure out who was who. A very tough job, I can tell you. And the ladder kept fraying with the weight of all those people, especially since some of the four-leggeds had sharp claws or hooves and the winged ones had sharp talons. The ladder from the lower world had to be constantly repaired. In your stories, you never hear that part because the people coming up the ladder only tell what they saw with their own eyes. They didn't have the responsibility for keeping that ladder safe. Fortunately, Mockingbird was there too and she took it upon herself to give the people their names as they came through.

"First were the Hopis, and while the other groups were climbing up, getting named, and settling in, the Hopis met Masaw, the guardian of the Fourth World, were tested, accepted as stewards of the earth, wandered all over the world, and eventually came back to the mesas. That's how long it took.

"They traveled a really long ways, leaving some people behind in different places, and in other places meeting up with people who had just emerged from the lower world. Sometimes the groups intermarried and sometimes they fought. But the Navajos began coming up a little while after the Hopis had settled onto the mesas. The land was pretty empty then, except for some ruins left behind when the ancestors of the Hopis and Pueblos moved on. And whereas the *sipapuni* for the Hopis had been where I told you, Cindy, in the Grand Canyon, by the time the Navajos came up through the reed, it was really shaking with the force of the flood from the lower world and the ladder had to be reattached up in Colorado. So that's how they came down here.

"Also, they needed a little tinkering with before they were ready for this world. See, the reason they had more worlds is that in their first world they weren't very much like people. They were more like bugs—grasshoppers or locusts."

"My teacher said we came from monkeys," one of the boys said.

"Your teacher doesn't know everything, and neither did Mr. Darwin. Maybe in the last world *Cindy's* people were monkeys but she's not Navajo."

"Some scientists think we were all fish to begin with," Cindy offered.

"If you had been, you wouldn't have had to leave the last world when it flooded, would you?" Grandma said scornfully. "Not everybody was the same thing. I understand from my white sister that her people were once thought to be small and have wings too, so maybe they're kin to the Navajo. I don't know. Anyway, when the Navajos emerged into this world, they needed some tinkering with. They still had the teeth, feet, and claws of beasts and insects. So, four beings whose English names would be called White Body, or in Navajo, *Bitsis Lagai;* Blue Body, in Navajo, *Bitsis Dotliz,* who is like the god now called Water Sprinkler; Yellow Body, or *Bitsis Litsoi;* and Black Body, who is the same as the one known to you as the god of fire, back then called *Bitsis Lizhin,* they visited the people four days in a row and tried to tell them something, but the people didn't understand them. Finally, Black Body stayed behind and spoke very loudly and slowly and told them that they were to be changed into more godlike forms, with proper hands and feet. However, Black Body also told them they needed to clean up before the ceremony and that the gods would return in twelve days.

"Well, the people bathed themselves really well and dried off—the women dried themselves with yellow cornmeal, the men with white cornmeal."

One of the boys' hands went up. "Why did they do that?" he asked. "Didn't they have towels or anything?"

The old woman gave him a look that would have frozen lava. "You wouldn't understand," she said. "It's a Navajo thing."

The girl in the plaid shirt, miffed at the rebuff of her brother—or maybe he was her husband—said, "I never heard any of this stuff. When I asked my auntie about the Navajo version of who made the world, she said Coyote made it."

The old lady said, "I'm coming to that. But your auntie had it wrong. Coyote didn't make the *world,* not that he wouldn't take the credit. I'm pretty sure he made the government, though."

"Grandmother," said the older man there, "it seems to me a

storm is coming. Would we not all be more comfortable if you continued your story inside the hogan? My grandsons will carry the loom for you."

"That is very kind of you, Grandson," Grandma Webster said.

Nell looked worried and asked Grandma something. Grandma nodded and said, "That is a very good question, Granddaughter." To the others she said, "Your auntie is worried because it is not good to tell stories during a storm. However, what I tell you now is not a story of the made-up kind but a true history I can personally say is fact. Besides, in this sort of thing I am a professional. I know when to speak of these things and when not, but the average person should go by the general rules." She said this with a self-deprecating smile, and repeated it in Navajo for Nell, who smiled, apparently satisfied.

Cindy noticed that the younger people now were treating Nell and Denise Tso with a little more courtesy, and the children scrambled to bring the fresh puffs and skeins of yarn the Tsos were working with into the hogan, too. Now the arrangement was different. The older man made a fire in the stove, which was good because the wind was picking up and it was getting cold. Cindy used the outhouse while things were being moved. She stopped on the way back to check on Chaco, who hadn't managed to untie himself and in fact, seemed perfectly willing to stay where he was the rest of the day if necessary. Little clouds clumped together to form big ones that blotted out the earlier bright blue of the sky and stampeded across it like sheep chased by wolves. The wind was cold and kicked up the dust. Small whirlwinds played out by the sheep.

Back inside the hogan, lamps were lit for Grandma and the Tsos to work by, and the two youngest grandchildren began carding as well. The women all sat on one side of the room and the men on the other, but all were close enough to hear and see.

Grandma Webster picked up the thread of her history as deftly as she picked up the yarn and thrust it between two or three warps to make the center part of a cross.

"The gods called out four times to announce their approach and then they were there. Blue Body and Black Body each carried buckskins. White Body and Yellow Body carried ears of corn, one white, one yellow, each perfect and completely covered with kernels, right to the end.

"The gods laid one buckskin on the ground, making the head face to the west. They put the two ears of corn on the buckskin and faced the tips to the east. Then they covered the corn with the other buckskin with *its* head to the east. They put a yellow eagle's feather under the yellow ear and a white eagle's feather under the white ear. Then the people all stood back as the wind blew through the buckskins and over the corn. A white wind blew from the east and a yellow wind from the west. While the wind blew, eight Mirage People came and danced around the buckskins and pretty soon something inside those buckskins began to move. The ears of corn were gone! Or rather, they had changed. The white ear had become a man and the yellow ear had become a woman. The wind had given them life."

Grandma tapped the plaid-shirted girl's hand and showed her, as she had showed Cindy, how the wind that gave her life had left its tracks on her fingertips.

"Really? Is that where they come from?" The girl and her husband and brothers inspected their hands curiously, as did the other children. Even the middle-aged couple took a furtive glance at their fingers.

Cindy was impressed. The Bible didn't go into nearly so much detail about the creation of Adam and Eve. Nell and Denise had been nodding while they spun, as if Grandma's story agreed with what they knew, so she felt the old lady wasn't making this up or that it was part of her delusion. It was no doubt the authentic creation story Grandma had learned somewhere—probably from her mother, since this sort of thing, from what little Cindy knew about it, tended to be handed down. But she had a question. "What are Mirage People?"

"You saw them earlier today," Grandma told her.

"I did?"

"When the heat made them rise in shimmers from the sand as we rode to Wupatki."

"Those heat waves?"

Grandma nodded. "Mirage People."

Cindy frowned, trying to take it in. Denise cleared her throat shyly and Grandma acknowledged her with a smile. "Back then everything was people, I think. I took a folklore course at college once and they talked about how in European folklore you have things called Elementals? Fire, Water, Earth and Air? That's like we have, with the Mirage People sort of—"

"They're like fire or heat, then?" asked Cindy.

"Yes, but also like real people. Because later on, some of First Man and First Woman's children married in with them, didn't they, Grandmother?"

Grandma nodded. "Yes. All of their children were twins. The first pair were hermaphrodites, each of them half male and half female, but after that they were sets—a boy and a girl in each pair of twins. They traveled to the four sacred mountains, which the gods named for them as they went. It's said that at the eastern mountain they learned of witchcraft and to wear masks. But they also learned something else, because when they came back from there, the brothers and sisters separated and that was when they married into the Mirage People, for they realized that one should not marry people to whom one is closely related. At this time, life went very fast. Women got pregnant and had their kids in just four days, and in four days the kids were adults, ready to have their kids. These grandchildren and great-grandchildren married people among the Kisani, or Pueblos, related to the Hopis and Zunis and the Rio Grande people, though everyone lived in different places then and everyone was moving around a lot.

"What about those herm—the ones that were both male and female?" one of the boys asked.

"First Man and First Woman made a big farm and the hermaphrodites were set as guards. One guarded the dam and irrigation ditch, the other guarded the field. The one that guarded the dam invented pottery. The other one invented wicker water bottles.

"The people learned about farming from the Kisani and made implements from animal bones. They learned to hunt too and to make masks.

"And eight years after they came from the Third World into the Fourth, the sky opened and out drops Coyote and Badger."

"So Coyote couldn't have made the world, I guess," the plaid-shirted girl said.

"Well, he sort of helped out with the people later," Grandma told her. "That's probably what you heard about. See, everything went along pretty good for a while with First Man and First Woman and their kids and grandkids. But then one day First Man went hunting like usual and brought home a nice deer like usual and First Woman cooked it and they ate it like usual. They were both gettin' a little out of shape with all the good eating in the world back then. First Woman wiped her hands and said—" Grandma said a phrase in Navajo that made the older Navajos and Denise smile. The younger ones looked cool, trying to pretend they understood, but they didn't. The kids just kept listening.

Cindy said, "Okay, I'll bite. What does that mean?"

Grandma laughed. "That's just what First Man wanted to know! Because what she said was 'Thank you, my vagina.' He said, 'Why are you thanking your vagina when it was me that went out and hunted that deer for us?' She said, 'You wouldn't have done it if it wasn't for sex, so I'm thanking my vagina. In a way, it's responsible for everything you do.' Now, the other women thought this was real reasonable but the men were mad. They moved across the river and took all the animals with them. It was okay at first because the crops had been put in and the women had lots to eat and they teased the men from across the river and the men teased back. But later on, they all started to get lonely and they got a little, what you would call perverted."

"You want the kids to leave now?" Cindy asked.

Grandma shook her head. "These kids grew up around animals. They know about this stuff. It just embarrasses the grownups, especially, excuse me, Cindy, among the *biligaana,* your white people, to think they do. The men pretended the animals were women and coupled with them and the women pretended all kinds of things were men and used them that way. But after a while, they couldn't stand it anymore and they all got back together. Too bad, but the damage had already been done. A little while later, the women started giving birth to things that were fathered by the stuff they used in place of men. Horrible monsters came of it. These monsters got worse as they got older and pretty soon they had eaten everybody except about half a dozen people."

At that point Grandma stopped speaking and weaving, and to Cindy's surprise, she could see that the rug was completely woven. Cindy had been so busy imagining the locust people Navajos, the Mirage People, the wind making fingerprints, and First Woman's early version of feminism and all of the strange results of that, that she hadn't paid much attention to anything but the lulling beat of Grandma's comb and the *shush* of the batten going through the warps. All of the yarn fluffs were spun now and piled into stacks of black, white and gray natural colors.

"We'd better take this off the loom and warp up the next rug," Grandma said.

The middle-aged woman said, "Jerry and Harold can help you and Denise and Auntie Nell with the loom. The rest of us will go get supper and bring it here."

"Good. Then I will continue my story."

"Just a minute," one of the boys was saying as Cindy trailed behind the plaid-shirted girl. "You mean *real* monsters? Like Godzilla and Jabba the Hut and Gargantua?"

"Worse than that," Grandma promised.

Cindy wondered when the older woman, whose name seemed to be Doris, had time to prepare so much food. A huge cauldron of simmering stew with big chunks of mutton, swimming in broth with potatoes and hominy, was the main dish. An equally big kettle filled with corn on the cob had been bubbling beside it, and as the food, plates, silverware, glasses and six packs of Coke, beer, and milk were carried out to the hogan, Doris and her plaid-shirted daughter, called Hannah by her mother, patted out circles of bread and dropped them in frying pans until a cookie sheet was piled high with puffy, fragrant bread.

Cindy picked up a stack of plates and was heading for the hogan with them, but Doris said something to the middle-aged man, her husband, Herb, and he took the plates from her.

"Really, I can help," Cindy said to Doris.

"No, no. Your auntie thinks we're bad enough already."

"We don't even know you—anyway, I don't and I don't think she does, though she and Mrs. Tso seem like old friends."

"They would be," Doris said. "Auntie Nell was brought up very traditionally. I was born here but I went to school in Flagstaff. Herbert, my husband, went to the same school. My dad worked for the railroad. Mom was always fussing at me when I was home about doing things the Navajo Way but really, she and Dad wanted us brought up so we could get along in the white world. Get educations and jobs. I probably don't know much more about those stories your aunt is telling us than you do. Neither do my kids. You probably can tell."

"Well, I have no room to talk," Cindy said, since of course she hadn't known the stories at all before today either.

"Yeah," Hannah put in. "But you're *biligaana*. It's not the same for you."

"The thing is," Doris went on, covering the fry bread with a clean tea towel of the touristy kind decorated with color postcard pictures of Phoenix, "my mom made it real hard on all of us. She was a very picky lady and even though she sent us away, she wanted us to act like Navajos too. Dad was never around till after he retired. When Auntie Nell got thrown out of her place, I felt mean and thought, So much for being a traditional Navajo. I feel ashamed of that now. I was afraid she'd be like Mom, just when I was getting used to running my own house. But she never has acted like that. And she's a lot more traditional than my mom was. That's why I thought she could make her rugs to help out."

"Well," Cindy said cautiously, "from what Grandma Webster—er—*my* auntie tells me, four rugs is quite a lot in a short time for most people. She seems to be coping, though."

"She sure is," Hannah said. "Who *is* she really?"

Cindy shrugged. "My guess right now is Rumplestiltskin."

When they both looked a bit puzzled, she explained, "That's a character in a fairy tale. A little dwarf who helped a princess spin straw into gold, which I bet Grandma could do if she wanted to. But as far as I know, she's just some lady I picked up on the highway. Said she'd been off visiting relatives and is on her way back to her place in some canyon. I was hoping maybe you folks were relatives—"

"Maybe we are," Doris said, shaking her head. "But I think she wants to stay with you."

They finished carrying the food to the hogan. Hannah's eyes almost popped when she saw that the rug that had just been finished was rolled beside a loom now redressed and with two inches of weaving already done at the bottom. "WHOA!" she said. Denise was taking a turn at the loom while Grandma busied herself with some yarn. When she turned back to take her food, she placed three baskets of different-colored yarn beside Denise—yellow, sage green and russet. Nell was smiling broadly to herself as she stopped spinning. Doris filled two plates, handing one to Grandma and one to Nell, respectfully. Grandma nodded her thanks. Nell's wrinkles were all turned up and her teeth shone in the dark leather of her face.

The wind outside howled now and whistled around the smoke hole. Cindy had barely taken her first bite when she heard hail start to hit. "Aw, horseshit!" she said, and covered her mouth, looking embarrassed. She had been under Pill's influence a little too long. She leapt to her feet. "Excuse me, I gotta go see about Chaco," she said.

"Sit down, sit down," Doris said and told the boy she'd called Jerry earlier, "Lead the horse in under the arbor and tie him there."

"I'll do it, Auntie," one of Denise's children said, and ran to the door barefoot. Before Cindy could step over everything and around everybody between her and the door, he had run out, untied Chaco, trotted with him back under the arbor, tied him securely beneath the sturdiest part of the overhang, and was back inside the hogan, shivering. Grandma Webster put her arm around him and patted his head. Her plate was empty.

"Now then, monsters," she said. "They were terrible monsters, water monsters, winged monsters, and all of them ate people. Except they were about to run out because like I said, there were only about six people, counting First Man and First Woman, left in the world."

"How about the Hopis?" Cindy asked.

"Oh, they don't count. The monsters weren't mad at them, because they hadn't left them to die when they were born. Besides, the Hopis were either out wandering or back up on their mesas. But the Navajos were almost all gone.

"They didn't know what to do. The gods weren't telling them anything now. I guess they were kind of disgusted with the Navajos for the way they acted when they separated. But then one dark night, First Man was wandering around because he couldn't sleep. It was very stormy, just like now, with thunder crashing and both straight and forked lightning jumping out of the sky. With so many monsters around too, it was very frightening.

"But in the middle of all this noise, First Man thought he heard a baby cry. The cry seemed to be coming from up on a mountaintop. The thunder boomed again, and once more he heard the crying baby. Well, he started climbing real fast. And at the top of that mountain, what did he find but a little baby girl! He took her back home and showed her to First Woman and the other people. They decided to call her Changing Woman. Like the other kids of the First People, Changing Woman grew up in four days. She was a beautiful young woman.

"She decided to have a nap by a stream and while she slept, the sun made love to her. She woke up warm and drowsy and decided to take a bath in the waterfall, and it too, caressed her. So in four more days, she bore twins, one for the sun, one for the water. The oldest one she called Slayer of Alien Monsters or Monster Slayer and the younger was Child of Water or Born for Water."

Full of food and drowsy, Cindy drifted off a little, seeing in her dreams the two young men trudging off to talk to the sun and get weapons to kill the monsters, and then take a long journey killing the monsters. The youngsters were having a good time with this part.

She jerked herself awake as she realized that suddenly it was silent. Grandma Webster had taken a breath, the plates were all cleared away, and the hail had stopped. And two rugs lay beside the loom. Nell was weaving now and a third rug was three-quarters done already.

Suddenly, not too far away, an eerie cry went up: "Ao ao ao aoooooowa! Yip yip yip yip," and was answered by a similar one.

Hannah had slipped into a leather motorcycle jacket and Howard's arm was around her shoulders. "This must be where Coyote comes in, huh?"

"Yeah, he's ready for his share of the story okay," Grandma said, laughing. "It happened this way. With so many people having been eaten by the monsters, once her sons had killed them all Changing Woman decided the world needed some more Navajos. She took a bath in white shell and dried off with yellow and white cornmeal and threw the bathwater into the ocean. A fog rose up from this and it became the Bead People, the Yoo'ii Din'é. There were two men and two women of white corn, and two men and two women of yellow corn, also two white corn boys and girls and two yellow corn boys and girls . . ."

Cindy stayed awake while the people went off on great adventures and one of the yellow corn men became a godlike white coyote. By this time, Grandma was showing Hannah and Doris how to card and spin as she talked and they were trying hard to suppress their giggles as they listened. Nell's weaving was almost complete when Cindy fell asleep.

When she woke up again, with her head resting on her forearm, she was covered with one of the rugs. All of the family were asleep, Doris with her head in Nell's lap, Nell's head thrown back against one of the beams of the hogan, Denise and Hannah and the children all in a swarm like puppies while the men snored from whatever position they had occupied when they dropped off to sleep. The loom was bare; one of the rugs covered Doris, two covered as much of Hannah and

Denise and the children as they could, though arms and legs and heads stuck out all over the place.

Grandma looked more like a woman who'd had a good night's sleep than one who had been up talking, spinning and weaving all night long. She stepped carefully around the legs and heads of the women, men and children and motioned with her spindle for Cindy to do likewise and they made their way out into a frosty, but rapidly warming, morning.

Chaco poked his gray muzzle out from under the arbor and stamped his hoof, as if impatient to be off. The scattered remains of what appeared to have been a substantial pile of grass hay lay at his forefeet. He'd been tied loosely enough to graze, she noted with approval. By his back hooves lay a couple of dumps, sign of his appreciation of his meal, and Cindy kicked these outside the arbor with her boot. Then she led him to the river and let him drink. When she led him back to saddle and bridle him, Grandma was waiting. The old lady handed Cindy the can of Coke she had left unfinished and Cindy downed it gratefully. When Grandma had mounted, Cindy climbed up behind her.

NINE

The Midas Touch

"THAT WAS AMAZING," Cindy said when they were well away from the settlement. "How did you do that?"

"Oh, I didn't do much. I just showed them how much better things went when they all worked together instead of pulling each other apart. It makes yarn and rugs strong, so it should for people."

"I can't believe we just met a whole family of total strangers and spent all night talking like that."

"It's a little like some of our ceremonies," Grandma said.

"Well, they sure opened up to you and really seemed to take your advice," Cindy said, thinking of a certain fairy god-mother again. But this woman was nothing like Felicity Fortune and except for weaving really fast, hadn't shown any signs of changing anything into anything else. Well, distant relatives into close ones, maybe. Maybe later, when Cindy was more awake, she'd tell the old lady about Felicity. They'd probably like each other.

"People always *do* seem to tell me their troubles," Grandma agreed cheerfully.

Chaco forded the river by merely avoiding the ponds and stepping over the stream threading them together like beads. The hailstorm had been brief and dramatic, but had not widened the river nor so much as dampened the ground that Cindy could see. Without any verbal agreement to do so, they let their course parallel the river as long as it went north. After a while, it took a bend toward the west, and it seemed only a few paces more and they were in utterly brown and gold desert that might never have seen even so small a river as the Little Colorado.

"Grandma," Cindy said, "you never did explain to me how the government could kick the Navajos off their land like that."

"Oh, that," the old woman said. "I guess I didn't get far enough in my history. Let me see, I guess it's cold enough here on Navajo land to tell a story now that it's not raining. This story is like one my white sisters told me about a king who wasn't too bad a man except he wanted everything he touched to turn to gold. He didn't realize that if his food and his family and all of his friends and all the animals and plants turned to gold, he would have a lot of gold but be very poor, and would even starve.

"It seems to our people like all the Europeans who came here must have been his grandchildren. Because our biggest troubles began when the Europeans came over. The Spanish and then the Americans. First the Spanish came and tried to make everybody belong to the Catholic Church, because then the People would have to tell them where they hid their gold. Of course, they didn't have any, but the Spanish thought, or hoped, they were lying. My white sister tells me that there was something real bad going on in Europe then, they were burning up lots of people and hurting them because of religion. Even if they were the *right* religion, if they didn't do it just like the priests said, they could get locked up and tortured and burnt at the stake. A lot of times this was about gold too, because once they were dead the Church and the government could take all their belongings.

"So they tried the same thing here. They said it was about religion, but really, it was about gold. Somebody had told them a big story about how the Indians out here had whole cities full of gold and they came and tried to get it. When they didn't find any gold, they got mad and murdered people. First Navajos and the Rio Grande people and then the Hopis—except by that time they were tired of just killing and decided to try to make people follow their religion instead. They forced them to drag big logs over a hundred miles from the mountains and carry them up the sides of cliffs to build the churches.

"The Navajos never had to do this because they didn't live

on mesas. They thought the Spanish were pretty good people for bringing them horses and sheep to raid. But the Hopis and the Rio Grande people suffered bad. The soldiers and even the priests messed with the women and tortured people to death for practicing their Native religion and honoring their own Holy People."

She sighed and said, "You know, my Hopi people are funny people. They are very nice mostly—very calm and friendly and peaceful. Except if you push them too far. Those early Catholics pushed them too far and the Hopis plotted with all the other peoples and pushed them out—way back to Santa Fe. They pretty much kept them out after that too. But the Navajos and the other Pueblos just kept raiding back and forth, back and forth, for horses and sheep and slaves. It was during this time that they learned to weave. The Hopi men already wove with cotton but the Navajos didn't stay in one place long enough to plant cotton. Now they had all those sheep though. It was easy enough for me to take one of the slaves aside and show her how to weave. As soon as the other women saw that the slave could make beautiful things, they all wanted to learn too.

"But anyway, when the Americans came, all the New Mexicans who were the children of the Spanish and some of the other tribes, all of them said that the Navajos were terrible raiders and always taking their animals and slaves. Well, they did take the animals and some slaves, but the New Mexicans raided just as often. The Americans believed them, though, and not the Navajos. A couple of times the American soldiers said they were making peace if everybody would give back their slaves and the Navajos did. But it was supposed to be an exchange and the New Mexicans never did give back any of theirs. They said the slaves had become Christian but it was mostly lies. They sprinkled them with a little water and said some words, but those people still talked to their Holy People and the Holy People visited them a lot so they wouldn't lose hope or stop being Navajo even when they were slaves."

"How do you know all this?" Cindy asked. She was still groggy, and the morning was at first chilly enough for her jacket, then became warm, and finally hot.

"I just do," Grandma said primly. "As if this wasn't bad enough, the Americans finally decided that they couldn't win against the Navajos on their own land, so they tried to take them away to another land. At first they didn't succeed and then they got a false friend of the Navajos, a man who knew them and who had once been trusted by them, to betray them to the soldiers. This man was Kit Carson. He told the soldiers to kill all the animals and burn down the crops and the beautiful peach orchards that had nourished the Navajos for many, many generations. This would starve them and break their hearts. And it did. Some of the people faced down the soldiers in Canyon de Chelly but eventually most were rounded up like cattle and made to walk hundreds of miles to Fort Sumner. They didn't live in the fort though, indoors or anything. They lived out in the open around the fort, in an area called Bosque Redondo. They were treated like slaves by the soldiers and forced to build nice houses for the Americans while they had to live in the open, in the rain and cold and heat. They got raided by the Comanches a lot too. It was a very bad time.

"During the walk there, many old people, little kids, pregnant ladies, anyone who couldn't make the walk, was shot by the soldiers, and at the camp many more died of disease and homesickness. Some of the Holy People went with them even there, though, to keep their spirits up. But they disguised themselves so only Navajos knew they were there and the soldiers didn't know it."

"Disguised themselves how?"

"Oh, say, as maybe a spider for instance," Grandma said, then added, "Chaco should go to the east here." She seemed to know the way, and Cindy let her take the lead. Cindy was no longer worried about Alzheimer's. There certainly was nothing wrong with the old lady's memory of events, places and people of the distant past, at least.

The sun was high in the sky when Grandma hopped down and began walking. "Chaco needs a break now. Even a very good horse shouldn't have to carry two of us all day."

Cindy felt a little guilty. The images in Grandma's story and the stories from the night before played continually across her mind. As the heat soaked into the desert sand, she imagined herself as a Navajo having to walk hundreds of miles in such heat or be killed. And she definitely could see the Mirage People rising up from it. She almost thought she saw them waving at Grandma Webster, and grinned to herself, shaking her head.

She was also still puzzling over the way the family had greeted them the night before. "It's so funny how Nell acted like she knew you right away," she said to Grandma. "Denise too and maybe the brother. Even that fellow back at the park. The one with the horse trailer. He wasn't really your grandson, was he?"

There was a long silence; then Grandma said, "Maybe you didn't see because you're not Navajo. But what I told last night was true. I *am* related to everyone and they are all kin to me—and to each other in one way or another."

"Well, us too, I guess, back to Adam and Eve, if you take the Bible literally. But that was a long time ago and it's easy to forget," Cindy said.

Grandma gave her a long look and said nothing. Cindy didn't say anything either because there really didn't seem to be much to say. She concentrated instead on Chaco. His wind was good, his pace steady. She'd checked his hooves before she saddled him that morning and they were free of rocks or thorns. His tail switched a little friskily. He seemed to be enjoying himself. He would be a good trail horse. He had a cheerful, cooperative personality without lacking spirit.

After a while, Grandma continued her story as if she had never stopped. "Finally, the Americans decided there wasn't any gold in the Navajo land—just a lot of desert and dead animals and nothing growing—and they got tired of spending *their* gold on the little bit of food they had to buy for the poor Navajos, who couldn't eat most of it anyway because it wasn't what they were used to.

"Barboncito, as the New Mexicans called the chief who had got himself captured so he could be with his people, talked them into letting the Navajos go home to the Dinetah, the land between the four sacred mountains.

"The Americans said, Okay, but don't raid no more. Barboncito said they wouldn't. They were a broken people. There were hardly any more of them left than there had been after the Alien Monsters ate them up the first time. All their sheep and horses were dead except for a few head they had at Bosque Redondo, their good crops had been destroyed, their houses and most of their relatives were gone. They were in sad shape.

"A lot of them wanted to settle as far away from the soldiers as they could, so they went waaaay out near the Hopi mesas to settle down. A lot of the people who had not been captured had been out that way too, hiding from the soldiers. The Hopis didn't care, then. There weren't very many Navajos and they were poor and hungry and ragged. There weren't very many Hopis either and they didn't have very much they figured anybody else would want.

"So nobody cared that they were all living next door to each other. But then over the years, the Navajo people, who are real smart and good breeders, increased their herds and themselves. They got to where they worked silver real good, wove real good, had lots more sheeps and horses.

"Now, most of the Hopis lived in their villages but they had always gone out on that land where the Navajos lived to gather fuel and material for their ceremonials and to visit their shrines, which were still all over at little springs and various places around, right in the middle of the Navajos. It was fine for a long time, but then the Hopis started noticing that there were a *lot* of Navajos there and some of them had started to think of that land as theirs and weren't real nice to the Hopis who came out there.

"Then the Americans got into the middle of things again. They wanted to make Hopi kids go to school, but there were some other Americans who had other ideas what Hopis should do and they were making trouble for the Indian agent.

"But since the land was, by the law of the Americans, open to everybody, the agent couldn't kick those other white guys off. So he had the government make a special area for Indians—back then it was for both tribes. Joint use, they called it. The Indian agent could do to the Hopis what he wanted, and the Navajos had a lot of the land they used to use, and there didn't seem to be much the Hopis could do about it.

"So then the Hopis sued the Navajos. See, they'd started

learning how the Americans did things. They said that was their land the Navajos were living on and the Navajos said no, it was joint use and the Hopis lived on the mesas while the Navajos lived on the flatter land. And that started a big argument.

"Finally, the government got into it again and split it up and gave half to the Navajos and half to the Hopis, but there were still thousands of Navajos living on the Hopi half. So the government has been kicking them off and it has been a great hardship. The Navajos feel they are being punished for being so good at surviving. They feel like they're being sent back to Bosque Redondo again. And the Hopis would just like to have some more land to do with what they want to because there are more Hopis now too.

"But what *I* think is that the government is doing just what it did when the New Mexicans and the Navajos were fighting. They get in the middle of it without knowing what's going on, but watching to see if there's anything they can take from anybody, like gold or something else valuable, while the Hopis and the Navajos are busy fighting with each other."

Cindy had been so caught up in the story that she was surprised when she suddenly became aware of a rushing sound and saw a streak of gray on the horizon. At first she thought it was another river, but then she saw the eighteen-wheeler with the red trailer bearing a logo she couldn't read. It passed before them like a shooting star and was gone.

"It's not far now," Grandma said. "We took the shortcut."

Though Cindy had thought it would be a much longer journey, in no time they were on the road to Tuba City from Highway 89. According to her map they were ready to dip to the south and traverse the Hopi mesas. They were already within the boundaries of the Navajo reservation, though because of their route, they'd seen no signs.

She started to remark as much to Grandma, but just then she noticed another whirlwind . . . rotating against the sun. The old lady had spotted it first and was totally preoccupied with watching it rise from a small column of dust and gust into a funnel that twirled down the road ahead of them, as if to herald their arrival. Watching it, Cindy was glad she was on a horse, not in a house, and unlikely to fall on any wicked witches.

TEN

The Wicked Witch of the Western Agency

ALICE BEGAY WAS not about to be deprived of the last thing in the world she could call her own. She had lost four babies on this land, and buried them. Her mother and father had both died here. She and her husband had lived here happily for many years until he left her, as she thought, for a woman who could give him children.

To finance her trips to publicize her battle to keep her home, she had sold all of her rugs, her jewelry, and her baskets. Her home was bare and wretched, but it was hers and she was going to keep it or die trying.

She had help. Not her own sister, of course. Her sister never got excited about anything. Thanks to Alice's efforts, nobody had been evicted yet. Alice had that young blond girl from Phoenix getting her father to put a court order against the BIAs if they tried to evict anybody. Alice had convinced the young people from AIM that they might need to make this fight as violent as the one at Wounded Knee if they were to save little old ladies like herself from being kicked out of their ancestral homes.

But her sister had not gone to the meetings or let the young people come to visit. She had not given up the beautiful jewelry Mother left her, and had donated only one rug to the struggle, though people said she was the finest weaver of the Ganado Red type of rug still living. Alice wove the Storm Pattern herself but she had not had time to weave for a very long time. Her loom had been scooted against the wall.

For a time, it had been interesting with all the people coming and going, bringing strange food and acting as if everything in Alice's life was a source of wonder and awe. But the Hopis had been keeping them out lately. The blond girl from Phoenix was supposed to be bringing her some papers. But Alice was terrified that it was too late now. The lease agreement had been signed by the government. Now she either had to sign to lease land that was already hers by right, where her babies and her umbilical cord were buried, or she would be put out like a dog.

That was not going to happen. No one could help her now but herself and she knew what she had to do. It was like that strange one she had met in the field had told her. No matter what she told the AIMs or the white people, she knew who was responsible for making her go. It was the Hopis. They had never liked Navajos. They had always had more power than the Navajos because they would do anything, even stuff to do with dead people. They lived up there in their cities and had everything they wanted—houses near their relatives and farms and their ceremonies and they didn't *need* any land. But they were going to take hers. Just because they had the power to do it. Because they weren't afraid to act like witches. Well, let them. But they weren't going to defeat her without a fight on equal terms. She knew that the one she had met, the one who claimed to be her husband's relative, was a witch. Some of her husband's ancestors had been witches too. Her husband had told her one time what must be done to gain a witch's power. The one who spoke to her out on the land seemed to assume she knew—people did, though they never alluded to it in public. It sometimes involved the little bone bead that the strange one with the shadow for a face had given her. She had made her decision not long after that and prepared what she needed, gathered some of the materials, planted the seeds of destruction. But one thing was left to do. A close family member had to die to give her the necessary power. And she knew just who it would be.

Anabah had been sleeping throughout the journey with her thumb in her mouth, but now that they were close to home, she couldn't wait to be there. Each bump in the dirt road was like a ride in the carnival. Soon she would see her own house and yard and her grandmother, and the sheep, and her horse.

The ride was bumpier than usual because her dad was taking his medicine again. That's what he and Mom called it, anyway. Anabah was only four, but she knew better. She knew medicine came in little bottles and Dad took his out of a big one. It made him cry sometimes, and very weak, and sometimes very angry.

Mom was in the hospital now, getting Anabah's brother, but Dad wasn't with her. He didn't have a job either. There weren't any jobs where they lived now. There were no sheep and no horses either. Not even any corn patches. There were some grandmothers, but they didn't say very much. Mom wouldn't let Anabah play outdoors because she said the older kids had made "gangs" and she was afraid of them. This was wrong. The BIAs had said the New Lands would be better. Maybe some of them were but where Anabah's family lived, they weren't. Mom had said there'd be a toilet that flushed, but it didn't, because there wasn't any water. The electric lights didn't work either and they had to use oil lamps, just like before, but it didn't smell nice there the way it did at home.

Anabah didn't know which she missed the most—watching her grandmother take the sheep's wool and spin it into yarn and build those yarns into a beautiful rug, strand by strand, all the time telling Anabah stories, or her horse, Sammy. Sammy was too young to be ridden yet and Anabah was too little to ride, but her Dad told her he'd tied her umbilical cord to a horse's tail and that would always make her get along with horses. She got along fine with Sammy.

Grandma came out of the house when the truck stopped and she smiled really big when she saw who it was.

"Get out," Dad told Anabah. "And take your stuff with you. Don't forget anything."

At his tone, Anabah hung her head and her thumb went back in her mouth, but then Grandma was opening the truck door and lifting her out and giving her a hug.

"You got to take care of her till Jenny's home, Ma. I can't handle her. She cries and whines all the time and it's all I can do not to blow up. She misses it out here."

Grandmother bounced her and said, in Navajo, "She just misses me, don't you, *shinali'*?"

Anabah liked it when Grandmother spoke Navajo to her. It reminded her of when she was little. She remembered Grandmother telling her that when she called her *shinali'* it not only meant "my granddaughter," it meant "my granddaughter who is the daughter of my son." She'd said all the Navajo names for relatives were like that, telling exactly how somebody was related to you. Anabah didn't care about that so much. She was just glad her grandmother could call her by a name that said exactly how and why she, Anabah, belonged with Grandmother. The little girl clutched her grandmother's neck tightly. She had her knapsack in one hand. Without waiting to see if she had everything else, Dad backed the pickup out and roared back down the dirt road.

Anabah called after him, but he couldn't hear her for the truck. Grandma set her down and Anabah thought she would go to her own house and see if her toys were there. Her real house was here, in Grandmother's camp, an old hogan with a tar paper roof that made a little waterfall beside Anabah's cot when it rained. But since it didn't rain very much, it didn't bother Anabah. In one of the corners, a spider spun a beautiful web. Grandmother said that she must be very careful and respectful of the spider, who was really Spiderwoman, the Holy Person who taught the Navajos to weave.

Anabah wiggled down and ran toward their house. But there was nothing there.

Grandma's cementblock house was still there, and the old storage hogan, and, just across the wash, Aunt Alice's hogan, and the little road connecting the two houses. It dipped around the thin crack that widened into the wash. But that was all wrong. There used to be Grandma's house and *three* hogans, Grandma's storage one, Anabah's family's, and Aunt Alice's. Now there were only two.

She looked back at her grandmother. Her father's mother didn't return her look but said, "I'm going to make us some beans and fry bread now. And peaches for dessert. How many fry breads can you eat?"

Just then Anabah saw Kittybitty run by and ran after him.

He was the most beautiful cat in the world. They weren't supposed to have cats or dogs in the new houses. Kittybitty ran under the lowest bar of the little corral and into the brush. Anabah stopped at the enclosure, wondering where Sammy was. He was probably out grazing. She picked up a handful of old hay from the side of the corral and set out to look for him.

Anabah's grandmother, Martha Tsosie, looked out the open window of her hogan, seeing her granddaughter running up over the rise, hay clutched in her little hand, looking for her horse. She didn't know how to tell the poor child that Sammy wasn't there anymore. The BIAs took him away when the family moved, as they'd razed the hogan and taken two-thirds of the sheep, even though all of the sheep belonged to the grandmother.

At least she was there to comfort Anabah. Jimmie would be no help at all, the way he was drinking and carrying on. He hadn't even stayed for supper, or brought her anything from town to help feed his daughter. Probably in too much of a hurry to get back and drink some more. She shook her head. She had never thought her son Jimmie would turn to drink. He had been such a happy little boy, out here with her and his grandfather, learning the names of the stars and the stories of the animals. She had raised him from the time he was no older than Anabah. She'd thought he would always be here with her. But the girl he married had been brought up in Gallup and she didn't like living out here. Jimmie had tried to get her to stay for his mother's sake, and that of his aunt, who had taken up with all of those *biligaana* people and those AIMs. Martha thought they just made things worse, though her sister said the BIAs and the Hopis would have dragged her out of her home by the hair a long time ago if the outsiders hadn't been there. They talked to the newspapers and television and their lawyers every time something especially bad or unfair happened—like the time the Hopi Rangers had torn down the hogan Hosteen Nazzie and his wife, Lillian (who were as old as Martha and had been dragged off to boarding school by the BIAs when she had been), were still using for ceremonies.

But Jimmie was not a fighter. He had always been a good boy, a respectful and considerate boy. He had not wanted to move, but his wife did. She said they would have a nice new house if they did, and she thought it was terrible to have to live with your relatives all the time. She didn't like it when Martha tried to teach her things about the old ways, and said it was all superstition and ignorance. For a time she got along with Alice, because Alice would sympathize with almost anyone who disagreed with Martha. Then one day she came back from Alice's all upset, and very soon after that she and Jimmie had signed relocation papers and left Martha all alone, except for Alice over there across the wash, and Alice never came over just to visit anymore. She was too important now, talking to all the outside people and even the President of the Navajo Nation about how the Navajos on the Executive Order Land shouldn't be forced to move.

At first Jimmie had come back really often, and told his mom how he missed her and the land and the sheep. His wife wouldn't let Anabah come, though, and after a few months, Jimmie stopped. Not because he didn't miss it anymore, Martha thought, but because he missed it so much he couldn't stand it.

But she would never have dreamed he'd treat Anabah in this way. He had always loved his daughter more than anything, had given her rides on his shoulders to find Sammy, had taught her everything he could think of about the land, the animals, the stars and tracking, even though she was only three at the time and a girl. Anabah had taken it all in. She had shy moments and sometimes didn't speak very clearly, but she was very smart, her grandmother knew. She always remembered the stories, and if Grandmother seemed to forget a line, Anabah would remind her.

Sighing, Anabah's grandmother turned to her cooking and was about to light the fire under the grease on the little Coleman stove on the counter when she felt something sting her in the neck. She reached up to touch it, and her fingers came away with blood on them. Not a bee sting, then. She suddenly felt more frightened than she had since the day her Lewis died. There would be a little piece of bone in there someplace, she bet.

The room began to spin around her and she sat down on the

floor between the counter and the wood stove. She could feel her heart beating very fast and her side started to hurt her, where her heart was. She should get to the door and call Anabah, and she would in just a minute.

Then suddenly the pain was very great, crushing her heart in a powerful witch's fist. The last thing that ran through her mind was that she was glad she hadn't put the grease on to heat yet.

ELEVEN

"WE'RE HEADING SOUTH," the T-shirted blond woman, whose name was Lindsey Fletcher, but whose Internet handle was Soaring Star, told the uniformed Hopi Ranger inspecting her van, its supplies and passengers. "To Two Tracks." She tried to keep the defiant edge from her voice, to speak to the ranger calmly, even gently, as she'd been taught in her classes on passive resistance.

"It'll save you time if you go around now instead of waiting till you get turned back at the intersection," the ranger told her. He pretended to be helpful but she heard the arrogant edge to his voice. This was going to be a confrontation. She knew it. Maybe he'd draw a weapon. If she faced him down, even the AIM people would have to recognize that she was a true sister to the cause, that she was one of them, not just some white woman with a checkbook and a big van.

But before the man could say any more, an elderly lady tapped him on the shoulder and spoke to him in what must have been Hopi, as Soaring Star by now had an excellent recognition, if not command, of Navajo. And yet, the old lady was dressed in Navajo clothing—not just everyday clothes either, but dress velvets with a great deal of turquoise. Behind her, astride a gray horse, sat another blond woman.

"Be careful, Sister," Soaring Star called to her, thinking she must be another one of the resistance workers, perhaps a new one, assisting this Navajo grandmother. "They'll impound your horse."

The blonde dismounted and led the horse over to Soaring Star's van. The Hopi Ranger and the old lady were in deep conversation by now. "What's going on here?" the horse-woman asked.

"My friends and I," Soaring Star said, referring to the sleeping Navajo woman and her child they'd picked up hitch-hiking; the Lakota elders—well, they were fairly elderly, middle-aged at least and one of them was practically a bona fide shaman—the somewhat younger Ojibway activist; the famous writer, Haskell Wainwright, who was sleeping since he'd taken Dramamine to keep from being car sick; and the paralegal she had recruited from her father's law office in Phoenix, "are on our way to bring provisions and assistance to the embattled families near Two Tracks. Are you headed that way too?"

"We're going south, I guess," the other woman answered uncertainly. "Anyway, I am." She peered at the piles of blankets, building materials and foodstuffs stacked in the back of the van. "Wow. Don't they have any grocery stores out there?"

"Sure, but they don't dare leave or these jackbooted gestapo"—she pointed at the Hopi Ranger nodding respect-fully at what the old woman was saying to him—"will run off their livestock and tear down their houses. They refuse to even let the Navajo families repair their houses."

"Gosh, why not?"

"Because they're trying to get rid of them. They want the Navajos to move off of land the government has arbitrarily as-signed to the Hopis so the greedy tribal council can sell it to the mines, who will rape Mother Earth and bring destruction on the people."

"Bummer," the other woman said sympathetically.

Warming to her subject, Soaring Star said, "Some of the people out there are in their eighties and speak no English. They've lived there all their lives, and so did their parents. They have never known another place."

"And the Hopis just want to shove them out into the—well, not the street, I guess—the desert?"

"Well," said Soaring Star, trying to be fair because after all, the Hopis were of the First Peoples too, "it's not the fault of the real true Hopi people, of course. Not the ordinary people.

It's the puppet council government set up by the feds. My Lakota brother Phil Medicine Eagle explained it at the Sun Dance." Actually, Soaring Star had known about the situation way before then, as the Phoenix papers liked to keep track of the troubles between the tribes. They did it in a condescending way, of course, to show how the Native Americans squabbled among themselves. As if that gave the lie to their naturally environmentalist lifestyle and superior spiritual enlightenment. But she wanted to let the other woman know that she, Soaring Star, had been guested at the Sun Dance. True, they wouldn't let her anywhere near the actual dance lodge since she had been on her moon then, but still, she was there.

"But I'd always heard the Hopis were such nice, peaceful people," the other woman said, not arguing, just looking surprised and actually, pretty tired and hot. Sort of dazed, really.

"Well, the ordinary folks are, and religious leaders like the ones who were with Medicine Eagle at the Sun Dance. They said he was right on. That Hopis and Navajos had always lived peacefully together before the U.S. government appealed to the greed of the Hopi leaders by giving them land they'll never even use and don't need. They deliberately set up this artificial division between the Hopis and the Navajos to undermine the lifestyle of all First Peoples and pit them against each other. As soon as our Navajo families can be shoved off their ancestral lands, the greedy Hopi officials will sell the mineral rights to some mining company that will rape Mother Earth and destroy all the sacred places."

"Was the policeman trying to stop you?"

"He's not a policeman," Soaring Star said scornfully. "He's just a Hopi Ranger. They're nothing but jumped-up tribal fish and game and agriculture inspectors but they think they own everything, including the public highway. They're trying to make us drive hundreds of miles around the reservation to come into Two Tracks from the north. They take away everything the Navajo families need to live, their sheep, their horses, their hogans, they persecute them for their religion, and now they're trying to stop us from bringing a little relief to them."

"Why are they being so mean?" the other woman wanted to know.

"To drive them away, of course. They're even arresting people who used to live here and were tricked into moving away who come back to their houses. They say the houses belong to the Hopis now. It's cultural genocide." Soaring Star finished with passion and suddenly felt it all ebbing out of her, she had told the same story so many times to so many people trying to get them to help. "So who's the grandmother you're looking after?"

The horsewoman looked around. The Hopi Ranger was starting back toward Soaring Star's van but no trace of an old lady in Navajo velvet and turquoise could be seen anywhere on the road leading out of Tuba City. "Excuse me," the woman said, turning back toward her horse. Then she looked over her shoulder. "Good luck."

The Hopi Ranger had a funny expression on his face as he stopped Cindy. "Your—friend—wants you to go with those people," he told her, nodding at the van.

"I can't do that," Cindy said. "Did she say where she was going?"

"She had something she had to do with my people," the ranger said. "Over at Moenkopi. But she said she'll find you."

"That's what I'm afraid of," Cindy said. "Do you know her? Does she have family here? I wouldn't want anything to happen to her, but actually I'm doing a job here, trying to train this horse, and I'm not sure what to do about her."

The ranger's expression was downright amused this time. "I guess you'll know when the time comes," he said, as if waiting for her to sit on a whoopee cushion. "Just go on ahead and she'll find you."

"She doesn't need to bother, really . . ." Cindy said.

With a full, broad grin, the Hopi Ranger said, "Oh, I don't think it will be any bother for that one. Have a nice trip now." He returned his attention to the van.

It was getting late and Cindy decided to see if she could find a place to stable Chaco for the night and get a motel room. This didn't work out. The only motel was a Hilton and the management had not had the foresight to provide horse housing facilities along with the rooms. Besides, it was booked solid. The minimart was a little more practical, however, and besides the corn dogs, jojos, antacids and gas, sold bales of grass hay. Cindy purchased a bale and, after loosening Chaco's cinch and removing his bit, fed and watered him. In front of a café, she saw an old-fashioned hitching post. Though she didn't see any other horses in town at the moment, she supposed that didn't mean there weren't ever any. Leaving a few flakes of hay for Chaco to nosh while she went inside, she sat near a window where she could watch him while she ordered an "Indian taco," beans, hamburger and salsa with a sprinkling of cheese and lettuce on a big puff of fry bread.

By then the shadows were lengthening and she decided she'd better ride out of town far enough to find a safe place to pitch her tent.

She reclaimed her saddle from behind the counter at the restaurant and walked out with her boots rubbing her blistered heels to resaddle Chaco. About that time the van she had seen earlier in the afternoon rolled up in the parking place beside her and the occupants poured out of the doors and into the restaurant, all except the blonde woman from the van who now sported a red bandanna around her head, headband style. Cindy could now see that her black T-shirt featured a picture of a sandpainting. She walked up to Cindy.

"Hi. People around here call me Soaring Star."

"Cindy Ellis," Cindy said, tightening the cinch under Chaco's belly.

"That Hopi Ranger seemed to like you."

"Did he? I don't know. I think he knew the old lady I was with."

"Yeah? Well, he seemed to like her, then. Anyway, I don't guess they would stop you from taking the road from just before you get to Hoteville on the highway up to Dinnebito. Not with you on horseback and them knowing your friend and all."

"I don't know if they would or not. I suppose they'll tell me if they don't want me back there."

"Yeah, well, I think that woman you were with must have some kind of pull. It's the first time I've seen a Hopi Ranger smile that he wasn't impounding somebody else's animals or wrecking somebody's house," Soaring Star said as bitterly as if it were her house and her animals involved. "So I was wondering if you maybe *would* go up there and take a message to a friend of mine, Alice Begay." She pressed an envelope into Cindy's hand and Cindy tucked it into a saddlebag.

"Sure, if I go up there, I will."

"You should. If you're going to be in this country, you need to know what's happening here," Soaring Star said.

"Uh, thanks. I'll check it out," Cindy said, but privately she was getting really tired of people telling her what she should and shouldn't do, where she should and shouldn't go.

She was relieved when Chaco took them beyond Tuba City, beyond the little Hopi village of Moenkopi, though she half expected Grandma Webster to be thumbing a ride by the side of the road.

According to the map, Coal Mine Mesa was twenty-seven miles away, Hoteville and Bacavi villages about sixty-two miles. It was too late to reach either. The road was hilly, up and down, and hard on Chaco so after a while, when the sky started streaking and the sun looked as if it was about to disappear behind the mesas, Cindy picked out a likely looking stretch of roadside desert and led Chaco off the road toward it. There wasn't much traffic on the roads at the moment. She removed Chaco's saddle and bridle, scoured the ground for a place free of prickly pear and rattlesnakes, popped up her dome tent and rolled out her air mattress and sleeping bag inside it, then began grooming Chaco for the night.

Sunset snuck up on her fast, and she was bathed in the ruddy light flaming through the sky as she finished currying Chaco and opened the flap of her tent.

About then, she heard a car and in another moment found herself frozen in the headlights, hearing the crunch of sand under boots as someone obscured by the lights walked toward her.

"You can't camp here," a man's deep voice said. "Non-tribal members are forbidden to leave the road or the villages."

Cindy had had a long day. "The ranger didn't say anything about it when I was back there," she said, pointing toward Tuba City and Moenkopi. "I checked at the motel and there was no room, and I'm on horseback. I can't make it to the next village tonight."

"You should have made a reservation earlier," the man said unsympathetically. He came closer, and she was relieved to see he wasn't armed. Surely he could see she presented no threat. Not that that was particularly comforting under the circumstances.

"I guess I should have," she said. "But I didn't. And this horse has had a full day already."

"I'm sorry about that, but you would have needed to make arrangements earlier."

"Well, actually, I was going to take a different route but I hooked up with this old lady and she knew a shortcut and then we ended up spending the night in this family's hogan while she told stories." She made it sound like fun because it had been fun but he didn't seem impressed.

He shook his head as if he couldn't believe her—what? Stupidity? Gullibility? She wasn't sure why the wonderful night they had spent with Nell Tso's family would make him act that way. His hair was worn long and curly, she could see it silhouetted in the light. His voice had the soft melodious undertone of an Indian accent but he spoke English unhesitatingly and with authority. "You should be careful who you take up with and where you stay."

"Maybe so, but Grandma doesn't exactly look like an ex-con and at least the family was nice enough to let me sleep at their place." She let *unlike some people* hang unspoken in the air between them. "And if I can't camp here, what am I supposed to do?" She realized her voice was getting shrill and squeaky with frustration and weariness and that she was close to tears. Which was embarrassing. She wasn't about to cry in front of this guy. He wouldn't care. He was just trying to push her around.

Or so it seemed until she realized he was actually giving some thought to her situation. He scratched his head and said slowly, "Well, I got a friend who has a place down by Rolling

Rocks who could take care of your horse tonight, maybe. It's about twelve miles from here, though, so you better ride with me. After we drop the horse off, I can drive you down to the hotel for the night. It's expensive, but this time of the year they usually have room. Tie his lead rope to the truck bed and he can trot along beside."

"That doesn't seem very safe," she said, stroking Chaco's neck. "What if he stumbles?"

The man gave a sigh that sounded more put-upon than was strictly fair. It was *his* idea to complicate her camping trip, after all. She could almost hear him mentally counting to ten and when he spoke, it was with deliberate patience. "I'll be going very slowly. He won't be carrying you." He made a move toward Chaco's lead rope and she took a step backwards and picked it up herself. Now he said in a low, reasonable voice, as if she herself were a skittish horse, "What you can do is tie a quick-release knot and hold the end through the window. That way if anything happens, you can free him up before he gets in too much trouble."

It was a sensible enough suggestion. Chaco was overtired for her to ride him and it was too far to walk along beside him. She decided that following the man's advice was probably the best idea. Of course, he could have been some kind of a nut. The kind he'd been warning her about before. But his voice had ended with a note of apologetic kindness that seemed all the more sincere because of his previous exasperation. And really, she would be no worse off riding with him than she was caught here in the middle of the desert with him, so what was the difference? It wasn't like Chaco was some trained attack horse who would rear and stomp him if he tried to hurt her.

So she struck camp, repacking her compact tent and camping gear into the saddlebags. She then secured Chaco to the truck, slung the bags and saddle into the truck bed on top of what looked like a load of railroad ties, and climbed into the cab of the truck. Rolling down the window, she grabbed the end of the rope, and with another anxious look at Chaco, said, "Okay." The man started the engine and drove back onto the highway, so slowly that Chaco, now released of the burden of his saddle and rider, almost outpaced the truck. She'd thought he was really tired and he was frisking like a foal! She relaxed, and the man beside her laughed. "This arrangement seems to suit your horse fine."

"I guess so," she agreed, taking her eyes off Chaco long enough to get a closer look at the driver.

He didn't *look* like an axe murderer. He had a pleasant face, even handsome in a rugged, irregular kind of way. Definitely Indian and probably Hopi from the possessive way he kept talking about the landscape.

He said, "I've been getting my consciousness raised by my niece or I'd ask you what a nice girl like you is doing—well, not here, because this is my home and I love it, but in the particular place you were at the particular time."

She shrugged. His voice was much pleasanter now, and when he turned to her momentarily, in the lights from the dashboard she noted that his eyes were really very pretty, dark brown and long lashed, expressive. To her surprise, because despite her looks she wasn't used to thinking of herself in those terms, she could tell that he was also deciding *she* was pretty. His authoritarian tone had definitely undergone a change.

"I'm training Chaco—the horse—for a rancher with a spread south of Flagstaff," she said, checking with a sidelong glance, to see that Chaco on his long lead was trotting to the side and slightly ahead of the truck. He seemed to want to drag race. "Or I was trying to. I didn't mean to trespass or anything. I was reading this book"—she pulled the Kluckhohn book out of the saddlebag beside her on the seat—"and he didn't mention anything about restrictions so I didn't really . . ."

The man said, "That book's about fifty years old and the restrictions weren't in force back then. You're not from this area, then, are you?"

"No. I'm from Seattle."

"Wow! That's a long way away. Did you bring us any of that rain you folks have so much of?" He didn't expect an answer but stuck a hand out sideways. "I'm Carl Loloma."

"Cindy Ellis," she said, shaking his hand. "Sorry, I didn't bring any rain. I left in kind of a hurry."

He didn't say anything, but there was an expectant silence. She glanced back at Chaco, who continued to act as if trotting beside the truck was a great adventure.

"I had a fight with my boyfriend, who is also my boss," Cindy told Loloma. "I needed to think things over. So when this opportunity came up, I took it. Actually, I wouldn't have come this way at all except that I met this old lady who needed help and then she disappeared when we got to Tuba City. I also met this woman in a van full of other people and she was telling me all about something to do with the Navajos. The ranger was making her take the long way around. But he seemed like he knew Grandma Webster—that's what the old lady says her name is—so he just let me come ahead this way. Except he didn't tell me there was no place to camp."

She felt as if she was babbling. Carl turned carefully off the highway and onto a gravel road, not the smoothest in the world but Chaco took it in his stride, slowing until he walked companionably beside the truck, paralleling its course as it bounced down the rather bumpy road. Chaco kept off the road and stayed in the dirt and sand by the side, veering slightly to avoid bushes and other obstacles.

"You just let the old lady stay lost?" Carl asked carefully, but she could tell he didn't think much of it.

"Well, I know what you're thinking. She sounded nuts to me too, but everyone seemed to know her and think she was taking care of me."

"Who's everyone? Who's she? I don't know any Websters in Tuba City or Moenkopi."

"Well, she's wearing a fancy velvet dress with silver buttons and a whole lot of expensive-looking turquoise jewelry. We met a man at Wupatki with Navajo Nation stickers on his truck and he and she were talking like long lost relatives. And when I asked him, he talked like he knew her and she wasn't lost at all. Then we met a family when we were crossing the desert, and she gave a spinning lesson to one of the women— she is an *amazing* spinner, and *they* seemed to know who she was, though nobody spoke much English so I couldn't understand. And then the Hopi Ranger seemed to know her too and treated her like she was a relative of his, but he didn't say so when I asked him, and told me she'd meet me later, so I figured, he should know, right?"

"Hm," Carl said shortly. "Yeah, well, if he thought it was all right, it probably was. There's the road back to Hamish's."

"Hamish?" They turned onto another dirt road. Chaco altered his course without any problem and looked at Cindy as if to say, This is fun. Why didn't we do it this way before? She signaled to him to pay attention to his own feet.

Carl was answering her question. "Hamish Secakuku. He runs the Rainbird Resort and Golf Course."

"A golf course? Out here?"

"Yeah, he was a pro in California, and when he moved back here he missed it. He got the idea of opening a golf course with the world's largest sandtrap and no water hazard. We get a lot of Japanese tourists in the summer who come to try it out. They have to stay at the hotel, 'cause the resort's still in progress. He's got a nice stable, though, and a small string of horses and gets one of the local boys to give horse tours. One of his horses died not too long ago, so there's an empty stall."

"Like I told you," Cindy said, "Chaco's not really mine, but I'm responsible for him." Chaco trotted along, his head forward, though, hearing his name, his ears were pricked a little bit.

"It's okay, Cindy. Hamish was taking care of horses before you were born. And he's honest, if that's what you're worried about."

It was, actually, though Cindy wasn't going to admit it. Nothing against Carl's friend, but you just didn't turn over a valuable animal to people you didn't know. A short distance farther, the road grew rougher, Chaco's stride shortened, and Cindy was ready to get out and ride the horse rather than spend any more time in a truck that could have used better shocks. She was relieved when Carl pulled into an open space in front of a collection of low, blocky buildings.

Hamish Secakuku limped out of his house and into the headlights of Carl's truck as they parked. Secakuku was middle-aged, she guessed, slightly built, and walked with the aid of a cane.

Carl leaned out the door of his truck and greeted the other man in Hopi, then said in English, "Hamish, I got a boarder for you." He gestured to Cindy to get out of the truck and did so himself.

"Who? Her?" Hamish asked, switching to English, too. "Nah, the missus wouldn't much like that. But say, Carl, did you hear . . ." and then he continued in Hopi.

Cindy had paused for just a moment to take in her surroundings. More desert, with poles in it, in front of the buildings. They looked like old mobile homes with adobe bricks built around them. The window curtains in the building before them were slightly parted and Cindy thought she saw the gleam of an eye inside. Mrs. Secakuku no doubt. But above them was a sky so perfectly what a night sky should be that it might have been created by Disney rather than natural. The stars, popping out of dark blue velvet, were as bright as Christmas lights.

"No kiddin'?" Carl asked and gave a low whistle. "Just today, huh?" and lapsed back into Hopi.

Cindy was already out of the truck, had released the knot, and was stroking Chaco.

"Oh, this is a fine one you got here, young lady," Secakuku said. His voice was cracked a little, as if he had a cold. As she led Chaco toward him, he reached out and stroked the horse on the neck.

"How much do you need for him to stay here?" she asked.

Carl said something again in Hopi and his friend said, "Don't worry about that. The stall's empty. But I could use a little something for the food and water. We've had to haul everything out here because the Navajos are sittin' on all the water. I could pry them loose from some, I guess, but I don't want any trouble. So, say, ten bucks maybe?"

"Fair enough," she said. "I'll just get him bedded down for the night if you'll show me where."

Carl said something to Secakuku in Hopi again and the older man said, "Nah, that's okay. I'll do it. Carl needs to get back down to Hoteville to pick up his niece and then home, so if you want a ride to the hotel, you better go with him now."

Cindy dug into her jeans pocket for the cash she brought with her.

"You can pay me in the morning," Hamish said, sounding ready to get rid of her.

Cindy hesitated. She didn't like leaving Chaco out here alone. "No, look. I'll be glad to do it. Maybe you could even let me put down my sleeping bag by him just till morning? I was going to sleep out, anyway."

"We'd rather you didn't," Carl said firmly.

"Too bad I don't have the guest cabins ready," Hamish said. "You and your horse'll have to come back then and you can stay as long as you want."

"Look, I'll bring you back up here myself tomorrow to get him," Carl promised.

"I'll feel a lot better if I feed and water him myself. No offense, Mr.—Secakuku." She stumbled slightly over the name, but tried to say it the way Carl had. "It's just that he's my responsibility."

"Okay by me, lady. Stable's over there. Water barrels and buckets beside the building. You'll find the feed. Carl, you can take a load off for a minute," he said, and they lapsed into Hopi as Cindy led Chaco to the stable.

She cooled the gray down, fed and watered him, and with a final pat goodnight, hefted her saddle and carried it out to where the men stood talking in the yard.

"We better get going now, Hamish," Carl said. "I don't like Sela away from home after dark."

Cindy tried to relax and tell herself not to feel so uptight. These folks seemed to be trying to help her. But she felt as if she was being herded more than Chaco, and she didn't like it. "It seems like a pretty quiet place," she ventured, when she and Carl were back inside the truck.

"I suppose it does to outsiders. And mostly it is. But you never know. I was just at the police station today—my niece identified a car she thinks might have belonged to drug dealers responsible for the death of a friend. They were gone by the time the police got there and it takes a while to run a license plate from here."

"Gee, are you afraid they saw her and maybe she's in danger?"

"Something like that. What about you? Why did you decide to train your horse right now? And where did you say you're from?"

"Seattle."

"Do you come this far every time you fight with your boyfriend?"

"Well, it wasn't really a fight. I just needed to think some things over, and I do my best thinking on horseback. Nobody I wanted to talk to was available and the people at Ray's house were part of the problem so . . ."

By the time she finished telling him about Pill and the job, which he still didn't seem to believe completely, they were turning off into a village. It was situated a little uphill, and had the flat stone and adobe buildings she was used to seeing in coffee-table books about Santa Fe, except these were decorated with nothing but moonlight and shadows, and once or twice she noticed a garland of strung corn hanging from a roof. Carl drove up to one of the houses that, in the dark, looked pretty much like the others. There was a soft light in the window, the curtain was pulled back, and two young girls emerged from the doorway, pushing back a blanket as they opened the door. One of them, plump, with a long black braid flipping behind her, waved to the other and grabbed the passenger door, saw Cindy, looked puzzled momentarily, then nodded and climbed in beside her.

"Are you one of those protesters from Berkeley who came out to help the Navajos who are trying to keep our land?" the girl asked. "Or has Uncle got a new girlfriend and been holding out on us?"

"I was *going* to introduce you," Carl said with a frown at his niece. "This is Cindy Ellis. Cindy, this is my niece Sela. Apparently no one informed Cindy that camping wasn't allowed here. She's riding a horse, training him, she says."

"So where is he?" Sela asked.

"At Hamish's. I was going to drop Cindy at the hotel. Do you need to go home first?"

"No, I'll ride along," Sela said, with a suspicious sidelong glance that made Cindy wonder if she wasn't more worried about Cindy being a girlfriend than a spy for the Navajos. "Did you hear from the police? Did they find out anything new?"

He shook his head, and spoke to her in Hopi.

She shrugged and then brightened and said, "Hey, did you hear that one of the rangers saw Kokyanwuhti?"

"We don't speak of such things in public," he cautioned her.

"Well, but she *appeared* in public. He said she was dressed like a Navajo, but it was her all right."

"The Navajos claim her as one of their Holy People too." He turned to Cindy and graciously offered an explanation. "The Navajos borrowed a lot of their religious ideas from us. As far as we can tell, when they first came here they didn't have much of a religion. They were just raiders and kidnappers, livestock thieves." His tone said he didn't think much had changed.

Cindy was listening, but felt caught in the middle, very much the outsider between uncle and niece as the truck took the hairpin curves and steep inclines and declines through the rocky prominences at speeds that would make even Ray motion-sick. Sometimes the road fell away into cliffs on both sides, sometimes she thought she saw a village clinging to the top of a cliff. Some of the rock formations looked to her as if they had once been part of buildings, now ruined and deserted.

At last the road leveled out a little and they drove a smooth stretch for a while. In another few feet they pulled into the parking lot of a large, squarish, flat-roofed building. "Here's the hotel. There's a good restaurant here. You can meet me at seven A.M. in there if you want. The blue cornmeal grits are good. I think you'll be comfortable."

"Thanks," she said. Sela opened the door and slid out, and Cindy grabbed her saddlebags from the back of the seat and followed suit.

Awkwardly Carl said, "It's kinda expensive. Seventy-five bucks a night this time of the year . . ."

"It's okay," she said. "I've got money." And she was glad for once that she did. Actually, not that much cash but Raydir was a great believer in credit cards and insisted that she have one under his corporate umbrella.

As she strode away, before the door closed behind her, she heard Sela say, "I'm surprised you didn't invite her home with us."

"Maybe I would have," Carl replied. "If I knew for sure she was what she said."

TWELVE

The Proper Way to Steal a Horse

WILEY SMILEY WAS very clever. The weather thermometer he'd taken from the side of Sela's house was in his hand and ready when she and her uncle pulled out of the drive. Chuckling to himself, he ducked into the piki shed and measured the temperature on the stone while it was still hot. Just to be sure, he did as he had seen Sela do. He had watched as she covered the bowl containing the remaining blue cornmeal batter and placed it in a dark corner. He retrieved it and, just as she had done, smeared some over the stone, sucking his burnt fingers afterward, licking off the cornmeal while waiting for the bread to cook.

The stone was cooling, so it took a moment longer than it had taken Sela—he'd timed her with his fake Rolex, which looked like the real thing, only silver. The guy who traded it to him said that was because Rolex heard that Indians liked silver better than gold and might want to make jewelry out of their watches, so they made a special Reservation Edition. The guy showed Wiley where it was stamped that way on the back. Only thing was, when Wiley tried to pawn it, the man at the pawnshop told him it was a fake and not worth as much as the average Timex. It had a second hand however. So he had timed Sela and knew how many seconds it took her to lift her flaky bread off the stone. He allowed a little more time, till it resembled what she made, and scraped it off. Ouch! What did Sela and the other women wear on their hands to protect them against that burning stone?

The stone smelled funny too. Maybe some special kind of oil. He'd ask about that too.

He lit the fire under the flat black stone again and heated it to precisely the same temperature as Sela had used, then smeared another dollop on. Damn! That piki was going to have some of his skin as part of it. When it had cooked, he removed it very gingerly, trying to fold it, and ended up crumbling it. That was enough for now. He had the basics down. He put out the fire and set the bowl aside, but forgot to cover it.

Then it was time to hitch a ride back to Gallup and try to find that woman who worked for the home shopping network again. Hint that he had something hot to sell—well, yeah, he did, actually. A few details to iron out then and he saw no reason why he couldn't find a cheap source of regular electric grills that would heat to the right temperature, sell the dried ingredients for the batter separately, along with the oil, whatever it was, and hey, maybe a special spatula to remove the damned stuff without burning yourself, or maybe a piki rolling utensil. This could spin off into a lot of different things. Sela said there were piki-making songs too. Maybe they could cut an album—even a video of Sela in her traditional dress, making the stuff—that would go over great with the yuppies. They could even offer it all in a little kit, tied up with bows of yucca strips or cornstalks. Wiley had to hand it to himself, he was a natural-born genius when it came to marketing. And now he had found the *perfect* product.

He went out on the road and waited for a ride. Pretty soon a guy in an old pickup hauling a horse trailer stopped. "Where you goin'?" the guy asked.

"Gallup," he said. "Or as close as you're going."

"I can take you into Window Rock at least, but I gotta make a couple of stops first. That okay?"

"Sure. You from there?"

"Yeah. I got some of my mom's relatives out here someplace, though." He leaned over and shook hands. "I'm Mike Blackgoat." He told Wiley his clans and waited for him to do the same.

"Wiley Smiley," he said. At first, when he was back on the reservation, he had made up clans for himself but rapidly found that was a great deal of trouble—a girl he might want to date could be a clan relative, and so could the person he was introducing himself to. So now he said nothing. Though it was impolite, a lot of Navajos didn't behave in the old ways that, according to the elders, had been protocol for them a few years back. "I stay in Gallup mostly but my girlfriend is Hopi, so I'm out here a lot."

Mike Blackgoat lifted his head slightly in acknowledgment. Wiley asked him what he did and he said he ran a herd of cattle on his sister's land, and was a carpenter on the side.

The rest of the time, Wiley did the talking, and was just telling Mike about the woman who worked for the home shopping network when Mike pulled off the road at Jeddito and parked his truck in front of a trailer between a hogan and a small corral. Another guy came out, bandy-legged, but Wiley thought there was something a little shifty about the guy.

Mike came back to the pickup and said, "I came out here to get a horse, Wiley." He twitched his lips toward the other man. "That's Charlie Etcitty. He has a good one he'll sell me but it's back up on his mom's property up near Two Tracks. You want to get out here and try your luck or ride along with us and go back with me?"

"I don't suppose he's got a phone?" Wiley asked. Well, maybe a cell phone. You never knew. There was a TV antenna on top of the trailer.

Mike turned around and asked Charlie and then shook his head.

"I'll just stick with you, I guess," Wiley said. He didn't know where that woman would be right now anyway. And it would be easy to get a lift from Window Rock for the few miles remaining to Gallup.

It was getting on toward late afternoon by then, clear, hot, a little windy. Once they saw a dust devil. Charlie looked grim. He clearly didn't like seeing the whirlwind, though Mike didn't seem to mind. Dust devils were supposed to be bad luck for Navajos. Wiley thought maybe if Charlie had been Catholic he would have crossed himself.

The road out to Charlie's mother's camp was bad, dust and sand blown over potholes, but Mike's truck was a good reservation vehicle and leapt the lesser potholes with a jolt. The larger ones it nosed down into and up out of with no trouble.

Finally they were on a clear stretch of road and in the distance could see the camp, which Charlie pointed out to them. Two hogans; probably one to live in, one for guests or ceremonial purposes, maybe both; a beat up trailer and a ramada. Charlie said he stabled all his horses out here, except Wiley didn't see any horses. Only a few sheep, a couple of dogs.

Mike was frowning and Charlie let out his breath in a long, disgusted hiss.

As they rattled into the yard, a skinny old woman came out to meet them. She was dressed old style, except her brown calico skirt's three tiers ended just below her knee, where they met what looked like support hose and sensible shoes. She wore a red blouse with a silver brooch at the neck, and turquoise nuggets at her ears. Her gray-streaked hair was bound back with white yarn in the Navajo hairstyle worn by both men and women, the *tsiyeel,* or bumblebee. Her right arm was bandaged but she was gesturing like crazy with the left one.

What she said was in Navajo though, and Wiley's command of the language wasn't all that good. "What'd she say?" he asked Mike.

"The horses are gone. Hopi Rangers took them away. Said they knew they belonged to Charlie and he doesn't live out here or have a permit, so they took them away. Charlie's mom tried to stop them and they hurt her arm."

"They got no respect? Doing that to an old lady!" Wiley said hotly. Carl Loloma was always looking at him like *he* was some kind of alien scum, but he didn't go around beating up on old ladies like those Hopi friends of Carl's. "That could have been their mother, you know. They wouldn't like somebody doing that to *their* mother."

Mike gave him a look that shut him up, but he didn't disagree with him.

Charlie ambled back to the truck, looking pissed and pensive at the same time.

"How bad you want that horse?" he asked Mike.

Mike shrugged. "What you got in mind?"

"I got an idea. Might involve a little night work up there." Charlie twisted his lips toward the south and the Hopi mesas. He grinned.

"They'd just send those rangers to get them back—they'd spot them right away as Hopi horses."

"Not if we ran 'em down to Jeddito."

"How many you figure? That horse trailer isn't all that big."

"Oh, I got another one. It's bigger. But we'll bring the horses to it, not the other way around."

"Isn't that stealing?" Wiley asked. He was very moral when it came to other peoples' deals, especially when they hadn't cut him in.

"What kinda Indi'n are you?" Etcitty asked him with what Wiley felt was an unjustified sneer.

Wiley wanted to say, An honest one, but felt that would open him up to further ridicule.

"Aw, Charlie," Mike said, "he's young. Lotsa the young people aren't being taught the traditions like guys our age. We should take him along and teach him. In the old days they thought having an apprentice along would bring luck."

"More likely bring the Hopi Rangers down on us," Charlie said with a little disapproving grunt. Wiley was disappointed that Etcitty wasn't disapproving enough to tell Mike he wouldn't have Wiley along. Wiley did not especially like the sort of adventures that involved other people with guns or badges. For that matter, he wasn't all that nuts about horses either. Etcitty gave him a look and broke into a grin, clapped him on the shoulder.

"Relax, brother. This ain't stealin'. It's tradin'. They took my horses without me knowin' and I was just gonna return the favor. *You* wouldn't call that stealin', would you?"

"We called it 'liberating' in the Navy," Mike said. Half of his mouth was smiling. His eyes weren't. Charlie's eyes had a hard glint in them that made Wiley realize this was no time for him to be his brother's keeper.

"Five-finger discount, kind of, huh?" he asked with his own version of Mike's smile. "Sure. Them Hopis act so holy but they shouldn't go pushing ladies around and taking other people's horses. I'll help you, hell yes."

Charlie nodded but gave Wiley a thoughtful look before saying, "My mom's making fry bread and mutton stew. You guys hungry?"

They ate with Charlie's mom, his two sisters and their kids. The kids, especially Charlie's teenage nephews, who'd been in school when it happened, were all stirred up about the Hopis coming to take their uncle's horses away.

Charlie said not to worry, they'd get them back, with interest. To Wiley's surprise, Etcitty's mother seemed pleased at the idea and began bustling around finding him medicine bundles and sticks and stuff like that.

"You gonna sing for me, Mama?" Charlie asked her.

She grinned. Charlie spoke to her in Navajo for a bit; then she nodded at Wiley and said something back to Charlie.

"What did she say?" he asked Mike, since Charlie was busy laughing.

"Charlie mentioned they used to think it was good luck to have an apprentice along and she said it would be his good luck if they caught you instead of him."

"I'm surprised she approves," Wiley said stuffily.

"Nobody ever tell you it's a Navajo's sacred duty to raid his enemies' horses when he needs 'em?"

"No. I—wasn't raised traditionally."

"That's for sure," Charlie said.

"Well, it is," Mike said. "See, the way our people figure it, we should have had horses all along. Horses were meant for Navajos. Changing Woman made them for us."

"Oh yeah? Well, according to my high-school history teacher, Navajos didn't even see horses until the Spanish came, and that was only a few hundred years ago."

"Yeah, but see, we were supposed to have had them first. Only Monster Slayer and Born for Water were really busy trying to kill all the monsters back in the beginning. They were asked to pick things for the People, and they saw the horses and they knew we would need them, but right then they needed weapons and magic to kill the monsters with, so they passed on the horses temporarily and the white man got them instead."

"That's why it's our sacred duty to take them back," Charlie said without a trace of humor on his face.

"Sacred duty, huh?" Wiley asked, feeling a little better.

"Yes," Charlie said. "Now eat up. We can't have all the things they used to have, like a Blessing Way beforehand and stuff, but we can build a sweat lodge and do a short purification before we go out. They used to do it for four days, my grandfather told me, but we don't have the time anymore."

"They used to not have sex for days ahead of time either," Mike told Wiley. "But since this is a spur of the moment thing, I guess it won't matter. I'm okay on that anyway, though."

"Me too," Charlie said, and they both looked expectantly at Wiley, who stammered and blushed and tried to remember what had actually happened, what he had bragged about, and what was nothing more than wishful thinking.

"Does last weekend count?" he asked finally.

Mike laughed and slapped him on the shoulder. "My *man*!" he said, congratulating Wiley. "You got lots of purifyin' to do."

Charlie's nephews wanted to go along but he said they were too young, in spite of all he had told Wiley. He finally said they could stand by the horse trailers and drive them away if necessary.

Then Charlie's mom had a few repairs she needed done. The roof was so full of holes, there wasn't a position anyone could sleep in so as to avoid all the leaks. And the corral was wrecked from where the horses had been broken out when the Hopis took them.

Wiley mostly watched because he didn't know much about house repairs. Charlie insisted he help him patch the roof however. Once Wiley started in hammering, Charlie said, "Now, Wiley, you do know this is against the law too, don't you? Navajos living on the HPL aren't supposed to repair their houses."

"*I* don't live on the HPL," Wiley said indignantly.

"Come to think of it, neither do I," Charlie said.

"Me neither," Mike said. "But, say, you don't know of anybody needs this kind of repair work done for money, do you?"

"You hinting you want to get paid for this?" Charlie looked bristly as a porcupine ready to give a dog a mouth full of quills.

Mike thought about that for a moment, then shook his head. "Nah, I ate your mom's food and didn't bring her anything. So I'm doing this for her. If you wanted to discount the horse a little, once we get him back, I wouldn't mind, of course."

Charlie snorted. "I don't guess you would."

"Why is it illegal to repair houses here?" Wiley asked. He wasn't much for reading the papers and his mind was usually too full of ideas of his own to pay much attention to laws that didn't even affect him.

"'Cause they're trying to get rid of my mom and the other people who live down here so the Hopis can start a mine or run their cattle over my grandma's and dad's graves."

They built the makeshift sweat lodge then, using supports that had been saved from a previous lodge, and a motley collection of tarps and hides. With Etcitty, and his nephews, Mike, and Wiley, the lodge was crowded. They had all stripped off their clothes, which Wiley didn't much like. He wasn't used to being naked in front of *men*.

Nobody paid much attention to him, though. Charlie and Mike both prayed in Navajo while the sweat ran off them and soaked their hair, and the boys mumbled along. Charlie sang a snatch of a song and Mike looked thoughtful.

"I feel like I should know more about this," Wiley said when Charlie had finished.

"Well, don't scratch yourself while we're out there—it's bad luck," Etcitty said. "And no talking, of course."

"In the old time they talked in a different way when they were raiding, even though they were talking Navajo," Mike said. He glistened with his own perspiration and it was starting to smell a little in here too, Wiley noticed. Didn't smell a thing like aftershave either.

"Like how?" one of the nephews asked.

"They'd sort of talk around things. I guess it was in case the enemy knew any of our words—any nouns, like, so instead of saying 'horse' they'd say 'the live one's plume.' "

"Was that a code?"

"Sort of. But it was also a way to flatter the horse and tell it how fast and light it was, like the plume of a live eagle."

"Huh. What else?"

Mike shrugged. "That's the only one I was ever told."

Charlie said, "If it was gonna be a long-distance raid, you weren't supposed to sleep on your back or your stomach, I remember. My old man used to bug me about only sleeping on my side—told me that was the way warriors did it. That was when he was still around. He wasn't very often. That's why I remember it."

Mike didn't say anything but stared into the steam. Wiley could only see faces now, the place was so hot. He was so hot and there was no place to lean—he didn't like this heat anyway, and he'd been raised in Utah, where it was plenty hot.

After a time Mike spoke again.

"Every time I used to see my girlfriend puttin' on one of those smeary white beauty masks, you know? I thought maybe she was going raidin'. I was always told we wore white clay when we were in enemy territory."

Wiley was too hot and too ready to get going to ask why but Mike continued, "It's from the old Enemy Way ceremony—mostly they just do it as a girl dance now, but in the beginning, part of the story was that Magpie offered to daub our warriors with white clay to drive away enemy ghosts."

"Lookin' like a ghost yourself scared the ghosts, huh?" Charlie said. "I never knew that one. I didn't think we used paint that much. I always thought that was movie Indi'n stuff."

"Nah. They used red and blue and black too, got themselves painted with bears and snakes, to be brave and scary, and the five-finger handprint, to show they were men after all. I guess we could do that, but if we're not having a sing, it probably wouldn't work."

"They're just Hopis anyway," Charlie said scornfully. "They'll just complain to the BIA. It's not like they do anything."

Wiley thought that if Carl knew he was involved in this, he might do plenty, but he didn't say so. He wanted to see what happened.

"We should pray some more," Mike said. "But all I can seem to think of is a line from the song we sang when our grandparents had us run at dawn, to make us strong. We thought it was for herding sheep, but later, I asked a *hathalie* about it and he said it's a war exercise song White Bead Woman taught her boys before they went to see their dad." He sat for a moment and then sang, just the one line, in Navajo.

This time Wiley had to know what it meant and asked.

" 'You were made for different kinds of horses, my son; run a race,' " Mike told him.

When they finally left the sweat lodge, it was already dark. Wiley wiped himself off with his clothes and put them on, gritty with sand and dust. When he reached for his boots, he was surprised to see that someone, maybe Charlie's mother, had drawn a big snake on the soles. Mike's and Charlie's boots were the same. Charlie saw Wiley's look and twitched his lips toward the boots.

"Mama's great-grandfather was a boy at Fort Sumner," he told him. "She remembers a lot of raids. She'll sing us the women's song while we're gone. The snakes on your feet will make us able to strike like snakes."

"Uh-huh," Wiley said, then, "wow. Cool."

The younger boys gave him a contemptuous look and put on their own snake-soled shoes.

THIRTEEN

Babe in the Desert, Prince Charming Returns,
The Great Horse Raid

ANABAH LOOKED AND looked but she couldn't find Sammy anywhere. Finally, she ran back to her grandmother's house, the hay still clutched in her hand.

"Grandma, I can't find Sammy. Grandma, where is he? Grandma?"

She flung open the door and looked around, but her grandmother wasn't there. "Grandma?" She took a step into the room, and then she saw her grandma's shoes, and then her legs and the hem of her skirt, peeking out from behind the wood stove. At the other end of the stove, her grandma's head lay against her arm. Her other arm was across her chest and her hand pressed over her heart.

Anabah didn't see how this could be right. It wasn't time to sleep. What was Grandma doing on the floor? It made Anabah feel funny and shy to see her calm, dignified grandmother acting in this way. Anabah decided to look at things from a different angle, something she often did. She turned her back to the room, bent from the waist, and took in the scene by peering between her ankles, upside down. It didn't look any better. She first tiptoed toward Grandma, in case she was asleep, but then, remembering that yelling hadn't woken her up, she ran to her, and tugged. Grandma just lay there, no matter how Anabah pulled at her. Once she gave a little groan.

If only Daddy had stayed, he might know what to do. But he would be out on the road now, heading back to the city. And Grandma didn't have a phone. And there were no neighbors except—well, there was Auntie Alice, but she was awfully cross and she always had all those strange people over at her house. Anabah didn't really like strangers very much.

This was an emergency though, and Auntie Alice was Grandma's sister, like the baby would be Anabah's sister or brother. She had to help with an emergency, didn't she?

Anabah dragged a blanket off the cot against the wall and put it over Grandma, then ran outside, over to the wash, and scurried down it.

Just then, as she looked up the other side, she saw Sammy gallop by with two boys on his back.

"Hey!" she yelled. "That's my horse!"

Grandma was momentarily forgotten as she clambered up the side and ran off after them, and then she realized that if she had Sammy back, she could ride for help herself and wouldn't have to ask Auntie Alice.

"Hey, come back!" she cried. Then she started calling, "Sammy! Buck them off and come here! Come here, Sammy! You come here right now, Sammy horse! I have a nice apple for you," she lied, and kept running after them. Once she looked back for just a second at Auntie Alice's house, but she didn't see any of the strange Indian men who weren't Navajos or the Anglo woman who hung around there sometimes. She didn't see their cars and she didn't even see Auntie Alice. So Sammy was her only hope probably. She wavered for just a moment, wanting to help her grandmother, not wanting to face her aunt, and not wanting to lose track of Sammy.

At least that didn't happen. Sammy's gallop had slowed and the boy who was riding in back turned around and yelled, "Hey, little one! I thought you wanted to ride this horse! Catch up with us and maybe we'll give him back."

So she started running after them again.

Alice Begay had seen her sister reach for her neck when the bone bead bit into it, just below her ear. She had seen the droplet of blood rise like a coral bead beside the turquoise nugget Martha always wore, one in each ear. She thought Martha looked like she was going to fall and she had been going to go in and see her, but then in the distance she heard Anabah, her niece, calling for her horse. The horse was no longer there. There was no car in the front, but that didn't mean maybe Jimmie or his wife weren't there too. One of them could have dropped the other off. They never came to see Alice. Jimmie used to, when he was little, but then it seemed like as he got older he took against her. She wasn't sure when it started. His wife didn't like her, she knew that.

It would be better to let Anabah or Jimmie or even that wife of his discover what had happened to Martha and come and tell her. Come to her for help. Then she would see what had to be done.

But she couldn't sit quietly or work on her papers or anything, so she started fixing some supper. She had grown out of the habit of regular meals, what with all the traveling she did and all the people coming and going from her place. Usually the Anglo kids did the cooking anyway, did a lot of the work, to help, they said. But Alice knew it was because they knew they owed her. It was funny in a way. When she was in the boarding school, she used to go to an Anglo woman's house and clean for her for extra money. Now she had Anglo kids wanting to clean her house for nothing. They didn't do it right, of course, but she was too busy to criticize.

Now she busied herself making food. A nice meat soup with plenty of corn. The smell alone would lure Anabah or her parents, since Martha might not feel like making supper. Of course, these things all worked differently, but you had to wish the person dead when you sent the bead into them. You didn't have to wish for it to happen in a special way, but Martha's heart was not strong, the doctors said. So Alice had thought about that heart stopping.

When she finished cooking, she looked out her own window and down across the wash. Smoke was no longer coming from Martha's stove. So. That meant there were no adults around or they would have made up the fire, they would have been over here by now. There was just the little girl. Alice wondered how close a relative Anabah would be considered, for witch purposes. Maybe two relatives would make better magic than one? She shuddered. She only wanted to be a witch so that she could beat the Hopis. It was one thing to wish her sister dead and shoot a bead at her and then not go see her. It was another thing to harm her niece. But she didn't know what kind of thing the other witches would want her to do next, except that it would be bad.

As she watched, the child ran up over the hill that rose in back of Martha's place and then down to the house, yelling something about Sammy. She opened the door, and stood there for a minute, then turned upside down, then went inside. She wasn't too little or too stupid to figure out that the next place to come would be to her auntie's house. Martha must be dead or at least dying. Alice wondered what she should do. Should she go in there where Martha was? That wouldn't be a good idea. If Martha was dead, her ghost would be really angry and would probably kill Alice and then it would have all been for nothing.

She hoped it had not been all for nothing, anyway. She and Martha had sometimes had good times together when they were little girls. In the old way, they might have been married to the same man. He probably would have liked Martha best, she thought, hardening her heart again. This thing had to be done.

Sure enough, Anabah came running out of the house again and scrambling down into the wash and back up over. Alice was about to go greet her, when the little girl turned away from her aunt's house and looked out to the east. Alice got to the door in time to see the child running wildly out into the desert, calling out for her horse again and for someone to stop. Alice yelled after her, but Anabah didn't seem to hear her. Oh well, she was too little to go very far and she knew this area pretty good. She'd be back. Maybe in time for her parents to come and get her, or the Anglo girl and the rest of Alice's company to return and help with the body.

Alice sat down to eat her supper but she found she wasn't very hungry.

"Hey, baby, your road warrior is home from the battles," Ray-dir called out as he entered the stables. "I brought you something nice," he said, rattling a jewelry box that caused the nearest horse to give him a long, considering look.

"Well, shit, sweetie-pie, I hope it's a can of snoose. I done run out and nobody around here has a chaw to spare," answered a voice pitched far below Cindy's range. This response was punctuated by a load of horseshit that flew out of a space two stalls down. The appearance of the horseshit was immediately followed by a face not much lovelier, and made even less so by a glower that could have curdled whiskey.

"What're you doing here?"

"Looking after your horses and the horses' asses who ride them," the older man said.

"Where's Cindy?"

"Not here."

"I know that. Look, I cut my tour short because I really need to see her. Where is she?"

"Didn't she leave a message with that heifer who answered your telephone and told her you couldn't be disturbed?"

"What heif—oh." Hannah the Heifer. Oh yeah. He had been a little miffed at Cindy, and Hannah had been doing an interview with him in the car en route and . . . well, surely Cindy couldn't expect— Maybe she did. "Okay, so I slipped up a little. But I love her, and I want to marry her."

"Yip. Pee," said the old man. Pill, that was his name. "Lucky her to get the likes of you. Not to mention all these fine folks living here. Buncha selfish, one-way deadbeats. Maybe I'm judgin' 'em too harsh, though, 'cause of all the prairie-dog holes I've seen that have so much more depth. If any one of you did something that was for somebody else the way that girl does instead of just moaning about your own breedin' practices, I think the world would end. Now, 'scuse me, boss, if you don't mind, I got some important horse puckey to shovel here."

"Good exit line, old man, but this is my place and whatever you think of me, Cindy is my girl. Maybe you're just trying to protect her, but I don't think she'd appreciate you getting in the middle of our relationship. If you know where she is, you ought to tell me."

Pill stopped shoveling and sucked thoughtfully on his handlebar mustache while watching Raydir with distaste. "Well," he said at long last, "how good are you at sending up smoke signals?"

When he finally stopped tormenting Raydir and told him where Cindy might be, Raydir stormed back up to the house and plowed through the mail on his secretary's desk. "Hey, Jeannie," he hollered. A woman with a shaved head, black lipstick and a tattooed cleavage turned around from her typing. "Where's that request I got from that outfit to do a benefit for the people at Big Mountain?"

Now the raiders-for-horses are setting out. Needs a Horse is setting out. Lost His Horses to Hopis is setting out. Coyote in Him is setting out. Big Snake is with them. Their moccasins are swift. Big Black Bear is with them. They are protected. Coyote is with them. Coyote is afraid. Coyote is also searching. Coyote is searching for an angle. Coyote is always searching for an angle. Coyote has no need of horses. Coyote is thinking what else he can get from raiding.

Now the raiders-for-horses find the place where horses live in houses like men. A man lives there too, but he sleeps in his own house. A woman lives there too, but she sleeps in the house with the man.

The horses are awake. Drawing near, the raiders-for-horses become afraid. The horses are not afraid. What should the horses fear? They don't mind who rides them.

The raiders coil ropes and throw them over the heads of three horses. One horse is white shell. One horse is black obsidian. One horse is blue turquoise.

With the swiftness of Big Snake, the raiders-for-horses mount.

With the power of Big Black Bear, the raiders-for-horses dominate their mounts.

With the ineptitude of Coyote, one falls from his horse, crying out to the gods in anger.

"Shut up, Wiley, or you'll get us all killed," like Big Snake hisses the one who Needs a Horse, otherwise known as Mike, to Coyote in Him, who was trying to avoid being stomped under the hooves of his excited mount.

From outside the house for horses, an owl calls. The owl

is named Howard and is Lost His Horses to Hopis' second sister's son.

Lost His Horses to Hopis, otherwise known as Charlie, looks outside and sees the light on in the house where the man and woman have been sleeping. "Shit," he says.

FOURTEEN

The Shivers

CINDY WAS EMBARRASSED by the nice accommodations at the Rainbird Hotel. She'd been planning such a rugged adventure, and here she was with two double beds all to herself, a bathroom with a luxurious shower, which embarrassment did *not* prevent her from enjoying, and a beautiful, even picturesque structure made to look like one of the pueblos, with a flat roof covering the guest rooms, restaurant, laundry, gift shop and museum. There were stairs to the roof back by the laundry room but they were blocked off.

The receptionist was friendly, surprised to see a sweaty, dirty blond woman check in with nothing but her saddle and saddlebags, but she asked about the trip and even apologized to Cindy that she had not been allowed to camp as she'd planned. "I guess you didn't know, coming all that way from Seattle," said the lady, whose nametag said "Marjorie." "Probably if you'd written to the tribal chairman ahead of time, it would have been okay and they'd have found you a place where you could camp."

"Thanks. I'll remember that if I ever do this again," Cindy said. The restaurant adjoined the reception desk. Cindy knew if she waited to eat until she had taken her belongings to her room, she'd never tear herself away from the shower in time to eat. Since she was hungry, as well as thirsty, she forced herself to drag her tack with her into one of the wooden booths with the Indian-blanket-print upholstery. The high-backed booths were decorated with what looked like pottery designs. She ordered a pitcher of water and once again ate an Indian "taco" like the one she'd had at the café in Tuba City, but better.

The place was empty at that hour and the waitress, a young girl about the size that Oprah had been before she discovered liquid diets and personal trainers, walked as if her feet were tired.

With deep gratitude for the Hopi regulations that prevented her from spending the night curled up next to her horse, Cindy took full advantage of the shower, though she took a short one, remembering how cracked and dry everything here was, washed out her dirty underwear, pulled on the T-shirt she kept for sleeping at nights and a pair of fresh panties. Then, well-fed and clean, she prepared to fall asleep in her air-conditioned room between crisp, clean sheets. She realized that she hadn't thought about Raydir most of the day, and her reaction, oddly enough, was to worry that he would be worrying about her. That he would call and find her gone and none of those so-called friends of his would know where she was because she hadn't told them. But then she remembered the condescending female voice on the other end of the line and thought, with a sigh of contentment that matched the sigh of the mattress as she sank into it, Aw, let him sweat. She was going to have to swear off worrying about people's feelings when they obviously didn't care about hers. Rosie had said more than once she worried about Cindy becoming just another co-dependent for Raydir.

She used the phone only to ask Marjorie for a wake-up call so she wouldn't keep Carl Loloma waiting for her in the morning. She was sure she wouldn't wake up till noon without it.

So she was surprised to find her eyes and ears wide open when the digital bedside clock said 12:00 A.M. The people in the room upstairs were stomping around. Probably just arrived, she thought. And then remembered that the building was one story. Maybe it was tourists, taking advantage of the flat roof, or kids who'd ignored the Keep Off signs and the sawhorses blocking access to the roof. She figured they'd get tired of it and go away pretty soon. She tried to go back to sleep.

The noise got louder. They must be having a party up there, she thought, and wearily dragged herself out of bed, pulled on her dirty jeans and shirt, and wrapped her poncho around her because by now it was very cold in her air-conditioned room.

The air outside was colder—crisp, clear, the sky almost blue rather than black and filled with stars. She had a clear view of it over an entirely empty flat roof. Not a soul was to be seen on top of the building in any direction. In fact, her bedside lamp was the only light she could see burning anywhere. She shrugged and went back inside.

The stomping started in again before she could lie back down.

She went back outside and surveyed the roof again. As before, it was entirely vacant.

She dialed the desk but this time no one answered and she remembered seeing a sign that said the reception desk closed at nine P.M. Now she lay fully dressed, pulling the covers up under her chin, listening to the stomping on the roof.

It grew into a somewhat predictable beat, and after a while, quite to her surprise, she found her eyes closing in spite of herself.

She seemed to sleep for a time, and then got up and went to the kitchen window, mostly to get a drink of water, but also to look out the window and see if she could pick out anything that was so important or interesting no outsiders were allowed even to camp out on this part of the reservation. She didn't see anything. Maybe a slight breeze rustled the mesquite and sage, maybe the shadow of a night bird flitted, but surely none of that was purposeful human movement? She was wondering whether to wash her cup in the sink when she remembered all at once that where she was standing in the kitchenette was not actually part of the room she'd fallen asleep in. That room had no kitchen, no kitchen sink, and the only cups were little plastic ones for brushing your teeth and so forth. There was no kitchen window either. Only one window opposite the bed she was—still lying on.

Oh, just a dream after all, then. She fell back to sleep, or moved from one phase of sleep to another. And heard knocking on her door. Who would be knocking on her door in the middle of the night? Struggling to open an eye, she checked the digital clock but it still registered barely past 12:30. Her wake-up call hadn't sounded. The pounding stopped and she dropped off again.

And all at once she saw, drifting from the place where the coatrack was in the back of the room, a raggedly clothed Indian man with short hair, grinning rather terrifyingly, floating a few inches above the ground across the room, past the foot of her bed, and through the closed door.

The pounding started again, this time louder and more insistent but by now she was really frightened—and still half asleep.

She woke up only when she heard voices outside her window, talking in fairly normal, if somewhat surprised tones.

The stomping had stopped. She pulled back the curtain and saw other hotel guests—and Marjorie—standing around in the dark, staring at the roof.

She had kept her clothes on from the night before and now pulled her jacket on and joined the other guests.

"Did you hear it too?" a young woman in a black leather jacket and pants asked—a biker probably. "I thought they were going to come through the roof."

"So it's not just me?" Cindy asked. "Good."

"Y'all sure must have big rats around here, Marjorie," a beefy balding man with a Texas accent said. He had on one of those Marlboro Man sheepskin coats over pajama bottoms and cowboy boots.

Marjorie shook her head and looked troubled. "Not rats," she said in a small voice. She seemed almost ashamed and a little scared.

"Has this ever happened before?" Cindy asked her.

The receptionist grimaced and gnawed her upper lip.

"I'd think it was steam heat maybe, but it was definitely coming from the roof," one of the guests said, "and the air conditioning is still on."

"The grass is frosted over," another one said. "I'm going up there and check for footprints."

"You're not going to find any," Marjorie said, and walked back into the hotel.

Cindy had had enough of weirdness for one night. She followed the others to the roof and they looked for the footprints, sure they'd find something. But the roof was sound, flat, whole, without leaks or even so much as a woodpecker hole in any of the wooden supports. There was frost, but the only footprints were their own.

"Did you only just now hear it?" Cindy asked the girl in the leathers.

"No, but Jaz and me were making too much noise ourselves for a long time to notice anything else," she said, with an adoring look at a very handsome young man also in leathers, his jacket open over, oddly enough, a Quantrill Raids black T-shirt. The couple had a Hispanic look to them, though the girl's hair was brilliant red.

"It took me a long time to realize there was no second story to this motel," the Texan said.

Cindy nodded, having had much the same thought herself. "What time is it?"

"Five," the Texan said, consulting an expensive-looking watch. "I heard them kids out here and decided maybe it had been them messing around up there. Then I saw they were as puzzled as me and we started talkin' and then the rest of these folks came out, along with that gal from the hotel desk."

"Well, maybe it's over with," Cindy said uncertainly.

It was. She slept fully dressed and in her jacket and boots under the covers until the phone rang. A man's voice told her it was her wake-up call and she got up, shook out her horsy-smelling clothes, undressed, took another shower, brushed out her wet hair and braided it. The undies she had washed the night before were already dry despite the chill. With almost zero humidity in the air it didn't take long.

It occurred to her that Pill should have returned to Seattle by now and was probably already helping the girls look out for the horses. She could call in directly on the stable line and if one of the girls answered, hang up, but if Pill answered, she would see how the—horses—were and if they missed her.

She also just wanted to hear a familiar, reassuring voice after her strange night.

The raid on the BIA holding pens did not happen. Charlie's nephews and brothers had the horse trailers ready, and on their first raid Charlie, Wiley and Mike had acquired new mounts to ride over there to free the horses, but thanks to Wiley's clumsiness and noise, Mike also had a very sore butt. He'd been hit by the buckshot in the old Hopi's shotgun and could hardly sit the horse he was on. Once they were safely out of range, he pulled his horse to a stop and slid off, almost falling to the ground.

Etcitty reined in too, and even Wiley noticed he was all alone after he had ridden another couple hundred yards. Etcitty rode back and dismounted. "What's the matter with you?"

"I'm all in for the night, Charlie. I got hit in the ass. You guys'll have to go without me or call it off and we'll do this another night."

Charlie leaned around and looked at Mike's rear end, swiped his hand across the horse's back. "Yeah, man, you're bleeding all over the place, leaving a trail. You want Ma to take a look at that?"

"No, man. We'll all get caught that way. He didn't see any of us. Let's get these horses loaded and I'll drive over to the hospital. I know one of the docs there, owes me a favor. Maybe I can get patched up and out of there before the old man can report this."

The boys had driven the horse trailers beyond the last Hopi Ranger checkpoint and hidden them at a place known to themselves and Charlie, a place that could be reached by horseback in about two hours. The plan had been to pick up Hamish Secakuku's horses, ride them off road to the impound corral where Charlie's horses would be at least for the night, distract the guards, free the horses and drive them down cross country to where the boys in the trucks would be waiting. The weather had been excellent for it. Clear, but with only a quarter moon, the ground hard but not yet frosty enough to show prints. A tracker would probably need daylight to follow them, and unless something went wrong—which it had—they should have been all right. Charlie had a fair amount of experience raiding, as it turned out.

All Mike wanted was that one horse. Not that gray one he'd been riding—the one Charlie had for him that was locked up.

Charlie shook his head. "I don't think so. You're gonna slow us down. Look, you find a place to lie low and I'll come back later with your truck, take you to a healer. You go to the hospital, they're gonna report you and then we're all screwed. You're not hurt real bad, are you?"

"Guess it wouldn't matter that much, would it?" Mike said, well aware that this guy didn't give a shit.

"I'll be back in an hour or so, take you to get fixed up, and you can come on back to my place. I can let you have one of these horses tonight—maybe two, for what you got in your pocket. Maybe you can sell them back near Window Rock and use the money to buy back that one of mine you want if I haven't stole them back by then. Or sell them for me, let me use the money to pay the fines due on mine, and I'll let you have the one you wanted for the money in your pocket."

"Gee, I don't see how I can refuse a deal like that, Charlie," Mike said. The guy had a lot of nerve to still be talking money after Mike had lost a piece of his ass trying to get those horses back for him. It made Mike mad enough to forget the pain for a minute, and he said, "I couldn't ride this one if you give him to me free. You take him with you. I don't want no cops finding him with me. Don't think they'd believe he was followin' me home so I'd ask my mom could I keep him. So you boys just run along. I'll find me a little den or something to hide in. Never mind about me."

"I'll be back for you later, man," Charlie said, taking the reins to Mike's mount, clucking to his horse, and giving it a little kick with his heels.

"Sure you will," Mike said under his breath. He watched him and Wiley leave, the breath of the horses making fog ghosts in the cold air, drifting back toward him. He was cold and sticky where the blood was dripping down his legs, soaking his jeans and leaking into his boots. He hugged his jacket tighter around himself. His hat was still back in the truck. He walked a few paces, stumbled really. Some of the shot seemed to have loused up a muscle or tendon or something. Hurt like hell to walk as well as ride. But he didn't have a whole lot of choice. He thought maybe if he could get to the road, someone would come from the north, off the land the Navajos held, maybe give him a ride. Get him out of there before morning. He'd hide if anyone came the other way. Or just lie down. That would be easy enough. He looked up. The stars were spinning. He walked a little more and the darkness started spinning around him too, rolling around him, making his head light, like it was trying to pull him up toward the stars. Instead, he fell flat on his face and lay there with the frost collecting on his upper lip and chin, hair and cheek, and the blood congealing on his backside.

FIFTEEN

MARIA CHEE'S SECOND night at her new assignment she spent on call for the emergency room. This meant she had to leave Dezi with Nicki out at Jeddito. She was supposed to catch what sleep she could on a gurney in an empty exam room while waiting to see if anybody needed a doctor.

She was very thankful for Nicki. The woman's house was extremely cramped with all of them there, but Nicki's mom was great, her twelve-year-old daughter treated Dezi like a little sister, and the sixteen-year-old boy was a good kid too and had been a lot of help loading and unloading Nicki's truck. Nicki had insisted they store the stuff under her house, covered with tarps, so Maria wouldn't have to drag it around in her car all day, making it more of a target for casual thieves. The Keams Canyon Garage had fixed her car that first day and it was now parked out in front of the hospital.

Fortunately, she wouldn't have to impose on her new friend much longer. Her father had told her she had relatives living out near Two Tracks, which wasn't too bad a commute from Keams. Probably if they lived out on the rez, a little rent money from a homeless relative would be welcome. She realized, of course, that the government and the Hopis had been causing some problems for the people out there, but if they signed the lease agreement they ought to be okay for at least seventy-five years, and maybe, with a doctor on the premises who worked for the government and treated both Hopis and Navajos, they would be spared some harassment.

She figured she'd go out there on her first day off, when she'd be able to take Dezi with her, and some gifts of food.

Meanwhile, Nicki insisted she wasn't imposing, that it was fun to have another woman her own age to talk to. Maria also had some hope she might be able to help Nicki regain the use of her legs by finding therapy for her within IHS's admittedly very limited resources. Nicki said when she went to the Flagstaff spinal cord clinic, there were always at least twenty or thirty other Navajo and Pueblo people, and one Ute and one Apache, who came, but they didn't seem very interested in anything that went on. She thought they mostly just sat in their houses and didn't even try to get out except to the hospital. She was the only one she knew of among them that drove, held down a job, and thought that maybe there was life after paralysis. And even at that, she wasn't exactly an activist for the rights of wheelchair-bound people. She confessed with more pain than anger that when people parked in the few spaces reserved for the handicapped, it was very frustrating having to get herself out of her truck, into her wheelchair and into work at Medical Records on time usually without help from anyone else, since she went to work rather early. She sounded as if she had to justify her right to the few concessions made for disabled people. A person in her condition in L.A. would have been screaming for the cops to come and put the boot on the offending vehicles, threatening to sue maybe.

Like a lot of the others, she'd been injured in an automobile accident. Her lover, whom she had regarded almost as a husband and who was the father of her youngest child, had been driving. He wasn't hurt badly. For a while he'd stayed with her and helped her out, but then decided he couldn't handle her disability, her dependence, as she saw it. He was Hopi and still lived up at Bacavi. Nicki still took her daughter, Tara, out to see the girl's grandparents. But Nicki stayed in the car. Her ex-lover had a new woman living with him. Sometimes the grandparents came out to the car to visit with Nicki. They still liked her, she said, and considered her their daughter. They didn't like the new woman, even though she was Hopi. She said all this trouble between the Navajos and the Hopis over the land made it hard for Tara in school. The kids teased her, even though there were a lot of kids who were both Navajo and Hopi.

Maria's night started off with a bang—almost literally—as

from the previous shift she inherited the victims of a car wreck. It had happened out on the highway at the intersection where both Bacavi and Hoteville let out onto the 264, according to the police who brought the victims in.

The doctor who had been on before Maria hadn't written orders on any of the patients, having given them all to the nurses verbally. He was just finishing when Maria came on. He gave her a brief rundown on the patients.

The police had told him that the pregnant woman and her three young children had been in one vehicle, an ancient station wagon. The kids had been strapped into kiddie seats and seat belts but the woman miscarried her fourth child before the ambulance reached the hospital. She also suffered head and spinal injuries. She and the kids had already been transferred to Gallup IHS hospital via helicopter. The man driving the other vehicle—a truck—reeked of alcohol and had a very high blood alcohol, .28, close to dying of alcohol poisoning if not the accident. He had a concussion as well as a compound fracture of the right femur and both clavicles, evident by examination according to Maria's predecessor, Dr. Loomis.

"Where are the X rays?" Maria asked him as he stood up and headed for the door.

"Can't get any films tonight," he said. "Not unless you know how to take them yourself."

"Where are the techs?" she asked. "Isn't anyone on call?"

"Yeah, but one of them is in the hospital at Gallup with a thrombophlebitis and the other one is way out on the rez someplace, no phone, at a funeral. She left before we discovered the phlebitis. They're s'posed to be sending a replacement up from Gallup or Flag."

"Supposed to be?" Maria asked. "Why didn't they send one as soon as they knew we were without one? How can we treat these people without X-ray capability?"

Loomis shrugged. "Medicine men did it a long time before we got here, I guess," he said.

"It's preposterous."

"In these little hospitals, these things happen, Doctor. Get used to it. Haven't you heard? The government is on a budget and we've been cut."

"What about a portable machine? Haven't any of the staff been cross-trained to use it?"

He shrugged again, and left without answering, but the receptionist said, "It's broke. The money to repair it hasn't been allocated yet."

Maria was outraged but there was little she could do except treat the patients as best she could with what she had to work with.

The adult male who had been in the truck that crashed into the woman and children was still in an examining room. Loomis had him on neuro checks q15 minutes—that is, every fifteen minutes throughout the night his pulse, blood pressure, respirations, pupils, response to painful stimuli and degree of orientation would be checked. So far he seemed to be doing okay. Because his was the larger vehicle and he had actually struck the pregnant woman's car while heading for a ditch, his injuries were less severe than hers.

While Maria was checking the accident victims, the police brought in a drunk with stab wounds. He was fighting mad, kicking the cops, the walls, running his handcuffed hands along the reception desk, knocking off the lamp, paperwork and phone, yelling slurred obscenities at the top of his lungs.

The commotion made it hard for Maria to concentrate on writing her orders, where she noted that the male accident victim should have had a chest X ray stat, seeing as how both clavicles were broken, and that as soon as the backup X-ray technician arrived, those films would be taken.

The drunk had shoved away the nurse who approached him so that she fell against a stretcher. Maria waved her back and said, "Get 100 milligrams of IM Librium ready."

The nurse nodded, looking dubious, and hurried to the med cabinet. Maria turned her attention to the drunk. Until he was calmed down, it would be difficult to treat anyone else.

Her own natural inclination had been to be indignant with drunks, back when she was beginning her training. That didn't work very well. But when she began working with the Indian Health Service at her first post in Oklahoma, she went out on some emergency calls with the ambulances. She was more shocked than she believed she could have been at the conditions people lived in—squalid, crowded trailer houses that made the cardboard boxes of the homeless look almost inviting. The despair and the depths to which drink had taken some of the people—the brutishness, the battery, and the lack of hope for themselves or future generations—were symbolized for her the most by seeing infants sucking on bottles containing whiskey. The mothers did it to keep the kids quiet, the EMT riding with her had said.

Later, she saw kids of ten who had to have portions of their stomachs removed due to huge ulcers caused by alcohol damage. She wasn't so quick to judge anymore. In fact, the drunks broke her heart. So instead of her usual brusque manner, she approached the man fighting off the cop who was trying to stanch the flow of blood pouring from his prisoner's wounds.

She came up beside the patient, between him and the cop, and put her arm around his shoulders. His hair was greasy and his skin had that pickled, sweaty sheen seen on old alcoholics too far gone for help. He was probably about thirty years old. "Hey, buddy," she said as if she were greeting an old friend she really cared about. "How's it goin' anyway? Hey, you got hurt! What's the matter here?"

The patient stopped fighting and turned to her with a look that told her he couldn't figure out if she was the mother he had always wanted but never had, the one who would always care what happened to him, or a hooker who had all of a miraculous sudden decided to give him her special demo freebie.

"Yeah, my coushin did this. Got mad at me. Don' know why hesh so mad . . ."

She eased him over to the stretcher, and beckoned to the nurse, who had the syringe ready. The 100 mg of Librium was a standard dose for calming down an angry drunk and letting them sleep it off. She kept talking to the man as she laid him down, allowed him to unzip his jeans in the interest of seeing if he had been stabbed below the belt line, and also so the nurse could slip the needle into his hip. He barely flinched, and fell asleep while she examined the knife wounds, which were nowhere near as deep as the bleeding had indicated, and prescribed the antibiotic, cleaning and dressing of the injuries.

One of the aides took over when she was done, and wheeled the patient off to a room until he had been observed long enough that he could be safely released to the cops.

A woman trailed by two young kids rushed through the door carrying a limp baby.

"What's the matter here?" Maria asked as the nurse approached with the paperwork. The baby was breathing weakly and with great difficulty. Maria touched her finger to his carotid pulse, which was thready and weak, even as she took him from his mother and to an exam table.

"His brother stuffed toilet paper down his throat. Anyway, that's what my husband says," the mother told Maria, following her at a run down the hall and into the exam room.

Maria was able to clear the airway only with great difficulty. The toilet paper was wet with secretions and clung to the little boy's mouth and epiglottis, even after she had cleared out the bulk of it. She could intubate, but that was likely to push the toilet paper into his larynx, where he would inhale it and it would decompose in his lungs, causing an incurable pneumonia. Meanwhile, he was all but dead anyway. She performed an emergency tracheotomy well below the level of the toilet paper, aerated the kid, got his little lungs moving and his heart pumping. Then she finished clearing the airway as best she could. This one would have to go out by copter too. If she had missed some of the toilet paper and complications developed, major surgery would be required to go in after the rest of it. If possible. She told the receptionist to call Gallup and order the chopper.

Mrs. Namoki, the licensed practical nurse on duty, intercepted Maria as she was about to go interview the mother. The woman had wanted to go on the helicopter with her son but there wasn't room for her and all the children, and the hospital couldn't assume responsibility for the youngsters. Besides, if the mom was to be believed, one of those kids had some tendencies that needed serious correction.

"Doctor, the patient in room four is awake now," Mrs. Namoki said, hugging her lightweight nylon cardigan around her polyester uniform top. She was an older woman, her hair tightly permed and thinning. Maria could see scalp through the curls. "His blood pressure is still real shocky, though, and he's real upset and talking in Navajo."

That was the accident victim from earlier in the night. "I'll check him and see if I can understand what he wants," she said. She had some doubts. She'd learned her Navajo at college, before she decided on med school. It hadn't been easy, though being around more native speakers had increased her fluency. It also decreased her confidence. She was often unintentionally amusing. Her native language was about as easy to learn as Chinese. She took a deep breath and went in to see the man.

The alcohol vapor had faded from his breath and apparently Mrs. Namoki had found the leisure to clean him up and change his ripped and bloody clothes for a hospital gown and sheet. He was also covered with a thermal blanket. Maria had been dashing around all night and she was sweating, but the steam heat in the old hospital needed tinkering with before anybody in the government was willing to admit it was winter and time to get serious about the heating system.

He tried to sit up but when she gently yet firmly pushed him back down, he extended his hand instead. He kept clearing his throat and mumbling something, the only word of which she could make out sounded like a name—Anabah.

His ID had been on him. His name was Jimmie Tsosie, age twenty-five. Driver's licenses unfortunately didn't list clans but she assumed if he reverted to Navajo when he was hurt, he must be a Native speaker from childhood and probably had a traditional upbringing. He was a nice-looking man, thick hair, fine features in a slightly rounded face with a sprinkling of acne scars on the cheeks. He was also minus a couple of teeth now. So, remembering her Navajo protocol, somewhat taught to her by her parents before visits to reservation relatives, but reinforced by those same relatives after she moved to Gallup, she began in the proper way, with her clans. "Jimmie, I am Navajo too. I am born to the Edge of the Water *Dine'e,* born for the Rock Gap *Dine'e.* I am your doctor, Dr. Chee."

Jimmie Tsosie gave a sigh, relaxed and sounded perfectly lucid now. He still didn't look directly at her. That was impolite to a traditional person. But he didn't look over her left shoulder and stare and stop talking, like some of the people did when they were afraid of her. "My sister, I'm glad to see you. My grandmother is Rock Gap *Dine'e*," he said. That did make her his clan sister. "Her name is Martha Tsosie. Anabah is with her. My little girl. I was drunk when I took her out there. I behaved badly and here I am dying and all she'll remember is how bad I was . . ."

"No, no," Maria said. Martha Tsosie was one of the names her dad had given her last night, one of the Two Tracks relatives. "You won't die. My father told me about your grandmother. I'll go see her. I'll tell her you're here so she won't worry and will look after your little girl."

"Good," he said, and stopped breathing.

She yelled for the crash cart and started CPR, and in about fifteen minutes he had been restored to a regular sinus rhythm, though he was far from out of the woods. The chopper had arrived for the baby just in time to transport him to Gallup as well, but Maria knew she had been very close to losing him. A spontaneous pneumothorax she hadn't expected. Damn. If they'd been able to get X rays, she would have been alert for it. He must have been crushed against the steering wheel or gear shift of the truck during the crash, broken a rib and, with the repetition of his labored breaths, driven the end into a lung.

The baby's mother was still hanging around when she finished. There had been no question of her being able to accompany the baby when the space aboard the chopper was needed for the other critical patient. The mother slunk around the waiting room like a beaten dog, her oldest child trailing her like a tail between her legs. She was young. Maybe not even twenty. Pretty, a little on the plump side. Her long hair was up in a curled black ponytail, but her bangs had what looked like peanut butter stuck on one side. The toddler she was carrying still had some on his (or her) hand. You couldn't tell the sex without a diaper change at that age.

At change of shift, Maria looked up from writing her admission orders and notes, some of which would be faxed to Gallup later, and saw that the mother was still there.

"Mrs. Manygoats, I think you could call Gallup now and see how your baby is doing," she suggested.

"I already called. He's in surgery again. I got no car."

"How'd you get here, then?"

"My husband dropped me and the kids off and went to Winslow."

"Isn't he coming back by to see how the baby is?"

She shrugged. "He doesn't care. He doesn't think Duane is his. He thinks I was fooling around. But I wasn't."

Hooboy. Probably wasn't one of the kids with those homicidal tendencies after all. Sounded like one for the cops.

"I got relatives in Gallup if I could just get there. I want to see my baby. He needs me with him." She was crying now and her older child started clinging to her and sniffling too, and the toddler in her arms began howling.

Maria told Mrs. Namoki to call the hospital social worker and see if she could arrange a ride for Duane's mother. Maybe the BIA police had to go into Gallup today for something?

She left the hospital not exhausted from lack of sleep as she had every right to be, but still pumped up from the adrenaline of the busy night. She stopped by Nicki's, left a brief note, and swept up the sleeping Dezi from the couch and went back out to the car. It was time to go visit the relatives.

Mike passed out, woke up, made it to his feet, walked a while, and passed out again. He could have been going in circles for all he knew but he thought he was heading toward the road. The night got colder and colder and he pulled his denim jacket tight around his arms, but he was still way too cold. He only had on a T-shirt underneath. His whole back and hips and legs hurt like crazy now, but he tried to keep walking. He didn't want to freeze to death with a butt full of buckshot over a horse he didn't even manage to steal for free. That would be really embarrassing.

He wondered if Etcitty was going to come back for him like he said. Maybe he would. He wasn't a bad guy. Just a horse trader. Mike kept thinking too, dreaming even, that there was something about that gray he'd been riding, something familiar, and some reason he didn't think it was a good idea for him to keep that particular horse. Some real good reason. It had to do with snakes, but he couldn't remember what it was right now.

He passed out in some prickly pear cactus, got up real quick again, pulled out some of the spines, walked a while more, and when he saw that he was going to fall again shuffled his boot over the place where he'd land real quick—which sent him into an even faster dive, of course. But this time there was no prickly pear.

He was still thinking about horses when he was passed out, but now there was a kid too—a kid who was crying, not because it was scared and cold, but because it was really mad.

"You guys stop that right now! Bring Sammy back! Sammy is *my* horse. Bring him baaaaaaaaack!!!!"

"Patience, little sister," Mike heard another voice say with a chuckle. "We're just borrowing him. We said if you could catch up, you could ride too. You know what's wrong with you, little sister? Your legs are too short! Isn't that right, my brother?"

"Yeah, her legs are too short. How do you ride a horse like this with such short legs, little sister? You aren't big enough to ride a horse. You should maybe ride a goat instead."

"I don't ride goats! I ride horses! I want Sammy back!"

Michael felt the air shift around him, the wind blow, not the cold blast it had been blowing all night but a soft slipping-by of wind, a swirl of wind that was almost warm, and a warm wet droplet landed on his face.

The child's voice shrilled right above him, "Give Sammy back! Please give him back. My grandma is sick and I want to ride him and get help."

"Why didn't you say so, then?" one of the boys asked, sounding almost serious. "Sick grandmothers are important. Of course, our grandmother never gets sick but if she did, we'd want someone to give us a horse to ride to get her help—if that would help her. But she never needs any help of course, does she, my brother?"

"No, my brother. Not our grandmother. Everybody asks her for help instead."

"Pleeeese give me Sammy." The child was begging now and her "please" was coming out *pweese,* like Elmer Fudd.

Michael felt sorry for her. If this wasn't a dream, he'd take the horse away from the two teasing boys and give it back to the child and help her find her grandmother. Sure. Right. He couldn't even help himself.

The child was crying nonstop now, with great big hiccups. Suddenly, a weight the size of a large feed sack plopped onto Mike's neck and shoulders and the crying was a screeching in his ears. Kids got opera singers beat all over the place when it comes to shattering glass, he thought.

"Little girl, get off my head," he said.

She shrieked again, this time really afraid, and ran off a little ways. The boys' voices were laughing, but distant. "Hey, little sister, why don't you get Uncle Horse Thief here to steal back your horse? He's real good at it. Right, Uncle?"

Mike cleared his throat and propped himself up on his elbows. "Knock it off, you guys. What kinda perverts are you, draggin' a little bitty kid like this way out here in the middle of the night?"

"Perverts? Uncle, you wound us! Why, we're not even horse thieves. See, little one? No horse!"

"Where'd you put Sammy?" she asked, startled into a normal voice.

"We never had him. It was just one of our little tricks. You wanted him so bad you just saw him. You better get Uncle Horse Thief to steal him back, like he tried to steal the horse our grandmother used."

Small feet thumped over the sand toward Mike. First he saw feet; then an upside-down face looked into his. "You okay, mister?"

"Freezing to d-d-death," he said. "Can you take me to your house?"

"Uncle Horse Thief is cold, my brother."

"We don't want him to die from being too cold. Grandmother wouldn't like that. He wouldn't say where her horse is, then. Here, Uncle." Something else dropped across him.

"What's this?" Mike asked, feeling thick heavy wool against his fingers.

"Magic saddle blanket. Our grandmother wove it but she'll weave us another one. Besides, it only works once. Just hold it over you to keep warm now. Later throw it over a horse you want to catch and he's yours. Nobody can take him away when he's wearing this."

"Thanks."

"Okay. Don't leave little sister with her auntie, though, whatever she says."

"Uh-huh," he said. He was wide awake now but he still couldn't see the boys. Just some shapes against the darkened sand. A sharp gust of wind, and even those were gone. Magic saddle blanket! Huh.

The little girl was freezing now that she wasn't running and crying. She had on a long-sleeved T-shirt and jeans and hugged herself tight and sniffled and shook, watching where the boys had been. She sank to her knees and hugged them to her, too.

With the blanket warm around his own shoulders, Mike tottered to his feet. Somehow the pain in his butt was less and he could stand easier, with the upper part of him warm. He managed to scoop the little girl up in as warm a hug as he had to offer and wrap the blanket around them both. "If you feel me start to fall, jump," he told her. "Where does your grandma live?"

"Over—there?" she said, pointing, then pulling her hand back and sticking her thumb in her mouth.

"Oh, yeah," he said. They were lost. The magic saddle blanket was warm and everything, but it would have been nice if they'd thrown in a compass and a flashlight while they were at it. Even the moon had set.

The little girl twisted in his arms and seemed to be looking behind him. He liked kids, but now was a heck of a time to have to take charge of one. She tugged on his T-shirt.

"What?" he asked.

She pointed. Dangling from the blanket and trailing behind them was a long, long piece of yarn that stretched clear back into the darkness. The magic blanket had apparently unraveled when the two boys brought the little girl to him. So, if he followed the ravel as far as it went, at least they should be going in the right direction. He gave the child a squeeze. "Good girl. When we get out of this, you gonna teach me to track, huh?"

SIXTEEN

"QUANTRILL STABLES," PILL's gruff voice answered. His tone said Quantrill didn't deserve stables and that he didn't like to answer the man's phone. It was a far cry from the gracious, folksy tone he employed when dealing with his own clients.

"Gosh, Pill, I'm going to have to speak to you about your telephone manner when you're representing the boss," she said with a somewhat shaky laugh.

"Well, hi there, Cin—young lady," he said, much more himself. "How the hell are you doin'? How's that cayuse of yours holding up?"

"I'll have to see," she said. "They wouldn't let me camp out here last night. I'm on the Hopi reservation. Nobody told me they didn't let you camp here, and one of the local guys found a stable for Chaco and brought me to the hotel. It was pretty strange."

"How strange was that?"

"Very. And I still don't know what happened."

"Nobody tried to—uh—hurt you, did they?" Pill asked, all the laughter cut from his voice.

"Nothing like that. Just funny dreams and weird noises."

"Well, strange buildings and all that—" he began. "Say, that boss of yours is—"

She had begun talking at the same time. "How's Raydir, is he—?"

"Back," Pill finished. "But not for long. You didn't say not to tell him where you were, so I did, and according to that snooty vampire housekeeper of his, he's headed down your way to do some kind of benefit for the Navajos gettin' kicked off their land."

"Where's he going to do that?" she asked. "There's police turning back people trying to go out that way."

"I don't know, honey. I'm not the man's goddamn roadie, for Pete's sakes. I just thought you'd better know he's going to be down there. He was pretty upset not to find you home."

"Good," she said.

"That's what I thought." She could hear the grin in his voice.

"I gotta go, Pill. I'm supposed to meet the man who gave me a lift to go back out to his friend's house to collect Chaco."

"You be careful, honey. There's some rough customers out there."

"There's rough customers everyplace, Pill."

"True enough." They hung up.

She repacked her saddlebags, slung them over one shoulder, hoisted her saddle into her arms and lugged everything to the lobby.

Carl Loloma was standing at the restaurant reception desk, talking to the cashier, an older woman with tightly permed hair. Marjorie was not around. The woman turned her attention from Carl to Cindy as Cindy came clomping in, carrying her saddle and bags. Carl turned toward her too, his expression still serious, then smiling, and then concerned as Cindy staggered a little under the weight she was carrying. Hank's heavy saddle was a bit too heavy for her to carry comfortably with loaded saddlebags. She had a little cart with wheels she could use to go to shows and such at home, but that kind of thing wasn't practical here. Carl took the saddle from her and nodded to the cashier, who led them into the restaurant and showed them to a booth.

A different waitress bustled smilingly toward them this morning—another young, heavyset girl, but this one had a wide, bright smile that was truly beautiful and a friendly manner.

"Wow, looks like somebody's going on a ride," the waitress said. Her nametag said "Carolina."

"Yeah," Cindy said. "But I need some coffee first. It was kind of noisy around here last night. Does that happen often?"

The girl's smile shut down. "I don't know. I can't afford to stay here, even if I wanted to. What can I get for you?"

"Number three for me with black coffee," Carl said.

Cindy tried the eggs and blue cornmeal grits with her coffee. The grits gave a little burst of corny flavor when she broke through the crispness on the outside.

"You didn't sleep well?" Carl asked.

"No. I had weird dreams and everyone here heard funny noises on the roof all night long. And nobody from the hotel seems to want to talk about it. I can't figure out what's going on here."

"I can tell you a little but let's wait till we're in the truck. You finished?" She was, after a last gulp of coffee. She asked the waitress to fill a thermos for her, too. Coffee wouldn't go down as well as water once it got hot again, but she needed the caffeine to stay awake. In fact, on the way out she set her stuff down long enough to get a couple of cans of Coke out of the pop machine, too.

Carl had already loaded the saddle in the bed of the pickup and was at the wheel when she reached the truck. She strapped herself in and he started talking. "Where the hotel is now there used to be a village, maybe not right underneath it but near here. We have a word in Hopi—*powqua*. It isn't always an insult but basically it means someone with powers—maybe even someone extra good-looking or what you might call charming. But mostly it means more like a witch. There were a lot of them who lived in this particular village. Our witches aren't like you think of them probably. No pointy hats or anything. But they want to control everything and they hurt people—they pervert ceremonies and plants and sacred things to selfish ends and want to keep everybody upset. In slang we call them 'the turds.' The kind of thing that happened last night to you and the other people has happened several times at the hotel, and certain sensitive people, both Indian and non-Indian, have had funny dreams there. We think it's because the witch energy is still there, still trying to work through people. So you have to be careful and not let it take you too far."

Cindy shuddered and sipped some of the coffee from her thermos. The man she'd seen floating certainly looked like what one of those witches might. Actually, he looked more like some kind of floating zombie.

"We'll stop and check on your horse but if you don't mind, I'd like to go out and dump these railroad ties on my grazing land and make sure my animals have enough water before I bring you back to Hamish's. Then you can follow me back to the highway."

"Well," she said, "I sort of promised this woman I'd take a message to somebody at Two Tracks. Do you know where that is?"

"I thought you didn't know anybody here," he said, his jaw tightening.

"I don't. She's someone I met briefly in Tuba City. She said she couldn't get to see her friend in Two Tracks and asked if I'd take a message."

"What's the message?"

"I don't know. I didn't read it. It wasn't for me. It's in my saddlebags."

"Did you get the name of the woman who gave you the message?"

"What's the interrogation for? I told you I don't know her. She was no more Indian than I am but she had some kind of made-up hippie name she said she was called around here."

He shook his head. "I can just imagine. Look, Cindy, I know you think we have a lot of rules here but this is not an easy situation for any of us in this country right now. The fact is, you couldn't have gone out to Hamish's on your own last night. The rangers aren't letting anyone past the highway."

"I didn't see anyone trying to stop us last night."

"No. That's because they saw us first and they know my truck. They were sitting off the road a ways, waiting. If you'd been on your own, you'd have been stopped."

"Oh. She thought it was okay because the ranger was so friendly with the old lady I was with."

"Well, maybe he knew her. But it still wouldn't have been okay. I admit part of this is to save us the hassle of having more people like your pal with her phony Indian name going out to give supplies to the Navajos who still haven't signed their leases and want to make us haul them out by force. We really don't want to do that. The lease agreement is more than fair to them and not entirely fair to us, if you want to know the truth. *My* lease on *my* grazing land is only for five years. Theirs are for seventy-five years and they're still not satisfied! And they steal stuff from us and ruin our shrines or try to keep us from getting back to them."

"I didn't know about any of that. The woman said they were just trying to help some old people who were being kicked off their land by the government and the mining companies."

"That's their story. Some of the people are even other Indians from Plains tribes and so forth who don't know anything about the cultures or history of this area. Some of those old Navajo ladies have gotten to be pretty good actresses by now, too."

"That seems pretty harsh. I mean, if it's their homes they're losing . . ."

"Look, Navajos are always moving around, except when you want them to. I don't want to put little old ladies out of their hogans, but they make it really hard to put up with them. And it was our land first. We let them come here after they'd all been imprisoned by the government. They guaranteed they wouldn't be any trouble. And at first they weren't. But they've been stealing us blind for years, and now they've lived on the land so long they think it's *their* ancestral land when it's actually ours."

"I'm glad it's not my problem," Cindy said. And then they got to Hamish's.

Hamish did not come out to greet them. Carl went to the door while Cindy went to the stable. The empty stable.

She looked out in the pasture, looked all around, thinking there had to be a mistake, when Hamish came out of his house.

She walked over there. "Where's Chaco?"

"Navajos got him. Along with two of mine. At least one of 'em also got an ass full of buckshot but it didn't seem to slow them down any."

"Did you call the police?"

He looked up at the sky, a sky unembroidered by wires of any sort. "Aw, you know how it is with these young cops these days. They forgot how to read smoke signals. So, since my truck's not running, I figured the best thing to do was wait until you and Carl came back here."

"We'll pick you up on the way back," Carl said, hopping into the pickup again. "If they were stealing horses last night, I'd better make sure my cows are safe. You coming?" he asked Cindy.

"Yeah, well, I guess it just became my problem after all."

Alice lay on her side and tried to go to sleep. She did not want to dream. And she did not want to miss someone coming to find Martha's body.

Anabah had not returned. Lost in the desert like that, she probably was dead already, unless she had found somebody else's house. They were scattered, and a lot of them left empty now by people who had relocated, but there were still some around. Behind her closed eyes she saw one, hidden in a hillside behind small trees and brush, made of stones and wood hauled from the lumber yard in Flagstaff. She knew, without ever having been there, that the man who had spoken to her in her sheep pasture lived there. Now she remembered who he had been.

At one time he'd been a powerful man, with an important job. Then he got caught stealing and moved out here. He had no wife or children anymore. He had no parents either. All his close relations died in accidents, one way or another, it was said. The rest of his relatives had moved away, like Alice's husband, or been among the first to relocate. They never visited him. Sometimes they sent him things. The lady at the post office said she thought maybe they sent him things so he wouldn't come to visit *them*.

Alice was walking to his door in her dream. She was saying, "Please come and help me with your truck. My sister is dying."

He was a very dark man and his hair was very thick. He wore it loose and wild when there was no one to see—or no one but Alice. He laughed and laughed. Howled with laughter. "Of course she is dying. That's what you wanted! What are you doing here, old woman? You should be with her—"

"But, if she is dead—?"

"Old woman, only good Navajos worry about the dead. If you're going to be a witch, the dead will be like your sheep, for your use. You will use their flesh and bones in your magic. You will wear their jewelry and sell it when you need money. You talk very tough with those BIAs and Hopis. Surely you're not afraid of ghosts?"

She didn't want to admit to this scornful man witch that she was still afraid of ghosts and only wanted to be able to witch enough to control some of the living. She didn't want to admit that she feared the reproach her sister's ghost would have for her. Martha in life had been maddeningly meek most of the time, but in death her *chi'in'di,* her ghost, could be all the more terrible with the wrath it had never vented in life.

"You shouldn't be here talking to me about this, old crone. You should be over at your sister's, taking the soles of her feet and the palms and tips of her hands, where her soul dwells, to use for corpse powder later."

The little bit of soup Alice had been able to eat threatened to come up. Cut flesh from Martha's hands that had woven such fine rugs? Cut the soles from the feet that had walked so many miles with her own feet, herding, going to school?

The man's words bit at her like the teeth of a wolf. "I thought you were strong and tough. I told the others you would be a good witch. You hated your sister and this is just a little thing we ask of you. There will be more, more and worse, later, until everyone will feel the things of power you do. None will know it is you, of course. Except us."

"I am expecting people. I don't know when they will come," she said.

"And you don't want to get caught? Do it then after she is prepared for burial—unwrap her and take the skin before she is in the ground. You will have her soul then, and your corpse powder."

He laughed again, like thunder, and cackled like cracks of lightning, and howled like a wolf.

And she woke up. It was still dark but she would not go to Martha, not now. She feared what she would do if she went.

She feared what would happen if she did not do it. The rest of the night passed very slowly.

By about eight o'clock in the morning, she was deciding that she would have to go to town and report not seeing Martha or Anabah for a while. First she was going to have to face Martha's body, though, in case she was just real sick and not dead yet. Maybe that would be the case. Then what would happen?

She was about to leave the house when she heard a car. Pretty soon one drove up and parked in her yard. A young woman and a little girl got out of the car. "Hi," said the young woman. "My name is Maria Chee. I think I'm your niece. I'm Rock Gap clan on my father's side and he said I had aunts living here. I'm a doctor and I got transferred to the hospital at Keams, so I thought I'd come to find you. This is my daughter, Dezbah. Are you Martha Tsosie?"

Alice greeted her with genuine and heartfelt welcome. She had been so afraid and lonely. It was just good to have someone to talk to again. "No," she said. "But I'm your aunt, too. I'm your other auntie, Alice Begay. Come in, come in. Sit down and have some coffee. It's a pretty good drive from Keams. Come in and rest and we'll go down and see if Martha is home or if she's up. Her granddaughter is visiting and they were probably up all night long with Martha telling her stories."

Nicki slept late since she didn't have to work that day. She found Maria's note and was a little disappointed. She'd hoped maybe when Maria got up they could go out to see her friend who had the gift shop over near Second Mesa. Nita knew everybody around there and she might know where Maria could find a place to live. Nicki didn't think it was a good idea for Maria and Dezi to live out on the HPL with all the trouble that happened. Especially she shouldn't live with relatives she hadn't even met.

But Nicki didn't say anything, since it wasn't really her business. However, she hadn't seen Nita in a while and it wouldn't hurt to just go out there and talk to her. Nita sold jewelry findings and tools too, and Nicki's boy was getting interested in making jewelry.

The parking lot was empty when she drove up. Nita's car would be around in back. The store was attached to her house.

Sometimes when it was like this, with no customers in the shop, Nicki would just honk and Nita would come out to the parking lot and visit at the truck so her friend didn't have to get out of the chair and everything. Other times she would come out to help her and they'd go inside and have a nice long visit. Nicki was in the mood for coffee in Nita's kitchen today, since she had some free time. She hoped her friend would be free, too.

Nita's kitchen connected her house with the shop. At one end was the jewelry counter, and there was a half door to get into the shop from there. But the kitchen table sat just out of the way, so Nita could have coffee while watching for customers. It was one of those metal tables you could put leaves in, and the chairs had cracked yellow plastic, upholstery "tastefully accented with duct tape" as Nita liked to say. The curtains were yellow too, and so were Nita's cats, who lay around the shop and house all day, waiting for someone to notice how beautiful they were and pet them.

Maria had been telling Nicki about some of the therapy they'd been doing for spinal-cord cases in Los Angeles, where she used to live. They had people to help you do the exercises to keep your muscles strong. Sometimes Nicki's kids helped her with the exercises, but they didn't always have time, what with school and everything. But in Los Angeles they'd also been having good luck, Maria had said, with these machines that gave little electrical shocks to the muscles and nerves and sometimes made them able to move on their own. Then, with a lot of physical therapy, some people, depending on how they were injured and so forth, could walk again. Maria had promised to go to the Flagstaff spinal-cord clinic with Nicki first thing tomorrow morning, after she got off shift. She wanted to talk to them about getting Nicki started, about where to find the little machines. About maybe helping Nicki to walk again. Nicki wanted that more than anything she could think of, and she was excited about it and wanted to talk it over with Nita. Nita always had good ideas for how to do things.

But just as Nicki was getting ready to honk, a long, dark green shiny car pulled into the lot, far down at the other end. A man, and a woman in a nice blue dress and high heels and stockings, got out of the car. They both had dark hair, like Indians, and were wearing sunglasses. They went into the shop. They looked rich, and though Nicki wanted to go see what they might buy, she thought maybe she'd stay out here and let Nita make her sale and then she could hear all about it.

She had a romance novel someplace she could read in the meantime. One of those set in Europe back in the old times. The Scottish men had already invaded the castle and were tearing it up and stealing everything and kidnapping and raping the ladies and killing the men. Lady Linnea and her nurse had just escaped through the secret passage. The Scottish chieftain, Laird Bruce MacTavish, better known as MacTavish the Ravisher, a name that struck fear into the hearts of the lords and ladies throughout the territory, had just gone outside to maybe see what else he could steal from the garden. He was looking at the castle chapel and that was exactly where the secret passage ended! Lady Linnea and her nurse would have to come out of there to get away, and MacTavish the Ravisher was right where he could see them.

That was when the well-dressed couple came out of Nita's store and got back into their car and drove away. Their hands were empty. No big sales, then. And New Mexico license plates too. A BMW. Nice car, but then, it could be rented. They might be tourists. But tourist ladies didn't usually wear heels and nylons on the reservation.

When they were way down the road, Nicki honked and Nita came out, looking a little mad. "Some people!" she said. "They were really rude and they kept asking who made this and who made that and, if they were young and just starting to carve or make jewelry, had they won any prizes. Which village were they from. What do they think I am? The Hopi phone directory? And after all that, they didn't buy anything. I bet they just wanted to go to people's houses and get them to sell to them before they sell to me."

"You think they were art dealers?"

"They pretended they weren't, but yeah, I bet they were."

"Where are they from? Are they Navajo?"

"No—they're not even from America, I don't think. At first I thought they were Mexican but the more they talked, the more I knew different. If they'd been nicer, I'd have asked."

About that time a battered pickup drove up. A young girl got out and Nita waved her over. "Hi, Sela. Do you know my friend Nicki Bedonie?"

"I don't think so," the girl said, and then looked more closely at Nicki. Nicki had seen her at some of the meetings for the disabled. She was helping take care of a grandfather who had bad arthritis and wasn't able to see anymore. "Oh, yeah, hi," Sela said finally.

"You probably didn't recognize me without my chair," Nicki said, without bitterness. At least the girl did recognize her. "How's your grandfather doing?"

"Well, okay, I guess. My neighbor is with him. Wiley got the use of a truck today, so I asked him to bring me over here for some more blades for my jewelry saw. I broke my last one yesterday."

They chatted for a while and Sela's boyfriend solved the problem of getting Nicki into the house by carrying her in while Nita brought the chair.

He seemed anxious to go, though, and finally said, "I gotta get this truck back."

Sela was still visiting and hadn't finished her tea and cookies yet. Like Nicki, she didn't get much time to herself, but this was her neighbor's day to watch the grandfather. The neighbor was a male nurse who worked at the hospital and supplemented his income with money or goods he earned relieving relatives who cared for elderly parents and grandparents. When Sela's uncle wasn't there to do it, the neighbor gave Grandfather his bath and washed his hair.

Nicki thought it must be nice, in a way, to have such close neighbors to help out. When she had lived in Hopi, she had always tried to help her neighbors just like the Hopis did with each other. If her man had stayed true to her, she might have someone to help her now, she thought bitterly. But she did okay. And there were ways she could still help people, even though some of them pitied her and thought she was worse off than they were. "I can give you a lift back, Sela," she said. "Stay and visit with us. Maybe you'll be interested to hear what my new doctor friend has to say—I thought I might try to talk about it in the meeting next time."

She barely noticed as she told her friends about Maria Chee that Sela's boyfriend Wiley slipped out the door.

Wiley was stopped by the Hopi Rangers, but if there was one thing he was good at, it was talking his way out of things.

"Only tribal members and residents allowed back there. You better go back," the ranger told him.

"Oh, gosh, but I promised my friend Carl Loloma I'd help him build a fence out on his land today," Wiley said. "I even borrowed this truck so I could help him haul stuff."

"You're a friend of Carl's, huh?" the man said.

"Yeah, I was just at his house today. Gave his niece Sela a ride up to Second Mesa."

"Well, I guess it's okay, then. Tell him to come around the office later on. Tell him Mitch Johnson said."

"Okay, Officer Johnson. Have a nice day," Wiley said, and drove on.

He didn't remember where they'd left Mike the night before exactly. They weren't on the road, 'cause that was the idea of taking the horses. Charlie had said just take the truck and park it alongside the road. He'd told Mike he should make it back to the road. But Wiley felt bad that Mike was hurt. Mike had been nice to him, and besides, now that Wiley had been seen driving a truck belonging to Mike, if Mike should be found out there and connected with the horse raid, Wiley would be connected too.

But he was almost back to the place where they had stolen the horses, and still saw no sign of Mike. He didn't like to just leave the truck there, like Charlie said. It was a good truck. He didn't like to just abandon it like that. If Mike had died or something, he wouldn't need his truck anymore, and even if Wiley didn't want to be seen driving it here, he could go sell it someplace and use the money to get something of his own, or trade it. Maybe finance his piki project.

He passed the turnoff for the golf course and kept driving on over to Two Tracks, which was where Carl's land was. Sela had said Carl was going out there, and as much as Wiley hated to face her uncle alone, he wanted to make sure and deliver Mitch Johnson's message and at least offer to help Carl so his story would check out. Of course, he would find some excuse to go back to town first. He was about halfway down the road between Rolling Rocks and Two Tracks when he saw the coyote come out of the scrub, with something dangling from its mouth.

A lot of things about being a Navajo still puzzled Wiley. One of them, sort of, was coyotes. Some people said they were evil, others said they were kind of jokers, and some even thought they were pretty good luck. He couldn't quite figure out what to think. This one was facing south, which was good.

The best thing was to kill it and drag it back over its own tracks, away from his path—the road.

He stopped the truck, reached for Mike's rifle and got out of the truck. The coyote looked at him and he looked at the coyote.

He raised the rifle. The coyote cocked its head and whined and—wagged its tail. Maybe it wasn't a coyote. Maybe it was a dog that *looked* like a coyote. Or maybe it was a tame coyote. A pet. He didn't want to kill somebody's pet.

He lowered the rifle. The animal bounded toward him, not attacking but like a happy dog greeting a friend-dog. Wiley was so surprised, he dropped the rifle. The coyote leapt up on him, paws on his chest, decomposition on its breath, and dropped what it was carrying in its mouth—a tangle of yarn— right under Wiley's chin, then licked his face. Maybe it was rabid.

The coyote yipped at him and he stared at it, fascinated. And began to see something there in its face—in its eyes. Something he saw when he looked in the mirror in the morning to shave the few whiskers he had and comb his hair just right. There it was, the same animal looking out of the coyote's eyes that looked out of his. So that's what it was. That's who he was. He had relatives after all. And one had recognized him and brought him a present.

Coyote jumped down, barked, tangled his paws in the yarn. Wiley helped him untangle. "That's okay, little brother, I know just how it feels," he said. With another wag, Coyote bounded back the way he'd come, along a long trail of yarn. He disappeared behind a bush and never reappeared.

But someone else did. About that time two people showed

up on the horizon, a child leading a limping adult. As they drew nearer, Wiley noticed that they were staring at the ground. Then the limping adult looked up and Wiley saw that it was Mike, and Mike, apparently, saw that it was Wiley—well, at least he saw his truck parked there. He waved.

Wiley went out to them and let Mike lean on him back to the truck. The guy was a mess. "Where'd you find the kid?" he asked.

"It's a long story," he said. "How did you know where we'd be coming out?"

"That's a kinda long story too," Wiley said and for once he didn't feel like talking about it right away. He wanted to savor the feeling of having a relative, a symbol of his own, something that recognized him, before letting people laugh at him again and tell him how tricky and unreliable coyotes were. Well, he knew different now.

"Where to?" he asked.

"Grandma's hurted," the little girl said. And pointed down the road in the direction he'd been heading. They got to where Carl Loloma's lease land was and she pointed toward it. Wiley looked for Carl as they drove down the dirt road that ran through his land, but didn't see him. Finally, though, they did see a cinderblock house and a couple of hogans. Carl's truck was parked in front of the hogan that was separated from the other one by a wash. In fact, Carl was standing in front of one of them.

Wiley stopped the truck.

"Is this your grandmother's place?" Mike asked the kid.

The child shook her head.

"Auntie Alice lives there," she said in a small voice, her thumb poised at her lips.

"Wiley, we gotta go to the other one," Mike said. His voice was thick and tired.

"Yeah, yeah. Just a minute. There's someone here I gotta see. I got a message for him."

SEVENTEEN

SOARING STAR HAD been really bummed not to be able to reach Alice's place when she planned, but she should have remembered that the universe had a way of doing things in its own good time. She called Earth's Children, the organization that sponsored her work with the resisters of government oppression, and told them about the new outrage—the blockade preventing her and her passengers from going through Hopi to reach their Navajo friends.

That was when she found out the good news. The cause was about to get a major, *major* publicity boost. Raydir Quantrill was coming through at the eleventh hour to bring attention to the plight of the Navajos who were supposed to sign the agreement that said that they were mere tenants on land that had been theirs for over a hundred years or face eviction. He was going to do a benefit for them. While it was true Alloy Rock was a little passé, still he had massive name recognition and she was sure people from all over the reservation would flock to hear him and in the process lend support to the beleaguered folks on the HPL.

And she, Soaring Star, was supposed to meet Raydir Quantrill here and be his liaison for the concert, making sure that he had what he needed, that everyone knew who he was and what he was doing there, that the publicity was as widely distributed as possible in the short time before the performance, and that the money collected got back to the home office to be funneled into the defense fund.

So she had to wait here in Tuba City for him to show up at the motel. Not that he'd stay there, of course. He had his own buses for himself and his tech crew. She'd seen them on the MTV special she watched before she got over such dumb superficial pursuits and came to the rez to do something meaningful.

Cindy fished Soaring Star's note from her saddlebag and opened it. Carl was driving over the rocky back road and she could hardly read for the bouncing of the truck.

"You can relax about the note, anyway," she said. "All it says is to let Alice Begay know that Soaring Star and the writer and Lakota elder she was bringing with her have been delayed. She says they're staying the night with friends in Tuba City and she'll check in with headquarters and if there's nothing new, be back at Alice's in time to help with the protest."

"Hm," Carl said. "Well, thanks for sharing."

She looked out the window at the rough-rocked cactus-tufted sand with its sparse patches of brown grass and low brush. Why would anybody want to fight over this country, anyway?

They turned off the road after a few miles and onto one that was even worse. Cindy got her exercise now opening gates to the many fences that crisscrossed the land. "Grazing control," Carl explained. "The Navajos don't understand about conservation and don't want to. They tend to graze all the land all the time and their sheep tear the grass up by the roots until the land is ruined for farming or other animals. The BIA and the Hopi Rangers put up these fences so the Navajos are forced to let some fields rest while grazing others, and rotating. Of course, the problem is the land has become so dry—much drier than when I was a boy—that it takes a whole lot of acreage to feed one animal. Our religion has continuous ceremonies and prayers to increase the rain, but when the grass is gone and the soil is so dry and porous it won't hold the moisture close enough to the surface for it to evaporate, there's very little left to go back into the sky. And the Peabody Mine is using millions of gallons an hour of fresh pure water to dump their slurry."

"I heard about that. Don't you get any of the money from it, though? It's not far from here, is it?"

"Money isn't everything. Once the land is ruined, reclaiming it will cost much more than we stand to gain from the mine. Our prophecies foretold that even the best corn land, that belonging to the chiefs, would be ruined, and that's happened already. It was also said that we'd be surrounded by lights, and that is happening."

"So what Soaring Star and her friends are saying isn't right? You don't want to take away the land from the Navajos and lease it to the mining companies?"

"Well, some people think it's a good idea and others don't. Just because all my people are Hopis doesn't mean they all agree on everything."

"Who does?"

"True. And we are the People of Peace because it really is part of our religion to be peaceful. But we have had bad disagreements—even fights in the past. The Navajos think they're being treated so bad because we're trying to get them to leave, but when my dad was a boy, there was a big fight in Oraibi about whether or not to allow our kids to go to the white man's school and a whole lot of people were kicked out of the village. You know where we came through Kykotsmovi? The other name for that village is New Oraibi. That's where my grandfather and the other men who didn't want the kids to go to school had to take their families when they were driven out by the 'Friendlies,' as the BIA called them. My family belonged to what were called the 'Hostiles.' Later on some of them went to Bacavi and then there was another split and those folks went over to Hoteville."

"So every time you have an argument you build a new village?"

"Something like that. Back during the migrations, before we settled here, it was worse than that, and one time—well, I'll show you something when we get back. Anyway, my father married a woman from Polacca and went there to settle, since the house and land belong to the women. So that's how come we live there. We *try* to settle things peacefully, without violence or bloodshed, these days. We try to follow the law and go through channels and procedures. But it ain't always easy. Especially when the Navajos break the law and mess with what little we have to help us survive."

About that time he pulled up to the remains of a fence. The posts were in the ground but that was about it. He jumped out of the truck, threw his hat down on the ground, and said something in Hopi that Cindy was sure wasn't polite.

"Fence is gone, none of the hay here I left for my stock, and there they are." He pointed to about five cows out in the scrub brush, munching what they could.

On Cindy's side of the truck, the flies were thick and bits of white stuck out from behind the brush. "Except maybe for this one," she called, getting out too.

One of his cows had been butchered, the hide and meat all gone, nothing left but offal and bones. The fleshy matter was gnawed and pecked and strewn around the bones. It stank, though the smell wasn't as bad as Cindy might have expected. It was cold of course, and the air was dry. To her nose, used to Seattle humidity, there was very little to smell out here. But this carcass announced itself.

"Damn," Carl said. "I *told* them I didn't care if they were here as long as they didn't mess with my stuff, and look at this. Come on."

"Where?"

"You had that message to deliver to Alice Begay? I have a message for her myself."

Cindy didn't like the sound of that. She didn't know this guy all that well, really. What if he got violent with some little old lady? What was she going to do?

He jumped back in his truck and she had to run to catch the door handle and jump in too before he drove off and left her. Just beyond a slight rise, the fence separated this area from a little cementblock house and two of the circular hogans. The house and one hogan were separated from the other hogan by a deep ditch—*arroyo,* in Spanish, Cindy remembered, or wash, the gullies that seamed this country like the lines on the face of a fairy tale witch.

In front of the solitary hogan four hay bales lay beside a stack of railroad ties. There was a car in the driveway.

Carl barely stopped at the fence in time to avoid running it down. Cindy got out and opened the gate and waited for him to drive through, then followed, closing the gate behind her and waiting until he climbed out of the truck to approach the house.

He knocked on the door and called, "Alice Begay, I want to talk to you. Open up."

The door opened and a young woman with a long black braid stood there, hands on her hips. "Who do you think you are, talking to my aunt that way?"

Inside the room, a child sat on a cot next to an elderly woman in a dark green calico Navajo skirt and a pale yellow velour blouse. The child looked curious and a little frightened.

Carl didn't seem to know what to say next, so Cindy took advantage of the situation and stepped forward to say, "Hi. A lady named Soaring Star gave me this message for Mrs. Begay. Mr. Loloma was nice enough to give me a ride out here and he just found some of his stuff torn up and one of his cows dead and he's a little upset, I guess . . ."

Carl glared at her as if to say he could speak for himself, but he seemed to be counting to ten first.

The old lady stood up and walked very briskly to the door and took the message Cindy had passed to the younger woman.

"Oh, too bad," she said, as if there was not an angry man about to huff and puff and blow her house down. "Soaring Star and Ernest Eagleclaw can't come right away. They were going to bring Haskall Wainwright, that writer. I was hoping you could meet them, my niece."

"Well, maybe another time," the younger woman said. "I mostly wanted to talk to you and Aunt Martha this time, anyway. If you people will excuse us, we have family business to discuss."

Carl said, "I don't mean to be rude, lady, but I still need to discuss why my railroad ties and hay are laying in your aunt's yard."

"Those are mine," Alice said. "My friends gave them to me."

"You should have asked them where they got them first," Carl said. He stalked over to the railroad ties. A red mark was on each end, clearly visible. "Funny they should be painted with the mark I put on mine," he called back to the house.

Cindy hated to be in the middle of the argument. She realized she should have been grateful that important personal information before this had been exchanged in either Hopi or Navajo and she couldn't be expected to understand. But she had a responsibility to Hank too. The niece cast a long, scornful glance at Carl and somehow, though Alice's face was not betraying much, Cindy had a feeling she was getting sort of a kick out of the whole thing.

"Please excuse Mr. Loloma," Cindy said to the niece, quietly enough, she hoped, so that her words didn't reach Carl, "but Hamish Secakuku's stable was broken into last night and the horses were stolen—including a horse he was boarding for me for the night. It isn't my horse. It belongs to a man I was training it for."

"Too bad," the niece said. "You hang out with Hopis and you're apt to take some of the flak. You should stay out of this. It doesn't concern you."

Alice, however, put her hand on her niece's arm and said, "Don't be so hard on the girl, Maria. If my Anglo friends had stayed out of this, I would have been forced from my land long ago. This girl is a friend of my friend Soaring Star. Maybe she just doesn't understand. You come in," she said to Cindy.

"Thank you, Mrs. Begay. I'm Cindy Ellis. And really, Maria—"

"Dr. Chee to you," Maria said.

Carl came back to the doorway in time to hear this.

Carl said, "Chee? You're the new staff physician at the hospital?"

"Yes," she said shortly.

"We'll be working together, then. I'm the substance abuse counselor for this area."

"No kidding. It seems to me you should be a little more enlightened, then. Going around trying to frighten old ladies and accusing them of stealing from you—"

"Doctor, you're new to this area. And I understand you're fairly new to the reservation, too. This problem has been going on for a long, long time. And I don't know what you would consider to be an enlightened attitude about theft."

"Well, for one thing, Mr. Loloma, it's a perfectly acceptable part of the Navajo Way to raid the horses of our enemies."

"Yeah, well, it was perfectly acceptable to the Anglos to hang horse thieves, too. You people have a funny way of trying to show you really want to stay on this land is all I can say. We've tried to work with you." He had calmed down by now and his words at this point were slow and measured.

"Well, your people haven't been very grateful for the protection we Navajos have given you either," Maria said. "By surrounding you, we've kept you from having to deal with the racism in the border towns. *You* weren't ripped from your homeland and made to walk hundreds of miles while your loved ones died around you. *You* didn't have your people enslaved and all of your food sources burned to the ground."

"No, but when your people had that done to them and wanted to settle here, we had compassion for them and said they could, but only if they behaved. And they repaid us by stealing our horses and our food and coming to our ceremonies and taking so much that we finally had to stop giving anything of value to our own people as well. As for protection, if Navajos have been protecting us, who's supposed to protect us from our protectors?"

Before she could answer, a truck bounced into the driveway.

The little girl looked around her mother's legs and pointed. "Mommy, it's the nice man who helped us the other day! He has a little girl."

And Carl said with a suspicious look at the driver, "Wiley, what are you doing here?"

The driver got out of the truck and came over to the doorway of the hogan.

"I was going to see if you needed any help with your fence, Carl. Sela told me you had a lot to do out here. And then a Hopi Ranger named Mitch Johnson told me to tell you you should stop by the office. And *then* I found this little girl wandering around out there and she's looking for her grandma."

"Anabah!" Alice Begay exclaimed, looking at the little girl in the truck. "I thought you were at Martha's."

The child tried to bury herself in the hole in the upholstery of the seat. Her thumb was in her mouth.

"Anabah?" Maria Chee said. "Aunt Alice, we need to go see Aunt Martha right now. It's about Jimmie—Anabah's father. He was in an accident."

"Gosh," Wiley said. "Anabah said something about her grandma being hurt too."

Cindy was looking at the people in the truck. She'd never seen Wiley before or the little girl. But the other man looked familiar. She left the doorway of the hogan and walked over to his side of the truck.

"Hi," she said. "I don't know if you remember me, but I'm Cindy Ellis. We met at the park. You were talking to the old lady I was with."

The guy looked really funny. His eyes were at half mast and his hair and face looked like he'd used a cactus for a pillow. He just nodded.

He was so obviously ill that she didn't like to continue, but she did. "You know, when I met you at Wupatki Ruins, the one with the snake pictographs?" No response, but she was sure this was the same man. He was still wearing the same clothes for one thing, except for the shawl or blanket, she couldn't tell which, wrapped around his shoulders. "That gray horse I was riding with my friend, the little old lady who called you 'grandson'?"

Now he turned his head slightly and gazed at her for just a fleeting second with something like horror in his eyes, then closed them, turned his head back toward the windshield and shrugged slightly.

"Well, I stabled it last night with a Hopi man not far from here and during the night while I was at a hotel, my horse and two other horses were stolen. I know you don't feel very good right now, but since you had a horse trailer on your truck, I guess you might be around other horsemen in the area and—well, if you hear or see anything of the gray, or even a horse you think might be him, for sale or anything, please please call me at the—I guess I'll go back to the Rainbird Hotel tonight. If I'm not there, leave a message and I'll check, okay?"

The man, a far cry from the jaunty, smiling person he had been at Wupatki, inclined his head slightly.

Wiley came over to the driver's side of the truck and lifted Anabah out over the steering wheel, set her down, let her wipe her eyes, and took her hand as he started down the narrow road to the other side of the wash. Alice Begay, Maria and Maria's daughter all followed behind on foot. Carl glanced at the railroad ties and the hay, then got back in his truck and followed the others down the road. Cindy shrugged and joined the walkers.

EIGHTEEN

Melting the Witch

As MARTHA LAY beside her stove, her body was still and her eyes were closed, but inside herself she sat weaving and talking to someone who sat beside her, guiding her willow stick shuttles, her fingers, her batten, her comb, so that the fine wool was joined thread by thread into one of the beautiful red, gray, black and white rugs that had supported Martha and her family through many hard times.

She sighed. "It is good that I will die this way. I will not have to leave this land for the New Lands, where you and the other Holy People will not be able to find me."

The being beside her laughed. "Children always underestimate their parents. We created this world, my relations and me. Do you think we have now become so old that we will not be able to find our own descendants wherever they go in the Dinetah?"

"But it is so far. And the white men have built us strange homes, like theirs. The doors won't even face east."

"My child, it is good that you observe the ways that have been given you. It is good that you still pray for the guidance of those who were before you. But do you think your great-grandmother had eastern-facing doors in the pits where our people lived at Fort Sumner? Do you think she had a round house to stay in on the long walk? Do you think *her* mother and grandmother had any of those things when the New Mexicans carried them off to their towns to be slaves and tried to make Christians of them?"

Martha—the part of her that was not unconscious on the floor, said, "No."

"And even if they stayed in those towns from that day to this, do you think they are not as Navajo as you? They are. Even Santa Fe is still within the four sacred mountains, child."

"I hadn't thought about that. But it's not my land. This is my land. My mother's mother gave birth to her here when she returned from Bosque Redondo."

"I know, my child. I was there when your mother's umbilical cord was buried beneath the loom. And yours."

The Old One spun out a long thread and Martha saw now that it was attached to her—it seemed to go inside her somehow. "Martha, you are not dead yet, you know. Not until I break this thread will you die. The thread is still strong because it was not your time yet to die. Someone tried to hurry you along. If you die, this person will gain a witch's power. She thinks it will help her be strong. What do you think?"

"It will destroy her, of course. Oh, Grandmother, she is my sister. She is the fighter. The strong one. The one with words. The one who will risk anything. I have no words. I don't write real well. I don't like fights. But I like my home. I love my family. Alice is angry with me because I haven't done more to help her, but I didn't need to. She does it better. All I know is my animals, my corn, my weaving, my children . . . Alice is the smart one. Why is she killing me and wanting to be a witch? She's done so much to protect the Navajo Way—but witches aren't part of the Navajo Way. They're the opposite. Oh, I should have helped her more. I should have given her more rugs. I should have said she was right more. But I was a little bit jealous—all those people coming to see her, asking her things, taking her places. I said to myself, 'She doesn't need me.' But I kept quiet and she forgot the most important thing."

"Yes. Well, and she's done something very bad. But if you don't die, she isn't a witch yet, is she?"

"Even though she wished me dead?"

"Have you never wished her dead? Ever? It is not our way to talk of these things, but in families, sometimes we do wish people gone . . . The bad wind has caught your sister. She has put herself in its way with her fighting. But there are ways to cleanse people."

"Yes."

"Now I will tell you another way, a traveling way, so that if you have to move, you will go in beauty, however heavy your heart is . . ."

Martha listened to the instructions of how to keep your spirit whole in foreign land, even if you can never return home. She was weaving it all into the rug she was making when there was a gust of wind and the door breezed open.

"Martha!" Alice cried, as if surprised to see her. Martha took her batten from her loom, set her comb in its basket, and returned to her body.

Alice bent over her, pretending to be concerned. For just a moment Martha was very angry, but then she called Alice by her girlhood name and said, "I got sick all of a sudden. I'm glad you came. Where's Anabah?"

A beautiful young woman with a long braid bent over her. Her face was intelligent and strong, like Alice's had been. She picked up Martha's hand and felt the blood pulse through the wrist on its way to the heart. "Anabah is fine, Aunt Martha. But you need to come to the hospital at Keams. It's okay. I'll be there to look after you. I am your brother's son's daughter, Maria Chee. I'm a doctor. My daughter, Dezbah, is here. Anabah is here too. And—Jimmie wants to see you."

"My nephew's girl? I have your baby picture!" Martha's own voice sounded whispery to her. "Alice," she said, reaching for her sister again. Alice's face was still hard. Martha put her hand to her neck and scratched with her fingernail until the little bead came away in her hand. Pretending to hold Alice's hand, she slipped the bead into it. "Maria, you must help with two kinds of healing. You must take the jewelry and the rugs I was saving for the fair and sell them. Give the money to Hastiin Irving Bitsui and tell him I want him to do a healing."

"Auntie, I—" Maria began.

"Both of you must work to heal me but the main part of the ceremony is for Alice." Martha pulled Alice close to her and said, "For you, my sister. You must be cured too. You have been fighting with the enemy so long you have become infected with their wickedness. This healing will help us both."

For a moment, Alice's face was closed and hostile, and then it softened and her eyes grew wet.

"Now," Martha said to her new niece. "Let's see how good a doctor you are."

Cindy was watching all of this from the doorway when she heard a voice behind her ear. "I see you have been very busy while I've been away, my sister's goddaughter."

She opened her mouth to ask, "Grandmother?" and turned around to look for the old lady, but the only ones there were Carl and Wiley.

"Shhhh," the voice said. "I have made myself small. I am behind your ear, hidden in your hair. Don't flick me off if I tickle you by mistake."

"Okay," Cindy whispered. Well, what could she say? She heard her friend speaking but couldn't see her. She didn't think there were any technological bugs involved way out here on the rez. And she did believe in magic now—sort of. She stepped away from the doorway and walked out beyond Maria's car, where no one could hear them. "Grandmother?" she whispered.

"Yes, my godniece?"

"You said I was your sister's goddaughter that time, not just daughter. Your white sister doesn't just happen to know an Irish lady named Felicity Fortune? Tallish, dresses in gray, turns motorcycles into horse trailers?"

"Of course. Didn't I say so? She is one of them anyway. There are many. It's a little like one of the Hopi women's societies, the way my sisters and I come together. Did Felicity never tell you of me?"

"No, but—"

"Ah well, it's a long story, my child. We will speak more of this later, when we are alone. Only in ceremonies do I choose to appear before this many people at once, when they have come to hear me or to speak to me. Otherwise I am better at what Carl Loloma would call one-on-one."

"Okay."

"You should tell Carl Loloma to take Alice Begay with him to the town. You ride with Wiley Smiley. Michael Blackgoat must go with Maria and Martha Tsosie and the little girls. Anabah likes him and is frightened, and besides, he and Maria are being drawn to one another. And he needs her help. He will wonder how you know this, but he will be glad for your help and I think you will get Chaco back."

Cindy said, "You know, if you ever want to get into another line of work, you'd make a great stage manager."

"Thank you, my godniece," the voice said with a low chuckle. "But I don't think there is anyone alive who would have time to read my resumé."

Mike was the only one who had not joined the group. Cindy went back up the hill to speak with him about the move before she spoke to Carl. He was out cold. His face was clammy and his breath came with difficulty. She ran back down the hill. Carl and Wiley were helping Maria load Martha into the back seat of her car.

"Tell Dr. Maria Chee that Mike needs her help too," said the voice behind Cindy's ear. "Tell her to get Wiley to help him from the truck but say nothing. Tell her to do this while you are talking to Carl."

"Right."

She went around to the side of the car where Maria had finished directing the transfer and was ready to take her aunt Martha to the hospital. "Dr. Chee," she said. "There's something wrong with Mike. I don't think he wants anyone to know but he needs your help. Mr. Loloma wouldn't understand, so if it's okay with you, I'll ask him to take your aunt Alice with him while you and Wiley help Mike and the girls into your car. Okay?"

"Yeah, sure, but let's get moving," Maria said, a bit snappishly, Cindy thought, because she was so preoccupied.

She called Dezbah and Anabah to her.

Cindy and the others followed on foot while Maria drove up the hill skirting the narrow end of the wash. All at once Cindy felt a tickle by her ear, and a sudden lack of a presence where one had been, and thought she saw something small and black half jump, half swing to the car. As it drew near the truck where Mike sat slumped against the window, Anabah began crying and stretching out her arms toward Mike. "Uncle, Uncle! Want Uncle Horsie!"

"Uncle Horsie?" Carl asked, frowning.

Cindy shrugged. She was barely keeping pace with Carl. He was not especially long-legged but had quite a good long stride on him. "Maybe it's his name in Navajo or maybe it's because he carried her here when she got lost. Anyway, it would be a shame to separate them. And the little girl really should go with Maria and the other little girl, and Carl, I think Alice Begay should go into Keams with her sister, too. Since no one is coming to be with her, I mean. I'd be glad to ride with Wiley if you would give her a lift."

"Why can't *she* ride with Wiley?" he asked.

Cindy thought fast. She felt a tickle by her ear again and after a small whispered prompting, said, "Because I don't think she'll go if she thinks your Hopi friends will come and tear down her house while she's gone. Couldn't you reassure her that her home and her sister's are safe until they get back from the hospital?"

First he looked put out and then he nodded and said, "Okay. That's only decent. I really don't want to hurt little old ladies either—even if they do steal my railroad ties. I *will* come and take the ties back, though."

"I think that's fair," Cindy said. From the corner of her eye, she saw that Wiley and Maria had bundled Mike into the front seat beside Dezbah and Anabah. Cindy saw that he had a blanket or something wrapped around his shoulders. Come to think about it, he'd been wearing it earlier. She thought Indian people wore Goretex like everybody else these days.

She went to Alice Begay, whose head was bowed and who could not seem to stop weeping, and gently helped her into Carl's truck, then hopped in beside Wiley Smiley. She slid in something sticky on the seat.

Wiley said, "Oh, I should have put something down. It's all bloody."

"Thanks for warning me."

"I'm sorry. Hey, you want to go to a trading post? They got

really good deals on kachina dolls. My girlfriend can probably get you a really good discount."

"Sorry. I can't carry anything like that safely in a saddlebag and I'm on—well, I was on a horseback trip until somebody stole my horse."

"Stole your—your horse?" Wiley asked. "Who would do something like that, I wonder?"

NINETEEN

CARL DROVE IN silence while Alice Begay sat rigid, staring straight ahead, as close to the door as she could. For a while, Carl was glad of that. The woman had been nothing but trouble ever since he got the grazing land adjoining her land. She was not his friend.

He negotiated a washed-out piece of road, hit a bump and drew an involuntary *oof* from her. He cast another sidelong glance. She did not think he was looking. Her face was not so impassive now. It was very troubled—terribly worried. Well, her sister was sick, her nephew had been in the accident, her great-niece had wandered the desert all night and only been rescued by a mysterious stranger, and she was about to be forced to sign a lease to stay on property she believed to be rightfully hers or face eviction. If you looked at it from her viewpoint, something Carl was professionally adept at, she had every right to be worried.

"Look," he said, "as soon as I get back to my office, I'll call the ranger headquarters, let them know that even if your place and your sister's appears empty, you're away on an emergency and you're coming back. I'll tell them not to bother anything until you get home."

She didn't say anything, which didn't surprise him. Navajos were even better than Hopis at giving someone the silent treatment. "You don't need to think this changes anything between us, because it doesn't," he went on. "I don't like having my animals messed with or my property stolen. The one thing that *will* be missing from your place as soon as I can manage is my hay and my railroad ties. I need those to feed and corral my animals. And you'd better speak to those friends of yours about where they get your presents from, because if I have any more trouble from your side of the fence, whether you sign the lease agreement or not, I'll have you evicted. Got it?"

She nodded with uncharacteristic meekness and said, softly, "Some of the boys get carried away. I didn't know they were yours. I'm—sorry."

He released his breath with a long sigh. "I'm sorry too, Alice. I'm sorry about your family problems and I'm sorry we got off to such a bad start. I can understand why you resent me and I hope you'll try to understand where I'm coming from too. Can we not try to accept things as they are instead of how we want them to be and get along as good neighbors? When this is all over and your Lakota and Anglo friends go home, it'll just be us Hopis and Navajos again. Some of our people have been good friends in the past. Maybe too much has happened now for us to be friends, but we could at least try not to make each other angry. I will respect you if you respect me. Deal?"

She regarded him for a moment with just a trace of sadness and bent her head just once.

Wiley Smiley hit every bump in the road, but Mike's truck was like a good horse and seemed to try to make up for its driver's inadequacies. Cindy thought she was going to need some serious dental work by the time Wiley finished shaking her teeth loose.

And he chattered the whole way. She had always heard that Navajos were quiet people. Not Wiley.

"Can I ask you something, Cindy? I mean, ask you as a member of a certain target group—the young, athletic, average city person?"

"Uh, I'm not sure I'd use that description but go ahead and ask," she said.

"Well, how do you think your friends and the people in your area would respond if they knew there was a new taste treat available—something long known to Indians as a staple food—thin, lightweight, nourishing, full of fiber, no fat, very low calorie. Delicious when hot, keeps a long time, can be eaten as a snack, a bread, or a breakfast cereal. Don't you think your friends would want something like that?"

"Probably," she admitted. "Uh—is it a secret or can you tell me what you're talking about?"

The truck dipped to its bumper into a hole and somehow bounced back out again. A piece of sky did a quick hop and settled back into place. A soaring hawk flew immediately and speedily out of range.

"Piki bread," he said. "Have you had any?"

"Nooo . . . what's it like?"

"It's this flake-thin bread Hopis bake on a hot stone and then roll up. Sometimes they crumple it up for corn flakes. They make a big deal out of how hard it is to make, but I think the process could be simplified and instead of needing a special room and a special stone and all that, I could manufacture an electric grill with a built-in thermometer to cook it on, do a mix with instructions and maybe bottle some of the special oil they use. I thought of putting it on TVM to sell to home shoppers. What do you think? Would people go for it?"

"They might," she said. "You never can tell. Fitness is a big priority right now, in Seattle, where I live, at least. Of course, most programs combine diet *and* exercise."

"Oh," he said. "Right. Hmmm."

They flew by the Hopi Ranger roadblock. The rangers were busy detaining someone else on the way in, anyway.

"Wait," she said, looking back at the roadblock Wiley had sped through without so much as slowing down.

"What?" he asked.

"I should have stopped to report my horse being stolen, and Mr. Secakuku's."

"Oh, well, Carl was ahead of us. He'll do that. He's good buddies with a lot of the cops. Don't worry about it."

"That's easy for you to say. It's not your horse. Not mine either, really, but I'm responsible for him and he's my only transportation."

"If it'll make you feel any better, I can take you down to Keams to the BIA police. They're the ones who'd investigate a crime, anyway. The rangers are just jumped-up agricultural agents."

Cindy had to agree. In fact, she was glad not to prolong the trip on the bumpy dirt road. She felt as if she could have jumped out of the truck and kissed the tarmac when they finally pulled onto the smooth highway. A few yards down the road, Wiley turned and parked in front of a two-story brown clapboard building with a sign that said it was an arts and crafts store with a Hopi name Cindy couldn't have pronounced if her life depended on it.

A green pickup truck and another car were in the gravel parking lot. Wiley said, "You want to come in? You don't have to buy anything, but they got jewelry as well as dolls and some nice Hopi plaques and pottery and stuff. You could just look."

Wondering how much of a kickback he got, she followed him inside. The store had been a regular house at one time, or maybe just the living room and dining room of one. There was a definite division for two rooms and not much floor space, after the shelves and counters were figured in. On one side of the store, there was a counter full of tools and jewelry findings and a half door and then, a step or two down, a kitchen. A young woman who could have been either Indian or Hispanic, Cindy couldn't tell, was showing a pair of men around. The men were admiring exquisite pottery and exclaiming over kachina dolls in a way that made Cindy think they were probably a gay couple thinking of feathering their nest in Santa Fe-style. At the kitchen table were Sela and another young woman Cindy hadn't met before. The second woman was in a wheelchair. One duct-tape-patched yellow-plastic upholstered kitchen chair had been displaced by it.

Wiley said, "Hi, Nita, I'm back," to the woman at the counter, who was explaining the finer points of a pot to the two men.

Sela looked up and said, "Wiley, you didn't have to come back for me. Nicki offered me a lift."

"I know, but I've got the truck longer than I thought I would, so I thought maybe you and me could go for a drive or something. This is Cindy Ellis, by the way."

"Yeah, I know," Sela said. "Uncle *Carl* gave her a lift *yes-*

terday." Sela's tone said that Cindy was making the rounds of the reservation, cadging lifts from every man who wasn't tied down.

The woman in the wheelchair gave Cindy a curious look and stuck out her hand. "Hi, I'm Nicki."

Cindy shook it, grateful for her friendliness. She decided to tackle Sela's unspoken criticism head-on. "Hi, Nicki. I really don't go hitchhiking with Sela's friends and relatives as a regular thing. Her uncle stopped me from camping illegally on the rez last night and found a place to stable me and my horse, Chaco. Unfortunately, they were separate places and after we left Chaco with a friend of his, horse thieves came and took *all* the horses."

The little voice beside her ear said, "Don't forget to mention the reward."

"I'm offering a generous reward for the return of that horse. He's not mine—I'm training him for a rancher, but he's a good horse and my professional reputation is going to be kind of tarnished if I can't ride two days on someone else's mount without having him stolen out from under me."

Wiley's eyebrows had gone up when she mentioned the reward okay. She was sure he knew something about the theft. Him and Mike both. Grandma had practically said as much. But he didn't say anything.

"Wiley was just telling me about his idea for marketing piki," she said, to change the subject.

To her surprise, Sela glared at him.

"It was just an idea, hon. I was thinking it would be great to do it for those TV shopping things and have you be the demonstrator while I did the sales talk. You know." Sela looked even more outraged and Wiley hurried on. "But Cindy here was saying how we would need an exercise gimmick to go with it. I thought sure all those big-city white people who are always wanting Indian secrets of survival would go for learning to make piki."

"Which is one of *our* secrets," Sela practically growled.

Nicki hadn't caught the undercurrents. "How about corn-grinding?" she asked. "Ceremonially, both Navajo and Hopi women and even other tribes do that and it really firms up the muscles of the arms and torso. If you could get somebody to manufacture fake grinding stones—maybe even have one of those kits where you make your own with cement and dye it the color you want—and then, oh boy, now *that* would make a great market for any surplus corn."

"Which you could then make piki out of," Sela said, now only a little sarcastically.

Cindy shrugged. "Well, I've been hearing a little from the Indian people up where I live about how some of the tribes are trying to find 'culturally appropriate' economic schemes to increase their revenue. It might not be a bad idea. I mean, if it isn't really a secret."

"Making piki isn't a secret," Sela said. "There's even a video about it for sale at the museum."

"There is?" Wiley said, disappointed that his wouldn't be the first.

"But if everybody starts trying to make it—well, for one thing, it's not that easy to do, and for another, in case you haven't noticed, Wiley, we haven't had a corn crop in three years. It will be a little hard for Hopi to supply the corn for your project, and even if we had it, what would we do if we sold it all away on television for rich people with big supermarkets nearby?"

"Maybe we could make a contract with someone else who grows it," he said. "Like, they'd have to pay us and do it under Hopi supervision or something."

Sela shook her head, then cradled it in her arms, crossed on the table. "Oh, Wiley," she moaned, her shoulders shaking and her voice unsteady.

He patted her awkwardly on the shoulder. "Don't cry, Sela. I just wanted to do something to make some money so we could get married. I was going to have you be the demonstrator—sort of the star."

Her shoulders shook even harder and she uttered strange, choking sounds.

"Sela, Sela, please don't cry," he said.

She looked up and her eyes were full of tears but she was grinning and laughing. "Wiley, only you would think up a diet food and exercise to be demonstrated by someone as fat as me."

"You're not fat, you're—"

"If you say pleasingly plump, I'll kill you."

"You're Sela. And if those rich people don't want to be like you, it's because they're not setting their goals high enough . . ."

"Ooooh," Nicki said. "He's a *good* talker, Sela. Watch out for this guy."

"I gotta," Sela said, rising to give Wiley a hug. "Somebody has to watch out for him. He gets in too much trouble otherwise."

Cindy started to say that she didn't want to break up the party but she needed to get to the police station and report the theft of her horse. But just then the door of the shop slammed open and a teenage boy dashed in as if the seat of his jeans was on fire.

"Close the door, Nathaniel," Nita ordered. "You think coal doesn't cost any money?"

She jerked a thumb to a stove just beyond the kitchen table. It was little more than a barrel and a pipe but it seemed to keep the kitchen warm, anyway.

"Mom, Raydir Quantrill is coming to give a concert over at Tuba City. Can we go?"

Soaring Star wondered what Alice was doing, if she had been able to catch a ride to town for groceries, if she'd been presented with her lease agreement yet, given the option to sign. Soaring Star wanted very badly to be there with her at that time. To help her tell them where they could shove their piece of paper. She seriously considered driving around, taking the chance that Quantrill's bus wouldn't be arriving for another day or two. She hated to just sit all this time. The concert was on Thursday. Advance publicity was already being spread in Phoenix, Tuscon, Flag and Albuquerque as well as the local towns, as far north as Salt Lake City and as far west as Reno. It would be great if they took in enough from the Anglos that they didn't have to charge any Navajos or, well, even the Hopis. Especially Hopi friends of the cause.

She was unprepared when Milt, the Ojibway videographer for Earth's Children, came rushing into the Mesa Café, his red-tied braids flapping behind him. "They're here," he said.

"Two big busloads of equipment, techs and band members. And they're looking like they'd just as soon leave again. The jewelry vendors are closing in, Star. You better get out there and do your thing."

Soaring Star had finally managed to score a completely veggie fry-bread taco, got them to fry the bread in Wesson Oil and everything, and had just taken her first bite. The ice was rapidly melting in her Coke, with which she had to make do since they didn't have any fruit juices here.

She didn't groan in front of Milt, though. His opinion of the Anglo volunteers wasn't especially high anyway and this job was considered one of the cushier ones. Milt was supposed to emcee the performance, making the plea for assistance for the last of the resisters, bringing out the inequities of the lease agreement, even emphasizing that the land the Hopis were supposed to be able to buy with the money the government was paying them did not have guaranteed water or mineral rights.

She took another bite of her taco, grabbed the Coke, and walked back to the motel, which was all but dwarfed by the two huge buses.

Some guys were hanging around looking antsy and one sleek redheaded woman, very well dressed, forest-green power suit and heels and hose, the whole bit, stood beside the bus, talking on a cell phone.

She finished her call and Soaring Star reached her. "Hi, I'm Lindsey, but call me Soaring Star. Everyone does. Are you with Mr. Quantrill? Earth's Children asked me to act as liaison for him and the people in our organization."

"I'm Belinda Benedict, Shooting Star, and you can do all your liaising with me," the redhead said. Her hair was pulled smoothly back into a ponytail, then fluffed out in billions of kinky curls. Very Nicole Kidman. "Raydir had some personal business to take care of and he won't be available till Thursday morning. Meanwhile, I'll give you a copy of the usual list of requirements, you can show us the concert site, and I'll give you some fliers to post. Oh, and where the hell is a liquor store? Our people are thirsty."

"I wouldn't know," Soaring Star said primly. "I'm not a drinker."

"Yeah, well, you're not a musician either, sweetie. These people are under a lot of pressure and they need outlets. Speaking of which, know anyone close by who has access to, shall we say, chemical outlets? No, no, don't tell me, you don't do chemicals either. How about herbal then? Grass? Comprende?"

"It's okay, Ms. Benedict," Soaring Star said. "I'm not Hispanic. You can use English if you like."

Belinda gave her a calculating look out of narrowed green eyes. "Then understand this, sweetie. Pull in your claws, and get your tight ass in gear. We have a show to put on. The money's horrible and our time is expensive. Why in the hell Raydir wanted to play this gig is beyond me—did you know this godforsaken place is used by astronauts to simulate the surface of the moon? I cannot believe we're here but since we are, let's get crackin'."

Soaring Star couldn't believe this appalling woman. She hoped to the Creator that any druggies among Raydir's people would keep their habits to themselves and not add to the problems on the reservation—or give the resisters a black eye. The government would just *love* to say they were all drug dealers. Old Navajo ladies like Alice, who wouldn't dream of doing anything so nontraditional! A little peyote made legal by the Native American Church maybe, certainly not the sort of drugs this woman was referring to. Why, oh why couldn't they have chosen a more health conscious celebrity? She supposed that was because if there were any, they were not very well-known yet.

Milt ambled over, as if he had just been passing by and had barely noticed the enormous buses with the custom paint jobs.

"Who's the guy in the pigtails?" Belinda asked in a low voice as Milt approached. Soaring Star might have believed he was as casual about the whole thing as he was pretending to be, except that his jeans were now clean and whole, he had covered his Red Power T-shirt with a red Western shirt with a sun-ray pattern in oranges and yellows, and donned about a ton of beadwork and turquoise.

"Milt Highwater, this is Betty—uh—Omelette—one of

Raydir's roadies." Two could play at the you're-not-important-enough-for-me-to-remember-your-name trick. Soaring Star, as Lindsey, had gone to a good back-East women's college, too.

Belinda gave her an "Oh, puh-leese" look, smiled a dazzling smile at Milt and extended her hand. "Hi, Milt, it's Belinda Benedict actually and I'm Mr. Quantrill's personal publicist, here to make sure everything goes smoothly."

Milt tried to look sexy and together and dangerous. Soaring Star had noted on several occasions that such a look was not hard for him to achieve. He was, as a matter of fact, older and somewhat more dangerous than he usually wanted people to think. "Pleasure, Belinda. I'm supposed to say a few words about him before the performance and during the intermission. Our people sure appreciate Raydir coming through like this."

"Great!" Belinda beamed, turning her back to Soaring Star. "That's just super, because I've arranged for TV and print coverage and I think it would just be a wonderful gesture if maybe you gave Raydir oh—an eagle feather or something—and adopted him into the Navajo tribe."

Soaring Star expected Milt to hit the roof. But he *was* a filmmaker after all, and conceivably could imagine that the Benedict woman might have good connections. He was also more sophisticated than he wanted a lot of people to think.

"Gee, Belinda, that would be okay except I couldn't adopt him as a Navajo on accounta I'm Ojibway."

"Then what are you doing emceeing the show?" she asked.

He shrugged. Soaring Star saw his tan begin to flush a little around the edges. "I dunno. Guess I thought I was representin' an organization helpin' the Navajo resisters. And about that eagle feather—that's not a public thing. It's a spontaneous gesture, usually from one warrior to another. If your boy does a good job for us, someone will probably think of it. But it isn't proper for you to suggest it. Or him."

"Whatever," Belinda said, and turned her back on him too and went inside the bus.

"Umm, nice lady," Milt said, watching her go.

"Not," Soaring Star said.

"Uh-huh."

"She asked me to score drugs for the band, can you believe it?"

"Yeah?" he said. "Now, that's real interesting."

Carl dropped Alice Begay at the hospital, and was surprised to find himself worried about the old girl. She had been very reasonable when he talked with her. He would have felt on more familiar ground if she'd laughed bitterly at him or spit in his eye. That was the Alice he'd grown to know, if not love. Worse, he didn't sense the change was an act to manipulate him; she seemed genuinely and alarmingly subdued. He was amazed to find he was actually concerned about her.

He realized he should have taken the long way back, stopped and picked up Hamish, or at least reported the theft of the horses to the rangers at the roadblock. He wasn't entirely sure whose jurisdiction this would fall under, or if it would be cooperative. But he'd promised Alice he'd call headquarters about her house anyway, and he also remembered Wiley's message to call Mitch Johnson, so he phoned the Hopi Ranger station first.

Johnson, Carl was fairly sure, had not been at the roadblock when he drove back through with Alice Begay. Actually, he'd had so much on his mind, he hadn't thought to look.

He asked to speak to Mitch and first told him about the raid on Hamish's place. Mitch said he'd see that someone was sent out there to investigate. His personal message for Carl had been about something else entirely. Johnson was a clan brother and it was time for the younger men to provide an escort for some of the elders out to a shrine in the HPL. Johnson had been going to do it, but extra security was required because of the influx of people expected for a concert Raydir Quantrill was doing at Tuba on Thursday. He asked Carl to substitute and Carl agreed.

He returned to his office. Though he had no appointments that day, he wanted to pick up other messages, see about appointments for the next day or two. There was a message on the machine from Theo Honahni, the tribal chairman, asking Carl to call when he got in.

He did and Honahni's secretary, Dina, answered.

"You just missed him, Carl," she said. "But you can probably meet him at the Hopi Cultural Center, in the conference room."

"I don't want to bother him if he's in a meeting," Carl said.

"Oh, but that was what he wanted to talk to you about. He specifically wanted you to be there."

"Well, then, I guess I'm on my way. Thanks, Dina."

He wondered briefly about Cindy Ellis, how she would get back to where she was to spend the night, but it had been her suggestion that they split up. He did feel a little responsible now, since her horse had been stolen from a place he'd assured her was safe. He'd try to find a ride for her back to Flagstaff tomorrow with someone, or take her himself, if necessary.

When he arrived at the Cultural Center, he headed straight for the conference room.

Theo Honahni, his chief political opponent, Alf Tewawina, and Alf's second-in-command, Jason Numkena, were already there. It was a little strange to see them all assembled in one place. However, the real surprise, for Carl, was also seeing Abercrombie and Firestone, the dynamic duo from Hub Honahni's hacienda.

"'Bout time you got here, Carl," Jason said. He seemed to think it was necessary to be snotty to your political opponents, but then, he was still in his early twenties.

Theo, a short stocky man with a moon face, eyes that missed very little, and, unfortunately, what the IHS doctors had diagnosed as pancreatic cancer, said, "Glad you got my message, Carl. I believe you've met Ed Abercrombie and Micah Firestone, from MEE, Mutual Energy Enterprises. They had a few thoughts they wanted brought before the tribal council at the next session, but since by then we should have a new chairman, it seemed best that all of us who have been or will be in a position of secular tribal leadership be here when these gentlemen make their presentation."

"Fair enough," Tewawina said.

Abercrombie and Firestone cleared their throats. Today Carl really was going to have a hard time telling them apart because they were wearing business suits—identical from what he could see, even to the ties. Some sort of corporate uniform maybe.

"Mr. Abercrombie," Theo said. "Perhaps you'd like to begin."

"Of course. We have had preliminary discussions with you, Mr. Chairman, and met Mr. Loloma under social circumstances at your cousin's. Also, we've visited with Mr. Tewawina and Mr. Numkena on separate occasions. We were rather disappointed not to have encountered a more positive response to our remarks regarding the future of what are now the Hopi Partitioned Lands and MEE. Mr. Numkena indicated that he would have to take the matter up with Mr. Tewawina, you, Mr. Chairman, indicated that you did not expect to retain your post long enough for your opinion to matter, and Mr. Loloma was cryptically kind enough to ask your cousin Hub to give us instruction in Hopi mythology."

Abercrombie didn't notice that his reference to Hopi religion as mythic created an angry murmur among the Hopis in the room. Except for Jason, of course, who probably thought that most of his own religion was a fairy tale.

Carl cleared his throat. "There was a purpose in that, sir. I asked Hub to tell you that story as an illustration of how Hopi values, even those of so-called progressive people, differ from yours. Perhaps you have believed what some of the people living on our land have said about those of us who would like a few more amenities for our villages—that we—and the tribal council—do not represent Hopi traditional values unlike some of the Hopi speakers who have publicly declared themselves in favor of letting the Navajos keep our land. However, I spend much of my time off attending to traditional duties, preparing for dances, participating in and conducting ceremonies in relation to my clan and assisting the elders in carrying out their functions. So my view is that most of us, whatever outsiders may label us, strongly espouse our traditions while using what the outside world has to improve our people's quality of life—sanitation, medical care, education—in a culturally appropriate way. This does not mean that, like some, our leaders are willing to sell to the highest bidder. For campaign money, or a new truck. You gentlemen may not have noticed but we're a long way from Manhattan Island here. Beads and trinkets won't cut it anymore."

Firestone leaned forward and said, "Okay, Mr. Loloma. I understand your point. And you may well be able to get your people to finally agree on something, talking stock market out of one side of your mouth and preaching mumbo jumbo out of the other. So I think it's time we gave you a little instruction in the way things work."

"Exactly," Abercrombie agreed. "Perhaps you'll explain, Micah."

"Well, pretty soon all the Navajos who don't sign a lease will be required to vacate the HPL, which has been awarded solely to the Hopis. I don't suppose it ever occurred to you guys that maybe it was a little unusual that a group of people as small, and not to put too fine a point on it, impoverished as yourselves should win a judgment against members of the largest, richest and most powerful tribe in the country."

"It crossed *my* mind," Jason said.

"You must remember, Mr. Firestone," Theo said, "we have a clear claim to the land as the first inhabitants, as evidenced by the tablets given to us by Masaw."

"Yeah, well, it may have escaped your notice but that sort of thing has never cut any ice with the U.S. government before. But MEE and its competitors pointed out to the government on several occasions that it would be in the best interests of national security and resource management to have the land cleared for use by a people who did not actually live on it. We made sure the law firms that handle our own affairs made their associates available to you regardless of the cost. But there was tremendous cost, gentlemen. And if you cannot convince your people to make the best possible use of the vacated land, under our auspices, I'm afraid the bills you will find coming in may be quite alarming, and in the ensuing court battles you may be surprised to find your luck has changed dramatically."

"That was not our understanding," Theo replied, "when the Hopi people contracted with the various law firms, gentlemen. I think you'll have a difficult time challenging the hege-

recently confirr

"And I think
with a grin. "As
You're too deep i
The Navajos sure a
perts after all that's
ronmentalist press i
your problems after
the government have
years. Think about it,
revenue to be earned fo
other expenses have be
source exploration we ⌐⌐⌐⌐⌐ ⌐rom any
taxes or excessive regula ⌐⌐⌐⌐ouncil."

Theo started to say som ⌐⌐ng, but the MEE representatives
had stood up. "It's been a pleasure visiting with you, gentlemen," Abercrombie said. "Be sure and give this information
as well as our regards to your council members and, oh
yes"—this with a smirk at Carl—"may the best man win."

The One Who Is Also a Wolf is there, unseen, when the
flunkey speaks once more with the MEE men, briefly, nodding and grinning. And then the men drive away and the
flunkey climbs into his own pickup, and, after a brief stop at
Carl Loloma's office, where he enters as if the lock wasn't on
the door, takes something from the desk, climbs back in his
truck and heads toward Gallup.

There, he knocks on the door of a closed shop.

Inside he meets a pair of people as dark-skinned as he is, a
man and a well-dressed woman, whose way of speaking is not
Navajo.

He tells them about Carl Loloma, his job, his family, and how
the niece is often alone with the old man. How she is known to
help her neighbors with little medical problems sometimes.

"She sounds like a nice girl," the woman says approvingly.

"Oh, yeah," the flunkey says. "Too nice. You'll have to kill
her—the old man too."

Elizabeth Ann Scarborough

220

"We are not murderers!" the m
sulted.

"Of course not." ,
"ness, okay, but
"What's another
flunkey asks wit
the police wi
there—sh
your c

woman says, as if she's in-

an sticks up for her. "A little busi-

id when you already killed that boy?" the
a shrug. "In fact, Sela and her uncle went to
your license number the last time you were up
e had your description from another kid who saw
ar at the boy's house when he died."

We are not fools," the man says, still huffy. "We have disposed of the car, obtained another vehicle."

"Yeah, but the MEE guys, they know who killed the boy too. They been feelin' bad about not tellin' the police 'cause you do them favors. You do them this one too, huh?"

The man swallows. He looks at his wife. She looks back and shrugs, cold as if it is cockroaches they're talking about killing. "Okay."

The flunkey explains what is to be done and gives them the bag containing the item he took from Loloma's office.

The One Who Is Also a Wolf sees and hears all of this. The woman smiles, her smile nearly as fierce as that of The One Who Is Also a Wolf. The smile says the boy's death is not, as she claims, the only one she's helped cause, but the woman herself says no more. Still, The One Who Is Also a Wolf thinks it is too bad she's not one of the People. She would make a good witch.

It was drizzling by the time they left Nita's store. Sela decided to ride back to her home in Polacca with Wiley after all, so Cindy got a firsthand look at a mesa-top village. The road up was narrow and lined with boulders. On either side was a sheer drop. The village itself reminded her somehow of a medieval castle, well defended by its height and inaccessibility, the face turned to her closed, as if its back were against the outside world.

Once they were within the tiny square, which seemed smaller than Raydir's living room, there was little room to turn the truck around, even though the horse trailer had somehow become disconnected. The adobe rectangles of the buildings—piled two stories high in some places, one in others, three in yet others—seemed to be made out of the mesa, just as the mesas had seemed to her, when she first came down from Tuba City, as if they were partially made from ruined villages.

Here and there the buildings were reinforced with corrugated steel or cardboard or bits of boards. A washtub hung against one outer wall, a faded and chipped Coke sign on the screen door of an adobe room that proclaimed itself to be the trading post. Signs advertised kachinas and silver.

At the end of the square, a man stepped from a dwelling. Sela waved. Wiley drove up to the front of the building, into the little yard, now rapidly turning from dust to mud.

The man came over to the truck as Sela got out. He had a dark face and short cut hair. Before she closed the truck door, he exchanged some Hopi words with the girl, and left.

"Good thing I came back," Sela said, still holding the door open. "Someone came up from the hospital and told our friend he was wanted on duty tonight, so he has to go sleep and I'll need to stay with Grandpa."

"I'll be back later. Keep you company," Wiley told her.

She said, "I don't know if Uncle Carl . . ."

"We'll have your grandad for a chaperone," Wiley said. "See you."

He backed up, turned around, and headed nose-down the narrow road while Cindy held her breath hoping they didn't meet anyone coming the other way. It was also getting slick and icy now, the drizzle mixed with big wet flakes of snow. The sky was oxidized silver, and wind rattled the truck.

Keams Canyon was a bit of a shock after the mesas and pueblos like Polacca. It looked like an army post, with rows of tidy squarish buildings uniformly painted white. "Who lives here?" she asked.

"Nobody much really, not that I know of," Wiley said. "It used to be the Indian Agency and the government boarding school down here. It was back when the government sent soldiers to drag kids out of their houses with their parents still hanging onto them. Sela says an awful lot of the Hopis didn't want their kids in school. Navajos didn't either. The schools were pretty tough on you and beat you if you spoke your Indian language."

"Wow, really?"

"Yeah, and sometimes they didn't let kids go home for years."

"That's awful," Cindy said. "Is the hospital far from the police station?"

Wiley looked suddenly shifty. "Uh—quite a ways in this weather. Let's check on Mike and the ladies and then I'll drive you over there."

TWENTY

Maria Chee got her aunt Martha, Anabah and Mike Black-goat into the emergency room. During the day, there was usually one doctor on call from hospital staffing, but since Maria brought the patients in, she wrote the orders.

Aunt Martha was feeling pretty well by the time Maria was able to do a proper exam. The EKG showed no abnormalities at all, much to Maria's surprise, the pain was gone, and her vital signs were stable. Normally, Maria would have ordered medevac to the Gallup cardiac care unit but there was nothing here to justify it. The doctors in Gallup would just discharge Martha on the evidence of such an exam, so Maria decided to admit her aunt and keep her in Keams Canyon for observation.

By the time she finished the exam and the charts, Aunt Martha had been moved to the main part of the hospital. The nurse said she'd fallen asleep almost at once.

The nurse nodded at the next exam room, completely ignoring the fact that Dr. Chee was no longer officially on duty. Maria rolled her eyes, took the chart from the plastic holder beside the door, and entered the room. Mike Blackgoat was lying on his stomach on an examining table.

Anabah and Dezbah stood off to one side, watching with grave wide eyes and whispering to each other. Anabah was supposed to be in a separate room by herself to be examined for any possible ill effects of the exposure she might have suffered from being out all night in the desert. She was wearing the gown the nurse had put on her. She'd also apparently been given a bath when the nurse checked her for wounds. Her hair had been freshly braided too, and bow-tied with gauze bandage, which looked a little like chiffon from a distance.

Maria gave Dezi a disapproving look and the youngster shrugged. "I saw Anabah leave her room, Mom, and I followed her so she wouldn't hurt herself on anything. An emergency room is no place for a little kid. I think she wanted to be with him though." She pointed at Mike.

Maria hunkered down and took one of Anabah's hands. "Anabah, I have to take care of your uncle now. Dezi will keep you company in the exam room until I can come and take care of you. Then we can maybe find someone to take you back home, okay? Your Daddy had to go to Gallup for awhile."

"Want to stay with Granma."

"We'll see," Maria said, not wanting to get into an argument with the child when she still had work to do—and on her precious sleep time at that.

She stood up and asked Romancita, "Would you please take Anabah back to her room?"

"I'll make sure she stays there, Mom," Dezi said.

"Okay, but stay out of the way."

"Doctor?" Romancita said, gesturing toward Mike.

"Yes?"

"This patient wouldn't let me examine him or clean up his wounds. He said he wanted to speak with you first."

"Okay, I'll deal with it."

Maria turned her attention to Mike.

He had apparently been awakened by the conversation in the room. He looked up at her with one eye.

"Okay, cowboy, time to tell the doctor where it hurts," Maria said.

"It's my butt, doc."

"Then take off your jeans. Why didn't you let the nurse clean you up? This is what she gets paid for and I can assure you, she's seen lots of men's butts before. You're using up time I should be spending sleeping to get ready for tonight's shift."

"Yeah, well, I'd like to sleep too," he said, climbing very

stiffly from the table, turning, and lowering his jeans just enough to uncover the wounds.

"God, we'll have to burn those jeans."

"Don't even think about it," he half-growled, half-mumbled. "You gonna stand there lookin' at the scenery all day or you gonna get the shot out of my derriere?"

She found her own instruments and a basin and washrag. She handed him the latter and said, "Clean off most of it yourself while I get your medicine together."

He began washing.

"You allergic to anything you know of?" she asked.

"Yeah, doc, I seem to have this real adverse reaction to buckshot."

"Penicillin okay, then?"

"Sure."

She filled a hypo with ampicillin and another with a mixture of Demerol and Phenergan.

"How did this happen?" she asked him.

"Well, that was why I didn't want the nurse to know, really, doc. See, my buddy and I were foolin' around and he thought his gun was unloaded and pointed it at me as I ran out the door, and well, it was still full of buckshot. I didn't want him to get in trouble or nothin'."

"Is that why you spent the night in the desert, then, rescuing lost little girls?"

"Well, you know how it is. We'd had a little too much to drink. I was going to go sleep it off in my truck and then remembered I'd lent it to this other fellow. I was going to meet him at the road, see, except I told him I'd be gone longer than I was."

"Why didn't your friend bring you here? Didn't he realize he might have hit something vital and you could have bled to death?"

He was hissing with pain when he washed near a wound, but Maria was getting a clearer picture now of where he was hurt. She took the rag away from him, rinsed it and the basin out, refilled the basin with clean Phisohex and water, and finished the cleanup, then swabbed the whole thing with Betadine.

"How long ago did you have your last drink?" she asked.

"Long time ago," he said, his voice tight with trying not to yell where the antiseptic solution burned. "Yesterday evening, maybe. Early."

"Okay, I'm going to give you a pain shot," she said.

"In the arm, okay? I think I got enough holes back there."

"Then one more won't matter," she said, and gave him the hypo. "You can lie down on your stomach now."

He did.

"Look, this would go a lot faster and be easier if I call the nurse in now to help."

"No, look, I didn't tell her what was wrong. Please, just you do it."

"Mr. Blackgoat, I think I'd better inform you that I'll have to put your diagnosis down as well as fill out a report for the police on this. I'm obligated to do so by law any time I treat gunshot wounds or any other suspicious injury."

"Well, I don't suppose you could delay it a little, could you? I mean, since I helped you out and all? I want my cousin to have a chance to report it himself first."

"I thought it was just a friend."

"Well, he's my cousin *and* my friend."

"Funny your accident should happen the same time as that man's horses got stolen."

"Hey! Do I look like I could ride a horse anywhere?"

"No, maybe that's why you were on foot."

His shoulder blades shrugged. "Maybe so."

She kept picking buckshot out of his rear end, and after a while he said, "Forgive me, Doctor, for I have sinned." And he told her about how he had come there to buy a horse but his horse had been stolen by the BIAs and he was really only helping the man he was going to buy the horse from borrow horses from a neighbor they didn't want to wake up in the middle of the night like that, so they could get back the horse trader's own horses so he could sell Mike the one he wanted.

"But I'm going to get them back," he said. "I won't tell the police where they are, no matter what, because I don't want to get the other guy in trouble. But I'll get them back if you just give me a little lead time before you report this. Okay?"

"Look, Mr. Blackgoat, Mike, I'm already in trouble with the administration for no real reason. If I give them a reason, I could get kicked out, lose my license, even go to jail—why should I do that for you?"

He turned his head around to where she was standing and half-grinned, half-grimaced. "I knew you were a trouble-maker from the time I first saw you. Just let me go and get busy for a half hour before you fill out your paperwork, will you?"

"You really going to bring the horses back?"

"Yes," he said firmly. "I am. Or I'll personally turn myself in and the guy I stole them with."

Maria wasn't gullible, and she preferred to follow the rules as she understood them, but she had heard about people's animals getting taken for so-called stock reductions. While she approved of conservation measures and all that, she felt there had to be a better way to do things, that the measures being taken were more punitive than useful, especially when trained animals were taken and the fines to get them back were exorbitant for the average poor Navajo family.

"There, that's the last of it," she said. "Can you stand?"

"Yes," he said, though he wobbled a little when he stood up, especially struggling to pull up the blood-caked jeans.

"You better rest for a while. I have a few things to do and my paperwork to fill out, but it may take me some time—half an hour to forty-five minutes."

"Thanks, doc."

Romancita poked her head in. "Doctor?"

"Yes?"

"There's a lady here to see the patient in room two. She says she's your auntie too. Also, there's a couple people here wanting to see you, asking about the patients you just brought in. Some blond girl and a kid says to tell Mr. Blackgoat that Wiley is here."

"Tell them to have a seat and I'll be with them pretty soon," Maria said.

Romancita left. Maria started to put her instruments in the sink for autoclaving later, and when she turned back, Mike Blackgoat was gone.

* * *

Cindy thought Wiley was right behind her when she arrived at the emergency room. She saw Alice Begay sitting uncomfortably on a folding chair. The old woman looked frail, holding her head in her hands.

"Have you been here long, Mrs. Begay?" Cindy asked her.

She nodded glumly.

"Where's Carl?"

Alice Begay made a noise halfway between a grunt and a hiss. "He told me sit here and took off."

"How about Maria?"

"She's busy. I don't want to bother her. Or could be she don't want to talk to me. Could be Martha died."

"Oh, I'm sure she would have told you if that were the case. Just a minute." Cindy asked the receptionist what had been done with Martha and led Alice into the room and to a chair by her sister's bed. When she returned, she realized that Wiley had not followed her into the building. She looked out in the parking lot. Both Wiley and the truck were gone.

Maria Chee came out of an exam room.

"Hi," Cindy said. "I went ahead and took your one aunt in to see your other aunt. But in the meantime, Wiley took off with the truck. I don't suppose there's a taxi service around here, is there?"

Maria sighed. She looked very tired, as if it was almost too much effort to shake her head.

She went into another of the examining rooms and came out a few minutes later trailing two children. Anabah, apparently relatively unscathed, was once more in her little jeans and long-sleeved T-shirt.

"Dezbah, you stay with her," Maria said, pointing to Cindy. Dezbah made a face and a large, exasperated shrugging gesture in which both shoulders rose almost to jaw level before being sharply lowered again.

Having been appointed baby-sitter, Cindy sat again. Dezbah sat too. She looked much like Maria, except that her complexion was lighter and her hair a soft taupe rather than raven's wing.

"So," Cindy said, "what grade are you in school?"

"Second," Dezbah said. "Or I was. Till we came here. I don't go to school right now."

"Really? Why not?"

"Mama hasn't had time to take me there yet. She hasn't been back to Nicki's to sleep since night before last."

"Who's Nicki?"

"Tara's mom. She's letting us stay with her 'cause we don't have a house yet."

"That's nice of her."

"She's really nice. I wish she could walk. But she was in an accident, Mom said, and hurt her back and now she can't. I hope Mom can cure her back." The little girl looked around the emergency room and sighed.

It was about three P.M. by that time, according to the big clock on the wall. Its hands moved very slowly as Cindy and Dezi sat waiting and Cindy realized that the tickle behind her ear was gone. "Grandmother?" she asked, but it was only Dezi who answered.

"Oh, yes. I have two grandmas and two grandpas but they're both in L.A. It was okay there, but it's prettier here. My auntie in Window Rock says the Dinetah is where Navajos belong, though."

Maria came back, holding Anabah, and said to Cindy, "I'm just going to take her in to see Aunt Martha. This little one is fine and there aren't any other relatives in Flag and with both her parents in the hospital, there's no point in sending her back there. I need to see what my aunts want to do." She and Anabah disappeared into room two.

A man in a three-piece suit strode into the emergency room from the main body of the hospital. He walked as if he owned the place. "Where is Dr. Chee?" he demanded of the world at large.

The receptionist in particular answered, "She's in room two, Mr. Nakai."

He didn't even say "thank you" but stalked over to the door, pulled it open without knocking, and barked, "Dr. Chee, I need to speak to you immediately."

A little slower than immediately, Maria emerged from Martha's room, Alice and Anabah behind her.

The man rounded on her at once. "Dr. Chee, I want to know, What is the meaning of all this?"

"All this what?" Maria asked, her arms folded under her breasts and her feet spread. The man was at least a foot taller than she.

"Do you think we don't have enough to do without your going out and beating the reservation for more patients in your off-duty hours?"

"Could you speak a little louder, Mr. Nakai?" Maria asked. "I don't think they can quite hear you in Tuba City."

"Don't be impertinent, young woman. Answer my question."

"Very well, but I think we should first of all get something straight. You manage administrative matters at this facility but that does not mean that you are my superior or in any way permitted to upbraid me in public, in front of patients and staff."

"I think you'll find I've got a lot more power than you imagine over your career," he said.

"Second," she continued doggedly, "I believe that I am not only permitted but obligated to offer medical assistance to people in a state of medical emergency whenever and wherever I find them. That's my understanding of my oath, at least."

He snorted, as if he couldn't believe her naiveté.

"Third, perhaps if you had been as good at administrating housing for the staff as you are at interfering in patient care, I would have no need to go onto the reservation during my off-duty hours because my child and I have come all the way out here to work and have no place to live. Now, if you'll excuse me, I need to attend to the disposition of my patients and then find somewhere to sleep so that I can be ready for my shift tonight."

"That won't be necessary," he said. "Dr. Morgan can take your shift. We got along without you before you came here and we can get along without you for a while longer until you learn what is expected of medical staff at this hospital. I'm placing you on administrative leave for the next three months, starting now."

"You haven't the authority."

"Haven't I? I thought I made it clear when you arrived that after the trouble you caused at your last assignment you have been on probation since your first day here. I think you'll find I have been empowered to discipline you *as* I see fit *when* I see fit, and I see fit now. Dr. Morgan can finish your work. You are dismissed. You'll be notified when you may return to work. In the meantime you are to have no contact with patients or staff in this facility."

"What did you administrate before hospitals, Nakai? Boarding schools? Prisons? I have records to complete and reports to Dr. Morgan to make before I can leave."

"Don't make me call Security, Doctor."

Cindy and Dezbah stood and followed Maria out, but Alice Begay remained behind, looking straight ahead, as if she didn't know them.

Maria looked calm and defiant as she left, but back at the car, she was so angry she was almost hyperventilating. "Dezbah, you and Anabah get in the back seat."

When the back door was closed, Cindy said, "I can't imagine what made that man think he had the right to treat you that way, Doctor."

Maria's expression was closed at first; then she turned away, took ten deep breaths, and when she faced Cindy again her mouth was twisted with wry humor. "I should be used to it by now. They can't get used to a woman with education and power around here. They think they can make me disappear by treating me like a schoolgirl. But I'll fight them in court, if need be. Whether Nakai and his old-boy buddies know it or not, there are organizations in this country to prevent or redress what just happened. People like Nakai can't be allowed to just run off anyone who threatens them. The Navajo Nation paid for my education and I want to repay my people by serving them. So do a lot of other young people, but this kind of thing keeps them from staying, or even from coming back once they leave. It drains our talent and brains away from the Navajo Nation along with the youth. I could get a high-paying position anywhere, *any*where, and not have to take this crap but I'm going to stay here and fight. I owe it to my people."

Cindy thought of Alice Begay's militant friends. "Wow, runs in the family, huh? I'd think your aunt Alice at least would be proud of you—" She glanced back at the hospital, worried. Nakai was standing at the glass door, his arms crossed, watching them. "The way she stayed behind, though . . ."

"Oh, she's going to stay with Aunt Martha. They won't dare kick *her* out, not with the reputation she's made championing the rights of Navajos to stay on the land here. Funny, I'd actually heard of her before, but I didn't know she was my aunt till I spoke with my dad. She's not one of the relatives we visited when we came out to the rez when I was a kid."

Cindy nodded toward the window. Maria saw Nakai and glowered. She motioned Cindy to get into the car.

"Listen, Aunt Martha and Aunt Alice have some chores for me out at their place and also they'd feel better if someone were staying out there while they're gone. I was going to see if I could find a neighbor to watch the few animals they have left and look after the place, but since I seem to be free and my friend's place is crowded, I may as well take care of things myself now. Shall I drop you at your hotel or would you like to stay with us for a night or two until you get your horse back?"

"That's really nice of you," Cindy said. "And to tell you the truth, I'm not crazy about spending another night at the hotel right now. But I left all my stuff in Carl's—Mr. Loloma's—truck. My saddle and saddlebags and everything. I thought I'd get it back from him here, but he didn't even come in with your aunt."

Maria shook her head. "Typical," she said. "I need to call my friend Nicki to let her know where we'll be and ask her if she'll take any messages for me. If Loloma is the substance-abuse counselor, he'll have a phone in his office. Why don't you call and leave a message for him and ask him to bring your stuff by? That way he'll know where you are when your horse is found, too."

"Sounds good to me," Cindy agreed.

They made their calls. At both places, they had to leave messages, since neither Nicki nor Carl were there. Then they headed for Two Tracks. The roadblock now consisted of only one officer and he was busy inspecting another car as they drove through.

Mike got Wiley to stop at the flea market in Jeddito and buy him some clean jeans and socks from a used-clothing dealer. They stopped at the Chapter House. It was open and empty. Mike used the toilet to wash up. He had to get Wiley to peel off his boots, though. They were real tight. Probably from walking around in the desert all night, but maybe his wounds made his feet swell. He didn't care. It hurt like hell anyway and he almost passed out. Wiley went back to the flea market and got him some red hightop moccasins to put on in a size larger than he usually wore. They threw his bloody clothes in the truck. He'd cleaned his boots up while Wiley was getting the moccasins.

The next stop was the Laundromat. He washed the jeans and socks and left them in the dryer. Someone would walk off with them before they noticed they had holes in the ass. That would take care of the most obvious evidence against him for now.

When he came out of the Laundromat, there was an old lady sitting in the truck, talking to Wiley. Mike stopped and stared for a minute. That was one familiar-looking old lady. He made himself limp onward to the truck. Trying to hide from *her* wouldn't do him any good.

She turned to him with a stern look. "Well, Grandson, you are as much trouble as my other two grandsons. The minute I get busy, you take up with coyotes and steal the horse practically out from under me!"

"I didn't know it was your horse, Grandmother. I—"

"The important thing is to get him back."

"It was dark, Grandmother," Mike said. "I didn't recognize the horse."

"In the dark you couldn't see that he was not your horse when you had no horses already? Pull the other one, my grandson."

"Mike?" Wiley asked.

"Huh?"

"How come your grandmother suddenly was sitting in the seat beside me when you left?"

"Ask her."

"How come?" Wiley said to the old lady.

She smiled. "You need more instruction from your elders, young man, if you don't know who I am. But I'll give you a clue. I rode behind your ear all the way out here till now."

"Hey! That was a serious question!" Wiley protested.

"She isn't teasing you, Wiley," Mike said. "She can do that."

"Your grandmother is magic?"

"*Our* grandmother, Wiley Coyote. She's *our* grandmother. Yours too."

"How can that be?"

"I don't have time to explain right now, Wiley," Grandmother said. "We'll speak more of this later, my grandson. When you two have stolen back the horse. Steal back those other horses too. Hamish Secakuku is also my grandson."

"We will, Grandmother," Mike promised. "I already told that pretty doctor I would. I got a feeling I wouldn't want her mad at me any more than I'd want you mad at me."

She patted them both on the cheek. "You're good boys. I'm going to be small again. Don't be afraid. I'll help you. You still got my blanket, Mike?"

"Yes, ma'am."

"You know how you must use it."

"Yes, Grandmother. There was that horse of Charlie's I wanted but I guess I'll just have to walk a while."

The old lady disappeared suddenly, except for a black blur that disappeared behind Mike's left ear. "Don't worry about it too much, my grandson. Maybe something will happen. Meanwhile, just don't scratch your head, okay?"

Milt Highwater hitched a ride to Hoteville to visit his Hopi friend Shirley, whom he knew online as tradmana@hopinet. com. Shirley was one of his best cyberallies, a good critical thinker, witty and articulate enough to dismember with a keystroke casual hecklers. The first time he met her, Milt had been kind of surprised to see her in jeans and a T-shirt, sitting at her computer instead of planting corn, grinding corn, dancing with her women's society, or any of the other traditional Hopi activities she spoke of so glowingly on the net. She wrote with such passion, telling of those who signed away the rights of their people, of the sewers disrupting Hopi prayer sticks and feathers.

Milt himself had abandoned a career in computer engineering after he learned to plant and harvest his earnings carefully. Now he had the time to devote to videography and his more spiritual pursuits. And another job he did not speak of, even on the net, though he watched and listened for matters that related to it.

He had visited Hopi twice before on this trip while he was helping out the Navajo resisters. He'd been back here to the Southwest four times in the last eight years. In between he went home and worked at disseminating information on the net, editing his films, upgrading his equipment and watering his investments.

He'd visited Shirley twice when he came to this area. Twice more Shirley had come down with some of her elders. In between times Milt kept in touch with her via his laptop, when he could keep the batteries charged and find a phone line.

He found her today, as he had before, intermittently typing and watching her screen for response. She looked up immediately when he appeared at the screen door, however, bounced to her feet and opened it, inviting him inside.

"Greetings, my brother," she said.

"Greetings, my sister. I have come to ask your counsel and have the honor of gifting you with these tickets to the Raydir Quantrill concert."

"Super!" she said. "Just let me sign off here and I'll be with you in a jiff."

It was a drizzly day and most of the family was sitting around the house. Milt leaned against the computer table and watched Shirl's fingers fly as she finished her message and logged off.

"How may I aid you, my brother?" she asked in the formal Red English they usually employed in their correspondence.

"It's like this," he said. "The tech crew and band for the concert have arrived. The publicist, a colonist of the worst type, more than hinted that we were expected to provide drugs as well as an adoption into the Navajo tribe and an eagle feather for Quantrill. I put the quietus on the feather and the adoption, I think, unless someone just volunteers that later on, but I'm not sure what to do about the drugs thing. I remembered you telling me that there had been dealers out here in Hopiland corrupting young artists—"

"*Killing* them," Shirley said. "My friend Joey is dead because of them. Surely you're not thinking of procuring for them?"

"No, but it seemed to me like maybe there's an opportunity here to kill two birds with one stone—look like we're trying to accommodate the guest artists and lure the drug runners in at the same time."

"You mean like put out the word that there's major money to be made from the *pahana* guest stars up at Tuba, and then—"

"At a crucial time, *before* the sale can be made, preferably to someone not connected with us, in fact, even more preferably to someone who's an obstacle to the liberation of our people, the police can move in."

"I can but put the word out, my brother. But it sounds brilliant to me."

Raydir Quantrill knew exactly where his buses were and for that reason he roared through Tuba City as if it were nothing more than another cactus plantation, like the rest of this desert.

Actually, he sort of liked it out here. It was all very Georgia O'Keeffe with its browns and beiges, yellows and golds, sagebrush and tumbleweed. He could have done without the drizzle and snow, but hey, that's what leathers were for.

He was off to find his girl and he wasn't about to let a little bad weather stop him. He was composing a song to that effect in his head even as he almost drove through the Hopi Ranger roadblock at the other end of the village of Moenkopi.

"Where you goin', mister?" the cop asked. The guy was stocky enough that he probably wouldn't have qualified as a bicycle cop in Seattle, but he looked pretty solid all the same.

Raydir put his finger to his lips. "I'm trying to keep that a secret, Officer. Have you noticed those two big buses back there by the motel?"

"Yeah, sure. Can't miss 'em, can you?"

"No, well, they're mine."

"Go on!"

"No, look, really." Raydir pulled out his wallet and showed the man his driver's license. "But the thing is, I had a fight with my girl and she took off down here on horseback someplace. You haven't seen a good-looking blond chick on horseback, have you?"

"No. Let me ask my partner." The officer turned to another cop with a fairly uncoplike figure. "Hey, Harvey . . ." he began in English and the rest of it was in Hopi, Raydir guessed.

"Nah," Harvey says. "Except for the one with the grandmother that Morey thought was Kokyanwuhti—the one that came through on that big blue horse. If that was her, she sure has a funny assortment of friends is all I can say . . ."

"Well, actually, she does," Raydir said. "Do you happen to know which way she could have been headed?"

The cop made a two-finger gesture, raising and lowering his hand with a flick of the wrist pointing down the center line. "This road only goes two ways right now, mister. That way or coming back."

"There's a nice hotel at Second Mesa," the cop called Harvey said. "The Rainbird. If I was you, I'd ask there. Then you can try the Hopi Cultural Center. Then the hotel at Keams Canyon."

"That's right," Morey said. "She came through too late to make it all the way down to the Navajo rez before dark. Said the motel in Tuba was booked."

"She could have camped."

"Not along here, sir. We don't allow it. No, try the hotels. She might have loved Hopiland so much she decided to stay awhile," he finished with a friendly grin, and waved Raydir through.

After Abercrombie and Firestone left, Jason Numkena and Alf Tewawina put their heads together and left the room, plotting, no doubt, how they could use the bombshell the MEE men had just dropped to their own political advantage. Carl sighed and rose to leave. It was still only midafternoon and he felt as if he'd put in a long hard day already, a day that was nowhere near over.

Theo Honahni was still seated. "What do you think about all that, Carl?" he asked.

"I think unless we signed something that legally obligated us to pay back those bastards, we're within our rights to say, 'Thanks very much for the help, it sure was altruistic of you. As far as the mine goes, don't call us, we'll call you.'"

"That sounds okay to me too. Listen, I hear you been seen around with some *pahana* girl. New girlfriend?"

Carl shook his head. "Afraid not. I'm still waiting for your little Mandy to grow up and marry me like she's been promising since she was three." He told Theo how he had met Cindy and just been trying to help her, and about the theft of Hamish's horses.

"You shouldn't have taken her back there. Only tribal members and people who live there. I heard today there was some Navajo kid claimed he was going back to help you."

"That was Sela's boyfriend. We only *think* he's Navajo, really. He was a foundling, so he doesn't actually know. Anyway, that's what Sela says. And I didn't think it was very reasonable to expect that girl to just keep riding because she couldn't find a place for her horse."

"We used to do it all the time," Honahni said.

"Yeah, but if something had happened to her, her relatives could have made a big stink about it, Theo. Made us look real bad in the press. Maybe even sued. We don't need that kind of trouble right now. It doesn't hurt to show outsiders that the Traditionals don't have the corner they claim on Hopi hospitality. And she wasn't one of those Earth's Children women.

She was just a tourist on horseback. Now she's just a tourist looking for her horse."

"You should check the impound corral. Maybe he got in by mistake with some Navajo horses."

"I don't think so, but I'll do it anyway. Right now I think if I'm going to get my railroad ties unloaded, I'd better drive back out to my property. I need to put the camper on tonight to take the elders out to the shrine at Yawpava in the morning."

He stopped by the Rainbird Hotel on the way out to see if Cindy had returned. He felt self-conscious now, asking about her, but she had left no word. So he phoned his office to pick up messages and sure enough, there was one from Cindy. She said she was going with Maria Chee back out to Alice Begay's place for the night. He frowned. He didn't like that and he was pretty sure Theo wouldn't like it much either. He hoped when this whole HPL business was over, everything wouldn't have to be so closely controlled anymore. Religious secrets were part of his culture but having to make continual choices between being self-protective and halfway hospitable was stressful. He was tired of always feeling on the defensive about what either the Earth's Children bunch or the Hopier than Thou crowd were telling outsiders, who innocently repeated the remarks when they came to visit. There were reasons to be wary, of course—thefts, misinterpretations, intrusions into rituals, all sorts of offensive and annoying things people did out of ignorance, greed or malice. It was tough when you had to develop a city cop's mentality about tourists.

As he pushed through the double glass doors at the lobby entrance, a sleek black Harley purred to a stop in front of the hotel. An equally sleek guy in full studded and fringed leathers, boots and an opaque black helmet swung himself off the bike and pushed past Carl into the hotel. There was something disturbing about him, but probably he was just here looking for silver jewelry to enhance an image he had obviously polished to a high gloss.

Shaking his head, Carl climbed into his truck, drove up the highway, and for the third time that day passed the roadblock and bumped down the road toward Two Tracks.

The drizzle and snow made the work cooler than usual, but he became aware of his age after the third railroad tie. Too bad Wiley hadn't been telling the truth about coming to help him. He was going to be sore as hell tomorrow. But he kept lifting and stacking, lifting and stacking, as the sky grew darker and the rain and snow became less rain and more snow, then finally thick snow, and darkness. He probably just about had time to go over to Alice's place and get his stuff loaded, get back here and unload it again before the roads got too bad. There was about an inch of white in between the brush now. He realized he might have to take the elders to their shrine by dogsled tomorrow if this kept up.

Anabah wouldn't go inside Alice Begay's house, so Maria decided that the four of them would stay the night at Martha's place instead. "Besides," she said, "Aunt Martha wants me to gather up some of her valuables and take them to a friend."

"Probably a good idea since you won't be around all the time. But won't your other aunt be back tomorrow?"

"I don't know and I don't think she does, really. It probably depends on how Aunt Martha does."

They went inside. Martha Tsosie's little cinderblock house was cold, but warmed up quickly when Maria built a small coal fire, starting it with sticks of kindling and bits of paper.

Anabah led Dezi by the hand around the house, digging out this or that treasure to show her. Pretty soon there was a scratching at the door. With it so dark and cold and snowy out here, and so remote, Cindy was startled by the scratching, but then it was followed by a plaintive meow.

"Kittybitty!" Anabah cried, and flung open the door to scoop up a fluffy orange tabby cat whose fur was dripping with ice and snow.

"Should we go see about your aunts' sheep?" Cindy asked.

Maria shook her head. "Not now. It's too dark. We'll round them up tomorrow. Today it was Aunt Martha or the sheep and I guess I was untraditional enough to choose Aunt Martha." She yawned and stretched both arms high in the air. "Shouldn't be hard to track them anyway."

"You look exhausted. Why don't you go take a nap and I'll get some dinner started."

They had stopped at the Keams Canyon minimart for groceries, but Cindy found the beginnings of the meal Martha Tsosie had been making for herself and Anabah the previous day. Cindy sniffed. With the weather turning so cold and the stove off, the meat had kept well. No reason not to use it.

Maria lay down and abruptly sat up again. "Darn! I forgot! I'm supposed to leave with Nicki for Flag first thing in the morning. I was going to go to her spinal cord clinic with her."

"Maybe you could go back to town and call her before it's too late," Cindy said. "You could meet at the highway and that would cut down the time. It's okay. I don't think they're going to miraculously find Chaco any time soon. I can stay here with the girls while you're gone."

Maria got up, went to the door and looked out. The snow was now about two inches deep on the road. "I don't think so. I hate to disappoint her."

"Maybe she'll go on her own."

"Probably, but I was going with her to see if they wouldn't help her get started on therapy with one of the Empi units— they stimulate the nerves. There's been pretty good luck with them in some cases."

"That sounds exciting enough she'll probably mention it to them."

"She's kind of shy. If the roads are bad too, she might not even go."

"Well, there's next time."

"Yeah, sure. It's just, she's been so good to us, what with our coming here with no housing and everybody down on me. She took us in."

Maria told Cindy of her frustration at being held back and harassed by certain male politicians of the Navajo Nation whose only concern seemed to be getting as much money and as many perks for themselves as they could.

"That's terrible, Maria. I'm sure glad your people have got folks like you to try to keep everybody straight."

"Yeah, if I don't get kicked out first. What about you? Why are you here?"

"You're probably not going to believe me," Cindy began. But she told Maria about Raydir and then backtracked to tell her about the stepsisters and Rosie. She even told how she had met Raydir on the search for Sno after the girl had been kidnapped. "And now I guess he's coming here to do a benefit for your aunt Alice's friends."

"You sound worried."

"Well, it's just that Carl has been so nice to me and I told him I wasn't involved in this whole land dispute thing at all and now he's going to think I've been lying . . ."

"You're not thinking about changing boyfriends are you?"

Cindy shook her head. "No. It's not that. Carl's really nice-looking and he's been great to me, well, after the first little deal with the camping. I know it's not his fault or Hamish's about Chaco. But he belongs here and it's real clear that I *don't*. I mean, look at us. Here we are talking like old friends already and yet I've spent a couple of days up at Hopi hanging out and hardly anyone but Carl has spoken to me. It's like people are always expecting you to grow an extra head or something. I could swear some of them are going to report me to my stepmother and stepsisters."

"Don't take it personally," Maria said. "This situation with the land has got everybody uptight. I even catch myself saying anti-Hopi things, and in high school I had so many Hopi friends that my Navajo friends got mad at me. The cultures are really different. I've done a little studying on both of them. Actually, I started in high school, before I went into medicine. My people live separately from each other, in family groups, with a lot of space between, and visit neighbors mostly for ceremonies and so forth. Well, at least, traditionally they did. They're pretty independent, but also it's scarier living out there by yourself when bad stuff happens, and I think that's why we have so many taboos. Some of them seem silly to me but my relatives explain them and they have perfectly good reasons behind them. Also, when it's just your family, you tend to take advantage of whatever's handy. You don't have to worry about neighbors too much. The Hopis all live clumped up together in their pueblos. I guess it gives them a lot of security from some things, but it makes them more worried about others—mostly things that help you get along with other people in close quarters."

"Yeah, and if they *don't* get along, according to Carl, they split up."

At that moment they became aware of loud thumping noises coming from the outside. Dezi and Anabah, who was clutching poor Kittybitty around the middle with both hands, ran to the door and looked out.

Maria and Cindy followed. A man was busy hefting large heavy objects into the bed of a pickup truck.

"That's Carl," Cindy said. "He told your aunt he was going to come back for those railroad ties. It's really late, though. He must be awfully cold, wet and tired, and it's going to be a rough trip back to town tonight, even in a pickup. After I dish up dinner, I'd like to take him up something hot to drink at least."

Maria shook her head. "No, tell him to come down and eat here when he's ready."

"Wouldn't your aunt mind?"

Maria shrugged. "How should I know? I just met her. But she's not here right now and he did help us out, too. I'm pretty sure that entitles him to her hospitality."

Cindy nodded and poured a cup of hot coffee, in case he couldn't spare the time for dinner, and walked up the slippery road to Alice Begay's hogan with it.

"Carl!" she called through the snow and the sound of the railroad ties first hitting, then sliding into the metal truck bed. "I brought you up some coffee. Nasty night, huh?"

He looked up through the snowflakes, caught a couple on his tongue. "Kinda pretty really."

He accepted the coffee and sipped a long steamy slurp.

"Maria said you should come down and have some supper with us," Cindy said. "I think it's mutton stew and there seems to be plenty."

He looked surprised. "That's really nice of her. I have to finish taking these over to my land first, though. Maybe if the snow has stopped and you ladies are still awake, I'll come back and take you up on it."

He took another sip of coffee. They both looked up through the swirling snow, crocheting a lacework of flakes, separating the night into millions of intertwining tunnels of blackness.

"The Qötsamanavitu, that's the snow maiden *katsinam,* are at work tonight. I hope these Navajo ladies have got their fuel in for the winter."

"I don't know," Cindy said. "There was coal and kindling in the stove already and a full coal bucket nearby. I don't know where Mrs. Tsosie keeps the rest of it."

He sighed and she thought he might be debating whether he ought to check. His anger at Alice Begay seemed to have evaporated, at least temporarily. Then he said, "No, I bet old Alice has had her helpers working hard all summer getting ready for this."

"Maybe so," Cindy said.

"I guess I should get back to this now. I have to put the camper shell on tonight so I can take some elders out to one of our shrines tomorrow. Got to clean out the truck first."

"Oh, shoot, I almost forgot," Cindy said. "Do you still have my saddle and saddlebags in there?"

"Good thing you reminded me." He broke off his reverie and hefted the last of the railroad ties into the truck bed, then went around to the front to take out the saddle and bags. He lifted them out and handed them to Cindy, who felt her knees buckle a little and her feet slide in the snow with the extra weight. "Here, let me give you a hand with these down the hill," he said. "I'd drive, but I don't know as it would be real easy getting back up again."

Once there, he agreed to a second cup of coffee and then decided after all that he could have a fast plate of stew before continuing work. Maria and the girls were just finishing theirs.

Maria regarded Carl with more interest than she had previously while Cindy ladled a heaping portion of cooling stew onto a white plate and gave it to him.

"So, Cindy," Maria asked with a mischievous twinkle in her eye. "Did you tell him yet?"

"What?" both Carl and Cindy asked at once.

"You know. About your boyfriend."

"She told me she . . ." Carl began, mumbling a little around a mouthful of stew. His long hair was soaked and he had spread it across his shoulders to dry. He was sitting with his back to the stove and little droplets kept falling off.

"Maria!" Cindy said warningly. But Maria wasn't being really bitchy—Cindy knew all too well what that was like. She was just playing around, encouraging Cindy to be a little more honest.

"Well, *did* you?" Maria teased.

"Not yet. But it doesn't matter, I guess."

"No, you should. You're being too modest. It gets dull around here. It's fun to know when there's a star in our midst."

"Oh, please!" Cindy said, exasperated. "I'm not a star. I just muck out the star's stables."

Maria wiggled her eyebrows.

"Well, okay." Cindy grinned. "More than that maybe. But I was seriously considering leaving him when I came down here."

"And now?" Maria egged her on.

"Now I don't know. Probably."

"It's okay if you girls just talk around me," Carl said, obviously very curious. "I never notice anything when I'm eating and I have to leave right away, anyhow."

"She didn't tell you who her boyfriend *is*?" Maria asked.

"No."

Cindy sighed. "Well, his real name is Ray Kinkaid and that's how I knew him, when I met him but he's a musician and his professional name is—"

"Raydir Quantrill," Carl said, with a snap of his fingers. "Sure! *That's* why that guy on the bike looked so familiar. That was Raydir!"

"You know him?"

"You think we don't get *People* magazine at the trading post? You looked a little familiar too, come to think of it. They had an article about you two finding his kid up in the mountains there in Washington." He looked—maybe—a little disappointed, but more excited really. "So that's why he's here. I heard he was giving a concert, but he's really here looking for you."

"I guess," she said. "But the concert is supposed to be for Alice and the other activists. That was entirely something Ray did after I left, Carl. I really didn't know anything about any of this when I came down here. I was just trying to train a horse . . ."

"No problem," he said. "You told me you worked for him, not the other way around. I'd appreciate it if maybe it didn't get to be too public knowledge, though."

"Could be embarrassing for you, huh?" Maria asked. "Cindy said you'd been telling her something about the historical differences of opinion in Hopi and how one group of people was always keeping another group from settling with them, or kicking them out. About the Oraibi split and all that. Did you tell her about Awatovi yet?"

"Well, no. It doesn't just come up casually in the course of conversation usually. My people don't much like to talk about it. I thought you were new around here. How do you know about Awatovi?"

Cindy said, smiling, "Maria had lots of Hopi friends in school and did a lot of reading about Hopi culture as well as Navajo culture, but don't tell her aunt Alice on her. And Carl, you don't have to talk about it if you don't want to. I'm perfectly capable of reading a book about it, too."

"No, no," he said. "I don't mind. Here I am, one of the People of Peace and I was a gunner on choppers in Nam. If I was going to be sensitive about something, I'd pick something I did personally. I was actually thinking of telling you about it, Cindy, when we were closer to where it happened—though nobody can go up there now. What version did you read, Maria?"

"Courlander's, in *The Fourth World of the Hopi.* Also Frank Waters's, in *The Book of the Hopi.* I mean, I can see where those guys were coming from in a way. Those early Castillano priests were real bastards."

"I heard something about the way the priests acted," Cindy said. "Either from you, Carl, or—Grandmother."

"And the Pueblo Revolt that followed, where we pushed

them back to Santa Fe?" Maria asked. To Carl she said, "We Navajos helped you guys then."

Cindy was nodding that she knew all this.

"Well, about twenty years later, the Spanish came back," Maria said. "They came as far as the outer villages. According to Waters, they were friendlier and one of the priests performed a miracle and that converted some folks. According to Courlander, they used force and trickery and started their same old cruel tactics again. But apparently some of the people really had converted this time and it made for a split in Awatovi. The old chief, who hadn't converted, if I understood it right, went to friends in—" she looked at Carl as if uncertain of her information—"Oraibi, I think it was, and Walpi. Waters sort of intimated it was all the villages, but Courlander said just those two. Basically, the chief told leaders in those villages that Awatovi had turned against the Hopi way and the only way to keep the villagers from causing the destruction of this world like the others had been destroyed was to kill them all and raze the village. To make a long story short, that's what they did. The men from those other villages caught the Awatovi men at a time when they were in their kivas and threw fire and chili peppers down. They killed everyone else except some of the women and kids that they took captive. It had something to do with the captives being from clans that were needed to complete the Hopi ceremonial cycle, I think, but according to Courlander, the captives were still mistreated and some even murdered in a fight over who got which women."

She looked to Carl for confirmation, but there was a faraway look in his eye. "You know," he said finally, with his fork halfway to his mouth, "I never went to the ruins until recently. We don't ordinarily go, but there was some tribal business I needed to help with going on around there. So I had no idea of the layout or anything like that. And I didn't learn that story as a boy, before I went away to Nam and all those years I spent off the reservation. Like you, Maria, I read about it. Except I really only read about it recently, when I was reading *The Fourth World of the Hopi,* too. Between going to school as a kid and leaving Hopiland when I grew up, I missed out on a lot of our stories and history. A lot of us these days are like that. Even our parents were kept at boarding school for years and they missed out too.

"But when I saw it, I had this sense of—whaddaya call it, when you see something you know you've already seen before in a dream?"

"Déjà vu," Cindy said.

"Yeah, déjà vu. Because before I went there and before I read the book, I had this dream. In it I was wearing clothes like I am now, and thinking as I walked down the road to— well, I knew it was my home village, 'Where can I hide these clothes and change?' I found some bushes and took off my regular clothes and hid them in the brush. Then from somewhere, you know how dreams are, I found some traditional type clothes—the kind people wore a long time ago, baggy white pants and a shirt woven from cotton. I put them on and walked the rest of the way into the village. I knew everybody and they all knew me and I remember feeling very much at home, knowing I belonged there. And then, the other thing I remember, the last thing, is that for some reason I was climbing up to the rooftop like we do when we have ceremonies and want to sit up there. But I went up and I was watching, looking for someone or something and feeling scared and saying to myself, 'I wonder which direction they'll be coming from?'

"When I saw the ruins of Awatovi I recognized the same ground plan as in the village of my dream and it gave me chills. I asked one of the elders about it, and he told me a little bit. Then when I read about Awatovi, I understood."

"I've got chills right now," Maria said, hugging herself. She glanced over at the girls. Cindy hadn't noticed how quiet they'd been, but both children were lying on the cot against the wall, fast asleep. Maria rose and pulled a blanket up over them.

"Me too," Cindy said. "Do you think maybe one of the women captives was one of your ancestors?"

Carl nodded. "I'm almost sure of it."

He looked out the front window and said, "Hey, if I'm going to finish up taking those ties to my property and unloading them and get back to town before this stuff gets too deep, I better hurry." He gathered his hair into a knot at the back of his neck.

"Wait a minute," Cindy said, and dug into her saddlebags, coming out with a navy blue fisherman's stocking cap and a pair of work gloves she thought she might need on the trip. "You could maybe use these if you're going to be out there a while."

He smiled down at the cap and gloves, then at Cindy. "Thanks. That's real thoughtful of you. Don't you girls worry about the snow now. Sometimes it gets real deep but it melts fast too. Then all you'll have to worry about is slick muddy roads instead of slick snowy roads."

"Yeah," Maria said. "That's how it is down by Gallup too, except there's more pavement."

"Cindy," Carl said, "you sure you don't want a lift to your hotel tonight?"

She shook her head and shuddered, remembering the story she'd just heard as well as the incidents of the previous night in the Rainbird. "No, I think I'll give the witches a miss tonight. Tomorrow will be soon enough to hear if the police have found Chaco yet and I'd—rather not run into Raydir again until *I'm* ready, if you know what I mean. I'll just stay here with Maria and the kids and ride back with her tomorrow. It'll be nice to have a little peace and quiet tonight."

"Okay, then," Carl said, pushing his knot of hair up higher on his head, stuffing the cap down over it and pulling on Cindy's gloves before opening the door to a blizzard. With a final wave, he closed the door behind him and disappeared up the road into the ever-thicker falling snow.

TWENTY-ONE

CHARLIE ETCITTY HAD said he would keep the horses in Jeddito, but they were not in his corral. Charlie's truck wasn't there either, and the horse trailer was also gone. None of Charlie's family was at home. His house was deserted.

"He's sold them already!" Wiley said. "And he isn't going to share the money."

Mike chewed on the inside of his mouth and considered. "Well, maybe. That would be quick, though. He may have taken them to another part of the reservation, or maybe down to Winslow. But these days there are a lot of horses out there. I don't think too many people would buy more horses that quick. He wouldn't take them back to his mother's, where the BIAs would find them. No, I think maybe he's hidden them, and maybe he and his family took the nephews and brothers back out to his mother's, so if the police come looking, they will say, 'Oh, we've been here all along.' Of course, he may have relatives in other places he could have taken the horses to, but if we're lucky, maybe they're close."

"If he had hidden them in Gallup or Winslow or even Farmington, I could find them," Wiley said. "But I don't know a lot about the outdoors and the desert."

From behind Mike's ear the small voice said, "Many of my relatives will be hidden beneath the snow tonight, or asleep in the cracks in the rocks. But some of us have relatives who, though normally useless, have good vision at night and can smell horses from far away."

"You mean my coyote relatives, Grandmother?" Wiley asked. "Would you call them again and get them to help us?"

"If I called them, they would run away," she said. "Coyotes and my people have not had good friendships since Old Man Coyote, the Hopi one, tried to look up at my privates when I was doing him the kindness of hauling him up the mesa in a burden basket I had woven. I dropped him and he never did catch what he was hunting. Another time, Old Man Coyote, the Navajo one, was being boastful and insulting, for no reason, to all of us, my people and the Swallow people. So my husband, also a weaver and spinner, and I spun a web around him and contained him while the Swallow people pecked him to pieces."

"Grandmother, I will always *always* treat you with the greatest respect and honor," Wiley said, sweating with sincerity in spite of the cold.

"See that you do," she said. "You can begin by calling your people and sending them out to look for those horses you stole from my godniece and my Hopi grandson."

"How do I do that?" he asked.

"You're the one who prides yourself on being a fast talker. You figure it out."

Wiley hated to get out of that nice warm truck and stand in the snow, but he did. He stood there, in the middle of the road by Etcitty's house, and howled once, like a coyote. He was howling to the east first. Nobody answered.

"Four times is the Navajo Way," Mike reminded him.

So Wiley howled three more times to the east.

"There's four directions too, don't forget. The coyotes and the horses could be in any of them."

Wiley finally understood and started to turn north but Mike and the little voice beside his ear both said, "Not that way!"

"What did I do wrong?" Wiley asked.

"Turning against the sun will bring nothing but evil, in the Navajo Way," Mike said. "Turn with the sun."

"But it's dark now!" Wiley protested. "It's snowing and cold and I'll get a sore throat."

"You'll get worse than that if you don't get those horses," the little voice behind Mike's ear said quite ferociously.

So Wiley turned south, then west, and only then north, howling four times in each direction.

He was shivering so hard, his bones rattled and his teeth chattered, but at last they all heard a howl, close by, from the east. Then it was joined by a howl from the south. An answer came from the west and finally the north.

And from all four directions, bounding across the snow-covered ground and through the snowblind darkness, came coyotes. There were four coyotes from the east, four from the south, four from the west and four from the north.

They hung back.

"Move away from the truck, Wiley," Mike said. "They're afraid of Grandmother."

"Oh, okay." He walked down the road a little and the coyotes all followed him, their eyes shining in the dark. They looked hungry. That worried him a little. But their tails, which normally hung down low and discouraged, were wagging and their tongues were hanging out. That encouraged him.

"I guess you're wondering why I've called you all together tonight," he began in his best pyramid-sales-pitch voice.

The coyotes sat down on their haunches and whined.

"I am looking for horses. Three horses. Maybe you can smell one of them on me." He gestured to Mike, who at first hung back, worried that all those coyotes would jump him and eat him.

"Go," the voice behind his ear whispered. "I'll wait here."

"Can I take my rifle, just in case?" Mike asked.

"What do you think? Go!"

Mike went and passed between the coyotes from the south and the coyotes from the west. They growled a little and their hackles rose, but Wiley said, "This is my friend Mike. You can smell one of the other horses on him. If you find these two, you can probably find the other one. Right around here, you'll probably be able to smell them too. Or their scent on the man who took them away from Mike and me. These horses are ours. We stole them fairly, and the leader of the raid, Charlie, the man you will smell here, did not give us our share. He hid them. Please go to find them for us."

The coyotes sat with their heads cocked and their tongues hanging out, but they didn't move.

"Please go find them for us *now*." Wiley said. Then he turned to Mike and in an urgent whine said, "It's not *working*."

"Well, even for a relative, would you go spend the night hunting through the snow for nothing? Offer them something, but *not* the horses."

"What?"

"What would you want?"

"Something to eat."

"What? What do you like best?"

"Piki. I love Sela's piki bread."

Mike looked exasperated. "Go ahead. They're your relatives. It's worth a try."

"If you will do this thing for me, I will see that you have all the piki you can eat. I could offer you meat, of course, but we two-legged coyotes are not nearly the great hunters that our four-legged relatives are. But we *can* make piki—or get others to make it for us."

Wiley thought it was a good speech. He might not be a great hunter but he *was* a terrific talker.

The coyotes yipped, wagged their tails again, and bounded off in the four directions from which they had come. "It worked!" Mike laughed.

Wiley knew he would have to be even more terrific at talking if he was going to get Sela to make piki enough for sixteen hungry coyotes.

After a time, the coyotes from the west returned. They brought nothing but their appetites. They sat down, their tongues hanging out, eyes shining and tails wagging, waiting for piki.

Four minutes later, the coyotes from the north returned. They also brought nothing but their appetites. They too sat down, tongues hanging out, eyes shining and tails wagging, waiting for piki.

Then the coyotes from the east returned. They were running and whining and chasing their tails, wanting to turn back the other way.

"They've found something!" Wiley said. "But they act confused."

And while Wiley was thinking what to do, the coyotes from

the south returned. They sniffed noses and assholes with the coyotes from the west and whined and yipped at each other; then they all came up to Wiley and grabbed at his clothing with their teeth and tried to pull him down the road with them, back up to the highway.

"Wait, brothers!" he said, when he was afraid he was going to end up with no pants and a shredded jacket before he'd gone ten yards toward the horses. "We two-leggeds have something to compensate for our missing legs. It's called a truck. Wonderful invention. You lead, we'll follow."

And so they did, down the road and left onto the highway, down steep curves and up steep hills for miles, they ran. They were close to the turnoff for Steamboat Springs when suddenly the coyotes turned right, left the main road and headed down the road leading to Toyei. At that point, some of the coyotes streaked off into the darkness and snow, while the others sat with eyes shining, waiting for Mike and Wiley.

The men parked and Mike painfully climbed from the truck while Wiley went after the coyotes, never seeing in the snow the fine gray thread that linked something behind Mike's left ear to the truck. At a whisper, Mike returned to the truck and grabbed the saddle blanket, then trudged over the prints made by Wiley and his relatives.

If Mike could not move very well, Wiley could, and the coyotes could. Wiley was thinking fast, now that he was with his relatives. He saw the horses—hobbled, he could tell, by their clumsily frantic movements—in a little box canyon with a rope strung across the mouth. Etcitty no doubt intended to move them soon or to wall up the canyon, but he wouldn't have had time for that yet. Meanwhile, Wiley's kinfolk circled the panicked horses, who whinnied in fear.

When Mike caught up to them, Wiley was talking even faster, trying to keep his kinfolk from eating the horses.

"Get rid of them, Wiley," Mike said as one of the horses reared and fell back again, over on its side onto the ground. "Jeez, we should have brought ropes or halters or something."

But the voice from behind his ear said, "That won't be necessary. Neither will the coyotes, anymore. Tell them to go away, Wiley. Now, you boys excuse me while I change."

Wiley gave his relatives his thanks and told them to go, which they were understandably, slobberingly, reluctant to do.

But all at once, an elderly lady appeared wearing heavy white leggings, Hopi-style, a blanket dress that seemed part Navajo-style and part Hopi, and a heavy, patterned chief's blanket over her shoulders and arms and part of her chest.

"Go!" she commanded the coyotes, and with a unified yelp they turned tail. The woman carried a spindle in her hand and she began walking and spinning around the horses while the coyotes fanned out in all directions.

"Thank you!" Wiley called after them again. "I'll be expecting you for breakfast, only give us a couple of days. Piki isn't easy to make. Yet."

By that time, the horses were in a finely spun corral. They looked cold and hungry. Charlie had not taken very good care of them.

"You must each ride one of them back to their stable," the spinning grandmother said. "You can lead the other one."

"But Grandmother," Mike said. "I couldn't sit a horse if my life depended on it. Literally. Maybe in a couple of days, but now—"

"Now is time for a little horse magic," Grandmother said. "You were injured for the sake of the turquoise horse. Horses are vain. They like to be flattered. Sing him this song and he will cure you so you can ride him."

She gave Mike the words, a phrase at a time. He recognized them from the Blessing Way, which he had heard a long time ago, when he was a little boy, before the songs grew shorter and the medicine men grew greedier and healing songs could be heard on the radio sung to pop tunes.

Before she began the song, she said, "Dig him up some grass first. You need a sacrifice."

Mike did so, his bare hands turning as blue with the cold as the horse. He held out the grass.

"Horse of the sun, who puffs along the surface of the earth, turquoise horse, I have made a sacrifice to you!" he sang.

The next lines described the horse's turquoise home, with rooms, floor, and trail leading to and from it of turquoise, and then got into the healing part.

*"When you have come upon me by means of your feet of
turquoise, you have thereby perfectly restored my feet, you
have wholly restored my legs . . ."*

The old woman said, "Here I think we will be more specific: *You have perfectly restored my seat by which I am
joined with you.*"

Mike recited that as well and went on with the rest of his
body, mind and voice.

The prayer ended with words from the old Flint Way, the
last bits, also cataloging Mike's body parts and finally the
four directions, seeming most appropriate. *"Do you cause me
to walk about nicely? May it be pleasant wherever I go! May
it always be pleasant in my rear where I go—"* and he continued praying to the horse for pleasantness to his front, and
all around him.

And then Grandmother took her spindle tip and broke the
web corral and the blue horse stepped out, whinnying softly,
and nosed Mike's face, chest, arms, torso, back, rear, legs and
feet, gently, the velvet nose oddly warm on such a cold night.
Lastly, Chaco ate the grass in Mike's hand.

"Now to show him you want to mount, brush the saddle
blanket I gave you and lay it across him, then get on his
back," Grandmother said. Wiley had already mounted the
black horse.

Mike did as she directed, and to his pleasure, if not surprise, he was able to leap lightly up on the blue horse's back
and sit as comfortably as if he'd never been wounded, except
for the bulk of bandages. He twisted and pulled them out from
under his jeans seat.

"Now," Grandmother said, "you must return them. Toss me
the keys to the truck."

The horses and riders followed her back to the truck, and as
she hopped in, threw it in gear, and roared off, it occured to
Mike that he had unwittingly made a sacrifice to her as well.

The One Who Is Also a Wolf doesn't need a horse, except perhaps to eat. The One Who Is Also a Wolf can have four paws
any time he cares to change his skin for a pelt and walk
around, run around, in the darkness.

Tonight the The One Who Is Also a Wolf is running toward a hogan near Two Tracks. He is angry. Alice Begay had made her decision to join his kind, as he knew from a dream and from the fact that the bone bead in its small plastic bag was no longer where he had left it. But then, after she had accepted his gift, she grew afraid.

She knew what happened to those who tried to defect, but still she lacked the will to kill and despite the consequences she would face, she failed to cause the death of her sister. The wind that blew through her was not dark enough. The Rolling Darkness did not take her completely enough.

So now The One Who Is Also a Wolf would have to finish the job. He would enjoy this.

All at once he smelled a man-smell, Hopi-smell, sweat-smell. A short-haired, Hopi-shaped man was pulling something from a truck bed, laying it on the ground. He was groaning and sighing. He was tired. He would be easy prey. Furthermore, he knew who this land belonged to and how glad certain people would be for the death of this man.

The One Who Is Also a Wolf dropped his pelt and became a man. It was not like it is in the movies, with pain in the changing and special effects making his nose grow longer. No. One moment he was a wolf. The next moment he was a man. A naked man, painted with chalk and adorned with quantities of turquoise jewelry he had ripped from the corpses of rich dead people. He found a heavy piece of wood the Hopi had used to build something. He walked up behind the tired man. His footsteps in the snow were as silent as his paw pads had been. He raised his makeshift club, took a swing, and the Hopi fell to the ground with a sigh that was his death rattle, for he would not have survived such a blow. Later The One Who Is Also a Wolf would return to harvest body parts, both for feeding and for magic.

Now he would settle up with Alice Begay.

Nicki blinked when she heard the ringing, and groped for her alarm clock. But the clock was ticking peacefully and the phone shrilled again.

She lifted the receiver.

"Is this a message phone for Dr. Maria Chee?" a man's voice asked.

"Yes, Dr. Chee is staying with me but . . ."

"I'm Tom Quiyo, a nurse calling from the hospital at Keams. Would you please tell Dr. Chee that her aunt has been asking for her. It seems pretty urgent."

"Oh. Oh, gosh. I'll try to get ahold of her," Nicki said. She called for Tara to get up and help her get dressed, leveraged herself into her chair, and opened the front door to see three inches of snow on the ground between her and her truck. "Push me, honey," she told her daughter. Together, they made it out there and Nicki climbed in the seat, telling Tara to go back inside, lock the door after her, and go back to bed.

Then Nicki tried to think how to get hold of Maria. The problem was, she didn't know where the aunties whose place Maria was watching lived. But Sela's boyfriend had known—he and the blond girl had just come from there. Sela lived in Polacca and Nicki did know her way around there. If she could just make it up that hill in this weather. Fortunately, her truck had four-wheel drive.

Sela's grandfather was in a talkative mood that night.

"The snow is falling," he said. "The evil is frozen underground now, Granddaughter. It is time to teach you more of our people."

Grandfather was just crippled up bad, his cataracts made him a little blind, and he had no teeth. There he was no worse off than a lot of elderly people in the villages, and in fact, Uncle Carl had brought him some false teeth from Mexico. They didn't fit very well but Grandfather had been a handsome man in his day and he was vain, so he always wore them, even when it was just him and Sela.

Unlike some old people, he had *nothing* wrong with his mind. He could remember stories he'd heard when he was three years old. He was smart too. When he was younger, he must have been a lot like Uncle Carl. He had been a Hopi Code Talker in World War II. Lots of people didn't realize there were Hopi as well as Navajo Code Talkers, but there were, and Grandfather had been one. That was why he understood so well what Uncle Carl had gone through in Vietnam, and sold almost everything he and Grandmother owned to have a healing ceremony for Uncle Carl. Grandfather wouldn't hear a word against his son either when Uncle Carl went off, away from the reservation all those years, the years when he got into a lot of trouble. Sela's mom had told her privately that Grandfather had cried for happiness like a little child when Uncle Carl finally returned.

Sela settled down by the fire with some mending. Grandfather was sitting up in the rocking chair Uncle Carl had brought him all the way from Oregon. A man at the Oregon County Fair had made the chair. It was made of sticks with their bark still on, all bound together for strength. Sela's mom had sewed a cushion for it out of the white cotton wedding manta Grandfather had woven for her when she got married.

Sela enjoyed some stories but some were meant to scold her a little and these were kind of upsetting. Tonight, Grandfather launched into the tale of the Female Masaw.

It was the story of a beautiful and talented young Hopi girl who was very hard-working and had all the other virtues Hopi girls were supposed to have. Except that she was a very particular girl, and couldn't seem to find a boy she wished to marry among the many that came to court her.

"In those days, men would come to court girls while the girls did their corn grinding. The men would stand at the window and try to get the girl to talk to them. This girl, she wouldn't talk to any of them."

Grandfather's voice was disapproving. Well, that didn't apply to Sela. She talked to lots of boys—she just didn't want to marry any of them—right now at least. They were all very young and none of them knew what they wanted to be. Some of the ones that her Grandfather would have liked her to consider, boys from prestigious families who had many associations with the men's and women's societies and came from important clans, Uncle Carl steered her away from. She knew this was because these boys probably had the kind of problems he dealt with in his work. Drinking or drugs. He had explained to her that sometimes, later in life, if a person lived long enough, they might see that such behavior was not good for them or for anybody else.

Then, sometimes, they would stop and go on to become the person their parents had hoped they'd be. But it wasn't good for a young girl to give herself to a person like that.

Grandfather went on, talking about how Masaw, the guardian of the Fourth World who had, after many tests, allowed the Hopis to enter his domain, heard of the girl, went to see her, and decided she would make a good wife for him. Masaw had a lot of different aspects. In one of them he was the lord of the dead, and in some of his guises he looked horrible, with blood all over his head and that sort of thing. Some people said this was a mask, and that the real Masaw was a handsome man. Some people said that Masaw really looked like his horrible self normally, but could magically assume the human guise of a nice-looking man or boy so that he didn't frighten people when he came among them, as he usually did when he wished to spend time with living people, often to help and protect them.

But he was a very lusty sort of god and he liked women and he really liked this young girl Grandfather's story was about. So he got all dressed up as a handsome youth and she couldn't resist him. They decided to marry with the blessings of her parents, but when Masaw said he had to go away on business, she said she wished to go with him. Masaw knew this was a bad idea, for he had to return to his duties among the dead and he knew that would frighten his bride, who still didn't know who he really was. So he told her that he would only agree to take her if she insisted on asking him four times.

The reason he said that was because when you really don't want to do something for someone, if they demand that you do by making their request four times, you just about have to do it or have extremely bad luck.

The girl went with Masaw, okay, and there she learned very much to her sorrow what Masaw's life was really like. Her duty as his wife was to live among the dead, to wear the clothing of dead people and the hideous Masaw mask in public and to take over many of her husband's duties of going about among the dead.

So even though the couple got together, it wasn't exactly "happily ever after." Especially for the girl, even though she had married a god.

Grandfather was just getting to the end of the story, which was always the same, when there was a knock at the door.

Sela knew right away it had to be an outsider, because nobody in her village knocked on another's door. You were really supposed to make a little noise so people knew you were there and wait for them to come.

She was right. Two complete strangers were standing out there in the snow. They were dark but didn't look like any Indians she knew of, though maybe they were Mexican. Since the village was officially closed to outsiders at five every day and there were guards, strangers at this hour were a real rarity.

"Can I help you?" Sela asked cautiously.

"Is this the Loloma residence?" the woman asked in a husky, accented voice a little like Natasha's on the *Rocky and Bullwinkle* cartoon videos Sela liked to watch at Shirley's.

"Yes," Sela said in a soft, shy voice. Her voice always seemed to drop when she was unsure of herself.

"Who are they?" Grandfather demanded, looking around the side of his rocker. The firelight and the light from the one lamp she had lit gleamed on the part of his eyes not clouded with cataracts. "What do they want here? This village is closed at night to outsiders. Tell them to go away and come back tomorrow!"

Sela was surprised again. Grandfather was usually pretty hospitable—but then, people they didn't know did not usually show up uninvited. He'd been mumbling lately, having bad dreams, he said. Maybe this was related to that.

"P-please don't send us away," the woman moaned, shivering hard as the snow soaked into her hair. She was too lightly dressed for the weather and was shaking, despite her husband's arm around her shoulders.

"My wife is diabetic," the man explained in an urgent voice. "I'm afraid your Hopi tacos aren't on her diet. She needs to take her insulin."

"Oh," Sela said, her eyes growing wide. "Gee." There were lots of diabetics on the reservations. The disease killed many people before they knew they had it, or if they didn't believe in going to the clinics. Sela, who gave her grandfather injections of vitamins, sometimes helped to give insulin shots to neighboring diabetic elders and children.

The man held up a vial of frozen liquid. "We came up here to see my old friend Carl Loloma just before the village curfew, but then our truck died and while I was trying to fix it, the vial froze. My wife is far past due for her medication. We were told Carl lived here."

"He does, but . . ." Sela began.

The woman gave a low moan and slumped against her husband. "She's going into a coma!" he cried and swept her up into his arms and through the door, which Sela swung open without further hesitation. She knew that a diabetic coma could quickly become fatal.

"You can put her on my bed," she told the man, and pulled back the hanging blanket that gave her some privacy.

When he'd laid the woman down and was starting to bring out the syringe, Sela noticed that it wasn't one of the little prepackaged ones with the tiny needle she was used to. He pulled out a tourniquet as well.

"When will my old friend Carl be coming back?" the man asked. The previously frozen vial now seemed to be perfectly thawed and he was mixing it with a powder, pumping the syringe back and forth with the needle still inside the bottle with the powder.

"Any—any minute now," Sela said, suddenly feeling trapped between the man and the woman on the bed, who was doing some uncomatose-like moaning and groaning, though now that Sela saw her a little more clearly, even in the shadows of her alcove, the woman's color didn't seem bad. "What's the tourniquet for? All the diabetic people I know get their insulin shots under the skin."

"Yes," said the man. "But in a case so severe, the drug must go straight into the vein. Like—so."

Sela, who had been sitting on the side of her bed while watching the man prepare the insulin, felt herself grabbed from behind, one hand pulled up behind her back.

The man tried to grab her other arm to put a tourniquet on, but Sela twisted. The woman, no longer lying comatose, pulled harder on her hand. Pain shot up Sela's arm and into her head and she was sure her arm was breaking. This time the man pinned her arm and popped the tourniquet in place. He pinned her free hand between his arm and torso and aimed the needle at the blue vein that had popped up.

Sela wasn't aware she had screamed, but she must have. Suddenly the man was falling forward, the syringe flying from his fingers, and Grandfather was clinging to his back, growling like a dog while trying to bite the stranger's ear off. The Mexican dentures weren't up to it, though. When the man flung Grandfather off, the dentures remained hanging from his lobe like some kind of new punk earring.

Sela thought she was giggling, but that wasn't the sound. The woman had let go of her arm in the struggle and was scrabbling across the bed, trying to find the syringe.

Grandfather lay in a heap on the floor. Sela saw blood.

"Grandfather!" Sela yelled, and tried to push past the pair to reach him. The man caught her and jerked her back, his arms so tight around her ribs, he knocked the breath from her.

"Oh, shut up," the woman said. She stood now, perfectly fine, holding up the syringe. It was still full and the tourniquet was still in place just above Sela's elbow. "People pay good money for this, you know."

Sela started to scream but the man clamped his hand under her jaw and held her head so high, her eyes could see nothing but the rafters of their house.

"She said to be quiet. If you do as you're told, this won't hurt. It will all be over soon."

"Now, darling," the woman told him in her soft accented voice. "Be gentle. It's her first time. And we want this to look as if it was her idea."

"What about the old man?"

She shrugged. The man had released Sela's head and covered only her mouth. She saw that the woman was dressed very elegantly in a high-necked black velour dress with a silver overlay necklace full of designs that were loose depictions of So'yokwuuti, a sister of the Ogre family that was always threatening to devour bad children at certain dances. Why was a rich woman like this trying to harm her? She was no one.

She had nothing. Sela wanted to ask, but she couldn't speak, couldn't scream. Couldn't move.

"I believe he'll do," the woman said, "if you just make sure of him before we go. It was convenient that he chose to struggle with you—it will genuinely seem as if it was she who struck him down while she was stoned out of her little mind. As if he caught her at it and was trying to stop her and she became violent."

Sela tried to breathe deeply and think calmly. Uncle Carl had taught her a few self-defense moves. Mostly when she first started seeing Wiley. One rule was to move in a direction your attacker didn't expect. She leaned back hard against the man, who staggered back, loosening his grip on her chest so she was able to turn and knee him in the groin.

She felt the woman lunge at her with the needle and half-dove, half-fell, out of the way. As the woman attacked, the man recovered from the blow enough to reach forward and they connected, his body blocking the woman's arm and the hand carrying the syringe.

This time it was the woman who screamed, and when she slumped against her partner, it was real. The man cursed and jerked out the needle but the syringe was empty.

Someone was hammering on the door. Someone, probably the man, had barred it, locking them all inside. Sela sprang for it and lifted the bar. Her head yanked backward and pain knifed through her scalp. The man had grabbed her hair. She shrieked.

But the door flew open and there stood Wiley, of all people, with Nicki Bedonie in his arms.

Beside them was an Indian man Sela had never seen before.

"Help her!" Nicki yelled to Wiley. "Just drop me!"

But meanwhile the other man came into her house, got hold of the foreign man's arm so that he released Sela's hair, and helped him raise the fallen woman and herd her toward the door. "Come on, you two," he said. "Before this idiot has a chance to think. The whole village will be on top of us at any minute."

"Who are you?" the man with the accent asked as the strange Indian pushed him and the woman out the door.

"Someone who's been looking all over the rez for you. Come on, snap it up. Let's go."

Neighbors were coming outside, but the two men and the woman had a head start. They threw the woman in the truck, jumped in after her, and the vehicle roared to immediate life, twirling around in the snow and plowing out of the plaza and down the long steep road to the highway.

Sela watched, hugging herself, hoping they'd fall off the Cliff, as her neighbors crowded closer, yelling questions. Wiley ran past her, out of the house, running after the truck, trying to catch it on foot.

It was no good of course, and he came back. Nicki Bedonie had crawled toward Grandfather, and was trying to take his pulse. Sela was almost afraid to touch him, but as she drew nearer, Nicki looked up and nodded toward his chest and Sela saw that he was breathing, at least.

There was a dark bruise forming on his forehead, and a pool of blood on the floor.

"Grandfather, can you hear me?" she asked, touching his face, nervous that she'd hurt him again.

Slowly his hand rose to his jaw and then his forehead and he opened his cloudy eyes and spat. "Some people got no manners," he said.

"It's okay, Grandfather. Wiley came and threw them out. Where are you hurt?" she asked, pointing to the blood and to his mouth.

"Not my blood," he said, and put a quivering finger to a little piece of gristly flesh lying in the pool. "I got him before my teeth came out."

Wiley came back in the house. "I couldn't catch them but I got the license number," he said, dropping to the floor and sitting there panting.

"That one may make a man yet," Grandfather said.

"You were right here when we needed you," Sela said, and the two of them helped Grandfather back onto his feet.

"The room's spinnin' a little," Grandfather said. Sela helped him sit on the edge of the bed while Nicki grabbed a leg of the rocking chair, pulled it over to her, and using her arms, swung herself around and into it. Then Grandfather lay down with an *oof* and swung his feet onto the bed.

"Gee, Sela, are you okay? What was that woman trying to do?" Nicki asked.

"They were those drug people," Sela said. "I think they knew I told Uncle Carl about them and he told the police. They were going to shoot me up and try to make me an addict, I guess, and were even going to make it look like I'd hit Grandfather, maybe even killed him."

She sat back down on the floor, shaking, trying to wrap her arms around herself but the one the man had pulled still ached like crazy.

Wiley hunkered down and half-hugged her, rubbing her arm. She was touched by his concern.

"Do you think it will feel good enough that you can make piki tomorrow, Sela?" he asked.

"Piki?" she cried indignantly and batted his hand away from her arm. "How can you think of piki right now?"

Grandfather said, "Some piki would taste real good right now. And maybe some coffee."

"Gee, Sela," Wiley said, "I wouldn't ask you if it wasn't real important. I promised my relatives, see, in exchange for this big favor they did me. I sure hope you can help me out. I really don't want to break a promise to them."

She just looked at him.

Nicki said, "Do you want me to take your grandfather down to the hospital in my truck?"

"Wiley can probably take him in that truck of his," Sela said.

"Uh—I can't right now, Sela. I don't have the truck, and I really just came over to ask you about the piki."

"In a snowstorm? You like piki better than a Hopi!"

"No, it's not for me. Like I said, for my relatives."

"What about you, Nicki?" Sela asked, smiling a little, woman to woman. "You get a yearning for piki for an evening snack too?"

Nicki laughed. "No, but it wouldn't hurt, I guess. No, I just thought maybe your uncle or Wiley would know where Maria's aunties live. The hospital called and said one of them was asking for Maria and it sounded like maybe—well. It sounded like I better go get her. My truck's got four-wheel drive."

Grandfather slapped his knee and barked a short laugh. "This sure is somethin'. Nothin' much out of the ordinary happens for years and then all of a sudden everything is going crazy. Reminds me of the Army . . ."

"Wiley wanted me to come in with him when he came to see you, Sela. I see why now. He needed me to protect him when he told you about the piki. But I'm glad he came by. That man who took off with those drug people flagged me down at the foot of the hill—practically made me run him over. I guess he thought I was local. And it was Homer Keams on guard duty tonight and he knows me from before . . . I was scared myself till Wiley came."

Wiley's chest was puffing out at the mention of his unintentional heroism, but his eyes were darting shiftily toward the door.

"I think Grandfather will be okay," Sela said. "If not, I got several neighbors who work at the hospital. They can help. Wiley, why don't you take Nicki out there to where her friend is? And while you're at it, will you see what's keeping Uncle Carl? He can't still be working out there and it's getting late."

"I can't. I—uh—someone's waiting for me. But I can tell you where it is, Nicki." He told her and drew a little map on the floor with a wet finger. And got up to leave.

"Wiley?" Nicki asked, holding up her arms.

"Oh—uh—yeah, excuse me." He picked her up and carried her to her truck and was gone before she had buckled herself in. Sela waved good-bye as Nicki turned her truck around. Wiley wasn't in the plaza anywhere. Where could he have gone and who could he have had waiting for him?

"Close the door, girl! It's cold in here!" Grandfather said.

Sela went back inside and closed the door.

"You didn't even introduce me to that pretty woman," Grandfather complained.

TWENTY-TWO

AFTER RIDING ALL over Hopiland and checking all the hotels, Raydir returned for the night to the only place that Cindy had been, the Rainbird. He was exhausted after riding all day, confused, lonely. He was always lonely without Cindy these days. He told himself she wasn't his type really, that he could get along without her. She was too straight. But she was the only one who didn't seem to want to own a piece of him, and the only one who already had a piece for the taking. She was trying to ride out of his life and he couldn't stand it. Whatever it took to keep her, he was going to try.

He fell asleep, as he had many nights after a concert, with his clothes on. This time it was weariness, not drugs or booze, that led him to pass out before he could brush his teeth and say his prayers or even grab his teddy. Not to mention removing his leathers and boots.

So he was a little surprised to wake only a couple of hours later, to the sound of a flute tootling upstairs, footsteps scraping and tapping around up there.

The player was a pretty good musician—better than Carlos Nakai maybe. Raydir found he couldn't drop back off while the flutist kept playing and decided he'd either go upstairs and tell him to knock it off or see if maybe they couldn't jam together. Hey! Maybe, if the guy was Native American, they could get him to do backup or a guest spot for the gig. That'd probably add a lot of political correctitude to the whole thing.

He stepped outside and looked up to see the room number and saw, at first, only sky. And snow. Lots of snow. In fact, three or four inches of it covered the courtyard between the rooms. The playing had stopped as soon as he opened the door. But while he was deciding what to do, a shadowy form appeared just beyond the edge of the roof.

"Hey, man, you've got a good set of chops there," he told the flute player.

The guy came closer to the edge. Looked like he was wearing some of those—whaddayacallem, antenna things, deely-bobbers, and a backpack that gave him a Quasimodo-type hump. Probably some stoned college kid, but he sure could play. "Thanks, I appreciate that coming from you. You're not so bad yourself, Raydir."

"You recognized me?"

"Sure! I hear most of your stuff out here, sooner or later, on the radio or someone's boom box."

"Well, hey, how about that. You sure are one hot player. I wonder if you could teach me a few licks sometime?"

"No problemo."

"Listen, I was kinda wondering, since you're so good, if maybe you might do a guest spot. Uh—are you like a real Native American?"

"Well—I guess you could say that. I've been here a long, long time. As for the guest spot, I don't know. I'm not much for the spotlight, y'know? But I might kick in with a few riffs now and then."

"Cool. I'll have my people get you a contract. You can sign when you show up."

"I don't do contracts, man. Just give me some cash and we'll be square."

"Well, I've only got a little on me. Would a couple hundred be okay?"

"Super. Just leave it on the ground there." There were footsteps on the roof and a beautiful wooden flute appeared on the edge, though the snow was swirling so hard Raydir couldn't see much of the person on the other end, just a shadow. "You take this now and I'll teach you a few things."

Maybe the hotel census was way low that night, or maybe the place was well soundproofed, but nobody seemed to hear the flute player except Raydir, and even after he started jamming with the guy, nobody seemed to hear him either. He started to hand the flute back when the fellow finally said Raydir had learned enough and it was time to call it quits. The guy said he wouldn't take it now, though. That Raydir would need it.

And just as Raydir was turning to go to bed, he saw two men and three horses galloping through the snow across the mesa in back of the hotel.

On an impulse, he walked out back and tootled a tune the flutist had taught him. The horses stopped, and the riderless white horse jerked its head sharply, pulling its reins from the hand of one of the riders.

The One Who Is Also a Wolf is running widdershins around the hogan of the failed witch. He is running widdershins around the hogan one time. He is running widdershins around the hogan a second time. He is running widdershins around it a third time, his feet leaving paw marks in the snow, his running paws leaving tracks in the snow. He is running around it a fourth time. Now the house is afire. Now the house is consumed by fire. Now blue flames are spouting from the roof of the house. Now red flames are spouting from the east-facing door of the house. Now white flames are running across the floor of the house. Now yellow flames are caving in the western wall of the house, where the window once looked out on the pastures full of sheep. Where Alice Begay used to watch her sheep. And in ruin the house is caving in. In ugliness the house is destroyed. In sorrow the house crumbles to ashes. In pain the beloved house is no more.

The One Who Is Also a Wolf sees the house of the sister who should have died. He goes over there. The big house is made of cinderblocks and the outside will not burn. The inside will. An old car is parked in front of the house. Smoke plumes from the chimney of the house.

The witch licks his big mouth, slavering. Human beings are within the house. A sacrifice will be made after all.

Running on four paws, he turns the car into flames in the same fashion as he turned Alice Begay's hogan into flames.

Running around the storage hogan, he turns it into flames in a likewise manner.

For the house, he must turn himself back into a man. He is a naked man, carrying a burning log from the storage hogan and bracing it against the door. He is standing there, a naked man, with a branch in his hand. He is standing there, a naked man with a branch reaching for the fire consuming the car. He is standing there with a flaming branch. He is standing there, breaking the window with the flaming branch and throwing it at the loom that stands against one wall.

The wool bursts into flames and he hears a child cry out. He licks his mouth again and waits for them to try to escape.

"Who the hell is that?" Mike asked, looking back at the black-leather-clad guy who had joined them. He looked a little Indian, maybe Cherokee or something, but sure not Navajo. Not Hopi either. He was riding the white horse. Bareback. He was playing it a tune on his flute.

"How should I know?" Wiley asked.

The stranger looked up from his playing, took the flute from his mouth and said, "Cool horses."

"What do we do now?" Mike asked. "Some stoned-out musician is horning in on our—uh—"

"You don't think it's a coincidence, do you?" the voice in his ear said. "No more than Wiley deciding to ask Sela for the piki when he did. The flute player is supposed to be here. Don't interfere."

Mike shrugged. "She says he stays," he told Wiley.

"Good," Wiley said. "It'll be like in the movies, with our own theme music playing. Hey, do you take requests?"

"Not tonight, man," the flute player mumbled, and returned to playing the piece that had summoned the white horse to him.

They rode on through the snowstorm, over the back of the mesas, Mike on the blue horse, Wiley on the black horse, the stranger playing flute on the white horse, until they came to the road that led off to Hamish Secakuku's wannabe golf course and resort.

"I got a question," Wiley said.

"Yeah?"

"How do we get back once we return the horses?"

"Maybe Secakuku will be so grateful we brought back his property he'll put us up for the night," Mike said optimistically.

"Yeah, and maybe he'll know what happened and shoot you in the ass again," Wiley replied.

"That is very likely to happen," the voice in Mike's ear said. "Just put the horses back where you found them. The Secakukus will not wake up while you're here."

That was what the men did. They put the horses back in their stalls, brushed them down, gave them hay and checked their water buckets, because Mike insisted that they do so, and then they walked back to the road.

"Hm," Mike said, looking right and left and hoping the voice in his ear would make a suggestion. The road was just a slight indentation from the sides now, the snow swooping across the desert in a smooth white coat. Only the tops of the bushes broke the evenness, and even they drooped under loads of snow.

"Wow, it's sure pretty out here, isn't it?" the flute player said, sticking his instrument in his jacket.

"Yeah," Mike said.

Wiley started walking down the road in the opposite direction from which they'd come.

"You're going the wrong way," Mike said.

"Oh, yeah? Well, I happen to know that Sela's Uncle Carl has property just a little ways down this road and that beyond that is the house where Dr. Chee's aunties live. I also know, if anybody had bothered to ask me, that Nicki Bedonie, Dr. Chee's friend, is going to be pulling up in her four-wheel-drive pickup to take Maria back to the hospital to see her auntie, who is calling for her. Even if we miss a ride with Nicki, we could stay in that nice warm house for the night and walk back in daylight." He stopped and said, "I bet there's even some groceries there. I'm sure hungry."

"Yeah, and I could use some more sleep," Mike said. "Somehow, I don't think I got my beauty rest out here last night when you guys abandoned me."

"I came back for you," Wiley said.

"Hey, either one of you guys seen a gorgeous blond chick on a horse around here?" the flute player asked. He seemed to be under the impression he was in a dream, or maybe he was under some kind of spell or something, Mike thought. Maybe that's what Grandmother meant by him being here. He sure wasn't acting normally for a guy caught on foot in a snowstorm with two strangers.

Maria heard the child cry first and heard the window break. She opened her eyes and was about to run to the children, when something hurtled through the window, and Aunt Martha's loom with the beautiful half-finished rug still on it went up in flames.

"Mama!" Dezi and Anabah screamed at the same time.

Cindy had stretched out her sleeping bag beneath the window. Maria couldn't see her for the smoke. She hoped she hadn't been cut to pieces by the flying glass. There was so much smoke, for just the loom fire. Maria covered her face with her shirttail and crawled through the smoke, cutting herself on the broken glass littering the floor, to the children's cot. "Get down, kids, get down. Cindy? Cindy, can you hear me? Open the door. Get some more air in here!"

And then, beyond the smoky pall, outside the window she saw the ball of flame that had been her car, and she knew someone was trying to murder them. And might succeed.

Cindy screamed back, coughing, "I can't. It's locked."

"Push hard! They don't have a lock!" Maria yelled, but the flames crackled like a factory full of popping bubble wrap and the children were screaming at the top of their lungs. Thank God the brand that had hit Aunt Martha's loom hadn't hit the cot instead. Damn those Hopis. Just when she was beginning to think that some of them still had some sense, they went to this extreme to try to get rid of her poor aunts.

Cindy had abandoned the door and threw the basin of wash water at the loom. The fire had spread only a little, to the wool

nearby, but wool fumes were pretty toxic. She was stamping
and coughing and falling.

Beyond the broken window, something half-laughed, half-
howled, a sound more chilling than the snowstorm and louder
than the fire.

Another brand flew through the window and this time it did
get the cot. Maria gathered the children in her arms and
crawled to the window. Cindy crawled over beside her.

"We can't go outside," Maria hissed. "There's someone
here, waiting to get us. I heard him. It."

Cindy coughed. "We can't stay here. The smoke will kill us."

She picked up her sleeping bag. Glass rattled to the floor.
Maria could hardly see what she was doing. Her eyes were
streaming and her nose and throat burning. The girls were
coughing piteously, unable to scream anymore.

Cindy pulled over the chair that was close to the window,
climbed up on it, her sleeping bag in front of her, and plunged
through the toothy maw of broken glass.

Cindy had intended to shove her sleeping bag back through
the window for Maria and the girls but there was no time. She
had landed against something and knocked it over backwards,
but now it was ripping the bag away from her. A full set of
razor-sharp claws tore through her jacket and something
snarled as she backed up against the cinderblock building.

Her eyes were streaming too and she could barely breathe,
much less fight the teeth and fangs that ripped at her when the
protection of the shredded sleeping bag was gone.

She kicked and bit and clawed herself, and was dimly
aware of the sound of a car horn blaring steadily above the
crackling fire and the snarling beast whose saliva burnt her
skin as its fangs dove for her throat.

Carl had been lying in the snow, half-frozen, having pleasant
dreams of being very warm, when the blare of a car horn and
the smell of smoke shocked him back to reality.

The cold had numbed him enough that he couldn't feel the
lump on his head where he'd been struck. He had no time to
wonder about that.

Alice Begay's hogan was ablaze, and by looks of the smoke and flame, so was her sister's place. Carl hauled himself into his truck and tried to start it. It was cold. Too cold. He tried again and again; while the smoke rose he heard screams over the blaring car horn, and some kind of animal sounds coming from over there.

Just as he was about to abandon the truck, it leaped to life and he threw it in gear. It plowed through the snow, but stuck by the fence in front of Alice Begay's hogan, now just a pile of embers and kindling. Down the road, a car was on fire and he made out two figures struggling. The other hogan down there was on fire too.

He half-walked, half-skiied down the hill, struggling to keep his balance and not end up out of control and colliding with the burning car. Instead he collided with something snarling, smelly and furry, and held onto it to keep his balance while he kicked the living daylights out of whatever it was.

Beyond it he saw a hank of black-streaked blond hair and Cindy Ellis's bloodied and frightened face. She picked up what looked like a sleeping bag and threw it over the head of the critter Carl had hold of—and also covered Carl's head so that he had to shake the bag off. The creature jerked itself free and turned on him.

He fell backwards and scrambled beyond the burning car. The damn thing ought to be exploding any minute, as soon as the fire hit the gas tank. He got to his feet and ran, and the thing he had been fighting dropped to all fours and bounded after him. It struck him and he doubled up and rolled away, off the road, just as a truck came barreling down the hill and caught the thing's head under a wheel.

The truck kept rolling, hitting the burning car, driving it back twenty or thirty feet beyond the house.

The face behind the wheel was terrified, but the driver threw the truck into reverse and backed up the hill just as the car exploded.

Carl doubled over and burrowed into the snow to protect himself. Flaming debris dropped onto his back and he rolled in the snow again to put it out.

If he were going to have combat flashbacks, this would

 have been a good time to do it, he thought, except that they hadn't had a whole lot of snow in Nam. Not in the part he was in, anyway.

He crawled to the thing and pulled it by the foot out from under the blazing sleeping bag and the burning car. The creature was on its stomach and Carl rolled it over. He stared at it, fell backwards onto his butt and sat rocking for a moment, looking at it.

Cindy had meanwhile extricated Maria and the children from the house. Maria was keeping the kids behind her, and standing well back.

"Maria, what is it?" the driver of the truck called as she drove in closer. Carl recognized her now. This was the Navajo girl who had been living with Sam Joseph's son. Sam was a client of Carl's. Nicki had been introduced to him once when Carl went to Sam's house to try to calm him down when he was on a bender. "Did I kill it?" Nicki asked.

"Looks like it," Maria answered.

Cindy Ellis knelt beside him and put her hand on his shoulder. "Do you know who he is—was?" she asked Carl.

"Yeah. He moved out here after being fired as some kind of official for the Navajos. Name of Wallace something or other."

"Wallace Curley? Is that *him*?" Maria asked, edging closer. "Jeez, he used to be the energy resources director for the Navajo Nation. I remember reading about him getting fired in the *Navajo Times*. He was taking all kinds of stuff in exchange for favors to the mining companies."

"Looks like he didn't stop doing that," Carl said, reaching out with a foot to prod the corpse.

Anabah was looking around Maria's legs. Her eyes were huge. Dezbah's face was just above hers. She reached up and tugged at Maria's sleeve. "Mom, that guy was like a werewolf, huh?"

Maria said, "Of course not. There's no such—well, actually, sort of, Dezi. People don't like to talk about it, though. He's what our people would call a skinwalker—a Navajo witch."

"No, Mom. Witches have pointy hats and cast spells. It'
werewolves who get all hairy and attack people."

Anabah stepped forward, as if to examine the body. The
snow was still falling, the flakes melting as they touched the
corpse. The explosion had scattered the fire. The crackling o
what was a dying blaze, the sizzle of snowflakes and the
steady thrum of the truck's engine were all that could be heard
for a moment. Everybody was kind of frozen, it seemed to
Carl—like the weather.

The little girl took another step and the truck half-drove
half-slid back down the hill toward them. Nicki cried, "Anabah, go back!"

Dezbah tackled the other child and tugged her away from
the body. Anabah screeched, screamed, and began to cry a
the top of her lungs.

"Navajos!" Carl said in a disgusted way. "He's not going to
hurt the little girl *now,* lady," he said to Nicki. To Cindy he
said, "They have this religious thing about dead bodies."

"Yeah," said Nicki, who was in earshot now. "Especially
witches. Don't think you're going to put that in *my* truck."

Carl looked at her. She blurred a little. "No," he heard himself say in a voice that sounded even to him as if it were coming from miles away. "The police will want us to leave it here
We'll . . ." He suddenly felt as if he'd been hit all over again
and he sat back down in the snow, holding his head in his
hands.

Cindy knelt beside him, asking, "Carl, are you okay?"

It could have been one of those Kodak moments maybe
but then three men ran down the hill from what was left of
Alice's place, and one of them hollered, "Babe! There you
are! Oh, man! What the hell happened here?"

TWENTY-THREE

THE SNOW STOPPED falling and Nicki's and Carl's trucks, both loaded with passengers, convoyed back up the mesa to the highway, and on down to the hospital. Carl stopped on the way to collect Sela and his father and have them checked, after Nicki and Wiley told him about what had happened to them.

Maria had herself and the others treated for smoke inhalation and went straight to her aunt Martha's room. The bed was stripped and empty.

Then a sweet little old lady dressed peculiarly in what seemed to be a mixture of Hopi and Navajo traditional dress came over and said, "You're looking for your aunties?"

"Yes."

"Oh, they were moved so they could be together," the little old lady said, leading them to a six-bed open ward. Only the first two beds were occupied. Oddly, she was carrying a spindle in her hand.

Aunt Martha was sitting up in bed but to Maria's surprise, Aunt Alice was lying down, hooked to a monitor and an IV. She looked as if she'd been in pain, but her respirations were strong and steady and when Maria took her pulse, she found it was strong and steady, too.

Maria couldn't bear to tell her about the house yet but Aunt Martha sniffed at the smoke in her clothes and asked, "What happened?"

The little old lady who had shown her to their bedsides said, "Go ahead, tell them."

When Maria finished telling of what had happened at and to their houses, the aunts were clutching each other's hands.

Their eyes shone with tears. "That bad one is *dead,* Alice," Martha said, referring obliquely to the witch. "You won't have to die now."

"Excuse me?" Maria said. "Did I miss something?"

Martha said, "When one of *them* dies, the spell is broken. That one is dead. The wind he had blown into Alice made her want to hurt me. She tried but by the time you came, she was sorry. Grandmother"—she nodded to where the old lady had been but when Maria turned she saw no one—"sat with me and helped me through the night because she knew I didn't want to die so that Alice would not be able to be a witch. But because she had ill-wished me, when I began to get better because of Grandmother, Alice began to sicken. Once you killed *that* one though, the evil went away and Alice will recover."

"But Aunt Alice's house is gone."

"She can live with me. That way she won't have to sign the lease paper. I will sign it and we will live where we've always lived, thanks to you and your friends and that Hopi. You say my house was not hurt too bad, just the shed."

"And my car. But we're all alive and we'll get through it somehow."

The elders backed out of the little cave near the spring containing their shrine. Carl could see in their faces that the shrine had been destroyed like so many others. He didn't know who had done it, of course. The witch didn't live far from here, but ordinary people did evil things too. The elders were shaking their heads. This was all very hard for them to understand. Who would do such a thing?

It was made harder because they lacked some of the proper materials for replenishing the shrines. The drought had killed many of the medicine plants and earlier in the year, the Navajos had denied the Hopis their god-given right to collect live eagles and raise them for the ceremonial feathers.

They trudged back sadly to the road where they had left the truck. To get here they had had to cross property occupied by some of the Navajos who didn't want to leave.

An old woman came out of the hogan they passed on their way back. She yelled something at Carl, something he didn't understand. He felt like yelling back in Hopi, but reckoned that she probably had enough troubles. Then three young men came out and one of them said in English, "My grandma wants to know if you're the Hopi that killed the person who burned down Alice Begay's house."

"I didn't kill him," Carl said. "I just tried to keep him from killing other people. He was hit by a car."

"Whatever," the kid said, and said something to the old woman. "My grandma says if you and your grandfathers are tired, you should come in and rest. When she saw you go by this morning, she made enough breakfast for everyone."

Carl didn't know what to say. It was the last thing he'd expected. "Just a minute," he said. "I'll ask the elders." He addressed the older men in Hopi and they answered that maybe it would be a bad thing to refuse something so rarely extended these days as Navajo hospitality to Hopis.

He nodded to the woman and her grandsons and he and the elders went inside and ate with them.

When the conversation, conducted mostly in English, was finished, the young men lined up like schoolboys under their grandmother's watchful eye.

"My grandma says to tell you that it is very wrong of you Hopis to want to drive us from our land," one of the young men said. "We were angry and we tore up your stuff up there," and being young, he pointed rather than did the Navajo lip twist, toward the shrine. "But when we heard that even though you and Alice Begay had caused trouble for each other, you helped her when her home and family was attacked, my grandma decided that you were a pretty good guy. That maybe you wouldn't do like they've been saying and dig up our dead—"

Carl shook his head. "That's not how *we* do things."

"No, well. Anyway, we tore up your stuff—your holy stuff, and we want to do something to make it up." They brought out four boxes, one for each boy and one for the mother. The boxes were full of eagle feathers. Carl thought perhaps some had been in the shrine, but others seemed newly acquired. "Please ask your elders if they will accept these."

* * *

By the time Maria was able to get some sleep, it was well after midnight and she had been up almost forty straight hours. After all that had happened, her uppermost thought was oddly enough how relieved she was that the x-ray technician had returned from her mourning in time for the most recent catastrophe. Not that she was needed. Maria was just glad to have her handy again.

Most of the injuries had been minor. She was able to re-lease Carl, Sela and Grandfather Loloma to go back home once their bruises, lacerations, and other wounds were daubed with antiseptic and bandaged. Tetanus shots were had by all and antibiotics when necessary. Nicki also returned home to be with her children. She was still shaking and talking a mile a minute, having something of a delayed shock reaction from the whole incident. She had taken a bad jolt when her truck hit the car, but the truck was okay and she didn't seem to be any worse.

The doctor on call for night shift was a Zuni, who said that the more ranting he heard from Nakai about Maria's uncoop-erative antics in the government hospital system, the more he had been dying to meet her. They worked together well, but poor Maria was exhausted, as were the children, Mike, Cindy, and Wiley. Raydir, who was the most alert of all, gave Maria's shoulder a sympathetic pat when he saw her yawning and, from the look on Cindy's face, surprised her by noticing how beat everyone was.

"You're all friends of my lady," he said. "And the roads are bad tonight. Stay at the hotel with us." And so they did. None was more glad than Maria.

Wiley was up early the next morning, however, and the slick roads did not keep him from being at Sela's in time for breakfast. He had not slept as well as he usually did, for his dreams were full of hungry coyotes. To his relief, Carl had al-ready left on business involving his clan elders. Still, Wiley hardly enjoyed his breakfast for watching Sela, how her arm moved, how she had to try to rotate it at the shoulder because it was so stiff, how large the bruises were when her sweater rode up on her wrist.

She noticed his regard but this time she was not touched.

"If you're wondering if I can make your piki this morning, no I can't. Piki is a lot of work. If you want piki so much, you can make it yourself."

"But—"

Grandfather was half-outraged, half-amused. "A Navajo boy making piki? Maybe the world is ending even sooner than we believed."

But Sela said, "Look, you're the great piki-machine sales-man. I'll help you and tell you what to do but you have to do all the hard work, because I can't."

She showed him how to grease the stone with watermelon seed oil and other things. He would never have guessed about the watermelon seed oil, though. And she showed him how, once he had taken the first piki from the stone and spread the second film of batter across in its place, he should take the first layer and put it across the one that was cooking, to keep it soft and pliant. By the end of the day, his arms were aching too and he only had about half the piki he figured he needed to feed all those coyotes.

"It's not enough," he said, rotating *his* shoulders to lessen the aches.

"Who are these relatives of yours?" she asked. "They all seem even hungrier than you!"

"You won't believe me," he said.

"Well, sometimes it's best that I don't, but I can usually tell when you're not telling me the truth, so go ahead, try me."

He told her. She laughed and said, "Oh, Wiley, only you would have that kind of a family reunion," and hugged him.

And they kept making piki. "I was right," he said finally. "This is an awful lot of work. You could simplify it by using corn oil on an electric grill heated to the right temperature, and use a premixed batter, maybe just use the regular kind of corn that's easy to get and have it dehydrated and ground in-stead of that long process you Hopis use and . . ."

"Wiley, I think you should definitely try to make some piki that way," Sela said. "And then you bring it over and you have some of yours and you have some of mine and you tell me what you think."

He didn't have to do that to know what she meant. Hers would be much better. "But Sela," he said. "I only wanted to make it for rich Anglos who won't know the difference."

"And then everyone will think Hopi piki tastes like the stuff you make? And they will think we're crazy or something to have that sort of thing as part of our diet. No, Wiley. Maybe the grill is a good idea but if you do it, you must do it right."

"Oh," he said, discouraged. "Well, I guess we better keep on if I'm going to have enough for tonight."

"I guess you'd better," Sela said. "You know how now. I have some studying to do. If you break my stone, I will feed you the pieces. Call me if you have any questions."

That was how at least one time Badger made Coyote do his own work.

But later on, that night, though there was no moon to howl at, Wiley howled and was answered. From the four directions came the sixteen coyotes to devour sixteen heaping platters of piki.

When the coyotes had gone, Wiley became aware of an old woman and an old man standing behind the pueblo in the darkness, watching him.

"Who are you?" he asked.

"Pardon us," the man said, "but when my sister and I heard the howling out on the mesa, we wondered why so many of our relations were crowding in so close to people tonight. Who are *you* that they come when you call and you feed them plates of piki?"

Wiley didn't mind people knowing, except that they'd think he was crazy, or say mean things about coyotes, so he told them about how he had been found at Smiley's trading post with no clue to his parentage and how he had always had this animal spirit and how he went to live with his Mormon mother and father and how his animal spirit got him in trouble and so he moved back to the reservation, and how he had been told to summon the coyotes to get back some horses a "friend" had "lost." He *did* mind telling the whole truth about that part, of course.

"Come closer," the man said. "In fact, come back with us to our place. There's something we'd like to show you."

They showed him a picture of their sister, who had run away with a Navajo at an early age, after which they never saw her again.

"She told us once before she ran off that her Navajo man was from over there where you were found," the sister said. "One of our cousins saw her in town one day and said she was going to have a kid, but we never heard another thing."

"Maybe you're the kid," the man said.

Wiley studied the picture. She was a fine-looking girl, with a thinner face and a leaner build than many Hopis, he thought. A bit on the skinny side, actually, just as he was. Just as, come to think of it, his host and hostess were. He held the picture closer to the light, and saw in her eyes the same animal spirit he saw in his own and had seen in the eyes of that first coyote relative.

"Yesss," the sister was saying. "I think so. I think you are our nephew. Are you sure you're Navajo?"

"I'm not sure of anything," he said. "Except that my relatives are coyotes."

"*We* are Coyote Clan and so was our sister, so you would be too if you're her child. You would also be Hopi, since it's the mother's side that counts," the man said.

"This is a happy occasion," said his sister. "We should have something nice to eat to celebrate. Are you two hungry?"

"I'm *always* hungry," the two men said together.

By the time Carl had finished escorting the elders to the shrines, it was late afternoon, but there was still time to leave for a professional conference he had been wanting to attend in Zuni. He was very weary, but also wired, in a strange sort of way, and felt more need to keep moving than he did for sleep.

He seldom stopped for hitchhikers when he was traveling these days, but when he saw the little old lady standing beside the highway on the way to Jeddito, he realized there was something disturbingly familiar about her. He stopped.

When she got in, he recognized her for who she was at once. "Grandmother!" he said. "Why were you hitchhiking? Where are you going?"

"I want to go visit my grandchildren in the New Lands," she said. "Do you mind turning off at Ganado and taking me as far as Chambers?"

"I'll take you wherever you wish to go," he said. The Zuni conference was important but this grandmother was an extremely important being. He would telephone from the trading post and tell them that if he made it at all, he would be late.

She patted his cheek. "You're a good boy, Carl."

That same night was the night of the concert. The weather had warmed again and most of the snow was gone. Raydir left before noon, roaring up the highway toward Tuba City. He'd called the bus cell phones from the hotel and learned that all hell had broken loose in his absence.

"Well, hey, I'm sorry about that, buddy, but I had stuff to do and I didn't want to be bothered," Cindy had overheard him say on the phone. "Belinda was stupid. Belinda *is* stupid. For one thing, it's in my best interests to keep the band clean and out of trouble. For another, she should know enough to figure out who she's talking to before she asks for something like that. *I'm* not paying her bail. Let her parents do it."

When he got off the phone, he ran both hands through his hair repeatedly. "I can't believe it," he said. "I can't effing believe the stupidity of some people."

"Why?" Cindy asked. She was oiling the leather on her tack, polishing the bridle, getting ready to resume her ride now that Chaco had turned up again in Hamish's stable along with the other missing horses, much to everyone's surprise. "What happened?"

"The dumb bitch Belinda started demanding drugs for the band from the concert organizers almost as soon as she got off the bus. I mean, I was pretty sure she'd been using but I didn't think she was anywhere *near* that far gone. Turns out the emcee is not only a pro-Dineh activist but also an anti-drug activist. A Hopi Traditionalist friend of his had told him about some creeps who were cruising the rez out here, trading art work for drugs with the kids. One of her friends died from an allergic reaction to some of their stuff. He got a description, got the Navajo Nation cops to wire him, and went looking for the people she described. He had them tracked up to your buddy Carl's house and if he hadn't hijacked that girl Nicki's truck, they would have done serious bodily harm to Carl's niece and her granddad. He and that Nicki and for some reason, that skinny kid Loloma's niece goes with, all turned up at once. He was afraid the Lolomas and Wiley would call out the village and have the dealers arrested before everything they needed to be charged with could be made to stick. So he got them out of there, took them up to Tuba, and got Belinda to negotiate her deal for the band. The cops closed in, the dealers and half my crew and band got busted, including Belinda, and I'm supposed to go bail."

"At least they got the dealers," Cindy said.

"Sure. I bet they made bail before the key was turned in the lock. Anyway, I gotta figure out how to play this with only half my people, babe, so I need to boogie on back up to Tuba. Coming with me?"

"Not right now. I'll come later with Maria and her daughter and aunts and Nicki and her kids. Mike Blackgoat said he'd give me a lift out to pick up Chaco. I think he just wants to see Maria again, though."

"Yeah. I can relate," Raydir said with a sad glance in Cindy's direction. "How about us, babe? What do you think?" He sat down on the bed beside her.

Cindy polished her bridle thoughtfully. "I think I need to be part of something real, Ray, not just attached to a collection of people too screwed up to do anything but hang out with each other and pretend they're important because they know someone they think is. I thought when we got together things would be different, that you realized Sno needed you and that you needed me."

"I *do*," he began, but she put her finger to his lips.

"You need to figure out your priorities. You're richer than God, but you don't do anything but pay to be surrounded by people who do stupid stuff like what Belinda just pulled. There are real people with real problems out here, Ray."

"I know, I *know*. Why do you think I agreed to play this concert?"

She looked him straight in the eye. "To try to get me back. But you didn't even know what this was all about first, Ray. You just believed what you were told and jumped in. You're a smart man, a talented man. You've got a kind of magic about you that makes people want to follow you. But you piss it away."

"I know, babe," he said, cupping her face in his hand. "And I'm trying. But I'm just a guy."

"Yes," she said patiently. "But you're just a guy who employs half the music industry in the Seattle area. And furthermore, you live with them and they don't want you to live with me as well."

He scratched the back of his head and said, "Well, yeah, I been thinking about that. You're right. I don't need to live with them. It's been a disaster for Sno, and frankly, it ain't that easy staying straight with so many people around who'd rather see me fucked up, y'know what I mean?"

She nodded.

"And I knew you were unhappy. I didn't know why. But this about tears it for me. Look, there's a place on Vashon Island for sale—nice little farmhouse, room for our horses—yours and mine and Sno's. Pretty good horse community there too, I understand. There'd be our own dock too and I could just tie the boat up over there and leave a car in Seattle—maybe pour a helipad, and we wouldn't need to live at the studio anymore. I think I might call my old buddy Folsom who built a terrific studio in his basement and get him to do something like that for me. Just for practice sessions. I'll keep the main stuff in Seattle. But we can unload that place and get something we can run ourselves—maybe with a couple of people *you* pick." He gave her a kiss. "You're the lady of my house and that's the way I want it. And just to make it perfectly clear—wanna get married before we move over there?"

Part of her wanted to shout "Yes!" and dance around the room, but the other, more cautious part, knew that there was a lot of difference between a plan formed in a desert hotel room and reality back in Seattle. "Let's see how things go," she said finally.

"They'll go great, baby, just you wait. Your wish will be my command." He made a silly bow. "Don't think of me as just another Prince Charming, my lady, think of me as Merlin the magician. You say the word and"—he waved an imaginary wand—"zip zip—or bibbity bobbity whatever, it's yours." He grinned, suddenly and slyly, walked over to where he'd hung his jacket and pulled out a flute. "Speaking of magic," he said. "Did I tell you what happened here the night I showed up? No, wait, let me play you something first. Did you know that Indian guys used to play the flute to get power over women?" He wiggled his eyebrows up and down, and leered at her.

"Like Kokopelli?" she asked.

"Who?"

"The humpbacked flute player who helped the Hopis get past the guardian of the Fourth World." She held up a battered copy of *The Book of the Hopi* from her bedside stand. "I borrowed a book from Carl."

"Carl, huh?" he asked, and raised the flute to his lips and played a melody totally unlike anything she'd ever heard before, from him or anyone else. Haunting, sensual, full of loneliness and longing, it spoke to every hope and dream she had had for the two of them. Her head was trying to remain skeptical but her heart and body had it outnumbered.

Sometime later, Raydir kissed her bare shoulder. "It works, huh?" and began pulling on his clothes.

He left not long after that.

Mike arrived in his pickup a short time later to take Cindy to Hamish's. In the seat beside him was a big baking pan with heavenly smells coming from it. Cindy's stomach rumbled.

"Have you eaten?" Mike asked. "I got some reeeal good banana bread in there. Talked the girl at the grocery store out of some bananas she was going to throw away and got Nicki Bedonie to show me how to make it."

"Banana bread? Really?"

"Yeah, you can have a piece. I made it for Maria, to help out with the party her aunts' friends are putting on for them. Later on, there'll be a real ceremony, with a medicine man and all but this time they're just going to have a party."

They got to where the checkpoint had been, but it wasn't

there today. Closer to Hamish's, Mike suddenly said, "I want to buy your horse."

"What?"

"I got four hundred dollars and I want to buy your horse. The blue one."

"Why?"

Mike said, "It's kind of a long story. And you might get mad at me. I'd rather tell you after you get him and we are away from Secakuku's place. But what do you say? Would you sell him?"

"He's not mine, really, but I could always call Hank and ask. I'm not sure he'd sell. He really wanted that horse for a trail ride he wants to do. And I think Chaco's worth more than four hundred dollars."

"Oh, he is. But how about if I not only paid him that but got him a really good deal on an even better horse for his trail ride than Chaco? A real reservation pony, trained for the rodeo. Real smart. You think getting in on something like that would be worth some money to him?"

Cindy smiled. "I don't know. He's a horse trader. Hard telling."

But when she noticed how Chaco greeted Mike, and the look in Mike's eyes when he ran his hand down the horse's face, she knew a team when she saw one. She thanked Hamish and paid him, and rode Chaco off his property and down the road, then stopped and signaled Mike to stop.

"Listen," she said. "You want to ride him and I'll drive?" He looked cautious, almost scared and she added, "Don't worry. If Hank doesn't go for your trade, I'm sure we can work out something."

"It's not that. It's just my truck is kinda temperamental. I'm not sure you can handle it."

But she did.

TWENTY-FOUR

PEOPLE TURNED UP at Martha Tsosie's house the next day raving about the concert. No one knew who the anonymous accompanist was who backed Raydir up on his new accoustic solos, but everyone agreed they had never heard anything more enchanting.

Cindy and Raydir had their arms around each other all during the party, except for when they were eating.

Mike's banana bread was a huge hit with Maria, and she kept looking speculatively at him all day.

Some of the Navajo Nation Tribal Council members attended the concert and were invited to the party as well. Maria had a chance to talk to some of the women on the council and found that they'd had much the same experience as she with the male powermongers among their own people. One woman in particular told her that Nakai had totally exceeded his authority in putting her on leave and interfering with the way a doctor did her job. She would go back to Window Rock and speak to her friends in the Indian Health Service. Mr. Nakai might soon find himself in someplace even more remote than Keams Canyon.

Nicki Bedonie arrived and asked Maria for a private word. "Since I—uh—hit that thing with my truck, you know? I been getting these feelings—pains I guess you'd say—in my back and legs," she said. Maria could see that Nicki was having to fight to sound casual about it.

"You *have*?"

"Yeah. I wonder, do you think I hurt myself worse or maybe—maybe—I haven't had any feeling down there in years . . ." Of course she hadn't. She was paraplegic. She shouldn't be feeling anything there, unless . . .

Maria did a couple of reflex tests and looked at Nicki, trying to keep her face from revealing the hope that she felt. "I can't tell from just a cursory exam like this. You should go into Flag and have some tests done, but, well, you said your original injury was a pinched nerve. Maybe something got jarred loose . . ."

Wiley brought Sela and also a Hopi couple Maria hadn't met, whom he introduced as his relatives.

Martha and Alice showed pictures of their new grand-and-godchild, baby Ninabah, Anabah's new little sister. As soon as Ninabah was old enough to be away from her mother, Jenny, for a while, Jenny was going back to work while Jimmie checked into a rehab clinic, the aunts had told Maria.

Milt Highwater and Sela's friend Shirley came later in the day, swaggering around like Mulder and Scully.

Raydir came up to Milt and said, "Man, I hope you know I had nothing to do with any of that drug stuff—"

Milt gave him one of Mulder's piercing looks and said, in a law-enforcement voice worthy of that same character, "We believe you, Mr. Quantrill. We got the folks who did. The couple who assaulted the Lolomas and were responsible for the death of Shirl's friend Joey are wanted by Interpol in several countries for terrorism and on drug-related charges. We found that out after we first placed them under arrest, and fortunately, after they had called two MEE executives, an Edward Abercrombie and Micah Firestone, to post bail for them. We confronted them with the Interpol charges while they were waiting for the MEE men to arrive. Whereupon the couple claimed the attack on the Lolomas was part of a conspiracy instigated by Mr. Abercrombie and Mr. Firestone on behalf of MEE. Mr. Abercrombie and Mr. Firestone were taken into custody when they came to post bail and have joined their co-conspirators. They attempted to have MEE post bail for them, but the company refused, disclaiming any knowledge of their activities. There will be further investigation, you can bet, but meanwhile the four people we have in custody will be looking at spending some time in beautiful Leavenworth, Kansas, enjoying accommodations courtesy of the United States Government. With Hopi, Navajo, and Lakota lobbyists all paying very close attention to the fate of these particular prisoners, they *will* be denied parole until they're all too old and shaky to hold a syringe."

"The same may go for your secretary, or whatever she was," Shirley added, sounding cheerfully smug.

Raydir shrugged and turned to greet his bass player, who arrived with Soaring Star on his arm. "Ray, can you believe this girl has actually lived out here with the Navajos and hauled water and herded sheep and everything?" he asked, smiling down at her. She looked pleased and embarrassed at the same time, and introduced Haskell Wainwright, Ernest Eagleclaw and the Lakota elders to everyone.

But the biggest surprise to everyone was when Carl Loloma arrived with a truck bed full of building materials.

He knew about the party of course, but as one of Alice's strongest opponents, he wasn't really expected to come, even if Sela did.

He looked very uncomfortable and embarrassed, but at the same time rather pleased with himself, Cindy thought as she watched him walk up to Alice and Martha and hand them a piece of paper. "It would be a bad joke to call this a house-warming present, since your house got way too warm the other night," he said. "But I have some friends on the tribal council and with the BIA. They said since Mrs. Tsosie had signed her lease agreement, it would be okay to go ahead with repairs on the house. I—uh—picked up some stuff in Gallup I figured you'd need. I had a chance to go down to that new part of the reservation the other day." He just shook his head. "You ladies don't belong out there."

"Like I told everybody, *this* is our home," Alice said.

Carl didn't say anything. He was thinking about Abercrombie and Firestone and their threats, the things they could do because they had now seen to it that two groups of people who had never got along would be so thoroughly divided that they would do anything to spite and destroy each other, to the benefit of MEE and the U.S. economy. Maybe the Alice Begays of the Fourth World didn't own this Hopi land, but before the U.S. government and MEE came along, both they and the Hopi people had understood that nobody owned the land. The people who belonged here were here only to care for the land. Alice had fought hard to protect her right to that, she had done anything, used anyone who understood that the land needed her here. Legally it was Hopi land and Carl wanted that respected, but he also felt that someone who fought as Alice did for her right to care for her land as the Creator told her, deserved respect as well. Many of the displaced Navajos in the New Lands seemed as if they'd been thrown into the ocean with nothing to hold onto, without their land. He was giving serious thought to doing some volunteer counseling over there.

But he didn't say anything except, "Well, I wish I had more time to help you, but maybe some of your friends . . ."

Raydir didn't like to be outdone at helping people, especially in front of Cindy. He pulled out his checkbook and said, "How much do you figure you'll need to hire a carpenter?"

Mike cleared his throat. "I'm a carpenter. Got good tools too. Be glad to give the ladies a bid."

They were arranging that when Alice put her hand on Carl's arm. "Loloma? Anybody messes with your stuff or any of your people's stuff or animals again, you won't need to call the BIAs. You'll find their hide nailed to my wall."

He didn't know what to say or do. He wasn't behaving like himself and she wasn't behaving like the old Alice he'd known. He behaved like somebody in a movie instead and picked up her hand and kissed it. Then they both turned away and began talking animatedly to someone else.

The whole time, no one seemed to notice the way their life threads were all being woven together into a finely intertwined web by a small being who was related to them all.

The warrior has taken the sun-haired maiden's place on the back of the sun's own blue horse.
He has been up on the Hopi mesas to visit his friends, but now he is going home again.

He is going home to the house he built.
He is going home to his wife.
He is going home to the children.
He is going home to the corral where the sun's own blue
*   horse can find something good to eat.*
As he rides, he sings to himself the last verse of the war
*   god's song, which was not too strangely about being*
*   surrounded by peace. Carl Loloma and his father*
*   would have told him that this was the best thing a true*
*   warrior wished for.*
Before me Peaceful
Behind me Peaceful
Under me Peaceful
Over me Peaceful
All around me Peaceful—
Peaceful voice when he neighs
I am Everlasting and Peaceful.
I stand for my horse.
And then because the peace is very new, very tenuous
*   and by no means universal, he adds, "In peace let it*
*   be finished."*

GLOSSARY

Navajo and Hopi Words

Bead People the Yoo'ii Dine'e (Dine'e is used in clan designation, and means tribe, race, people or nation plural. Dine' refers to the Navajo Nation or *the* People and is used also when speaking of a single person or man or Navajo).

Biligaana white man or American (may also have derogatory connotations).

Black Body (Navajo) Bitsis *Li*zhin, the god of fire.

Blue Body (Navajo) Bitsis Do*t*liz, similar to the god Water Sprinkler.

Chi'in'di Navajo for a ghost or spirit—Navajo ghosts are always bad spirits and feared no matter how good they were when alive.

Dine'e or Dine'h The People, the Navajos (as used in the book this is the meaning it has).

Dinetah the sacred Navajo land between the four sacred mountains.

Edge of the Water Dine'e a clan.

Female Masaw The wife of the Hopi god Masaw, who is guardian of the earth and keeper of the dead among many other functions. The female Masaw helps her husband with his functions, which, despite the fearsome aspect of the couple, are often helpful and beneficial to the Hopis.

Hathalie Navajo singer or medicine man or chanter. This person must learn the long healing songs and ceremonies, also called Ways or Paths, know how to make the healing sandpaintings and so forth. Although the hathalie has the curative functions of a shaman, harmful or nonbeneficial aspects of a shaman are considered to be the province of Navajo witches.

Huruing Wuhti   (Hopi) the Sea Woman or Woman of Hard Substances, one of the Holy People.

Ketoh   (Navajo) something that looks like a leather bracelet with a piece of silverwork but which was originally a bow guard.

Kikmongwi   (Hopi) the leader or chief of a village.

Kinaalda   (Navajo) the Navajo girl's puberty or coming of age ceremony.

Kisani   Navajo word for the Pueblos.

Kokopelli   the humpbacked flute player (sometimes depicted as a locust) who helped the Hopis get into the Fourth World. This character appears now in many other American Indian cultures.

Kokyanwuhti   Spiderwoman, who is the first person made by Dawa or Tawa in Hopi creation stories. As Spiderwoman she is also the person who taught the Navajos to weave.

Masaw   (Hopi) guardian of the Fourth World, keeper of the dead, and many other functions—one of the main Holy Persons of the Hopi.

Nakwakwusi   (Hopi) prayer feathers.

Pahana   (Hopi) white people, non-Hopis.

Pahana (the)   (Hopi) The Lost White Brother of the Hopis. So far, none of the races they've met have met the requirements of the Pahana who will have a missing piece of Masaw's stone tablet with him.

Pahos   (Hopi) prayer sticks.

Piki   (Hopi) thin, flakey bread made from (usually) blue cornmeal.

Powqua   (Hopi) someone with powers, often a witch.

Qotsamanavitu   the snow maiden kachina.

Shinali'   (Navajo) my granddaughter who is the daughter of my son.

Sipapuni   (Hopi) the place of emergence.

So'yokwuuti   (Hopi) a sister of the Ogre family.

Tsiyeel (Navajo bumblebee) the traditional Navajo hair-style, in which the hair is tied with yarn bindings into a figure-eight-style bun worn vertically at the back of the head.

Tushi (Hopi) a foodstuff.

White Body (Navajo) Bitsis Lagai, one of the people who helped make the Navajos into more human-like people when they entered (to them) the Fifth World.

Yah-ta-hey Navajo greeting.

Yellow Body (Navajo) Bitsis *Litsoi*, another of the Holy People.

Yoo'ii Dine'e the Bead People (a Navajo clan).

Navajo and Hopi Place Names, Concepts, and Deities Not Formerly Mentioned

Alien Monsters mutant monsters (big ones) born to the first Navajos created in this world. They were abandoned by their mothers and the other Navajos and hence, were angry with the People and ate all but a half-dozen.

American Indian this is used in place of Native American at the request of one of the author's informants and according to Indian Country today is now considered equally politically correct.

Badger Clan a Hopi clan.

Basha's a supermarket in Window Rock.

Big Black Bear a personified bear spirit helpful to horse raiders.

Big Mountain a particularly embattled portion of the Hopi Partitioned Lands.

Big Snake a personified snake spirit helpful in keeping raiders stealthy and quiet.

Black Mesa a formerly sacred place to both Navajos and Hopis, now being strip-mined by Peabody Coal Co.

Blessing Way a Navajo ceremony.

Born for Water or Child of Water the second of the Hero Twins of the Navajos. Child of Changing Woman and a waterfall and one who helped his brother, Slayer of Alien

Monsters or Monster Slayer, save the Navajos from destruction.

Bosque Redondo Spanish name for the area around Fort Sumner, New Mexico. This is the area in which most of the Navajo Nation was imprisoned after being force marched for eighteen to twenty days. Many who weren't killed starved to death or died of disease.

Canyon de Chelly very sacred canyon to the Navajos, also an ancient home of the Hopis and earlier cliff dwellers. This was the place where the great peach orchards grew and is also the location of Spider Rock, traditional home of Spiderwoman.

Changing Woman very special Holy Person to the Navajos. Mother of Monster Slayer (by the sun, Tawa), and Born for Water (by a waterfall).

Child of Water (see Born for Water).

Coal Mine Mesa mesa that has rich deposits of coal.

Coyote Many cultures but to Navajos and Hopis is the trickster, messenger, fire-bringer. Very analogous to Raven in many northern indigenous cultures.

Coyote Clan a Hopi clan with coyotes as the totem animal.

Coyote in Him story name for Wiley Smiley.

Creator the supreme being as called by American Indian cultures (and translated into English, of course).

Darkness a whirlwind.

Dawa sign also Tawa sign—the sun sign with the radiating rays in the four directions, a frequently seen Southwestern design.

Dinnebito a place on the border of the Hopi Partitioned Lands.

Enemy Way a Navajo ceremony to cleanse Navajos who have been associating with outsiders too much, have moved away and returned to the reservation, been in the military, or experienced other spiritual contamination.

First Man/First Woman the first human beings created by Dawa—mortal human beings, not Holy People such as Spiderwoman, Changing Woman, or the Hero Twins. Particularly important in Navajo stories.

The Fourth World   to the Hopis, the present world is the Fourth World.

The Fifth World   to the Navajos, the present world is the Fifth World.

Fry bread   a puffy fried bread similar to a sopapilla.

Ganado   name of town on Navajo reservation. Home of the remaining trading post of Lorenzo Hubbell, a trader who helped Navajos develop their artistic skills to sell to the outside market. Particularly helped with Navajo rug styles, an example of which is the Ganado Red, a rug whose colors are a combination of the natural sheep colors of black, white, and gray plus red.

Havasu City   where London Bridge is.

Hopi Partitioned Lands   actually, this is a U.S. government concept, very complex. This land is a consequence of acts and laws that made a separate Hopi reservation in the middle of the Navajo reservation. The Hopi reservation is about a fifth the size of the Navajo. The Hopi Partitioned Land and the Navajo Partitioned Land is the part of the designated Hopi reservation the U.S. government arbitrarily divided in half and said "No Navajos settle here," "No Hopis settle here." Unfortunately, some Navajo families had already been settled on the designated Hopi area for well over a century. The situation is described in this book and also in excellent nonfiction books and articles.

Hoteville   Hopi village originally settled by a group of "Hostiles" or Hopis who did not wish to conform to any white ways, particularly education of their children.

Kachinas or kachina dolls   kachinas are the Hopi and Pueblo Holy People and beings who come down from the stars to bring blessings and instructions to the people. They are personified by dancers, often masked. In order to teach children about them, they are also carved as dolls and given as learning aids to children as well as (these days) sold to tourists.

Keams Canyon   a settlement on the eastern end of the Hopi mesas where the old government boarding school used to be and now other U.S. government services are located.

Kykotsmovi   another name for the Hopi village of New Oraibi.

Lost His Horses to Hopis   story name for Charlie Etcitty.

Magpie   the magpie bird personified in stories.

Mirage People   sometimes called the Illusion People—these people were among the early ancestors of the first Navajos. They intermarried with the first couples in order that there would not be incest. They are the personifications of the heat waves rising from the desert.

Mockingbird   a personified mockingbird. This character is the one who gave peoples their tribal names as they emerged into the present world.

Moenkopi   a Hopi village.

Monster Slayer   child of Changing Woman and Dawa or Tawa (the sun), elder twin of Born for Water. Monster Slayer is also called Slayer of Alien Monsters and with his brother slew the mutant monsters who decimated the early Navajos.

Needs a Horse   story name for Mike Blackgoat.

New Lands   the area the Navajo Nation purchased to resettle their people who agreed to relocate from the HPL.

New Oraibi   a Hopi village currently called Kykotsmovi.

Old Man Coyote   nickname for personified coyote character in stories.

One Who Is Also a Wolf   story name for the Navajo Witch or Skinwalker in this book.

Oraibi   a Hopi village.

Polacca   another Hopi village on First Mesa.

Rock Gap Clan   a Navajo clan designation.

Rolling Darkness   a bad whirlwind that rotates counterclockwise and brings evil with it.

Sacred Mountains of the West or Light Always Glitters on Top   the San Francisco Peaks—one of the Navajo four sacred mountains and for the Hopi, the place from which the kachinas descend from the stars.

Sea Woman   a Hopi holy person also known as the Woman of Hard Substances.

Second Mesa   the second finger of the Hopi Mesas.

Shipaulovi   a Hopi village.

Shiprock   a landmark on the Navajo reservation, as well as a town named for the landmark. Shiprock is supposedly the petrified body of a great bird monster slain by the Hero Twins.

Skinwalkers   Navajo witches who can shift shapes, usually into a wolf or coyote but also into other forms. In this story the skinwalker is called The One Who Is Also a Wolf. He is a male Navajo witch.

Slayer of Alien Monsters   another name for Monster Slayer.

Snake Clan   the Hopi clan whose totem is the snake. Their clan is supposedly descended from the Snake People.

The Snake People   shape shifters who were snakes sometimes and people sometimes. A woman of these intermarried with an early Hopi and they brought back all sorts of medicines and the gift for making rain to the Hopis.

Spiderwoman   a holy person to both Hopis and Navajos. She is the first holy person created by Taiowa, or Tawa, in Hopi creation. For the Navajos, she is the holy person who brought them weaving and resides at Spider Rock, a very tall monolith in Canyon de Chelly.

Storm pattern   a Navajo rug pattern, very complex, with lightning symbols as a part of the design.

Sun, The   principle deity of Navajos and Pueblos who created the Holy People and human beings as well. Known to the Hopis as Taiowa and more generally in the Southwest as Tawa or Dawa.

Sun Dance   a sacred dance introduced by the Lakotas to the Southwest.

Sun-haired Maiden   Cindy Ellis's story name.

Swallow People   personified swallows from a story.

The Third World   a more prosperous world for the Hopis, where they fell into evil ways because of idleness. The Navajo Third World was also one they had to leave because they misbehaved.

Toyei   a place name.

Traditionals   Hopis who wish to follow Hopi ways and religion.

Tuba City   where the farthest west Hopi village is on one side of the highway and a Navajo village is on the other. This is also about the farthest west Navajo village.

Uncle Horsie   Anabah's name for Mike Blackgoat.

Walpi   a Hopi village.

White Bead Woman   a Navajo holy person.

Witch   a Navajo witch, who may be either male or female, and has the power to shapeshift. No association with wicca and is always an evil, self-serving person.

Wupatki National Monument and Ruins   a place sacred to the Hopi Snake clan, once inhabited by their ancestors, the woman of the Snake People and her Hopi husband.

Cast of Characters and Individuals Mentioned in Text (Not Already Named)

Abbott Sekaquaptewa   a former Hopi tribal chairman responsible for many modern innovations on the Hopi mesas, including the Hopi Cultural Center and hotel.

Alf Tewawina   political opponent of Theo Honahni, acting Hopi tribal chairman (in this story, not in real life).

Alice Begay   Navajo resister on the HPL and sister of Martha Tsosie, great aunt of Anabah, aunt of Maria Chee and of Jimmie Tsosie.

Amy Honahni   Hub Honahni's deceased first wife.

Anabah   Navajo child, daughter of Jimmie Tsosie, granddaughter of Martha Tsosie, great-niece of Alice Begay. A horse-child, owner of Sammy.

Barboncito   a great Navajo chief who voluntarily underwent the Long March and captivity with his people at Bosque Redondo to encourage and help them and form a liaison with another great chief, Manuelito.

Belinda Benedict   publicist for Raydir Quantrill.

Bill Gates   a wrangler.

Carl Loloma   a Hopi Vietnam vet, substance abuse counselor, a possible candidate for next tribal chairman.

Carlos Nakai   the real-life famous Navajo flute player and musical innovator.

Chaco a gray stallion whose color is known to Navajos as blue or turquoise, the color favored by the sun for his own horse.

Charlie Etcitty a horse trader and sometimes raider.

Charlie Smiley the trader at whose door the foundling later known as Wiley Smiley was found.

Cindy Ellis protagonist horsewoman from first Godmother book. Stable manager and lover of Raydir Quantrill, trainer for Chaco, companion to Grandmother.

Clyde Kluckhohn scholar on Southwest Indian matters and author of *To the Foot of the Rainbow*.

Commissioner Becenti a Navajo politician.

Courtney a young stablehand at Raydir Quantrill's stables.

David King a talk show host (fictitious).

Denise Nell Tso's daughter.

Dezbah or Dezi Maria Chee's daughter.

Dico Miller from the previous two Godmother books, a street kid who later went to Ireland to study music.

Dina Theo Honahni's secretary.

Doris niece of Nell Tso.

Dr. Loomis staff physician.

Dr. Morgan a colleague of Maria Chee.

Duane Manygoats an infant patient of Maria Chee.

Ed Abercrombie representative of Mutual Energy Enterprises.

Edison Nakai (fictitious) hospital administrator.

Ernest Eagleclaw a Lakota AIM member helping the Navajo resisters.

Felicity Fortune a fairy godmother.

Flunkey the disgraced Navajo politician who later works for Firestone and Abercrombie.

Folsom a sound engineer buddy of Raydir's.

Fred Moran from first book, social worker Rose Samson's fiancé.

Ginjer a stablehand at Quantrill Stables.

Grandfather Carl Loloma's father, former Hopi code talker in World War II, Sela's grandfather.

Grandma Hilda Raydir Quantrill's former mother-in-law, maternal grandmother of his daughter, Sno.

Grandma Webster, Grandmother, or Grandma   the mysterious and powerful old woman who guides Cindy Ellis's journey through Hopiland.

Grossnickel   The real name of Raydir Quantrill's pretentious housekeeper is Phyllis Grossnickel, not Pagan Platero, as she calls herself.

Hamish Secakuku   Hopi entrepeneur and founder of the Rainbird Golf Course and Resort.

Hank   Chaco's owner.

Hannah   Doris's daughter.

Harold   one of the boys in the household of Nell's brother.

Harvey   a Hopi Ranger.

Haskell Wainwright   a carsick writer.

Hastiin Irving Bitsui   a hathalie or healer.

Heather the Heifer   a journalist who answers Raydir's cell phone.

Herb   Doris's husband.

Hogeye   Raydir's chef.

Homer Keams   guard at entrance of road to Polacca.

Hosteen Nazzie   a Navajo man.

Howard   young nephew of Charlie Etcitty.

Jason Numkena   second-in-command of Alf Tewawina.

Jaz   a biker's boyfriend.

Jeannie   Raydir's punk secretary.

Jenny   Anabah's mother.

Jerry   a boy in the household of Nell's brother.

Jimmie Tsosie   Anabah's father.

Joey   a classmate of Sela's.

Kit Carson   Indian Scout, first friend and then betrayer of the Navajos.

Kittybitty   Anabah's cat.

Lewis   Martha Tsosie's late husband.

Lillian   Hosteen Nazzie's wife.

Lindsey Fletcher   aka Soaring Star, the representative of Earth's Children who is helping Navajo resisters in general and Alice Begay in particular.

Mandy   Theo Honahni's daughter.

Marjorie   receptionist at the Rainbird Hotel.

Martha Tsosie   sister of Alice Begay, grandmother of An-
   abah, aunt of Maria Chee.
Micah Firestone   a representative of Mutual Energy Enter-
   prises, colleage of Ed Abercrombie.
Michael Blackgoat   Mike, Navajo carpenter and rancher/
   horseman.
Milt Highwater   an Ojibway activist/videographer and
   computer buff—Shirley's Natchat friend.
Morey   a Hopi ranger.
Mrs. Manygoats   mother of abused infant Duane.
Mrs. Namoki   a practical nurse.
Mutual Energy Enterprises (MEE)   a large multinational
   energy corporation.
Natchat   the Native chat line on the Internet.
Nathaniel   Nita's son.
Native American   in this book, this term is used only by
   outsiders. On the reservations, most people refer to them-
   selves as Indians and the author had a specific request from
   one of her informants to have the Indian people refer to
   themselves as American Indian, which is apparently now
   equally politically correct.
Neddy   Raydir's promotional manager.
Nell Tso   a relocated Navajo from the HPL and a weaver.
Nicki Bedonie   wheelchair-bound Navajo friend of Maria
   Chee.
Ninabah   newborn sister of Anabah.
Nita   a gift shop owner on the Hopi reservation.
One Who Is Also a Wolf   a Navajo witch or skinwalker.
Pagan Platero   Raydir's housekeeper, aka Phyllis Gross-
   nickle.
People of Peace   nickname for the Hopi.
Perdita   stepsister of Cindy Ellis.
Phil Medicine Eagle   a Lakota.
Pill   Cindy's former stable boss.
Punkin   Cindy's horse.
Puss   a talking cat from The Godmother.
Quantrill's Fiery Lawrence   aka Larry, a Thoroughbred.
Ralph Sakiestewa   a former client of Carl's.

Raydir Quantrill   born Ray Kinkaid. Professionally known as the King of Alloy Rock. Cindy's lover and boss.

Romancita   an ER nurse.

Rose Samson   social worker friend of Cindy's.

Sam Joseph   a client of Carl's.

Sammy   Anabah's horse.

Sela   Carl's niece.

Shirley   Sela's Hostile, Traditional, computer-wizard pro-Navajo resister friend from Hoteville.

Sno   Raydir's daughter.

Soaring Star   nickname of Lindsey Fletcher, activist working with Earth's Children for the Navajo resisters.

Spiderwoman   a Holy Person, ancestor of the Hopis and the Navajos, taught the Navajos to weave.

Tara   Nicki's daughter.

Theo Honahni   present Hopi tribal chairman (fictitious).

Wallace Curley   the name of a character.

Wiley Smiley   Sela's boyfriend.

Wyatt Emory   a client of Carl's.